ARDNEH'S SWORD

TOR BOOKS BY FRED SABERHAGEN

ARDNEH'S SWORD

FRED SABERHAGEN

A TOM DOHERTY ASSOCIATES BOOK **TOR**® NEW YORK

ARDNEH'S SWORD

Copyright © 2006 by Fred Saberhagen

This book is printed on acid-free paper.

A Tor Book
Published by Tom Doherty Associates, LLC
175 Fifth Avenue
New York, NY 10010

www.tor.com

Tor® is a registered trademark of Tom Doherty Associates, LLC.

Library of Congress Cataloging-in-Publication

Saberhagen, Fred, 1930–
    Ardneh's sword / Fred Saberhagen—1st ed.
        p. cm.
    "A Tom Doherty Associates book."
    ISBN: 0-765-31210-7
    EAN: 978-0-765-31210-5

    PS3569.A215 A73 2006
    813'54—dc22

                                    2006040364

First Edition: May 2006

Printed in the United States of America

0 9 8 7 6 5 4 3 2 1

ARDNEH'S SWORD

ONE

THE NIGHT WAS NO LONGER THICK WITH DARKNESS, AND THE chill air had the feel of early morning, when the flapping and thrashing noise exploded atop the covered wagon's canvas roof. The noise jarred Chance out of some kind of pleasantly mournful dream, whose content vanished entirely, leaving only a feeling behind, the instant his eyes came open. His first conscious thought was: *This time Mitra's made a really rough landing. Stupid damned owl.* His second thought was: *Something's seriously wrong.*

In the next moment, all thinking was shocked into a temporary halt. A little more than a meter above his face, the canvas sagged alarmingly. The slender wooden hoops that held it above the wagon's body were giving way, as if the whole weight of some creature considerably heavier than a giant owl had suddenly been dumped aboard.

It was a rare event, though not unheard of, for the bird to come down on the wagon's top. Mitra's preferred and much more practical landing place was right at the front, on the narrow bench of the driver's seat, which was otherwise unoccupied at the predawn hour when the owl generally returned.

Chance called out: "Mitra?" His voice cracked in the middle of the word, as it sometimes did these days. By now he was sitting up straight, confusedly brushing dark hair out of his eyes. The movement had brought his head close to the inward-bulging fabric just above, and the slash that came next, as if in answer to his call, opening up tough canvas like so much gossamer, sounded deafeningly loud. He threw up his hands to shield his face.

First the bird's large predatory foot appeared, armed with razor claws. Next there dropped into Chance's hand a diminutive object that felt like a loop of fine chain with one small, irregular lump attached. His fingers closed automatically on this unexpected offering, just as the owl's foot vanished. Its place in the opening was immediately taken by a monstrous face, totally strange and alien, looming within an arm's length of Chance's own. The sheer visual shock of the apparition knocked him flat, cringing on his back.

Two staring eyes, somewhat mismatched in size but each fully large enough to have been human, peered down into the wagon through the fresh gap in the canvas. They flanked a vaguely human nose, that no one could possibly mistake for the great bird Mitra's short but powerful hooked beak. The eyes now boring in at Chance seemed something either more or less than animal, and they were certainly all wrong for any bird. They glowed in a way that no owl's ever could.

Instinct sent Chance's wiry, fifteen-year-old body rolling sideways, trying to put space between him and the hideous vision. Even as the boy moved, the thin, curving, wood supports upholding the wagon's roof sprang back into place above him, affording no clue as to just what solid weight had so deformed them, or what had happened to suddenly relieve the pressure. The fresh gap in the overhead canvas, abruptly emptied of nightmare, showed only the grayish blankness of the predawn sky.

Horror had vanished, or at least retreated, but uproar continued. Chance's ears informed him that the noisy presence had already left the wagon's top, landing with an audible thump and wounded-sounding flutter somewhere on the nearby ground. The great bird was still uttering cries that were almost musical even in its terror.

Springing into a crouch, shoeless but clad in shirt and trousers, Chance tossed blankets aside, jumped to the canvas door flap and pulled it wide open. The huge owl, one of its long wings extended in a way that suggested injury, met him in the doorway. The bird was struggling to get in, to reach the safety of its sheltered nest inside the wagon even as Chance kept trying to get out.

"Mitra? What was it? Mitra?" The bulk of dark, puffed-out feathers magnified Mitra's apparent size to that of a large dog. The boy bent himself out of the way as best he could, the bird screaming tunefully in his ear as she squeezed by. If Mitra was trying to utter words in answer to his question, as he halfway expected she must be in this situation, he could not make them out.

Bursting out into the open air, he stepped over the narrow driver's bench and dropped lightly to the ground, frosty grass shocking his bare feet. Around him in the grayish predawn light, the compact campsite of the small caravan was so far showing no great signs of alarm. The other two wagons, and the row of soldiers' small tent shelters just beyond them, were dark and still. In the dimness Chance could see movement only at the doorway of the larger single tent nearby, the shelter of the military captain of the expedition—he was the only soldier with a shelter big enough to stand up in. Certainly there had been enough noise to begin to stir things up. Even the phlegmatic loadbeasts, night-hobbled beside the stream an easy stone's throw distant, had raised their heads alertly.

The small central fire had burned itself away to graying embers. Many days ago, before the caravan had even passed the first of several borders, Captain Horkos had thought it necessary for the camp to keep a fire going all night to ward off beasts of prey. But that routine precaution had gradually been abandoned. On the great plain over which they had been traveling for the last few days, large predators were rare to the point of nonexistence. And wood for fires was scarce; the only plentiful fuel was chips of the sun-dried dung of wild herdbeasts, and even that was often in short supply.

The single sentry currently on watch, a trooper uniformed in the colors of Sarasvati, was standing some thirty meters off, and beginning to take an interest in the proceedings. Like everyone else he was used to the bird's comings and goings, which sometimes tended to be noisy. Evidently the soldier had not seen anything wildly out of the ordinary, for his concern had not yet risen to the point where he would raise an alarm, and his short sword was still sheathed at his side.

None of the sentry's comrades were yet stirring from their places in the row of low shelter tents and blankets, though they would soon be out and about. At first light, one of the privates in the military escort routinely began to build up the central campfire with the intention of brewing tea and cooking breakfast.

Hastily Chance made his way around the wagon, looking carefully under the vehicle and in all directions. He could see no sign anywhere of any intruding bird or person, no trace of any more exotic creature that might have landed weightily on the wagon's top, then ripped it open—of course the big owl's formidable beak or talons could have accomplished that. In any case, the owner of that ghastly face had disappeared.

As completely as if it had been a vision, or a dream. . . . Chance had been deceived by dreams before, though he had never experienced one as sharply detailed and realistic as this. Dreaming was part of an ancient family tradition, considered by some to be a curse.

A vague awareness that his left fist was still clenched reminded him of the object dropped into his hand. Looking down stupidly at his closed fingers, Chance for the first time became fully aware of a tingling in that palm, a sensation that was already fading. It continued to do so as he turned over his hand and opened it, to reveal . . .

Nothing. It was as if whatever the owl had given him had dissolved into the air, or somehow melted into his skin. Of course, he must have let it fall somewhere.

In a moment he realized that at least one bit of solid evidence of the visitation was still in sight. It appeared that someone—or something—might have been using a net to try to catch the owl, because there was an abandoned net, of a size that might have snared a big bird. One end of it was caught somehow atop the wagon, from which modest height it hung down like coarse lace drapery along one curving bulge of canvas.

Chance grabbed quickly at the net, his mind working on some half-formed impulse to prevent this second bit of evidence from disappearing. The small mass of coarse mesh easily pulled free from the wagon and he began to look it over. He had barely started to do this when he caught sight of Jervase, the Scholar, leader of the expedition, emerging from his private wagon. A few paces away, Horkos, commander of the cavalry escort, was stepping out of his own wagon, a luxury to which his military rank entitled him. In a moment the pair of them had reached Chance's side.

Horkos had his sword in hand, but Jervase had not bothered to bring his along. The Scholar was half a head taller than Chance, and approximately twice his age. His brown hair and beard had been kept neatly trimmed despite the inconveniences of camp life. Moving at his usual brisk pace, his lean, half-clad body blanket-wrapped in the frosty dawn, Jervase was first to reach the boy.

"What have you got there?" the man demanded in his precisely articulated voice, staring at the net. Then, more urgently: "What's happened to the owl?"

Chance was shaking his head, still trying to clear his mind. He wanted to stop and think before he got into a discussion of the vision of that ghastly face. All he said was: "Strange things are going on. I think the bird is hurt." The fingers of his left hand, which remained empty, were opening and closing as if of their own accord.

Meanwhile, Mitra had disappeared into the familiar haven of her nest, from which invisible source there drifted out a fluttering, hooting uproar. Jervase reacted with alarm to the news about the owl, and moved at once to follow Mitra into the wagon. Captain Horkos, about the same age as Jervase, stocky yet nimble, had already sheathed his sword and turned aside to begin questioning the sentry, who had moved closer.

In a moment Chance had joined the Scholar under the canvas top, where the boy immediately began to soothe the injured bird, while Jervase tried to inspect her wing.

Mitra's hooked beak opened, her small tongue vibrated, and she garbled words at Chance, recognizable sounds mixed in with other noises that might or might not have been crafted to carry meaning. Judging by his many past attempts to gain useful information from the owl, Chance thought it unlikely that Mitra would ever give anyone a coherent explanation of what had just happened. Certainly they weren't going to get one while she was still excited.

Jervase had given up trying to inspect the wing, his efforts simply driving the owl deeper into a panic. Now he crouched under the low wagon top making awkward little motions with both hands, as if determined to do something useful but not sure just what it ought to be. Chance was actually more experienced in caring for the bird; he had been acting as its chief caretaker for almost a month, not at all the way he had expected to spend his days when they were setting out from home. His official title on the expedition was the vague one of special assistant to Jervase. In practice, this had turned out to mean spending a great deal of time keeping the bird company whenever the Scholar himself was absent—which was coming to be a greater and greater portion of every day and night. Among other things, Jervase thought it important that someone should write down everything that Mitra said—or seemed to say.

Captain Horkos had rejoined them, having concluded his brief talk with the sentry, and three humans were now inside the wagon, whose whole interior was not much bigger than a good-sized double bed. Though it had never contained more than the one bird and was aired out every night while the owl was absent, its interior atmosphere assailed the nose with the spicy mustiness of a coop heavily populated with barnyard fowl.

All three of the current human occupants were long used to the stink, and none were paying it any attention. The Scholar was scowling up at the ripped canvas. "What happened here? Mitra did that?"

"Yes, I believe she did." Having got that far, Chance hesitated, clearing his throat; he wanted to give his report calmly, so the leaders of the expedition would not think he had been dreaming, or had gone mad.

But the proper moment had not yet come—the Scholar was fussing with the owl again. One of the bird's wings did seem to be hurt, and it appeared unlikely that the owl was going to be flying for at least a few days.

The door flap of canvas moved again, and another human head intruded, this one's dark hair styled distinctively above a middle-aged woman's sweet, still pretty face. Her usual air was one of purposeful competence.

The enchantress Ayaba spent the nights sleeping or working in her own private wagon. Most of her daylight hours were also spent under its painted canvas, from which she emerged at intervals to pass on to the Scholar or the captain information or suggestions she had received from her unseen powers.

Now she, the Scholar, and the military commander were all demanding to know what was going on. "My Lord," was how the Lady

Ayaba, being something of a stickler for formality, addressed Chance in her soft and pleasant voice.

"Lady Ayaba." Chance answered politely, with a nod that had in it something of a bow; women of her profession were generally given that title by courtesy, regardless of what rank or lack of rank might be their due because of family connections or lack thereof.

IN ODD CORNERS OF THE WAGON, AND UNDER THE NEST OF OLD blankets, were a few small bones. Mitra had now and then brought home a small mammal or reptile of modest size for her own dinner. Big owls were a rare, exotic species, and of their number only a few possessed the power of speech. Mitra was one of these, but rarely spoke, and never when excited.

The quivering bird was silent. Chance thought she was not only in pain, but terrified.

When a moment came in which no one else had anything to say, he offered: "I think I know what scared her."

People gave Chance their attention, and he ran through his story. The tale was very short, but he was sure that he would have to go over it several more times.

"Then I thought Mitra dropped something into my hand," he concluded, holding it out palm up. As he spoke he flexed the fingers yet again; by this time all trace of the tingling sensation had also disappeared.

The lady was studying him keenly. "Dropped something? You mean deliberately?"

"I thought so."

"What did she give you, Lord Chance?"

The young lord spread his eight fingers and two thumbs. "I don't know. It felt like—like a small chain. With some object f-fastened to it. Like . . ."

"Like an amulet or locket?"

"Yes."

"But you say that it then vanished."

"That's it."

The bird's eyes were shielded with a soft hood and the enchantress furnished a light—it appeared in the form of a small, half-animate, darting thing; a minor servant of the Lady Ayaba, coming and going at her bidding. The people in the wagon searched the floor minutely, but they found nothing remotely resembling Chance's description among the odd bits and fragments that might be expected in any living space used by a large bird and several people.

Lady Ayaba produced from somewhere a short wand, with which she conducted a brief magical survey of the young lord's person and the wagon's whole interior. The curious stone set in her thumb ring flashed. Soon she put her wand away, signing that she had discovered nothing.

Her voice was calm and reassuring, and she spoke to Chance as if to a child. "I don't think it could have been of much importance, whatever it was the owl dropped into your hand."

But I wasn't dreaming it. While his audience was still making a desultory attempt to scan the wagon's floor, Chance tried to explain what had happened. "I'm certain there was someone—or something—else on top of the wagon with the bird. For just a moment, when it landed. I saw an odd . . ." He stalled again.

Jervase was brisk, though patient, determined to be thorough. "An odd what?"

"Face. Very odd."

For a moment all three of Chance's listeners stared at him in silence. He could plainly hear the chorus of unspoken comment: *Having nightmares again, are we?*

The enchantress ducked outside, murmuring that she wished to look around.

It was the captain who offered the first spoken observation. "This whole business doesn't make any sense, young sir. Not the way you're telling it. Bird's not going to be able to pick up a human being, even a small child, and carry him home like a rabbit." The captain himself had once held a considerably higher position, in civilian life, before a certain event had happened to bring about a sharp demotion. Chance didn't know the precise nature of the catastrophe and had no particular desire to find out.

Horkos still tended to slide into an easy informality with people who were nominally well above his current rank, as for example young Chance Rolfson, who was not only a member of an ancient and illustrious family, but the lineal descendant of Rolf himself. That was quite all right with Chance, who did not care much for formality under any conditions, and ceremony of any kind seemed definitely out of place while camping in the wilderness.

"No, of course not," Chance agreed. He was shaking his head before the captain was halfway through with his objection. At the same time, Chance was insisting stubbornly, in his own mind: *Someone, or something as heavy as a man, was really up there.*

There would be no use in trying to argue the point. "I didn't say the bird was carrying anyone. And I don't suppose the . . . the thing, the person, whatever it was . . . carried the bird home either. But *something* besides the owl was up there." And Chance jerked a thumb toward the overhead.

Judging from the expressions on the faces of his audience, he was perfectly sure that none of them believed him.

"Truly, I wasn't dreaming," he added finally. "Some of you must have heard the noise."

The enchantress Ayaba, remaining properly formal, rejoined them inside the wagon, carrying the net that she had just picked up outside. Favoring Chance with an intense gaze as she made her way completely inside, she studied the interior of the wagon, half of the small space occupied by the bird's nest, the other half strewn with the modest litter of Chance's personal belongings.

Presently she declared that whatever might have happened, no particular magic seemed to have been involved.

Her small, capable fingers stretched out the net to allow everyone a good look at it. She said: "The bird must have become entangled in this somewhere, and that threw her into a panic. She dragged the net with her, and she was home before she could get free of it."

THE THREE WHO HEARD CHANCE'S DESCRIPTION OF THE MONSTROUS intruding face all attributed it to his somewhat overactive imagination—somehow they connected that with sleepwalking, which had afflicted him a couple of times earlier in the journey. From early childhood he had had a tendency to vivid and often frightening dreams.

Still, there was the hole slashed in the canvas. And the strange net, which resembled no piece of equipment that the expedition had ever carried.

Eventually the three leaders were able to agree on what seemed to them a plausible explanation.

The lady summed it up: "The net must have been set in a tree somewhere, as a snare, by someone who was trying to catch another kind of bird—or some kind of flying creature.

"Somehow Mitra accidentally became entangled in the mesh, but managed to tear herself out of the tree and fly home. She was in a panic, flying almost out of control, and landed atop the wagon instead of on the driver's seat as usual. Then she clawed open the wagon top before she could get free of the net."

Her colleagues' heads nodded in agreement. All members of this company had at some time taken a good look at Mitra's talons, which were not only sharply pointed, but razor-edged for half their considerable length. Chance could see that the three leaders were ready to find this explanation satisfying. He was not convinced, but it seemed pointless to argue, unless he could come up with some new evidence. This time he knew what he had seen.

Tying on his shoes, he climbed out of the wagon again and looked around. Daylight was growing, though the sun had not yet actually made it over the horizon, and the camp was peaceful in the morning light. A loadbeast made a lowing sound. The sergeant hovered in the background, waiting calmly for the day's orders. The rest of the men of the escort, by now all thoroughly awake, were grumbling and murmuring their way into the routines of breakfast.

be—if they could find it at all—the mere intersection of two faint desert tracks. He estimated that point to be about ten kilometers away, a fair day's journey for loaded wagons over rough country.

In a matter of minutes last night's campsite had been abandoned. The caravan's five wagons were creaking on, following the tracks of the Scholar's ridingbeast. The two vehicles not devoted to private use or to the bird were loaded with tents and various supplies. Two loadbeasts pulled each wagon, and several more were herded along as spare draft animals. Troopers rode on either side of the small caravan, or sometimes went scouting into the desert.

The owl was snug in her mobile nest, hurt wing extended, feathers still quivering with the shock of whatever had been done to her in the predawn darkness, her eyes hooded against what little daylight filtered in. Inside the wagon that carried the great bird, the soldier who generally repaired damaged canvas, a former tentmaker, crouched in an awkward position, doing his best to sew up the gash in the overhead covering even while the wagon tilted and jolted on its way. Roads marked on the ancient map tended to be anything but smooth, when any trace of them could be found at all.

BEFORE RIDING AHEAD, THE SCHOLAR HAD DETAILED CHANCE TO take the morning shift as wagon-driver, and the young lord welcomed the slight change in routine. Driving a wagon was not one of the skills that members of aristocratic families were required—or even encouraged—to learn. But Jervase had taught him that in the business of hunting ancient artifacts, the more practical things a worker knew how to do, the better.

Chance's parents, back in the capital city of Sarasvati, had expressed their wish that his taking part in this research expedition—one of the few activities they could approve of that Chance also found interesting—would acquaint him with the joys and virtues of a hearty, outdoor life. That in turn, they hoped, would cure him of

TWO

FOR MOST MEMBERS OF THE EXPEDITION, THE MORNING ROUTINE had been only slightly disrupted, and no one suggested any reason to change it further. The Scholar, as usual unwilling to waste time, had soon gulped down his customary morning tea and was astride his ridingbeast, canteen at his belt, with a scroll of age-cracked map in hand.

Several days ago, with the first appearance of evidence suggesting a bandit presence in the desert, the Scholar had begun to wear a short sword at his side. He had belted on the weapon, opposite his canteen, and Chance thought it looked as incongruous as a quill pen might have done at the captain's side.

In his saddlebags, Chance knew, Jervase carried sketches and notes on the subject of ancient artifacts, many of them copied into his notebook from antique documents he guarded jealously inside his wagon. Some of these were in almost-forgotten languages that only the Scholar and a few of his learned colleagues were able to decipher.

Jervase rode ahead, after telling the others what he had in mind as today's goal. The map that he considered his most reliable showed a crossroads, and when they reached it, it would doubtless turn out to certain dreamy, unambitious tendencies. They were pleased that he had not insisted on occupying a private wagon of his own, a privilege to which his social rank would certainly have entitled him. Instead their son had chosen to focus on his duties by sharing the bird's conveyance.

Oh yes, his family were all proud, in their own way, of Chance's scholastic achievements. But they would be prouder if he were able to excel in the ways of leadership and power.

Toward this end he heard from them—not frequently, but still often enough to be maddening—gentle hints and reminders regarding his illustrious ancestor, Rolf of the Broken Lands. To tell the truth, Chance was more than a little weary of hearing about the great deeds of the illustrious and legendary Rolf, and how proud they all must be to bear the Rolfson name.

CHANCE ASSUMED THAT HE WAS GOING TO SPEND A GOOD PART OF this day as he had spent the majority of his days since leaving home: staying close to the owl, keeping his ears open for anything the bird might say that could possibly have a bearing on their mission of discovery. It seemed to Chance that he had already spent a good portion of his life straining his eyes in the dim interior of the covered wagon doing his best to faithfully record the owl's utterances. That sometimes meant jolting along beneath a double top, extra thicknesses of dark fabric to protect the half-tamed bird from direct and glaring sunlight.

Anyway, Chance was having serious doubts about the usefulness of all this note-taking. It seemed to be one of the things that scholars did, endlessly, but when he reread the notes he had taken from the owl so far they all seemed utter gibberish.

So much, he thought, for the hearty, outdoor life. Still, he did not regret coming on the expedition. It brought, at least, the chance of something new and different every day.

GRADUALLY THE MEMORY OF A GHASTLY FACE POKING THROUGH THE wagon top receded into the background of Chance's thoughts. Hour by hour he was beginning to waver in his belief in the reality of that vision. Suddenly it struck him to wonder whether it might have been not a true face at all, but some kind of mask—but in that case, who had worn it?

In moments when his mind was otherwise unoccupied, the question tended to return: What would an object most likely be, that felt like a loop of fine chain, with one hard, small, irregular lump attached? The possibilities seemed to narrow down to a rather ordinary kind of jewelry, or possibly a magic amulet. But ordinary jewelry would not have disappeared—and the enchantress, who everyone agreed was good at her profession, had as much as told him that no magical transaction had taken place.

That seemed to leave the possibility that he had been dreaming, or imagining things.

Chance could almost begin to suspect that Lady Ayaba could be right. The bird had simply got entangled in the net somewhere by accident, fluttered home in a panic, and ripped the canvas. He might, after all, have dreamed the rest of the experience.

He could almost believe that—but not quite. When he looked beneath the driver's bench, he could see the strange torn net still lying where he had tucked it away. Chance knew in his bones that the simple explanation for its presence was quite wrong.

SCHOLAR JERVASE'S MIND WAS THOROUGHLY SATURATED WITH AN-cient tales of the transcendent being, the legendary champion of humanity, known as Ardneh.

It was not, of course, that Jervase believed all the old stories that were told, in Scripture and elsewhere. Indeed, he seemed to have a devotee's faith that some of the legends regarding Ardneh, filled with miraculous accomplishments, could *not* be true.

Facts were what the Scholar doted on, things that could be verified and documented. Since well before the expedition got under way, Jervase had been almost feverishly hopeful that the bird would prove to be the key to its success. Mitra could provide them with the very clue they needed to settle the detail that was foremost in the Scholar's mind: determining at last the precise location, and perhaps the exact date, of what he considered one of the pivotal events in human history—Ardneh's death, in combat with the legendary archdemon Orcus, approximately a thousand years in the past.

But pinning down the exact time and place of that fatal struggle was not the only goal of the Scholar's expedition, and perhaps not its most important. For centuries rumors, legends, and speculations had circulated regarding some fabulous legacy, a treasure that Ardneh was supposed to have left for the benefit of his beloved human race. For centuries people had sought to locate this inheritance, frequently combing the broad stretch of this very valley—a vague, gentle saucer-shape between two distant mountain ranges.

Jervase had his own ideas about Ardneh's treasure. To the Scholar's thinking, no friend of the human race, certainly not the great wise benefactor that Ardneh was supposed to have been, would ever have played people such a foul trick as to leave them a vast accumulation of gold and jewels, essentially useless trinkets they would be certain to kill each other over.

Instead, Jervase envisioned Ardneh's inheritance (if indeed there was one; he was doubtful about that) as a trove of knowledge. Perhaps the great wise benefactor would also have included some kind of art, beauty meant to be shared by all the human beings of the world.

These days, according to Jervase, there was general agreement among scholars that the stories of Ardneh and his times, as related in Scripture, could not be entirely correct. But precisely which parts should, and which should not, be taken literally was still much in dispute. Again, Jervase had his own ideas on the subject, but stood ready to be proven wrong.

The Scholar's lack of interest in accumulating vast wealth was not widely shared. The king himself, a distant relative of the Rolfson family, did not view the idea of material treasure so indifferently. He had quietly provided backing for the Scholar's expedition, including a detachment of mounted troops to keep Jervase and his entourage safe while they traveled the somewhat risky desert—and especially as they made their way homeward with their loot, if they should come up lucky. Gold and jewels might not be what the Scholar was looking for, but if he found any he would not be so witless as to fail to bring them home to those who could properly appreciate their value.

The royal interest was expressed in the form of a small company of twenty troopers chosen by the able Captain Horkos and under his command. Chance had heard of several spirited discussions, while the expedition was in the planning stages, on the subject of how strong an escort should be provided. The final decision had been that sending many more troops than twenty would only be likely to call unwelcome attention to the enterprise.

There was no need to create unnecessary interest among the king of Sarasvati's rival monarchs in their respective countries—he who ruled in Yasodhara, for example, was known to nurse suspicions bordering on madness. The territory where the Scholar intended to carry out his search was not claimed by any power that Chance's great-uncle, the king, felt duty-bound to recognize.

All evidence so far had tended to confirm that a score of soldiers were going to be more than enough. There were reports of ragged bands of bandits in the region, and visual evidence of their presence in the form of the demon-altars that such outlaws had a habit of erecting in hope of gaining demonic help. But there was no reason to think that any of them would have the nerve to attack a company so strong. The Lady Ayaba had a reputation for being able to deal with demons if any should appear.

SPRING WAS MAKING STEADY INROADS ON THE WILD COUNTRY, THE broad, sparsely inhabited plains, crisscrossed at rare intervals by faint, winding roads. The ridingbeasts of the cavalry and the load-beasts that pulled the wagons had some tender green grass to eat when they were allowed to stop. On clear afternoons there were certain hours when the sunshine began to feel as warm as summer.

It was rarely possible to find a road that would take the caravan in precisely the direction Jervase had decided they should go. Simply rolling a train of wagons cross-country was a slow process inevitably plagued by mechanical breakdowns; an expedition of explorers might have managed better without wheeled vehicles altogether, and Chance wished they could have done so. But that had not been possible, for one reason because of the daily need to shield the owl from direct sunlight while traveling. Also the enchantress had wanted a private wagon, and the Scholar had insisted on bringing along key items from his library and his collection, and having some sheltered space in which to work. Above all, Jervase thought it essential to have transport available for a bulky volume of new discoveries.

Patches of snow still lingered on the shaded sides of the occasional rock outcroppings, and the small stream that diligently carved its trough between two gentle slopes was running high between low banks, though Chance thought it looked no more than knee deep anywhere. A few days ago, a lone herdsman, the first human they had met for several days, struggling to keep his scrawny flock together on its bank, had informed the travelers that this stream was called the Rivanna.

Chance, as Jervase's assistant, had seen the maps, and one notable feature held in common by almost all of them was the daunting amount of blank space, denoting unknown territory, that they contained. Jervase, frowning as he pored over these hand-drawn and -lettered documents, kept insisting that this stream, whatever its proper name, was bound to meld itself into some larger river before it found the ocean. But no one in the expedition was sure which great waterway that would be.

LADY AYABA HAD BROUGHT ALONG HER OWN SMALL ENTOURAGE OF helpers—none of them human. All were minor immaterial powers, that generally remained invisible, and needed no wagons, solid food, or shelter from the elements. The only member of this crew Chance had ever actually seen was the one who had provided light in the dark bird-wagon.

On the evening of the day of Chance's dawn adventure, sitting cross-legged on the ground at dinner with the other leaders around their small campfire, she reported almost casually that her attendant powers were gone.

That got the attention of everyone in the small group. Jervase blinked at the enchantress from across the fire. "Gone?"

"Gone, Scholar Jervase. I think it likely they have simply taken flight."

Chance, though not one of the expedition's leaders in any practical sense, topped them all in social rank, and so was routinely accepted in their discussions. Now he asked: "What would cause them to do that?"

The lady turned her face to him respectfully. "I do not know any specific cause, Lord Chance. It is as if my little helpers dread something that lies ahead of us more than they fear any punishment for disloyalty I would be likely to mete out."

"And what could the thing be that lies ahead? That t-terrified them so?" Chance hated his occasional stutter, but there seemed nothing to be done about it. The most annoying aspect was that it tended to make him sound frightened, whether he was or not. The present company had learned to pay the trivial defect no attention.

The Lady Ayaba made a graceful gesture, signifying ignorance. "Thousand-year-old traces, perhaps, of the king-demon Orcus." That had been the name of Ardneh's arch-antagonist; the two mighty powers had disposed of each other in a spasm of mutual annihilation. "But there is no real harm in such psychic relics, and I see nothing to suggest we have any cause for alarm."

THE NEXT DAY'S SUN HAD CLIMBED AS HIGH AS IT WAS GOING TO GET in this latitude and at this season, and was well along on its afternoon descent, when the caravan, having with some difficulty covered about ten kilometers, caught up with Jervase. This morning Chance was astride his own thoroughbred ridingbeast.

The Scholar had dismounted, and was surveying some rocky outcroppings as he stood on the rim of a miniature canyon, its depth three or four times the height of a man, carved by the small river as it began to make its way deeper and deeper into the earth. Scratches and small cavities showed where the explorer had already been poking and digging, not wasting any time. The Scholar had decided that a stream bank, where new layers of earth were constantly being exposed by running water, was the most likely place to seek artifacts. The sight of this reminded Chance of yesterday's predawn incident. Since then he had tried several times to question the owl Mitra, to find out what if anything she had really dropped into his hand. But the bird, as was more often the case than not, was refusing, or simply unable, to answer questions.

Again and again Chance told himself that if the Lady Ayaba, with all her proven skill, could find no trace of unknown magic newly attached to him, there was no reason for him to worry.

There were still several hours of daylight left, but as the Scholar wanted to use them searching and digging in this area for more Old World artifacts, he decided this would be a good place to camp.

Routine patrols were sent out, while most of the troopers dismounted and set to work in a well-established routine. During the past few days, ever since the caravan had begun following the river, they had had no problem finding water; they had been following the river fairly closely as they made their way steadily downstream. Here and there trees grew in clusters along its banks, making a narrow winding strip of woodland where handy firewood could usually be gathered with little trouble. Grass grew more thickly here, providing forage for the animals. As foragers and scouts who had been paralleling the line of march came in, they were put to work erecting tents.

WITH THE WAGONS HALTED, THE SCHOLAR CONTINUED TO CONCEN-trate upon his search for surviving shreds and traces of the ancient world. If Jervase followed his usual procedure, he would settle into the wagon after sunset and spend an hour or two listening to the bird's vocalizations, trying to induce it to undertake something like a real conversation. He seldom succeeded in this effort, but he kept trying.

Later in the evening, if events followed their usual course, the enchantress would take a turn as Mitra's companion and scribe. Jervase thought it important to have someone who could write in the presence of the owl at all times.

GRABBING CHUNKS OF BISCUIT AND SAUSAGE TO TAKE WITH HIM FOR a belated midday meal, Chance went out by his own decision, telling the others he would try to find some tidbits for the owl. As he was about to leave the camp Jervase called after him, reminding him to look for artifacts from Ardneh's era whenever he had the opportunity.

This time Chance was walking—just because he wanted to stretch his legs—and when on foot it was easier to make a close inspection of the ground and the walled high banks.

THE SOLDIER WHO SERVED AS VETERINARIAN HAD ANNOUNCED THAT Mitra's injured wing did not appear to be broken. But the owl was still favoring the member, and it seemed doubtful that she would be able to fly and forage for herself during the coming night. Chance thought that even if the wing was functional, the owl might be too frightened to make the attempt. It crossed his mind to wonder if the bird could be cunning enough to fake an injury, so that no one would try to make her fly when she was frightened.

The bird was on reasonably friendly terms with Chance—as much as it was with anyone. About the most that could be said for the relationship was that Mitra tolerated her human caregivers, and declined to escape from them, putting up with their presence and their questions in return for the guarantee of a safe nest and steady diet. Chance seldom failed to take an opportunity to get away from the creature for a time. It was also good to have some time away from the sight and sound of other people.

MUNCHING ON AN END OF SAUSAGE, CHANCE HAD WORKED HIS WAY about two hundred meters farther downstream, and was stepping carefully along the narrow bank, one wall of the small canyon close enough for him to lean on if he put out an arm. At certain places there appeared to be the faint remnant of a path.

The air was comparatively warm down here, out of most of the breeze. He was advancing slowly, keeping his eyes open for anything that might serve as owl-food—he doubted stranded fish would do—for half-buried artifacts, for anything of interest. He was think-ing that the stream must have recently risen slightly, for there was no muddy rim of shoreline visible at water's edge. But the tag-end of winter was still hanging on, the weather had been too cold to hope for turtle eggs . . . not that he was even sure the bird would ever eat that kind of thing. . . .

"Hello." The voice was tentative, small, and childish.

THREE

C HANCE LOOKED UP SHARPLY AND SLOWED HIS PACE. THE GIRL appeared to be no older than seven. She was standing up to her slender ankles in the brisk ripples not twenty meters ahead of him. Until this moment, it seemed, the child had been so motionless that Chance's eyes had failed to register her presence. Wild hair of a startling red, stirring in the faint currents of air, framed her pale face. Her clothing was unusual, what appeared to be a single tight-fitting garment, a kind of sheath that covered her body and limbs to wrists and ankles—like long underwear, but far more trim and sleek and stylish. Its color, a mottled, vaguely metallic gray, blended into the background of rock and earth and bits of driftwood so well that it seemed to be trying to establish the illusion that—except for her exceptional hair—she was not there at all. She wore no ornament of any kind.

The girl's body was bent slightly forward, her dainty right hand clutching the circular rim of a small fishing net. Her arm was angled, cocked like the trigger on a crossbow, ready to lash the net into the water with a scooping motion the next time a suitable target appeared at the proper spot in the shallows. That this method might be more effective than seemed likely at first glance was evidenced by the presence of a couple of small fish, twitching slightly on a tuft of grass that adorned the nearby riverbank.

Chance blinked, coming to a halt. "Hello yourself."

"Seen any big fish upstream?" the girl asked him brightly. She had flashed Chance a brief smile, and now dropped her gaze to the water again. A serious fisher-girl, very calm and self-possessed. "I know they're in there."

"No. But then I haven't been looking for fish." Chance hesitated, then added: "You must live somewhere nearby." His eyes were drawn back to the net, which at second glance was odd enough to deserve some attention—the mesh of it was fairly fine, of remarkably even workmanship. He couldn't tell just what it had been woven of—as if the string, or cord, or thread, was as translucent as glass. The second interesting net that Chance had seen recently, this one seemed to have little in common with the first, which was still stuffed under the driver's seat of the bird's wagon. That was of a coarser, stronger mesh, made to catch much bigger creatures.

The girl shrugged. "Just camping, sort of. My family does a lot of traveling. My name is Zalmo, by the way." And her eyes flicked at Chance as if she were wondering what he thought about the name.

It was the first time he had ever heard of anyone or anything named Zalmo. But it would hardly be polite to say so. "I should have introduced myself before this. I beg your pardon. My name is Chance."

"Is Chance your only name?"

"Chance Rolfson." Now, possibly, he was about to discover whether his family's fame had spread this far from home; but of course it would be unlikely to get a positive result in such a matter from a small child.

But Zalmo only nodded and smiled, as if that was the answer she had been expecting. Then she shifted her stance slightly in the stream, looking for fish again. Chance had tested the water earlier, and found it still carried winter's cold. But the girl did not seem to mind standing barefoot, up to her insteps, in the swift bubbling flow.

Feeling a sudden protective impulse, Chance asked her: "Zalmo, do you feel safe, out here alone?"

She cocked her head, seeming to think about it, then offered another brief smile. "Yes, here I feel secure. I wouldn't everywhere, though." She paused. "There are a few places that I might like to visit—but I don't dare. And there's one, a very special one, where I really want to go but I just can't get in." Her smile grew. "Anyway, I'm not alone any longer, am I?"

Chance had to smile. "No."

"Do *you* feel safe, Chance Rolfson?"

He blinked. "Yes." He looked around. "I guess so. But I . . ." Today he had come out exploring, as he usually did, unarmed except for the sturdy hunting knife he commonly wore at his belt, more as a tool than as a weapon. He didn't think it necessary to add that within range of a good loud shout he had a company of soldiers ready to come galloping or running to his defense. ". . . I'm not exactly alone either."

The girl seemed determined to be curious. "You said you weren't looking for fish. What are you looking for?"

"Well . . ." He wasn't going to attempt a detailed answer to that question for any seven-year-old, not even the most articulate and engaging. "Old things," he finally offered. That was true enough, as far as it went.

That reply seemed only to sharpen Zalmo's interest. The girl straightened, relaxing the arm that held the net. As if she were giving up a pretense of being interested in fish, and it was time to get down to business. When she did she surprised Chance again. "I like old things too. I really do, I *really* find them fascinating. What sort are you trying to discover?"

"Well . . . things that are *very* old." Chance shook his head. In a different tone he added: "Actually I was also hoping to find some food, to feed my owl. I know that sounds strange, but—"

"Does your owl eat fish? Would you like to take her these?" Zalmo nodded toward the bank.

Chance shook his head. "I can't remember that we've ever given her any fish. And she's never brought home any water-creatures, so I doubt they're part of her regular diet. I had better decline with thanks."

"Having an owl is a little strange. But I could tell you stranger things than that." Zalmo gave him a sly smile.

Chance's own childhood was still fresh enough in his memory that he tended to be wary of mischievous children. It seemed time to change the subject. "That's a neat fishnet you have there."

"Thank you. I made it myself."

"You did?" Chance saw no possibility of believing such a thing, but he wasn't going to argue. "You are a girl of many surprises."

Red hair streamed in the light breeze. "A boy who has a pet owl is surprising too. Don't you think?"

Chance's eyes were searching the upper banks, the canyon rims an easy pebble-toss above. "I guess maybe I am an odd person, really. Some people in my family think so. Is your family camped very near here?"

"Not far away."

Chance looked up and down the stream. There was no sign of anyone else. "Are they fishing too? Your father and mother?"

"They're not far. Neither is my brother—he's probably closer than they are. He likes to swim."

"Does he?" Here it would be like diving into a shallow bath of ice water, half-filled with nearly frozen rocks, with every now and then a chip of pure ice drifting down. "Well, in that I wish him luck," Chance said. One of the odd things, he thought, about this odd little girl was her voice—though just what was so strange about it he couldn't quite decide. Actually her accent in the common language was quite familiar, something he wouldn't have expected to encounter this far from Sarasvati.

Now she had returned her concentration to the possibility of fish. It seemed that none were appearing, though. After some delay he offered: "The bird's not exactly a pet."

"Oh? What is it, then?"

"Well . . ." Somewhat belatedly it struck Chance that talking about the owl, in connection with a search for old things, might lead the conversation too close to their expedition's real purpose. "We were hoping to train it as a hunter. You know, the way some people do with hawks."

She nodded wisely. "I have heard that there is good hunting in these parts. I suppose the owl brings you things from time to time. Things it catches. Or things it finds."

Had there been a slight, sly accent on that last word? "Oh yes. Sometimes."

The girl nodded wisely. She still seemed perfectly content to remain barefoot in the frigid rushing stream, and Chance's own toes, warm and dry in his scruffy hiking shoes, were beginning to ache in sympathy. He asked her: "Water's pretty cold, isn't it? Aren't your feet freezing?"

"The suit I'm wearing keeps them warm!" Eagerly, as if he had raised the very subject she had been waiting to discuss. "Haven't you noticed it?"

"Yes, I did notice your special—garment. Very pretty. But it doesn't cover your feet."

"It doesn't need to!"

Chance shook his head. "Then there must be some magic woven in."

Zalmo nodded calmly. "There is. Along with other things. It's special magic that offers great protection. It's called *technology*." The girl seemed proud of the big word. "Have you heard of the Old World?"

This time Chance paused, and his voice was different when he answered. "Yes, I have. You're saying your suit is from that time? More than a thousand years ago?"

"Much more. Yes it is. Do you have anything from the Old World with you?"

"I . . . no."

"Oh, that's too bad. Would you like to try on a special suit like mine?"

Polite society held an ingrained taboo, that was well-nigh universal, against accepting any kind of magic offered by a stranger. The corollary was, of course, that it was considered bad manners to make such an offer. "Well . . . possibly. But I don't think your suit would fit me."

"Silly boy!" Zalmo was almost condescending. "I didn't mean mine. I mean, if some item of a proper size should be made available. It might even do *more* for you than keep your feet warm." Her flashing eyes seemed to promise some truly amazing benefit.

"I'd like to find out more about your suit. What makes you think it came from the Old World?" Chance wondered uneasily if there was any possibility that this child might know what she was talking about—and, if so, whether her parents had any idea she was on the verge of giving away treasure.

Whatever her degree of knowledge, whatever her ultimate purpose, the girl was serious. Tossing her net ashore beside the fish, as if they had all served their purpose, she persisted: "You could have a suit like mine to start with. And then, other things."

Chance looked up and down the narrow, curving canyon. "Which way are your parents? I'd like to talk to them."

"I don't know if that's possible just now . . . but come this way."

Zalmo, abandoning her fine net and her catch without a second thought, turned and began splashing downstream.

Chance followed, remaining on the bank, trudging downstream along the faint riparian path. He was surprised to find that he had to move briskly just to keep up with her short splashing strides.

Over her shoulder the girl called: "If you were lucky enough to get your hands on something that was really from the Old World, would you have to show it to your friends? I mean the people you are traveling with?"

"Yes, of course. Why wouldn't I show it to them? As you say, they are my friends."

"But not if you had promised to keep it secret. That would be a different matter, would it not? Chance?"

"I haven't made any such promise."

"But if you had."

This conversation was not leading anywhere that Chance wanted to go. "I'd have to know more about it. This mysterious thing, whatever it is. Exactly what I was promising."

"Maybe your friends don't really care that much about old things. Not as much as you do." Zalmo kept splashing steadily along.

As they moved he tried to look more closely at her suit. Except for the neat exactitude of the fit, it did indeed resemble nothing so much as long winter underwear, if such a garment could be woven out of metal. But the usual rear trapdoor built into such garments was not visible from a couple of meters' distance, and the mottled pattern was certainly unusual.

The garment did not in the least resemble any Old World artifact that Chance could remember seeing, or anything he'd heard the Scholar talk about. Of course the best way to get more information from the girl might well be not to seem too eager. This seemed like the proper time to roll out the expedition's official cover story. This would be the first time Chance had tried it out.

He said: "If you seriously want to know, or if your parents do, what we're really trying to find, I can tell you. It's the infirmary run by the Servants of Ardneh. We've heard that they've built one, a place to care for sick people, out here in the desert."

Evidently the girl had to think that over, for she fell silent for a time. Chance maintained his downstream pace, with the girl still splashing effortlessly along beside him. From her expression, Chance got the impression that his new companion did not think much of the Servants of Ardneh.

When Zalmo spoke again, her voice had become smaller and more distant. With a toss of her flaming hair she finally said: "I've heard those people are not as good and kind as they pretend to be. Not always to be trusted."

"Oh? We have Ardneh's Servants in our homeland, Sarasvati, and they have a fine reputation there. Some of them spend all their lives taking care of poor people, sick people." He decided not to mention that his mother, only a couple of years ago, had been one of the organization's original sponsors.

"Then doubtless you know them better than I do." Now the girl sounded somewhat put out that he was not pursuing what ought to have been a tantalizing suggestion of a secret present. She tossed her hair again, the strands impressively active in the breeze.

Then she hit Chance with another unexpected question: "Have you had any . . . adventures on your journey?"

"Adventures? No." Judging by the experience of the expedition so far, whatever bandits prowled through this wasteland might still be hundreds of kilometers away.

"Tell me, does your owl, that is not a pet, ever fly out at night?"

"Yes, of course she does. On most nights she flies out. T-that's what owls do."

"If she does what owls do, then maybe she has had adventures."

"I can't argue with that. But if she has, she hasn't told me about them."

"But she does bring you things."

"Sometimes."

"But you don't want to talk about them." Zalmo nodded encouragingly. "That's all right. We don't have to talk about anything you don't want to discuss."

Chance answered that one with a grunt. He kept trudging along, looking for some sign of his new companion's parents or brother up ahead, and failing to discover any. The girl kept wading briskly with him. How far had they come? No enormous distance, something between fifty meters and a hundred. Rounding a bend brought Chance in sight of a place where one of the stream's banks rose sharply into a miniature cliff, topped by a rounded outcropping. Just at the peak of the little cliff there arose a crude but obviously artificial structure, where several weighty slabs of rock had been arranged to form a table-like form, waist high to a human adult, and broad as a wagon bed.

Chance squinted, puzzled at the sight. It looked like some of the demon-altars the expedition had passed several days ago, but this was bigger. Those altars had been built of pebbles, compared to this. Someone—not just someone, but a whole group of people, to judge by the rocks' substantial size—had put considerable effort into the construction.

Zalmo had stopped at Chance's side and joined him in looking upward. She sniffed. "I would say that is an altar, and that it is crudely made."

"Well . . . yes, I suppose it is."

HE HAD NEVER APPROACHED ANY OF THE OTHER ALTARS ANYWHERE near as closely as this. Curious about this discovery, Chance briefly scanned the bank in front of him for the easiest ascent, then went scrambling up the steep slope, provoking a miniature landslide of dirt and pebbles. In a couple of moments he was at the top, standing beside what was obviously an altar where someone had quite recently been making offering to some nameless but no doubt evil power.

The girl had made the climb just as swiftly as Chance, and more surefootedly, kicking down less dirt and gravel, wasting less energy in scrambling and waving her arms for balance. Her red hair streamed more furiously than ever, as if the light breeze passing near her picked up energy and speed. Her small shoeless feet seemed as indifferent to the rocks on the steep bank as they had been to those of the river bottom—it could well be that her magic suit really worked.

If it was truly an Old World artifact . . . well, in that case Chance could not begin to guess what might be possible. Several times he had been allowed to see some of the Scholar's greatest private treasures, the ones he brought out of hiding only on special occasions—they were all small bits of that ancient and marvelous technology: a glass that made small things look large, and a knife blade that seemed impossible to dull.

FOUR

L OOKING AROUND, CHANCE FOUND NO ONE ELSE IN SIGHT. THERE were no dwellings, no other signs of human habitation, not even a thread of smoke, anywhere out to a distant horizon rimmed in places by mountains so far away that they looked blue-gray.

Nearby were a few bushes, and a natural jumble of stones of widely assorted sizes, raw material for more construction if anyone wanted to put in the time and effort.

But the buzz of an insect brought Chance's attention back to the altar. In the center of the broad, flat horizontal stone were several reddish brown stains of what appeared to be dried blood, still fresh enough to interest flies.

More of the same substance had been used, with some care, to mark out words. Chance's recent studies with the Scholar enabled him to decipher most of the lettering's ancient characters. At last he made out:

Nathan Gokard

"I wouldn't touch any part of it if I were you," cautioned Zalmo, in her quietest voice yet.

"I wasn't going to."

Chance could see that what was probably a second name was also here, inscribed above the first, in a different array of larger symbols. A knotty little symbol, and three more words, had been carved between the two names, linking them—like some happy couple announcing to the world that they were sweethearts. Parts of the lettering were crudely smeared in some dark repulsive substance that Chance wasn't going to try to identify. It must be blood, he thought, thickened with something else. He wasn't going to try to guess just what the other ingredient might be.

In a few moments he had puzzled out the whole inscription:

AVENARIUS

& his faithful servant

Nathan Gokard

The little girl was looking very serious. "Can you read the two names there, Chance Rolfson?"

"I can." His voice was very quiet. "Yes . . . I'm pretty sure I can."

"Read them, then, and remember them both. The lower one belongs to a man, and you can say it. But never try to pronounce the first one. Not even in a tiny whisper. Certain words should never be said aloud." The girl stopped, waiting with wide eyes for a response from Chance.

It seemed to take a long time to get out the simple words. "I never will."

Zalmo nodded. She had come to a halt standing not quite close enough to the rude, smeared pile of stone to touch it. Wide-eyed, gazing at the crude construction, while holding her hands behind her back, she told Chance: "I have seen these clumsy things before. Many people call them altars."

"Yes, I'm sure that's what they are." A new uneasiness was growing in Chance, quite apart from any anxiety about making Old

World discoveries, or revealing the goals of the expedition. He couldn't pinpoint the moment when it had started, but it was focused on the girl.

He said: "T-traveling through the desert we've seen a few others, none as big as this. They were all dedicated to various demons. Or so I was told."

Zalmo stepped forward to rap boldly with her tiny knuckles on a bloodstained stone. "Bandits, like this one who signs his name here Nathan Gokard. Dangerous people who hate other people, make these things and scrawl their names on them. This altar is even more poorly built than most. *I* would never place an offering on any of these altars. Unless I had no choice. I wonder if you would do that?"

Chance was signing that he would not. Involuntarily he had backed away from his new companion by half a step, and he was staring at her intently.

"I believe they do have something to do with demons," Zalmo observed brightly, in her little-girl voice. "Creatures whose names are best not spoken aloud by human beings. These crude stone altars, built out in the middle of nowhere." She put out a hand and rocked a loose stone back and forth, then shook her head in disapproval. "Whoever put this one up has much to learn about building anything."

"Yes." Chance could hear that his own voice had fallen to a whisper. "Demons." Like most people, he had never seen a demon and never wanted to. Now it seemed that he had read the name of one, but he had no intention of saying it. Every time he had passed near one of their altars it had increased his uneasiness.

According to the Lady Ayaba, as well as a number of old scare-stories Chance had heard in childhood and half forgotten, they sometimes appeared in human shape.

Zalmo had turned her face toward him. But the little girl was only looking past him, through her flaming curls of hair. She said: "Someone is calling you."

Chance had heard no call. He turned, looking out over a wilderness of scattered trees, jutting rocks, and barren land, still hearing nothing but the whisper of a breeze and the continuous plashing of the stream in its small canyon a few meters below. From the slight elevation of this high bank he could see the modest cluster of trees behind which he knew the camp had been established. About halfway to the grove, at a distance of a little over a hundred meters, one of the uniformed soldiers was coming toward him atop the high bank of the stream. Chance immediately recognized Vardtrad, a veteran private, dark hair peppered heavily with gray.

At a slight sound, Chance turned back, to see that Zalmo had fastened her gaze on him intently. She asked cheerfully: "What's that you're wearing around your neck?"

Chance looked down. His fingers, groping inside the loose collar of his shirt, discovered a fine chain, from which depended a small, hard weight. Pulling this out from under his chin, he held it under his nose and stared at it stupidly. This could hardly be anything but what the owl had dropped into his hand. Though he had never actually seen the object before, the feel of it was recognizable.

How he came to be wearing the chain around his neck was utterly mysterious. He had dropped the owl's gift somewhere in the darkness of the wagon, had never pulled it on over his head.

Had he?

The little weight supported by the fine links was no heavier than a large coin, only a little bigger, and almost flat enough to be a piece of money. It was carved or molded of a stone or ceramic substance, mottled black and white and brown, like a morsel of marble. To Chance its contours suggested the idea of a somewhat misshapen key.

Zalmo was pointing at it with a tiny finger. "Looks to me like the key to Ardneh's workshop," she announced, matter-of-factly. "If I were you, I wouldn't let anyone know I had it."

The key to . . . what? Ardneh's workshop? Chance had never heard of such a thing. But in his confusion he remained silent. *Certain words should never be said aloud.* Fighting inner turmoil, Chance turned his back on the girl, looking for help, some kind of guidance.

Vardtrad, seeing that the young lord was facing him again, lifted an arm in salutation, meanwhile continuing his patient advance. When the soldier had come a few meters closer, he called out in his hoarse voice: "Lord Chance, the Scholar wants you. Seems you're due for another turn at bird-sitting."

Chance turned back to the little girl, meaning to say good-bye, and half hoping to get some explanation of what she had called a key. But Zalmo and her magic suit had totally disappeared. Of course it was no surprise that any girl—any human—might suddenly go shy, and dart for cover, at the sight of a sword-wearing stranger in uniform. Chance told himself that Zalmo could have done just that. There were a number of sizable bushes and large rocks, offering possible concealment, studding the ground up to a few meters from the demon's altar.

Though Vardtrad had already delivered his message, he was methodically continuing his forward progress. Suddenly the soldier paused, having evidently just recognized the altar for what it was. Squinting at the pile of stones, as if he saw something he did not like, he moved forward a few more paces, stepped sideways to get a different angle, stopped again in his tracks, and continued gazing at it for the space of several breaths.

Vardtrad put out a hand as if to touch the clean side of the stone that had been defiled with blood, then let his hand fall back to his side without making contact.

"The little girl told me that is some demon's name," said Chance, pointing at the upper word.

"Little girl, sir?" Vardtrad looked around.

"You didn't see her as you came up?"

"No sir." The soldier did not appear much interested.

"What do you think of this, Vardtrad?" Chance asked as they were walking back to camp. But when he reached for the chain inside his collar, it had vanished again. His hand could find no trace of anything there but his own skin.

The man beside him was blinking amiably. "What's that, Lord Chance?"

"Nothing. Never mind. I had—I had an idea, but it went away."

Vardtrad trudged on imperturbably. "Sir, mine tend to do that all the time."

BACK IN CAMP, CHANCE IMMEDIATELY SOUGHT OUT THE SCHOLAR. Jervase had retreated inside his private wagon. It was slightly larger than the other wagons, and fitted out for business, not for luxury. One side of the interior held a bunk, too narrow for more than a single occupant. On the opposite wall of curving canvas there hung a large map, drawn on waterproofed leather, showing the valley of the Rivanna and vast reaches of the surrounding wastelands. In this setting the Scholar spent many waking hours studying the samples of his precious collection that he had brought from home. Most of them dated back to the Old World, though there were some items from the later time of Ardneh.

The collection consisted mostly of fragments of unidentifiable items, personal ornaments, pieces of what Jervase explained was probably cookware. There were scraps of parchment-like substance, faintly marked with what was indubitably writing in an unknown language. The Scholar had brought a variety of specimens with him on this trip to aid him in comparing and classifying any new discoveries that might be made. So far, there had been discouragingly few.

Chance found Jervase sitting cross-legged on the wagon's floor, in front of the tiny table that was built in below the map, in quiet contemplation of the few genuine specimens he had so far been able to gather on this trip. Spread out on the table before him were parts of what appeared to be a broken bracelet, half of some kind of writing implement, other bits of exotic material about which Chance could only guess.

The Scholar's own magical ability was as limited as Chance's, but he had consulted specialists to determine the age of his collected specimens. Items from the time of Ardneh's legendary combat against the demons of the East were dated at approximately a thousand years. For many thousands of years before that, the powerful, mysterious humans of the Old World, Ardneh's creators, had ruled the earth, largely by the power of their own peculiar branch of magic called technology.

Today Jervase, searching along the stream in the opposite direction from Chance, had made a minor discovery, a new fragment of one of the ancient artificial materials, that had him somewhat excited.

He raised his head abstractedly as the boy appeared. "Chance, I'm glad that Vardtrad found you. Would you be good enough to take another turn with Mitra? She seems inordinately restless today."

"Of course." Chance wanted to talk about the mysterious object on the chain, the owl's gift that had gone away and then come back again. But what seemed of more immediate importance was his strange encounter with a peculiar little girl, who wore what she claimed was a magic suit and had told Chance that it came from the Old World.

Those last two words got the Scholar's immediate attention, as

Chance had known they would. Jervase put down the fragment he was fussing with, and frowned. "A suit? What was it made of? Did you get a close look?"

"Not a very close look. It was very tight-fitting, and covered her down to wrists and ankles. It looked like it might have been of some kind of metallic cloth."

Jervase's tentative excitement drained away. "Never heard of any ancient garb that looked like that—never heard of any cloth, metallic or not, surviving for so long . . . did you mention the Old World before she did?"

"No. I did tell her that we were looking for old things."

"Well, then . . ."

As soon as Jervase was sure Chance had brought him nothing more solid than a story, he effectively ceased to listen. In a moment, the Scholar had returned his attention to his collection of artifacts.

Now was not the time to raise the subject of the Key to Ardneh's Workshop—not when there was nothing he could show. Chance also thought of mentioning the demon-altar; but as the expedition had encountered other similar structures over the past few days, and this one was not that much different from them, he saved his breath and went to attend the bird.

ON HIS WAY TO DO SO, CHANCE SAW CAPTAIN HORKOS AND THE EN-chantress nearby and stopped to tell them about the altar and the peculiar girl. They were as politely uninterested as Jervase had been.

"She was wearing a strange-looking garment," Chance repeated. "Some kind of metallic cloth. Swore it kept her feet warm, though it didn't cover them."

At last the Lady Ayaba seemed to be starting to take him halfway seriously. A faint vertical frown line appeared in her forehead. "If you please, my Lord, come with me to my wagon for a moment."

Inside the wagon, a little smaller than the Scholar's but furnished

more elaborately, the enchantress drew a short wand from somewhere, as she had done on the morning of the bird's injury, passed it
over Chance, then nodded with routine satisfaction when her ring
winked light.

"No doubt the child was quite as odd as you say, my Lord, but she
worked no significant magic on you, whatever her peculiarities may
have been."

Somehow Chance got the impression that Lady Ayaba still suspected he was making the whole thing up. He said: "I didn't really
think she had cast any spells on me." Automatically he flexed the fingers of his left hand, then silently ordered himself to stop doing that;
the gesture was rapidly becoming something of a habit. Besides, the
Lady Ayaba's wand had again touched the hand in the course of her
latest examination, and nothing had happened.

When the enchantress opened her little cabinet of paraphernalia
to put away the wand, Chance was looking over her shoulder, and
caught a glimpse of several oddities. He had never shown or felt any
particular aptitude for magic, but tended to find its trappings fascinating. These included what appeared to be a miniaturized carpenter's set, far too small to be of any mundane use, even had the blades
been steel and not mere imitations carefully shaped in wood. In the
next compartment nested a gnarled, fist-sized object whose two eye-
less sockets seemed to be looking back at Chance—either a
shrunken human head or a great imitation of one. He quickly
looked away.

The lady's voice was matter-of-fact. "I'm surprised we haven't encountered more people, these last few days. We've been sticking
pretty close to the stream, and that's where people are likely to show
up, if they're anywhere in the vicinity."

FIVE

THE WEATHER HAD TURNED A LITTLE WARMER. CHANCE ATE HIS evening meal sitting as usual beside the small campfire with Jervase and Horkos and the Lady Ayaba. After that he carried his blanket under the bird-wagon rather than inside, wanting to escape the heavy atmosphere of confined bird-stink.

Lying down to sleep, the boy fully expected that he would dream. On most mornings he awakened with the feeling of having wandered extensively through the fantasy land of sleep, though it was rare when he retained any firm memory of what his dreams had been about. The few that did leave him with a lasting impression were almost invariably unpleasant.

. . . TONIGHT HE FOUND HIMSELF IN SOME KIND OF CAVE. HE WAS frightened by a deep subterranean rumbling, rocks falling from overhead, and then an eruption of darkness from the earth. . . .

. . . But on a second look, the place where he found himself was not exactly a cave. The structure surrounding him seemed to have all the design and decoration of a mighty palace though it was somehow sunken in the earth. Something compelled him to go forward, but the way in front of him was blocked by a closed and formidable door.

. . . He was holding in his hand one of the Scholar's scrolls, and he knew, with the secret knowledge granted only in dreams, that the scroll was somehow the key he needed to pass the barrier. He knew also, with the same dream-certainty, that the monarch who had ruled in this palace was dead, and that it would be a terrible thing to find him where he must be found, lying in state in one of these awesome rooms. Still the dreamer had no choice but to push on. . . .

But it was not the royal corpse that lay on display in front of Chance when the door stood open. He found himself gazing, without understanding, upon the dead body of the Lady Ayaba, formally displayed in a ponderous and ornate coffin, attended by the faint, whining song of invisible and eerie powers.

On the wall above the bier hung suspended a strange, massive sword, far too big for human arms to wield—or so it appeared to be at first glance. As Chance moved closer he could see that the sword was only a flat image, marvelously detailed, somehow emblazoned on the wall.

The coffin and corpse had disappeared. Standing beneath the imaged weapon was a smallish man, with upswept graying hair and glittering eyes. Leaning with folded arms against the wall, he smirked at Chance and laughed a wicked little laugh, and told him: "I will make the worst promise that you have ever heard."

Waves of fear, like the stench of something rotten, came washing outward from the little man, starting to make Chance sick. But still there was a question he had to ask the man. He was given no choice about it. "What must I do?"

The other leaned forward. With the air of one who took tremendous joy in delivering a curse, he whispered: "You must open the door to the next room!"

With that, the man was gone. Chance, unable to do otherwise, moved toward the door ahead of him. Somehow it opened, and he passed through.

And now it seemed that he was no longer underground or in a palace, but simply out of doors, moving under an open sky of swirling clouds. Powerful tall figures, mostly in the shape of men and women, but some borrowing the forms of animals, stood about him waving swords in ritualistic patterns. They seemed to be performing a kind of dance, or formal combat. Whatever it really was, it was more than he could understand. . . .

HE STIRRED AND TURNED, HALF WAKING, THEN SLEPT AND DREAMED again.

Once more he was walking through the Rivanna's narrow canyon, worrying because he had somehow become separated from the soldiers who were supposed to be guarding him—and suddenly he was confronted by a man with bright red hair carrying a large net in each hand—and then behind the first man was another and another, all of them identical, like figures escaped from a hall of mirrors. Their swinging nets swirled everywhere, and there was no escape . . . until the little chain tightened around Chance's neck and, somehow without choking him in the least, yanked him swirling into the clouds—

HIS DREAM WAS SHATTERED, ITS FRAGMENTS SCATTERED OUT OF memory, by the quavering voice of the caged owl, coming from inside the wagon, saying something at once outrageous and fascinating. But by the time he had awakened enough to grab for his slate and chalk, he could no longer remember what it was.

"HOW'D YOU SLEEP, LORD CHANCE?" VARDTRAD ASKED HIM, IN THE morning twilight, as they passed each other, coming and going, on the way to the latrine trench.

"Well enough." Chance knew there had been dreams, but could remember almost nothing of them.

Riding the bird-wagon through the morning's daylight hours, Chance was glad to see that Mitra was now holding her injured wing in something close to its normal position while she slept.

MORE HOURS HAD PASSED, AND A WARMING SUN WAS HIGH IN THE sky, when the bird, stirring in her daytime sleep, made a little preliminary noise that seemed to come from deep in her owlish throat. It was the usual sign that she might be about to talk. Chance heard it from outside the wagon and moved quickly to climb in.

Chance worked at copying his recorded fragments of possible bird-speech, as usual, with a piece of chalk on slate. Many times he couldn't be sure if a sound was a word or not—then he did the best he could, and added a question mark.

Jervase, who was determined to give the owl every chance to be of help, would be certain to look at these notes soon. Then the Scholar would copy whatever snippets of talk he thought worthwhile onto his own private parchment scroll. Depending on what he thought Mitra had said, he might make some new marking on his growing map. In the month since the expedition had left home, there had been several versions of the Scholar's map, each painstakingly amended in turn, until its general shabbiness convinced the maker it would be wiser to start over.

CHANCE THOUGHT THAT MIGHT BE ALL THE OWLISH CONVERSATION for the day, but he was wrong. Toward sunset, waking up, the bird said very clearly, out of nowhere: "Ardneh's key." And in the same moment Mitra made an awkward gesture with one leg, pointing with one claw at Chance's chest. Looking down inside his collar he saw that the crooked marbly chip had reappeared, suspended on its fine chain.

He made a small note on his slate—then rubbed the two words out with his finger, telling himself it was unlikely that the owl had really said anything of the kind. Had he dozed off himself, and dreamed again?

One possible explanation came to mind: He might have repeated Zalmo's words in his own sleep-mutterings, and the bird might have picked them up that way.

His first instinct was to yank the chain off over his head, but his darting hand aborted that motion before it had got fairly started. Instead he simply held the little object up in front of his nose and squinted at it in puzzlement.

ON THE FOLLOWING NIGHT, A THUNDERSTORM CAME AND WENT during the very early morning. Chance heard a noise and had to get out from under the wagon and climb inside, to make sure that Mitra was all right.

In the flare of lightning from the middle distance, only a kilometer or two away, Chance could see the owl's beak quivering. What sounded like three words came forth.

Nothing like *Ardneh's Key* this time. Chance wiped the wetness of rain from his forehead. "Again. Repeat for me, please, Mitra."

Requests for repetition often were not met, but this one was.

This time he heard the three words plainly, the same sounds in length and tone, but sharpened into clarity: *The Beastlord comes.* Chance had not the faintest idea what they might purport to mean. At least this time there was no possibility that he had simply dreamed them.

He would be sure to tell the Scholar what the bird had said: *The Beastlord comes.*

Yes, tell him, but first be conscientious and write it down. Chance got out his slate again.

THE TENTMAKER SOLDIER HAD DONE A NEAT JOB OF REPAIRING THE hole in the bird-wagon's overhead fabric, closing the rent tightly enough to repel rain and keep out ordinary light. Now a narrow crevice of opening at the canvas door showed brightening sky, but it was still very dark inside. The bird's keepers had learned that one small candle, or oil lamp, did not much bother the owl's great yellow eyes, as long as they were closed and its head was turned away.

But now the sun was coming up.

On days of bright sun, Mitra soon grew frantic unless her nesting area was covered with an extra layer of dark blanket. Chance thought that if they were still hauling the bird around a couple of months from now, when spring warmed into summer, the inside of this wagon was going to get infernally hot—but there was no use worrying about that this early in the spring, when the general concern was still about keeping warm.

CHANCE EXAMINED HIS RECENT NOTES AGAIN. HE NOTED, WITH A feeling of vague concern, that he had not written down *Ardneh's key*, despite the Scholar's insistence that he wanted everything that sounded remotely like a word. Chance told himself that those two words had probably not really come from the bird at all.

But what about *the Beastlord comes*. What did that mean? The name *Beastlord* irresistibly reminded him of the frightening apparition he'd glimpsed through the hole in the wagon cover.

When Chance confronted Jervase with *the Beastlord comes* it got an immediate reaction. Jervase turned a frowning stare on his assistant, but at first said nothing.

Chance's questions were generally encouraged. He asked: "Who would 'the Beastlord' be?"

Jervase stretched his back and rubbed his eyes. If he was consistent—and he usually was—the next time he paused in his work he would descend from the wagon to give his long legs room to stretch. His answer when he finally gave it was mild enough. "Well, on that point I can enlighten you. Though I might have thought your reading had already done so. It's another name, or title, for Draffut."

"Sorry, Jervase, but I don't think I ever quite—"

"You should have come across that name, if you've been doing the reading I assigned." The reproof sounded more tired than angry. The Scholar had recommended—his polite way of making something a firm requirement—that his student and apprentice read extensively in Scripture. Unfortunately, spending more than a few minutes in a session with crackling, faded scrolls and blurry lettering had tended to put Chance to sleep; relating their contents to the real world was not something that he did instinctively.

Jervase had given reasons for his recommendation. "The scrolls of course are filled with legends and wonders, many of which are pure fiction and can be safely disregarded. But they also contain nuggets of solid fact regarding the Old World and the succeeding Age of Ardneh—facts that are available nowhere else."

Chance signed agreement. "I have been reading as you suggested, Scholar, and I did run into the name. But it wasn't clear to me just who or what Draffut was. He—it—didn't seem to be human."

"Certainly not, though appearing invariably as a great friend of humanity. A close companion of Ardneh, and the patron of all healers and all animals."

"Not a demon, then."

"You can't have read very thoroughly if you have to ask that question." Jervase uttered a little grunting sound. "I should say the very opposite of demonic."

"I don't understand. What would the opposite be? Like Ardneh?"

"Ardneh's helper." After a moment's thought the Scholar went burrowing into his chest of scrolls and came out with a drawing, an illustration in one of his hand-lettered documents. Chance squinted at a two-legged furry monster with an incongruously almost human head and face. In each hand the monster was crushing what appeared to be a tiny, stylized demon, while in the foreground there cowered two small humans who looked to be in need of help.

ACROSS FROM HIM, JERVASE WAS SAYING: "... MODERN THOUGHT tends to interpret Draffut as purely legendary, a personification of certain forces beneficial to humanity." Presently Jervase went to take his own turn with the bird, and tried to get Mitra to repeat the phrase, but the owl could not or would not.

CHANCE CAME AWAY WITH THE UNDERSTANDING THAT DRAFFUT was as ancient and mysterious as Ardneh himself—and no more likely to show up suddenly in the real world.

As Jervase pointed out, Scripture itself contained only a few mentions of Draffut. But according to Jervase there were other writings, thought to be of equal age, that told much more.

According to the Scholar, descriptions of this being were somewhat varied. One thing the stories did agree on was that Draffut was definitely of a material nature, never appearing in any shape but one, and his only mode of travel was to walk on two feet like a man. In Ardneh's day he had presided over a marvelous healing facility known as the Lake of Life. The Lake had been destroyed in one of Ardneh's final battles, and its exact location was now in dispute.

Draffut never injured a human being, whatever the provocation. Some legends made him six meters tall, others as much as nine. Always the Lord of Beasts was defined as a close, dependable ally of Ardneh, though (as Jervase had pointed out to his student) in none of the stories did the two beings ever actually appear together.

TODAY JERVASE SEEMED TORN BETWEEN AN EAGERNESS TO PUSH ON, and a fear that an additional advance might only take him farther from his goal. He had been secretive about that, telling no one, not even the other members of this party, exactly what he thought he had deduced from ancient records, maps, verses, and minstrel's tales. Chance had decided that the Scholar had no exact, pinpoint location to aim for, only a gathering of hints, faint and mysterious clues from various ancient sources.

At last Jervase said: "We'll camp here. My maps indicate that we are very near the place that the old writers call ground zero."

Night was coming on again, and it remained to be seen whether the owl was going to fly.

BACK IN THE WAGON AGAIN, CHANCE SAT FOR A LITTLE WHILE steadily regarding the bird, while she looked back at him. One moment he could imagine that he saw profound wisdom in her dark eye, and in the next it looked as witless as a worm.

SIX

A T DUSK THE OWL HAD EMERGED FROM HER NEST ONLY LONG enough to stretch her wings. Evidently still not quite satisfied with the condition of the injured one, Mitra chose not to fly, but retreated again into her wagon. While Chance spent the night dozing fitfully beside the nest, Mitra ate, drank water, nursed her sore wing, and occasionally mumbled something unintelligible, before falling asleep once more at the approach of dawn.

Since morning of the day after his encounter with the little girl, the expedition had struggled approximately another ten kilometers or so downstream, to establish its latest camp. The day's travel had discovered no further sign of human presence in the land. In the late afternoon Chance once again walked alone beside the river, which still threaded the narrow bottom of the canyon.

Today's section of the stream seemed very little different from yesterday's, except that here the running water had cut its way a little deeper into the earth. A bright spot in the middle of the high bank on the river's far side caught Chance's eye, a whiteness that was almost a gleam, suggesting a fragment of Old World metal. He splashed, ankle-deep, across the shallow stream to take a look, noting in passing that today's river felt just as cold as yesterday's.

The object he had spotted yielded almost at once to the point of

Chance's probing knife, revealing itself to be only another disappointment.

He juggled the oddly-colored pebble in his hand a couple of times, then threw it spinning, flat side down, in an unsuccessful attempt to make it skip across the relatively smooth surface of a pool. Well, he would keep looking. Several days had passed since either human or owl had brought in anything that caught the Scholar's interest. Nor had Jervase managed to find anything to please himself.

Now and then Chance's hand strayed up to feel inside his collar. But since the moment when he had turned his back on Zalmo and the demon's altar, he had been unable to discover any trace of the chain or its mysterious burden.

Still he had made no determined effort to discuss the series of odd events with any of his traveling companions. If he tried to convince them of such a story without anything to back it up, no one would believe him. Certainly not when the Lady Ayaba insisted nothing magical had been happening to him. He would simply be put down as letting his imagination run away.

It seemed to Chance that Jervase had unfairly dismissed the idea of protective clothing as Old World artifacts simply because he had never heard of such a thing before. Chance found himself wishing that he might encounter Zalmo again, just to see if she would seem as strange as she had at their first meeting.

Rounding the river's next sharp bend brought him in view of a somewhat broader pool whose farther rim at that very moment erupted with a violent splash, suggesting that some creature big as a human being had just jumped in, or else that a great fish leapt. But great fish, as Zalmo had remarked yesterday, were unlikely in this small stream. In the next moment Chance decided the effect must have been caused by nothing but the chaotic plunge of current entering the pool.

Another kind of movement at the far end of the small pool, just where it narrowed into a rushing stream again, attracted his attention. He found himself staring at an elaborate toy waterwheel, whirling and solid and vertical, thin and fragile-looking, almost a meter high in its upright diameter. This device stood spinning swiftly, its bottom continuously shoved forward by the miniature millrace running between two rocks only a hand's-breadth apart.

At first glance the wheel appeared to have been constructed out of nothing more solid than twigs and grass, with here and there a bit of string. But at a second look there did appear to be some minimum of solid frame beneath. The skill of the design put Chance in mind of Zalmo's superbly crafted fishnet, though the two objects were widely different in shape and in the materials employed.

Fascinated, Chance moved closer, stretching out his arms to keep his balance as he shifted his weight from one rounded streamside rock to another.

Chance was still staring at the spinning wheel when an explosive eruption at the pool's center sent him recoiling a step, so that he nearly fell. With a great splash, and a dash of water from a swing of long red hair, there burst into view the head and upper body of a twelve-year-old boy, clothed in a tight-fitting, mottled garment very similar to Zalmo's.

In a moment Chance had regained his balance. "Hello," he ventured to the apparition now standing waist-deep in the center of the pool. The wet, green-eyed face grinning up at him seemed utterly harmless.

"Hello!" The boy's high voice had a somewhat familiar accent. "I bet your name is Chance, isn't it?"

"That's right. You must be Zalmo's brother." The similarity of bright red hair and suit rendered any other conclusion practically impossible. The half-formed fear that Zalmo might have been something other than human had just taken a heavy blow. Demons might sometimes take human form but they did not have brothers—did they?

Chance added: "She told me that you like to swim."

"That's right!" the youngster piped. "My name is Moxis, and my sister told me about you, too. And about your owl. Do you like my waterwheel? I built it myself."

"Did you now?" The family might be strange but there was little doubt about its talent; Zalmo had claimed to have made her fishnet. "It looks very ingenious."

"Thank you. Want to join me for a swim?"

"No thanks." Chance shivered faintly. "I'd say you have to be freezing—but I suppose that suit you're wearing keeps you warm."

"Indeed it does!" Moxis almost yelled in his enthusiasm. "I can loan you one very much like it. You must want a bath, after many days and nights in the bird-wagon."

First, it sounded like some agent of the red-haired family must have been spying on the expedition. Second, putting on a suit to take a bath would seem to defeat the purpose. Chance grunted something.

The boy was leaning toward him, looking eager. "How about it?"

Once Chance had seen the king's bathtub in the royal palace at home, and it was not a whole lot smaller than this pool. "It seems a bit cold and rocky for me. And I don't t-trust a s-stranger's . . . magic." His words trailed off; groping inside his collar, his unconsciously exploring hand had just discovered that his neck was once more looped by the half-familiar fine chain, supporting its customary odd burden.

A quick lunge sent Moxis halfway across the pool to the far bank, where he pulled himself out of the water to sit on a handy flat rock close beside his wheel. The movement revealed that his body, like

Zalmo's yesterday, was covered down to the ankles by the suit, leaving his exposed feet to dangle in the refreshing current.

In the next moment Moxis, grabbing at his own collar as if in imitation of Chance, pulled the tight-fitting fabric away from his neck. "I've got another suit ready for you, Chance. Want to give it a try? Put it on, then slip into the cold water a little at a time. You'll see it works!"

Chance was about to say that he didn't see any such garment available, when Moxis pulled one into view from where it had been lying folded beside the waterwheel, its mottled pattern serving as excellent camouflage.

Suddenly the young boy's voice dropped, almost to a whisper, as if he were talking only to himself. "Of course you might not even need this, given what you wear already." And he patted the folded outfit in his lap. Then he whispered what sounded like two more words. They were too faint for Chance to be sure of them: but he wondered if they had been "*Ardneh's Key.*"

Chance decided to ignore the possibility. "All right," he agreed slowly. "I might give it a try, if you can tell me where it came from. Do you and Zalmo weave your own protective charms? The way you build your nets and waterwheels?"

Moxis cradled his right elbow in his left hand and rested his chin on his right fist. He appeared to be giving the question serious thought. "We might weave some things, but not these." He patted the folded suit again. "We found these, we didn't make them, I believe my sister told you that. And I'm certain 'weaving' is not the right word for how these suits were put together."

"Zalmo told me they were from the Old World. But a friend of mine said that was unlikely."

The green eyes squinted almost shut, apparently in concentration. "Chance, if you were given something from the Old World, would you feel you had to take it to your friend? Are you afraid of what he might do if you kept secrets from him?"

"I'm not afraid of him. Why should I be? But why should I keep secrets?"

The eyes snapped open. "Sorry, I didn't mean you're cowardly. Of course you're brave. You are a Rolfson. Don't be angry." Now Moxis started pulling the sleeve cuff on his left wrist loose with his right hand, and letting it snap back, as if he wanted to keep Chance's attention focused on the suit. "We found these garments in a secret place, one that we might show you sometime. You'd like that place, for it holds many other marvels."

"Yes, Moxis, I think I might like to see that. Is it anywhere near here?"

"A few days away, for travelers in slow wagons."

"In which direction?"

The boy was slowly shaking his head. "I'm not quite ready to tell you yet."

All right. "Then how about telling me where your mother and father are?" Yesterday Chance had asked a similar question of Zalmo, but she had vanished before answering.

Moxis looked upstream and down. He shrugged. "Somewhere around. With my little sister." He appeared to be carefully planning what he wanted to say next. Finally he settled on: "Do you like my wheel, Chance Rolfson?"

"It's very clever. Yes, I like it. Do you have more than one sister, then?"

"I'd make you a present of it, but it would be difficult to carry." The boy reached out a hand to make some delicate adjustment near the hub. "I can build bigger and better things than this," he announced with confidence. "Much better. You'd be surprised. You really would." Then he frowned. "But you see—the problem is—I can't build everything I need to have."

Chance scratched his head. "I suppose hardly anyone can do that. Unless you're willing to live in a poor hut, or a cave, and just eat what you can pick up off the ground."

Moxis dismissed the plight of such unhappy people with a shake of his head. He didn't want to get off the subject of Old World marvels. Lifting the folded suit from his lap, he brandished it in the air.

"You see, Chance—I could just give you this. That's what I was going to do. But now that I think about it, it wouldn't be a good idea for you to just take it and go away. We should have a serious talk first. There are much greater marvels in the world than this, and you may gather them into your hands. If we work together."

"What would be the subject of our serious talk?"

"You told Zalmo you had come here looking for old things. The kind of things that certain people mean when they say treasure." It sounded somewhere between a plea and an accusation.

The uneasiness Chance had begun to feel yesterday was coming over him again, full force. He said: "You want my help finding old things, and you're willing to give me some. But you're saying you don't want anyone else to know about our arrangement?"

Moxis was signing his agreement. "That's about it."

"I don't understand. Why does it have to b-be me who serves as your helper?" Chance noted that his own right hand was resting on the hilt of his hunting knife. But it made no sense for him to fear this unarmed youngster scarcely two-thirds his size.

Moxis was speaking earnestly, slowly and distinctly, as if to someone not quite bright: "All I'm saying is, maybe we can help each other. If you help me, I promise I can lead you to the things you want. But—you see—if your friends are going to know everything we do, that could be trouble. It could be dangerous. I might not be able to help them. Just you. Chance Rolfson."

"Why just me?"

Moxis slid from the rock back into waist-deep water. Thin as his garment looked, clinging to his lean body like a second skin, it really did seem to render him immune to cold, or at least to shivering. Leaving the spare suit behind him on the rock, holding his arms folded like a Sarasvati judge, he came wading without a trace of shivering straight across the pool. His eyes were fixed on Chance, not menacing but unnaturally intent. He piped: "You also told my sister you were looking for the Servants of Ardneh."

Chance caught himself taking a step backward, and determinedly regained half the distance with a forward shuffle. "Well. I can be looking for two things at the same time, can't I?"

The head of wild red hair nodded readily. "Of course. I do that a lot. Usually I find everything I look for."

"Do you know where their infirmary is?"

The boy let himself sink into the pool neck-deep, as if to underline the fact that no, he still wasn't getting cold. "Actually I do. And I don't mind helping your friends find that. This will show you I wish them no harm, and I can be trusted. And I know what I'm talking about."

"So—?"

Moxis nodded. "Keep following the river downstream for about another fifteen kilometers, and you will see the walled place where they are. It's not a hundred meters from the canyon, tucked away behind a grove of trees."

"Thank you. We will look there for the Servants. Does your family belong to their group?"

Moxis, looking solemn and standing straight again, ignored the question. "Now I have given you help; when the right hour comes, and I ask it of you, you must do the same for me."

It seemed that the boy was about to add something else, but instead he hesitated, raising his eyes until he was looking up into the sky, somewhere over Chance's head. At that moment Chance heard a distant noise, like a roar of voices on the wind, that made him turn his head and look around. Nothing was visible that he had not seen before: only the nearby riverbanks and the stream between them.

When he turned back a moment later, the boy had retreated again to the far side of the stream, where he seemed to be focusing all his attention on adjusting his wheel, making his toy turn just a little faster.

"What was that noise?" Chance heard himself asking the question as if he expected a real, informative answer.

He got one. Moxis replied calmly, without looking up from his adjustment of the wheel. "The people you travel with are being attacked by bandits."

SEVEN

B ANDITS!"
"But don't worry, your cavalry escort should be able to handle it." Moxis flashed a sudden, wild grin. "Maybe it's just as well that I haven't given you a suit today. You probably wouldn't put it on anyway. Later you will understand things better. Don't worry, Chance! My grandmother will come to see you."

"Your . . . who?"

With a swift lunge, the youngster abruptly plunged into the middle of the pool.

Chance kept calling: "Your—*what?*—will what?" But trying to question someone who had disappeared completely under water was an exercise in deep futility.

Chance supposed the warning about bandits might have been some kind of prank, but he wasn't going to argue or delay by trying to find out how long Moxis might be able to hold his breath. The young lord did not wait to see if bubbles were coming up. He had turned his back on pool and waterwheel, and was scrambling at full speed to get back to camp.

BEFORE CHANCE HAD COME WITHIN A HUNDRED METERS OF THE wagons, it was grimly obvious that the warning of an attack had been no joke. He caught blurred glimpses of arrows and slung stones arcing through the air, flying in about equal numbers toward the encampment and away from it. Hoarse cries were going up, some of them in measured yells of command, other voices breaking in panicked screams.

Chance's hunting knife was still sheathed at his belt, and he clamped hand on hilt, but immediately broke off his forward movement and dodged behind a tree. For the past two years he had struggled doggedly through the early stages of the formal weapons training expected of any able-bodied young aristocrat, putting up with occasional sprains and innumerable bruises, doing well enough to satisfy his instructors. But he was a total stranger to real combat, and did not look forward to the experience. It was good that none of the Rolfson family were expecting him to hew out a career as a warrior.

Unconsciously his left hand had come up to clutch the Key of Ardneh's Workshop, still very much present on its fine chain. He had stopped in a clearing in the thin woods, only a stone's throw from the actual fighting, screened from it only by a line of saplings and scrawny bushes. Any of the combatants who took the trouble to look in his direction ought to spot him fairly easily. But at the moment Chance was being totally ignored—all of them had more urgent things to claim their attention.

In front of Chance the expedition's five wagons had been pulled into a rude approximation of a circle. Close around the circle, outside of it and inside but all facing outward, men in familiar Sarasvati uniforms, dismounted and brandishing an assortment of weapons, were popping up from behind rocks, bushes, and wagons and ducking back again to shelter. A number of these Sarasvati men were letting fly with slings and arrows; where the rest of the expedition's people might be Chance could not be sure.

Meanwhile the attackers, irregularly clad and armed, more numerous and scattered over a wider surrounding area, were making a lot of noise, and putting to use their own long-range weapons. Though only a few were actually visible at one time, Chance had the impression that they had Horkos and his troop outnumbered.

There fell a bandit, an arrow right through his neck. To the young lord's inexpert eye and ear, it appeared that the captain and his company were at least holding their own so far in the struggle. And as far as Chance could see, his own barging ahead into the middle of it might prove his bravery but it wasn't going to do anyone any good, least of all himself.

In the next moment he caught a glimpse of the Scholar, who seemed so far uninjured. Jervase spent most of his time crouching under the front of the bird-wagon, popping out into view now and then as if he just wanted to see how things were going. With the military leadership in the capable hands of Horkos, Jervase had to do little more than grip his plain short sword and look determined. But Chance had to admire the Scholar for looking more angry than afraid. An effort was under way to steal, perhaps even to destroy, his artifacts, his journals and his scrolls and maps—and that would be a truly monstrous crime.

Chance kept trying to see whether the caravan's people had managed to get their ridingbeasts and loadbeasts to relative security inside the barricade of wagons, or whether the enemy had managed to run the animals off. Chance relaxed slightly when he saw that at least some of the livestock were visible toward the center of the defended space.

It occurred to Chance that if he just stretched his neck up a little farther, he might be able to get a better look. . . .

The slight noise of a foot crunching on dried leaves cut through the battle tumult with amazing clarity . . . because the sound had come from directly behind him.

Chance spun around. In an instant the blood seemed to freeze in all his veins, and he let out a very faint, unheroic sound of terror, half groan, half gasp. Two heavily armed men, both muscular and bearded, garbed in shabby clothing typical of the bandit gang, and sweating despite the coolness of the air, were standing no more than a good spear-thrust away. The pair had come ghosting silently out of the thin patch of small trees, very nearly following Chance's own line of approach to the small clearing. Their clothing and their weapons made it obvious that they were part of the attacking force, either scouting or trying to play their role in some plan to encircle the beset camp.

The man on Chance's left was very tall, wearing a dagger at his belt and the leather thongs of a sling wound round his left shoulder, and seemed to be sweating a great deal. His shorter, older partner gripped a sword, and had a battle hatchet slung at his waist, as well as a small shield on his freehand arm. Both had crude water bottles strapped on as well.

By reflex Chance had drawn his knife, a futile, automatic gesture that must have been the result of training. He needed a moment to realize that the wiser course might well have been to turn and run, or even to surrender.

Another moment after that his next impression struck him, struck hard with a sense of fainting wonder. How he reacted to the presence of the two men might make no difference—because neither of them were looking at him. Their eyes, as alert as you might expect of men in combat, were busy searching past the young lord who stood directly in their field of view, staring past him and through him as if he were not there at all. They were completely absorbed in studying the fighting, as Chance himself had been a moment earlier.

Chance's shock of sudden terror and momentary relief were followed in rapid succession first by puzzlement, then anger: Was he of such small importance that enemies did not bother to notice his existence?

Even as they ignored him the pair of intruders were advancing step by cautious step. It seemed to Chance that the taller one, moving as if with unconscious courtesy, actually detoured a step or two to go around the boy who happened to be standing in his way. The bandits exchanged a few words with each other in the common tongue. And then the pair of them were in motion again, unexpectedly stepping sideways rather than plunging ahead right into the fighting.

The awkward part was that Chance once more happened to be right in the tallest bandit's path.

Frozen in fear and puzzlement, Chance remained motionless until the fellow was almost upon him, then made a jerky movement to avoid contact. In his confusion he actually stumbled on his own feet, accidentally propelling himself right into the tall sling-carrier, who tripped on Chance's leg. Man and boy both tumbled to the ground, the bandit swearing mightily.

"Ardneh's ass, what's with you? Drunk?" the other one demanded, turning fiercely on his partner.

The bigger man, regaining his feet, snarled back. Still he did not even look at the lad who had made him fall, who was sitting beside him with a drawn knife, in good position to remove him from the fight and maybe from the world by slicing a tendon or artery in his leg.

It's true, neither of them can see me! On the verge of hysteria, Chance shouted something, meaningless words that jumbled into stuttering and a kind of hysterical laugh.

The burst of maniacal cackling, close at hand, frightened the men, and set them spinning and stumbling this way and that, unable to find its source.

The one who had a sword in hand turned wildly, stabbing and violating the air—fortunately none of the wild strokes came near Chance.

But the next thrust, or the one after that, might kill him by sheer accident. Unaware of making any conscious decision, Chance was on his feet again and had dropped his knife. Stepping in behind the shorter bandit, he grabbed the fellow by the collar. It was childishly easy to pull the man off balance, send him tumbling on the ground, from which position he bounced up an instant later in blind panic.

Both bandits were yelling, scrambling and stumbling to get away, convinced that they faced some overwhelming magic. The shorter one as he ran pulled out something on a leather thong, evidently a defensive charm, from inside his own collar. But he did not wait to see if it would do him any good against the invisible power that had hurled him to the ground. In another moment the pair had gone blundering away in the direction they had come from, a frantic retreat that carried them quickly out of sight behind the trees and rocks.

CHANCE STOOD STARING AFTER THEM, LISTENING TO THE POUNDING of his own heart, vaguely aware that in the time it had taken him to draw his last few breaths, the volume of battle noise in the background had drastically declined.

Overwhelming magic. Yes, no doubt, but . . .

Looking down at himself as he slowly picked up his knife and replaced it in its sheath, Chance was relieved to note that he could see his own clothing and body as clearly as ever. Had he become invisible or not? He could hope that only the eyes of enemies were clouded. The mysterious object that the two uncanny children had called Ardneh's Key was still solidly in place on its thin chain around his neck.

Meanwhile, what was happening in camp? A couple of the wagons had been tipped over, which seemed an ominous sign; whatever people were still present were keeping out of sight. Anxious about the course of the fighting, and unable to see any of the details from where he was, Chance soon decided to accept the risk of moving closer, and began slowly working his way, a few steps at a time. Three or four such advances brought him to a position behind a jutting rock, from which vantage point he could see a larger portion of the field of combat, without exposing much of himself.

No missiles were flying at the moment. Every few heartbeats he looked down, verifying his own visibility, at least to his own eyes.

Now he thought he could begin to understand what course the fight had taken. Apparently there had been an attempt to charge the wagons, involving mounted attackers as well as some on foot, and the attack had not succeeded—there was Jervase, and there was Horkos, looking very capable and still in charge. There were more troopers, resting at the moment, but ready for whatever happened next.

A couple of ridingbeasts, and more than a couple of men in dull peasants' or beggars' clothes, were lying motionless, one man with the shaft of a Sarasvati arrow protruding from the middle of his belly. Chance could easily suppose that more of the fallen were hidden in tall grass.

Chance remained for some time in his new observation post, standing almost motionless, cooly deciding that he had best remain at a distance from the fighting for a while. He was pleased at his own ability to stay calm in this situation. From time to time his fingers, half-consciously searching inside his collar, confirmed that Ardneh's Key was still firmly in place.

He soon caught glimpses of Horkos and Jervase again, both still looking unharmed. But where was the Lady Ayaba? Involved in his own struggle, Chance had missed much of the action, but now he thought her wagon was one of those tipped over. Magic was never at its most effective when swords were out, and the enchantress would not be blamed if she were seeking shelter inside or underneath a wagon.

OVER THE NEXT FEW MINUTES, CHANCE CONFIRMED HIS IMPRESSION that whoever had assigned Captain Horkos and his company to the expedition as its bodyguards had chosen well. Then somehow, before he realized what was happening, the skirmish seemed to be completely over. There were retreating calls and whistles. The enemy, most of whom Chance had never got a good look at, had vanished from the field, leaving behind a scattering of dead and wounded.

WHEN THINGS HAD REMAINED ALMOST QUIET FOR THE TIME OF A dozen breaths, he slowly got to his feet, then warily walked out into the open, toward the wagons. His fingers, checking at his throat again, told him that Ardneh's Key had once more disappeared. He wondered if he should accept that as reliable evidence that danger was past.

Several Sarasvati soldiers were sprawled or sitting on the ground, with others tending their bloody wounds. People looked up alertly at the sound of Chance's approaching steps, then showed visible relief. He shared their feeling when he was sure that they could see him.

Jervase and the captain both looked up from their tasks of keeping people on alert and assessing damage, and the face of each lightened considerably when Chance, clearly unharmed, came back to join them.

Captain Horkos was the most parental in his reaction. He seemed the angriest, and at the same time most intensely relieved. Forgetting his manners, he demanded: "Where in all the hells were you?"

Chance was looking soberly around, at bleeding, groaning men and damage. "Down by the river. I started to come back when I heard fighting, but when I saw what was happening, I kept out of the way." *And I'm not going to try to tell you what else I've seen and heard. Not just yet, anyway.*

"Best decision you could have made!" The captain rasped that out with obvious sincerity. Then he turned, shouting orders to a sergeant: "Get me some kind of count on how many of 'em there are. Try and find out how far they ran!"

Chance didn't want to let Horkos go without making an effort to pass along important information. When the captain would have turned away, Chance caught him by the arm.

"I met a boy there, who told me bandits were attacking our camp. He couldn't have seen what was happening from where we were."

Horkos was scowling, mouth open on bad teeth. "You met a what?"

"A boy, an odd one. When we heard the fighting, he acted as if he might have known about it ahead of time."

That caught the captain. But right now he had a hundred pressing things to do. He barked: "Some bandit brat, then. Tell me the story later!" and turned away.

The minds of everybody in camp were naturally still filled with battle, and talking to them now about his own, somewhat tamer marvels seemed impossible. The young lord moved on, feeling slightly dazed. Here was Vardtrad, wholly occupied in trying to stop the flow of blood from the wound in another soldier's arm. There were a couple of other wounded in the company, but Chance gathered from scraps of talk that only one of the captain's troopers, a man Chance knew little about, had been killed outright. A burial detail was already being organized.

Jervase, his sword sheathed again, was standing at a little distance, looking at Chance. The Scholar's expression suggested that he had information he wanted to convey.

"Where's the Lady Ayaba?" Chance demanded of him as he drew near.

The older man nodded, as if that was indeed the proper subject to begin with. His voice was even quieter than usual. "They're putting her in her wagon, as soon as they get it back up on its wheels. She was hit badly, and I fear she's dying. One of the first slung stones broke her skull."

"Oh." Chance could feel the impact of that news in the pit of his stomach. Not that he and the lady had been closely attached in any way, or ever would have been. But still . . .

"So, overall, we were lucky," the Scholar was going on. "And of course it was more than luck. The captain and his men fought well. Very well."

Chance murmured something vaguely appropriate and moved on. He reached the wagon of the enchantress just after it had been tipped back up on its wheels. Three troopers, moving slowly and carefully, were gently lifting the wounded woman inside, where someone had already created a kind of nest of blankets. Chance moved forward, hoping to discover that the enchantress was not as badly injured as Jervase had said. If that was not to be, he hoped at least to be able to exchange a few words with her.

The troopers who had done the lifting were glad to leave the lady in the young lord's care and hurry away to other tasks. Chance was alone with the enchantress in her private wagon, both of them surrounded by a mass of magical materials that had spilled from drawers and cabinets to mingle with the chaotic spillage of clothing and supplies that any woman of her class might bring on a trip. Oblivious to all this the Lady Ayaba lay silent, eyes closed, still breathing, but only barely. Her head had suffered a serious gash, the distinctive styling of her hair in bloody ruin. Someone had put on a hasty bandage, but blood was soaking through. A bruised swelling extended down across a quadrant of her face.

Chance started to climb out of the wagon, thinking he could do nothing for the lady, then changed his mind and came back to sit beside her. Her body seemed to have shrunken in size. At this moment it was impossible to believe that she was not as vulnerable as any other mortal woman. Chance took her hand, but could feel no response in lifeless fingers. He murmured a few words of encouragement, hoping the Lady Ayaba could hear them, squeezed her hand gently, and moved on, hoping to make himself useful somehow.

Casualties had evidently been fairly heavy on the bandits' side—one trooper was moving about the area attempting a body count. Chance got a hasty look at a couple of the fallen who seemed beyond help but were not yet quite finished breathing. Neither had been a member of the pair he had encountered earlier.

A couple of Sarasvati troopers, under the direction of a sergeant, were recovering a few useful-looking weapons from the field, and turning out the pockets, pouches, and the occasional backpack, of the enemy fallen. Chance supposed the searchers would be helping themselves to any valuables they came across—no doubt the official purpose was to discover anything that might show just who the attackers were, or where they had come from.

NO STARTLING INFORMATION CAME TO LIGHT. AFTER A QUICK CON-ference with Jervase, the captain gave orders to break camp and move on as soon as the business could be managed. Horkos was worried that the attackers might return with reinforcement, and wanted to reach some more defensible position before nightfall.

"I know which way we ought to go," Chance suddenly volunteered, taking advantage of a momentary silence.

The two leaders looked at him.

"Just before the fight started, t-there was a boy who warned me about bandits—a-and he was right about that. He also told me where the Servants of Ardneh have set up their hospital."

A hospital might certainly be helpful for the wounded—those who could be brought to it in time. In a matter of minutes the battered caravan was under way.

———

HOURS HAD PASSED, A NEW CAMP WAS ESTABLISHED. NIGHT HAD come, and chance had lain down to sleep beneath the bird's familiar wagon before it occurred to him that he really ought to be making a more serious effort to inform the Scholar and the captain on the subject of the strange children and what he had heard from them. He should be reporting to Jervase and Horkos about their elegant fishnet and toy waterwheel, about the odd garments they offered as protection—and, above all, he should pass on their peculiar warnings.

Belatedly Chance remembered how the one who called himself Moxis had volunteered his help, and his sister's, to enable Chance and his friends to find the old things they were looking for.

By the river, during the last few days, Chance had been exposed to plenty of strangeness, seen and heard things that were certainly worth reporting, had received word that he ordinarily would have passed on to his people immediately on coming back to camp. But conditions had been far from ordinary. The fight had intervened, Chance's first such violent encounter with blood and death. The fight, complicated by the puzzle of his own spell of invisibility, had forced all lesser events into the background of his thought.

But was that all? From somewhere in the bottom of his mind a suspicion came welling up: Was his failure to speak out due simply to the shock of combat, and the puzzle of invisibility? Or was some other influence, too subtle for him to be clearly aware of its presence, holding him back?

He had not been surprised, not really, to discover when the fight was over that the chain and its key-shaped burden had once more disappeared. And the skilled magician who had as much as told him, with bland assurance, that no such object really existed, was dying in her wagon, perhaps already dead. Jervase was sitting with her now.

The business was certainly too important to be ignored. In the morning, first thing, he would be sure to tell Jervase and Horkos all about it, whether they thought it all interesting or not. Everything that had happened. Yes, in the morning. . . .

The last thing Chance seemed to hear before sleep claimed him was the echo of a whisper: *There will be another attack, and you will need more powerful protection.*

My grandmother will come to see you.

EIGHT

A T DUSK THOSE WHO WATCHED THE BIRD WERE RELIEVED TO
see that she flew out as usual. Tonight Mitra took wing accompanied by fervent wishes that she would return with some solid
information about the bandits. No fires were lighted in the expedition's camp. The soldiers rested in shifts, with half of the uninjured
troopers continually on watch while the other half slept with
weapons at their sides.

It was well past midnight when Vardtrad came to the bird-wagon
to find Lord Chance, stretched out in his blankets below it, and
shake him out of an uneasy slumber. His sleep had been infested by
dreams that filled him with a sense of urgency but, as usual, evaporated from his memory the moment his eyes came open.

"It's the Lady Ayaba, M'lord. She's come t'herself, a little bit, and
says she wants to see you. But she don't look good."

"I'll be right there."

Stumbling to his feet and rubbing his eyes, Chance peered into
the wagon and noted with little surprise that the owl's nest was still
empty. Pulling on an extra shirt against the morning chill, Chance
observed that no small chain currently looped his neck. Ardneh's
Key—he still had no other name to give the owl's mysterious
bestowal—was absent. The only consistent explanation he had been

able to think of for the Key's comings and goings was that it appeared only when danger threatened; of course that would mean that the strange children who had named it for him were themselves somehow dangerous—in their presence it had been visible.

Whether the gift had come from the owl or from some other power, it had almost certainly saved Chance's life. If it was the Key's magic that had rendered him invisible, then Chance was deeply indebted to whoever his benefactor had been. It must have been someone more intelligent than Mitra.

THE LADY AYABA'S EYES WERE PARTLY OPEN, BUT SHE SEEMED BARELY conscious, breathing slowly and irregularly. Power had gone from her face, and it looked strangely younger than before. Now did not appear to be the moment for Chance to tell her she must have been seriously wrong in her judgment of the thing the owl had brought him.

Her eyes opened fully when Chance climbed into the wagon. With a gasp and a gesture, the enchantress indicated that she wanted Chance's help in sitting up. He did his gentle best; her shrunken body was alarmingly easy to move.

Vardtrad had followed Chance at a little distance. And a few moments later Jervase also arrived. The lady's feeble hand made one gesture to bring Chance closer, and another to shoo away the two leaders of the expedition. She wanted to try to speak to Chance alone.

With a great effort, the dying enchantress managed to get out a few words: "Give me your hand."

As soon as her fingers clasped his, the lady's eyes came open wider.

Her weak voice murmured: "Something has happened to you, lad. Changed you. I can see it now."

"Yes." *But—has it changed me? How?* Of course the lady's mind was probably wandering.

She breathed: "I was wrong, was I not? You have received a gift."

"I . . . yes."

The lady nodded slowly. "I thought . . . I thought no magic had touched you, my Lord. But what had happened was too great a thing for me to see—when I was standing very near it. Now . . . when I am about to pass . . . I see more clearly."

Whatever she saw clearly awed the enchantress, but also caused her concern.

Part of her admonition was a warning against the dangers to human beings posed by demons. And, rousing herself, her voice suddenly loud and harsh, she added a few words of heartfelt curses against people who trafficked with those fiendish creatures and tried to purchase their aid with human sacrifice.

Her eyes were filled with terror, and urgent warning. "You must be careful, boy! Avenarius is near, and . . ."

Before Chance could even try to put a reasonable question, the Lady Ayaba died. The suddenness of it took him by surprise. He could see in her eyes the great change taking place behind them. The moment came and went, and carried her away with it, and only the small woman's body remained for him to see.

Chance held her hand a moment longer, then let go.

Jervase had come up quietly to the doorway and now put a hand lightly on Chance's shoulder. As Chance would have expected, the Scholar's first comment was practical. "These wizards, men and women alike, all have a certain company of helpers who are not human—nor animal. We're in for a spell of nasty tricks if we don't show them some respect."

The young lord reminded him that those immaterial creatures had already fled in fear.

"Not all of them, perhaps. However that may be, we'd best get her body under the earth."

MITRA RETURNED FROM HER SCOUTING FLIGHT AT DAWN, SHORTLY after the last shovelfuls of soil had been dropped on Lady Ayaba's unmarked grave. In certain circles, the corpses of dead magicians were prized for certain exotic properties they were reputed to possess. When Jervase asked the bird whether she had been attacked again, or bothered in any way, he got a prolonged *no-o-o-o* as answer. More questioning elicited disturbing news.

"If Mitra's telling me the truth," Jervase was reporting to Horkos a minute later, "and I think she is—the bandits are being heavily reinforced. They're mobilizing over there"—he pointed—"no more than five kilometers away, in numbers the owl seems to think amount to a small army. Even allowing for the fact that she isn't very good at horizontal distances, or counting. . . ." The Scholar concluded with a shrug.

The captain nodded briskly. "The conclusion is, we'd best be on our way at once, in the opposite direction."

After a hasty fireless breakfast, dried meat and fruit and fish washed down with river water, the caravan quickly broke camp and moved on, the more severely wounded men once more enduring a jolting passage inside the baggage wagons. To make room for them there, several large containers had been shifted into Mitra's vehicle.

For the time being, everyone was occupied with the immediate practical considerations of defense and movement. There was no time or inclination for any further discussion about demonic altars and peculiar children.

CHANCE SPENT THE EARLY HOURS OF DAYLIGHT RIDING INSIDE THE Lady Ayaba's wagon, confronting her extensive inventory of magical equipment, while a trooper drove. The Scholar and Horkos were leaving it up to him to decide what disposal to make of her things—everyone knew it could be risky to treat a wizard's tools and materials carelessly. The trouble was that no one remaining in the party was qualified to decide exactly what should be done. Chance and the Scholar, who probably had more magical training than anyone else who still survived, had pondered the question of whether it would be better to destroy any of these objects at once, or if they had better be preserved.

The Scholar sounded vexed, in his dry way. This business was taking time that he would rather spend in study, planning, and contemplating his artifacts. "Yes, it might be better to burn some of them. But no one remaining in our party has the skill to know which ones—and I believe it likely that destroying the wrong ones would be worse than doing nothing."

The lady's sprites having all already fled, they were going to be of no help. It seemed the people on hand had to muddle through as best they could.

"It worries me," Jervase confided to his assistant, "that we seem to have left ourselves practically unprotected in that regard. My own powers are pretty much limited to determining the age of things, and something of their history."

So far there had been no psychic disturbances. Jervase commented that their absence in these circumstances was almost ominous. "I fear it may mean that they are still afraid to be with us."

AS THE CARAVAN DREW WITHIN A FEW KILOMETERS OF THE PLACE where Moxis had told Chance the Servants were to be found, Jervase mounted and went scouting ahead. This time Chance rode beside him.

Topping a small rise, the two riders came in sight of what had to be the compound of the Servants of Ardneh. A sturdy wall of whitish stone enclosed something like half a hectare of flattish ground, separated from the river by a grove of trees.

The fieldstone wall surrounding the compound rose everywhere as high as the head of a mounted man, but lacked any ditch or trench in front of it to increase its effective height as a defense. It surrounded a cluster of half a dozen low buildings constructed mostly of the same material. Some of these structures, and large sections of the enclosing wall, were stained and crumbling, and might have been in place for centuries, for all that Chance could tell. Other buildings looked newer, though of a somewhat cruder construction.

Here and there a few people were visible, distant figures all garbed in white, going about a variety of tasks. Outside the walls, between the compound and the rim of the river's canyon, the outlines of what appeared to be an extensive garden had been scratched into the earth.

People living in this isolated spot would need to grow most of their own food, and healers would of course want certain roots and herbs. A couple of white-robed figures inside the outline appeared to be poking at the ground with sticks, evidently carrying out the first tentative steps in spring planting.

In the background, well behind the compound, more than half a kilometer farther from the river's twisting canyon, an outcropping of rugged rocky hills erupted from the gradual, kilometers-long slope of the plain. Out of these hills a small stream came winding down, carving its own small gully, to add its modest volume of flow to the Rivanna.

Trees on the hills grew taller and also much more thickly than on the plain, and most of them were putting out their tender new spring foliage. Prominent in the center of the clustered hills was the top of a stark, sharp-edged mesa. The near side of this formation, half hidden behind the heights of tree-clad nearer hills, showed a broad curve of dark shadow. To Chance this looked like the barely visible top of a large concavity in the mesa's rocky face, raising in his mind the suggestion of some vast grotto or cave.

Chance noted these things in passing; he and his companion had focused their attention on the walled compound, located just where Moxis had said the Servants of Ardneh would be found. Here they were, their flag flying from a short pole atop the modest building positioned centrally within the walls.

Chance said: "It's definitely the Servants' banner, Jervase— almost pure white, with a few little dark squiggles—I forget what they're supposed to mean. I recognize it from my mother's dealings with the group. And all the people I see are wearing white, as you'd expect."

Prominent over the gateway of the compound, just below the flag, was mounted a slab of some strange-looking artificial material. The mottled colors of the slab's surface were different from those on the suits worn by the strange children. Instead they reminded Chance of the pattern on the thing he had been told was Ardneh's Key. Automatically his hand went up once more to his throat—as usual, there was no trace of the mysterious artifact. Was that an indication that it would be safe for him to approach the compound? Well, he had no reason to think otherwise.

Riding forward with the Scholar at his side, Chance decided as they drew near that the slab bearing the inscription could not be made of stone, though it looked a lot like marble; any mass of solid stone as big as that would be too heavy for ordinary human beings to hoist it into that position.

On the slab was an inscription, and as he and Jervase drew closer Chance paused to study it:

AUTOMATIC RESTORATION DIRECTOR
NATIONAL EXECUTIVE HEADQUARTERS

Jervase spelled out the acronym for him—ARDNEH—just in case Chance had missed it—which he had not.

NINE

CHANCE FELT UNCERTAIN OF SEVERAL WORDS IN THE ANCIENT inscription, but they were all well within the Scholar's capability. Jervase smoothly read the whole text aloud.

"Have you seen it before, Chance?" he added. "It is the full, formal name of Ardneh, and it appears in at least six other places in the valley of the Rivanna. I have seen three of them, on previous expeditions." Jervase's voice was hushed, almost reverent—Chance knew the man well enough to be certain that it was not Ardneh who inspired such a worshipful attitude. Rather it was antiquity in general, and its wealth of ancient knowledge waiting to be regained for humanity.

Large segments of the surrounding walls and buildings had recently been restored and rebuilt. According to the signs of fresh construction, the job was still in progress. Immediately below the embossed slab a regular gate had been installed, of very recent construction, timbers of raw wood hanging on enormous posts.

The arrival of the small cavalcade of escorted wagons created a stir, but no alarm. More and more white robes were drifting into visibility, one or two at a time. About a dozen had gathered near the gate by the time Chance and Jervase were close enough for conversation. The first people to greet the new arrivals were a trio of young, white-robed novices of the new order, two short girls and a tall, stooped youth who appeared to be two or three years older than Chance.

Ardneh's Servants seemed more pleased than alarmed by the incursion of uniformed troopers—at least this particular variety of mounted men, who came wearing and carrying the Sarasvati colors. But the mood in the compound quickly changed when its people heard the Scholar's first words, an immediate warning about a powerful force of bandits.

Captain Horkos cut short the resulting babble of questions. "All in good time. If you folk are in the healing business, we've got some material for you to practice on." He waved a wagon forward. "Bring our wounded out!"

The call to duty immediately changed the mood again. People hurried to attend the wounded, with what impressed Chance as professional skill and knowledge.

Their immediate concerns having been dealt with, the visitors were generally made welcome. There was nothing here to remind Chance of the demon-altar. What blood was spilled within these walls would be a result of surgery, never in anger or in sacrifice.

When one of the troopers whispered to Chance a question as to why these people wore white, he explained that it was to demonstrate the cleanliness of body and mind they considered necessary in those who would practice human healing.

Jervase, like the captain, was impatient with so much jolly good will. "Who is in charge here?"

A low, crisp voice, that jogged Chance's memory as soon as he heard it, announced: "I am the Director, my name is Kuan Yin." The lady who spoke had just emerged from inside one of the larger buildings, wiping her hands on a white cloth. She was diminutive and energetic, looking a little older than Jervase. Her head was bare, her straight black hair cut short. Like her associates, she was dressed in plain white garments, simply cut.

Chance was the first visitor to speak up. "Director Kuan Yin, it is good to see you again." Then, realizing that he must be the only member of the arriving party who had met her before, he began to perform introductions.

When the formalities had been concluded, the Director moved closer, watching him dismount. "Lord Chance, you are a good bit taller than the last time I saw you—only one year ago? Or was it two?"

Chance remembered this woman as possessing a kind of inner happiness, and it was still in evidence. "Actually somewhere between two and three years, I believe, my Lady. You had come to our house to talk to my mother about money."

She spread out small, work-hardened, ringless hands. "Alas, the days of our lives fly away from us, continually escaping. I have been forced to spend a great deal of time trying to raise funds. Your mother was very generous. I trust she is in good health?"

"Excellent, when last I saw her." There followed queries on other members of Chance's family. While Chance was bringing the Director up to date on conditions back in Sarasvati, she was joined by a white-robed girl a few years younger than Chance and almost as tall.

Chance needed a moment to recognize the Director's daughter, Abigail. She had also been present on her mother's visit to the Sarasvati capital, but the girl whose bright blue eyes now gazed with some surprise at Chance seemed to have little in common with the chubby child that he remembered. Now her slender body had begun the transformation into womanhood. Chance thought it unlikely that she was ever going to be credited with great beauty, but she did appear healthy and quietly energetic. Her long hair was as dark as her mother's, but her eyes a somewhat startling, striking blue—perhaps no one word could describe the color adequately.

Kuan Yin was saying to her: "Abigail, if your memory is as keen as it should be, you will remember Lord Chance Rolfson, whom we met in Sarasvati."

Bowing and murmuring his own acknowledgment, Chance consulted his memory, wondering whether there were other people in Kuan Yin's family about whom he should politely ask. No, he wasn't aware of any—he did recall that the girl's father had died years ago.

MORE MEMORIES OF HIS LAST MEETING WITH ABIGAIL AND HER mother were returning. It seemed to Chance that at the time of their previous meeting he and this girl had disagreed about something. Could it have been the nature of Ardneh?

At the moment, Abigail was looking at him as if his presence here might not be entirely welcome. Maybe their disagreement at their previous meeting had been more vehement than he remembered it.

When Kuan Yin graciously introduced Jervase's young assistant to the growing assembly of Servants, it was obvious that several additional members of their company immediately recognized his name. One or two proclaimed themselves honored to play host to a member of the eminent Rolfson family. Chance heard a background murmur, familiar in a way that he had come to find unpleasant: "Not just a wealthy family. Actually has a prominent place in Scripture!" Here, standing before them, was really Rolf's lineal descendant!

Inwardly he shrank, while his face continued wearing a polite smile.

AMONG THOSE WHO SEEMED MOST IMPRESSED BY THE FAMILY NAME was the young male novice called Benambra, who had begun edging marginally closer, as if he sought to draw the eminent visitor's attention to himself. Benambra was tall and rather stooped, though only two or three years older than Chance. He had wispy, colorless hair that seemed already to be thinning, and large pale hands that gave the impression of being always in motion—grasping, counting, rubbing themselves together.

Noticing that the youth was wearing what appeared to be a full purse tied at his belt, Chance said, by way of making conversation: "I see you are entrusted with the treasury."

Benambra nodded slightly, acknowledging a compliment. "I strive to be worthy of the honor."

"I fear we cannot spend much time on pleasantries," Captain Horkos was saying. He explained in a few terse words that one of the wagons held the working materials of a recently deceased enchantress, which had to be somehow disposed of.

"And the lady's body?"

"Was quickly buried. We had no time to spare."

The Director turned to her daughter. "See what you can do, Abigail. Disposal of a magician's tools and materials, if done improperly, can certainly cause inconvenience."

"Or sometimes worse than that." Abigail's face changed expression, and she drew up her small frame. Suddenly she looked considerably older than she was. "It is a specialty that I have never studied—but I will do the best I can. Who was last to see the lady alive?" A professional tone had come into her voice.

Chance thought the apprentice enchantress might be going in beyond her depth—all the more reason for others to be as helpful as possible. He raised a hand. "I was."

"Then, if you would, show me her things."

LADY AYABA'S WAGON HAD BEEN PARKED WITH THE OTHERS IN AN open space toward the center of the compound. Walking in that direction with Abigail, Chance paused beside Jervase, who was standing on the ground looking up at Captain Horkos. The captain had wasted no time in climbing to one of the low, flat rooftops, at which vantage point he stood scowling with fists on hips, surveying practically the whole compound with professional disapproval.

The captain was growling his opinions. "Cultivating her garden is going to be the least of the lady's problems. This place is not defensible against anything worse than a couple of prowlers."

The Servants who happened to be nearby were beginning to take alarm. One of them asked: "Can it be made so?"

"Hah, yes, it might be. If I had a good number of days in which to work, and several hundred sturdy workers and fighters."

One of the white-robes had climbed up beside Horkos, and now tentatively pointed out: "There are walls . . ."

The captain made a low savage noise. "Half a kilometer of wall, and none of it high enough to discourage anyone who's not terminally lazy. It's a sure thing we're going to have more trouble from those damned bandits—I call 'em that, but I fear me they are something worse."

Jervase, who was still paying close attention from ground level, gave one of his meditative grunts. "Worse than bandits? In what way?"

"I don't know. Not my business to meddle in politics. But they seemed more than a shade too well disciplined. And there were just too bloody many of them for any ordinary band. I tell you straight, we won't be able to fight them off from inside these walls."

Abigail's mother, coming to join the group, said that some of the Servants had military experience, and would stand ready to defend the place.

It was the captain's turn to grunt. "If you say so, my Lady. I respect their spirit. But I doubt any of 'em are going to whip off magical disguises and reveal themselves to be a regiment of pikemen."

The discussion was going on, but Abigail caught Chance's eye and briskly jerked her head toward the wagons. "We had better proceed on our own task."

As he turned to follow her, Chance could hear Jervase smoothly agreeing with the Director that a serious discussion about their common defense was necessary.

Walking beside Chance, Abigail explained that all of the Servants' most skilled magicians were for various reasons absent. One was on leave, others were traveling in distant lands, having been dispatched on missions that had seemed vital when they were proposed. None of the people on hand were real adepts. What little magical knowledge any of them had was in the field related to healing.

"That's unfortunate."

"But it is the situation. What can you tell me about the lady whose belongings we are about to inspect?"

When Chance thought about it he had to admit that he knew very little of the Lady Ayaba's background or abilities. "Probably Jervase could tell you more."

The girl sighed. "I may ask him later. For now, let me see her things."

Soon they had climbed into the wagon. Opening several bags and boxes, Chance began spilling a strange variety of objects out of them, spreading them for examination on the bed in which the lady had died.

"It looks a hopeless muddle," was the young woman's quick comment, as she surveyed the jumble.

"There was fighting going on at the time, and this wagon was overturned. The soldiers piled things back in as best they could. None of the rest of us have any magical skills at all."

"Few people of your lordship's social status do."

Chance cleared his throat. "I wish you wouldn't call me 'Lord.' No one in our caravan does."

"Really? I'd be willing to bet that none of the enlisted soldiers would dare to address you in any other way." The Director's daughter sounded older than her years.

"Oh well, the soldiers . . . that's true, I suppose. They do what the captain tells them, and it's not up to me to interfere with military discipline."

"No, of course not." Abigail's tone infused the words with more than a shade of mockery. "And the servants in your household . . ."

Chance could feel himself blushing, as there came to his mind, for no particular reason he was aware of, a certain servant girl who had worked there until about six months ago, and a certain very private arrangement he had had with her.

Being caused to blush was irritating. "Look here—Abigail? I see I must be careful with the form of names and titles. Would it be better to call you Lady Abigail?"

"Certainly not, Lord Chance. We Servants make no pretense of rank and distinction."

Now he was sure that she must be remembering some old problem between them, even if he had totally forgotten it—which he had. "Except for one of you being the Director."

"That is different."

"Ah. Well, look here, then. The last time we met, I-I may have somehow given you the wrong impression." He couldn't recall the details, but an impression was growing in his memory that something of the kind had happened.

Now Abigail, too, was ready to change the subject. Her professionalism was being challenged. "Let us try to concentrate on the job we have to do. What's this?" She held up in her small, sturdy fingers an object that seemed to Chance totally out of place. A mere toy? It might have been a mundane doorknob, but why would anyone carry a doorknob while living in a wagon with canvas walls? "Did it get mixed in here by mistake?"

"That's quite possible."

Both of them trying to concentrate on business, they continued working their way through the assortment of objects, tossing aside the occasionally identifiable mundane item which had become confused with the tools of magic.

As he handled one item of power after another, Chance began to nurse the hope that one of them would trigger the visible presence of the object that—sometimes—hung around his neck. If he could show this girl Ardneh's Key, he would be able to call her as an independent witness to the fact of its existence.

But of course the Key refused to cooperate, keeping itself maddeningly out of sight. For all the effect produced by the tools of the Lady Ayaba's trade, they might as well have been a trunk full of children's toys.

IT SEEMED TIME TO DELIVER A PRELIMINARY REPORT TO THEIR RESPEC-tive leaders. As they walked away from the wagon together the girl told him that this ruined compound had been chosen as the location of the Servants' infirmary partly because of the inscription over the gateway. That slab of exotic material had been dug out of the earth somewhere nearby.

"I see. But . . ."

"But what?"

"Well . . . why here?" Chance made a sweeping gesture. "I mean, if I was going to establish an infirmary, and hoped for a lot of business, I might want to put it in or near a busy city, where many more sick people would find it accessible."

"Yes, of course. Many more would seek us out if we were in among crowds. Here we are so far getting only a few herders or travelers, who move on as soon as they are able. But mother fears that swarms of patients would be too much for us to cope with, as we still try to become organized. Eventually, of course, we will be established in the cities too. But our Order is a new one, and before we try to serve people in great numbers we must find out who we are, and what we can do."

"If you are physicians, you surely must have a pretty fair idea of that already."

"Each man or woman among us knows what he or she has already done. But we must also learn what we can do together, as Ardneh's Servants."

IT WAS EASY TO SEE THAT THERE HAD ALSO BEEN PRACTICAL ADVANtages to establishing a base at this location. The faint traces of ancient paths—for all Chance could tell they might once have been real highways—suggested that there had been a crossroads. One of the intersecting roads had forded the river here, at a place where the little canyon's steep walls had conveniently crumbled. Eventually, he supposed, there might be a crossroads and a ford again. There might even be a town or city, if and when the balances of trade and population once more shifted. A good supply of water was readily available, even without counting the river—Abby pointed out a bountiful well within the compound's zigzag stone walls, no doubt the chief reason why one building after another had occupied this spot for centuries.

Abby added: "Mother does worry about how we are going to manage the garden, though. All the cultivation we need will require a lot of water-carrying."

The compound was hardly more than a stone's throw from the river, but the stream here was still running at the bottom of a narrow, winding canyon, even deeper than it had been where Chance walked its banks. This would make it inconvenient as a regular source of water, and impossible to reach if the place ever fell under siege.

DURING THE HOUR OR SO CHANCE HAD SPENT INSIDE THE COM-pound, he thought he had been able to look closely at all its occupants. None of the forty or so people he had encountered had bright red hair or spoke with the flat, clear accent of Zalmo and Moxis. And so far he had seen no children.

Kuan Yin admitted that she claimed no gift of magical foresight. But in certain matters she had learned to trust her instincts. "I agree with you, Captain. We must act on the assumption that those who attacked you yesterday will follow you here, and that they may be reinforced. But I wonder what originally made them bold enough to attack you in your camp? You are a strong party, after all."

Horkos seemed vaguely amused. "They were not polite enough to offer an explanation."

The Director persisted gently. "Are you carrying objects of great value? Ordinarily, of course, that would be none of my business. But in the circumstances . . ."

Jervase answered. "It's a fair question. You want to know if you will now be called upon to help us defend our loot." He made a dismissive gesture. "Personally I consider the antiquities in my collection extremely valuable. I would even call one or two of them priceless—but many are mere broken fragments, and there is nothing among them that bandits would ordinarily prize, or hope to be able to sell. Nor would robbers even be likely to know I carry them."

His gaze shifted to Chance. "It's much more probable that the rare object they have in mind is of a very different kind: I mean the direct descendant of Rolf, who travels with us." He nodded toward the young lord. "One who might be kidnapped with great hopes of collecting a large ransom."

Kuan Yin was signing agreement. "That may be. Also, we ought not to be too surprised when people behave irrationally. Sometimes the worship of demons will drive humans into madness."

She frowned suddenly as her thought moved to a different subject. "Speaking of magical matters, Abigail, have you and Lord Chance come to a decision on the disposal of the Lady Ayaba's things?"

"Not yet, mother. We thought it best to bring you a preliminary report."

AS A SERIOUS DISCUSSION OF THE PROBLEMS OF DEFENSE GOT UNDER way, another member of the little group of white robes added: "And also find out what kind of help we can expect—from Draffut and from Ardneh."

There was a little silence. Then the Scholar said, in his dry voice of certainty: "I assume you are speaking allegorically. Ardneh—whatever the true nature of that marvelous being—has been dead for about a thousand years. And it seems doubtful, to say the least, that the wonder-working creature called Draffut ever existed."

TEN

THE STATEMENT PRODUCED A SOUND OF SHARPLY INDRAWN breath from a couple of the novices who were standing by, followed by a few moments of pin-drop silence. People were looking at the Director, Kuan Yin.

Her reply was quiet, but very firm. "You are wrong on that point, Scholar Jervase."

Captain Horkos, momentarily turned diplomat, suggested: "Whatever the metaphysical situation may be, we had better concentrate for now on a discussion of matters relating to our common defense."

Jervase made his little throat-clearing sound. "Yes, of course."

CHANCE AND ABIGAIL HAD BEEN SENT BACK TO FINISH THE JOB OF sorting the Lady Ayaba's magical goods. He thought the girl's attitude toward him was somewhat improved, but it could use some further enhancement, and he was working at it. "They tell me that the Rolf in Scripture was my umpteen-great-grandfather. But I doubt I'd feel any different if they suddenly told me that our whole family story was some huge mistake, and my ancestor a thousand years ago was cleaning stables. And when you think of how many generations have lived between Rolf's time and ours, it would be strange if a majority at that time were not peasants or stable-cleaners."

"I think you would, though."

"Would what?"

"Feel different." She said: "You are a Rolfson, in the line of lineal descent. A number of the people here are much impressed by that."

"I can see you're not. But I haven't asked you to be. If something I said two years ago upset you, I don't remember what it was."

Abigail blinked at him and said nothing. She seemed to be still in the process of making up her mind on what her attitude should be.

They sorted a few more objects.

Presently Chance offered: "Scripture says that Rolf himself was a peasant."

His young companion nodded calmly. She was obviously the kind who had an answer for everything. "Until he was chosen by Ardneh, to do great things."

Chance couldn't tell if she was urging him to take himself more seriously or not. Maybe she felt he was not accepting his responsibility to the noble line. "Well, I haven't been chosen for anything." Then something prompted him to add: "As far as I know."

The next subject to come up was the Scholar. In particular, his boldness in practically denying that Draffut had ever existed. Chance wanted to know what the novice Abigail Yin thought of that? It seemed like an attack on all that she and her colleagues were doing here.

When Abigail seemed reluctant to answer, he pressed her further. "Aren't there some people who maintain that Ardneh is also still alive?"

Her lip curled with scorn. "Of course Ardneh has been dead for a thousand years; everybody knows that, even your Scholar. We Servants believe in him as a great guardian and teacher of humanity, whose influence still persists, whose teachings still live in those of us who follow him." She raised her eyes to stare at Chance directly. "And we also believe in a Draffut who is still alive."

"I see."

"But of course you don't see. You merely accept what your great Scholar has taught you."

They sorted a few more things, while he thought the matter over. At last Chance said: "Well—yes, I believe most things the Scholar teaches. Not that he is always right—he himself would admit that."

"Really."

"Yes. Maybe you don't believe it, but I've been living with him for several months, talking with him every day. What Jervase really favors is the idea of people thinking for themselves."

"But he does not hold that the Beastlord lives."

Chance stopped what he was doing and just looked at her. "What did you just say?"

"I said 'the Beastlord.' It is another name for Draffut. Sometimes he is called High Lord of Beasts."

"Is that so."

"Yes! Why?"

Chance said: "Yesterday the great owl we carry with us said something that sounded to me like: 'The Beastlord comes.' I wrote it down, I can show you if you like. But it's often difficult to tell when Mitra is trying to say something meaningful, and when she's j-just b-babbling."

"Yes, one of your people mentioned that you have a talking owl." At last it seemed that Abigail was allowing herself to be impressed. "They're very rare. That's what your bird said? 'The Beastlord comes'?"

"That's what it sounded like to me. Jervase says that in Ardneh's day they were comparatively common."

Abby asked questions about the owl, and Chance began to tell her about the strange return of the injured bird one recent morning—

leaving out the monstrous face and the eerie gift Mitra had brought him. Now that he had found a willing listener, the words poured out. It was a relief to be telling someone these things at last, and Chance almost told her more than he wanted to . . . almost.

Kuan Yin's daughter seemed increasingly intrigued. "And you say no one believed your version of the event? Whyever not?"

Chance fidgeted uncomfortably. "I am sometimes accused of confusing my dreams and reality. Sleepwalking, and similar things that it seems nice people just don't do. That's happened, but very rarely."

"Oh?"

"I think one reason my parents allow me to study with the Scholar, and were in favor of my going on this trip, was their hope that what they called 'the hearty outdoor life' would do me good. Cure me of certain, well, 'dreamy tendencies.' "

She was smiling slightly. "And has it cured you?"

"I'll let you judge that for yourself. It's not that my family really values what the Scholar does. They're engaged in business that they think is much more important than digging up old tricks and miracles. That's what one of my brothers called it: 'tricks and jokes and miracles.' One of them actually denies that Old World magic could accomplish anything beyond the power of our wizards today."

Abby's hands had ceased their sorting, discarding a pair of what seemed ordinary buttons. Her expression suggested that anyone who said that was a fool. "What we generally call magic is one thing, and what the Old World called 'technology' is something else. Your Scholar Jervase is right about that, at least. But your brother—" The young woman shook her head. "Has he never seen an Old World lamp? And Ardneh himself was created in Old World times. Now, what is this?" Abigail held up what might have been the stub of an ordinary candle, except that it seemed to have been burned at both ends.

They sorted a few more magical objects, to the best of their ability. Chance felt vaguely relieved that the shrunken head, if that was really what he had seen before the enchantress died, had disappeared.

He drew a deep breath and spoke impulsively. "While we are on the subject of peculiar objects, have you ever heard of something called Ardneh's Key?" He got the question out without giving himself time to think about it.

That gave her pause. Again her hands stopped moving. This time her face grew unexpressive. Her voice was quiet. "Why do you ask me that?"

"Why? Because I'm curious. A couple of days ago I met someone who mentioned it."

At last Abigail seemed to be taking him seriously. "And who might that have been?"

Of course Chance had first heard those syllables from the bird. But he didn't want to return to the subject of the owl. "Uh, another traveler. Someone I just met in passing. It just sounded like something . . . interesting."

"Yes." Abigail was still looking at him strangely. "Interesting," she repeated.

"What can you tell me about it?"

Abby seemed to be taking counsel with herself. Then she came to a decision. "Lord Chance, what do you know of Ardneh's legacy—sometimes called Ardneh's Sword? You've heard of that?"

"Yes." He didn't want to come right out and name it as the prime object of their expedition—to say that, at least, it held that place in the minds of all the members, with the possible exception of Jervase himself. "I've heard of such a legacy—never heard it called a Sword, though. I suppose the Key has some connection?"

Abigail explained in a few words: The Key was a magical implement of some kind, its appearance varying from story to story. But in all versions it offered means of access to the legendary underground chambers where the secrets of Ardneh's power and wisdom were still supposed to exist.

She went on: "There's a name for that place too: 'Ardneh's Workshop.' And in the Workshop, of course, is where the great treasure, the centerpiece of the legacy, is supposedly waiting to be found: Ardneh's Sword."

"Now we have a Key, a Workshop, and a Sword. What next?"

Abigail ignored the question. "Naturally we Servants are interested in anyone who makes a claim concerning Ardneh. Just who was this other traveler you spoke with?"

Once more the boy's fingers sought the inside of his collar. As usual, they could discover nothing that he might display as evidence. "Well, there were two of them, actually. Two children. On successive days, just before we arrived at your compound."

"Children!"

"Yes. Abigail—can you tell me, please . . . if someone claimed to have possession of this Key—I mean if someone actually did have it—what would happen?"

Surprisingly, that seemed to relieve Abby's mind. She had a lovely laugh. "People can and will claim anything, Lord Chance. You didn't believe two children when they said they had it?" She was ready to laugh at him for a lordly fool if he said yes to that.

His shoulders slumped a little. It seemed the safest course to allow this girl her slight misunderstanding. "If I knew what the Key was, I might be better able to know what to believe."

Her look suggested that she regretted laughing at him. "All the versions I have heard say that Ardneh's chosen champion will bear the Key." She smiled. "Don't worry. You said you've never been chosen for anything."

THEY SEEMED TO BE SUCCEEDING WITH THEIR SORTING JOB. ABIGAIL, sounding confident, began to talk of magic. When she became hard to understand, hinting in magician's jargon of great powers and strange possibilities, Chance grew, annoyed with her and muttered: "I wonder that you don't have red hair."

She heard him, and it made her scowl. "Obviously I don't. Neither do you. What in the world does hair color have to do with anything?"

"Lately I've met a couple of people with red hair. And they were . . . strange."

"The strange children again?"

He nodded.

HAVING SORTED THROUGH THE LADY AYABA'S TOOLS AND MATERIALS, and come to the conclusion that nothing special needed to be done with them for the present, Chance and Abby at last were able to rejoin the others. It did not seem to be a good sign that no one paid much attention to their return. Chance could see that an edgy tension was well on the way to developing between Kuan Yin and the Scholar.

They were two people who viewed the world differently, disagreeing on matters of philosophy and historical interpretation. When they had time they would argue over some artifacts she had discovered locally.

NO ONE TRIED TO ARGUE WITH CAPTAIN HORKOS WHEN HE CALMLY assumed command of the compound's defense. After talking with the captain briefly, Kuan Yin gave him her blessing.

Relieved to have his authority accepted, the captain went into some detail. "In the first place, your wall here is just vastly too long a wall to try to hold with twenty men. Or thirty, even if I could muster ten more good fighters from this roster of pill-rollers. Or forty, or . . . in the second place, I have no doubt we're due for another fight. I really don't want to have it here, but I'm not sure what our options are."

Kuan Yin nodded, understandingly, and sighed. "I did not want to mention it until I was sure we could cooperate; but there is one option. We have a nearby place of sanctuary."

"Sanctuary?"

"I suppose it really qualifies as a fortress—but you will be the best judge of that. I'm talking about a large cave, up among the hills, less than a kilometer from where we stand."

"Large enough to hold all these people, yours and ours?" Jervase, sounding doubtful, swept an arm around in an inclusive gesture.

The Director nodded with quiet confidence. "Oh yes. Plus all the animals, and your wagons. There will be room to spare."

The captain got to his feet. "I'd better saddle up at once and take a look."

The Director sighed again. "While you are doing so, I think I had better gather my people. A retreat to the cave would appear to be inevitable. We've been keeping it provisioned against just some such emergency as this."

Horkos was skeptical. "It's really defensible? I don't want to be trapped in a hole in the ground."

"You shall see for yourself. The one entrance is accessible only by a narrow trail, and it has its own underground water supply."

Everybody got moving.

HORKOS AND JERVASE HURRIED AHEAD TO CARRY OUT A PRELIMINARY inspection of the cave, while the Director, seeming confident of the result, got her people packing, preparing to evacuate the compound.

When the move got under way, Chance was driving Lady Ayaba's wagon, while Abigail rode inside, still considering the legacy the older enchantress had left.

The improvised caravan heading for the cave included a total of about fifty people, including both Servants and the members of Jervase's expedition. A short migration required as much packing as a long one.

The move got under way with what Chance considered amazing speed. It seemed possible that everything that was to be moved could be carried in a single trip—or everything that could not be moved in one trip would be abandoned—none of the people involved in the evacuation were burdened with excess baggage. Kuan Yin walked at the head of the little column, leading the way. The Servants were evidently not wealthy. In the way of transport, they owned only a couple of ridingbeasts, perhaps two wagons, and a few draft animals.

KUAN YIN WAS THE LAST TO LEAVE THE PLACE WHERE SHE HAD SO RE-cently begun to live and work, where her recent plans had been so suddenly disrupted. She swept a quick, sad gaze around one empty room after another before taking her place at the head of the caravan. The Director, like most of her people, would be walking to the sanctuary, while the children and the wounded rode.

The Scholar, perpetually on watch to discover something, was keeping her company during this ritual of farewell. Also, there seemed to be no end of details regarding the move and their joint defense that needed to be discussed between the two of them.

During most of this time Chance accompanied his mentor. He and Abigail also saw to the packing and transportation of the Lady Ayaba's magical equipment—one small chest being brought along.

The novice Benambra had also been among the group making a final inspection of the compound to make sure nothing of value was left behind. Gazing at the now-abandoned garden space outside the walls, he mused: "It's just as well we didn't get much planting done. It would all have been wasted effort."

AS THE MOVE ACTUALLY GOT UNDER WAY, JERVASE WALKED BESIDE Kuan Yin. Their heads were close together most of the time, continuing their conference. Since there were troopers and swift mounts available, the possibility had to be considered of dispatching a rider or two toward the nearest Sarasvati outpost, or some nearby ally, urgently requesting aid. The leaders came to a quick agreement that such an appeal was impractical, all likely sources of help were much too distant.

In the next moment, one of the Servants, possibly Abigail, asked if the talking owl could be used as a messenger. Jervase and Chance both shook their heads. They agreed that Mitra might understand what was needed, but would be hopelessly undependable in that role.

"Trying to send her off with a message would be an utter waste. We are going to need the bird with us, she's invaluable as a scout."

WHILE THE WAGONS WERE LOADING, THE CAPTAIN HAD DISPATCHED two veteran scouts out on fast animals to search the country back in the direction from which the expedition had come. Their mission turned out to be a short one, and the caravan moving at a walking pace toward the cave had not reached its goal before the men returned.

Gloomily, the scouts confirmed that the force which had earlier attacked the expedition ("Whether you want to call them bandits, or irregulars."), now much reinforced, was advancing across the desert in the direction of the Servants' abandoned compound. They estimated the strength of this ominous gathering at several hundred, four or five times the number of people in the Servants' compound.

"This combined outfit of ours is leaving a huge trail, and it won't take 'em long to discover it once they find the compound's empty. They might have got that far by now, except maybe they were waiting for reinforcements."

Jervase was keenly interested. "Reinforcements from where? What did they look like?"

One of the scouts was sure that he had seen the colors of Yasodhara's mad king being worn by some men in the ominous gathering.

Twice in the course of the short journey Chance dismounted and helped to wrestle one or two of the heavily-laden wagons around the difficult curves in the narrow, twisting road that switchbacked up a steep and barren hillside. Abby was at his side, leaning on the wood with all her slender weight.

The trail the caravan was following wound in among the wooded hills, among many signs of spring's new life. It continued curving back and forth, tending steadily upward. The fragmentary road leading back into the hills had obviously been very little traveled in recent years, and was almost overgrown with grass and straggly bushes. But there were no obstacles serious enough to keep a wagon from getting through—not as long as the people making the effort were determined. The narrow, gradually ascending path turned out to be just wide enough for a rolling vehicle propelled slowly, with much cursing and pushing by dismounted troopers for help over the hard spots.

Growing steeper, the twisting road wound its way halfway up the slanted side of a low mesa before vanishing over a lip of rock. When the explorers had climbed to that lip, the mouth of a huge cave, almost entirely hidden until this moment, suddenly appeared in the hillside ahead.

Chance's first look at the cave's broad, gaping mouth, now directly ahead, made him pause and blink in wonder. From where he stood the trail to the cave led down again, then up once more; and when he and the other sweating wagon-pushers had fought their way up the final twisting path and could see deep into the cave's interior, he stopped to stare, aware that Jervase at his side was doing the same thing. In childhood Chance had poked his head into a small cavern or two, but he had never imagined anything like this.

NOT ONLY WAGONS, BUT ALL THE LIVESTOCK—LOADBEASTS, CAVALRY mounts loaded with bags of fodder for their own maintenance, two cows that the Servants kept for milk—had to be maneuvered up the narrow path, then down inside the cave to where some ancient occupants had created cattle pens.

The mouth of the cave was broad enough to allow in a large amount of daylight. Reflecting from one surface of light-colored rock to another, it cast useful illumination into chambers that were tens of meters below the surface.

As soon as he got inside, the Scholar looked about him with great interest. As usual, he was the most persistent questioner. "How far underground does this extend?"

The novice Benambra answered. "It goes down deeper than any of us have ever explored. We have not tried to count the branches and the rooms. The lower levels hold more space than we will ever need, if we were ten times as many as we are." Kuan Yin smiled lightly. "That is true. If you doubt me, take a look."

Right at the lip of the entrance, at the spot where the trail came in, natural defensive barriers had been reinforced by a rearrangement of small boulders and some carving of big ones. Horkos pronounced himself well satisfied that with no more than twenty men, only six or eight on duty at a time, he could defend this doorway against a vastly larger force.

"This is much better than I expected when you proposed hiding in a cave. Yes, we could do a lot worse than this," the captain agreed, nodding grimly as he looked around at the massive curves of sheltering rock.

"Then you are confident that here we will be safe?"

He had one wry caveat. "Always provided that no tricks are worked against us. That's where the impregnable fortress always fails—if it's going to fail."

ELEVEN

AFTER THE PROCESS OF UNPACKING HAD BEGUN, AND THINGS were being arranged inside the cave, troopers and Servants alike were ready for a rest. The transfer of people and goods had been accomplished in less than a day, more quickly than Chance would have believed possible. It had been necessary to send only one wagon back for a second trip.

Jervase was considering an idea that had come to him when the cave was first mentioned: that Ardneh's Workshop might actually be here, part of this cavern, or connected to it by some underground passage. Signs of old construction were visible in several rooms of the cave, and common everywhere in this area.

A thousand years ago, according to the Scholar, Ardneh's auxiliary machines—if the stories were true, there must have been an army of such devices—had carried out an extensive tunneling operation, trying to build a great system of defenses against Orcus, the archdemon, and his allies.

Most of that defense was thought to have been obliterated in the final battle. But Jervase now wondered whether some part of that effort might have been to connect Ardneh's stronghold with the natural cave complex that the Servants had now chosen for their sanctuary.

Down through the centuries, ever since the day when Ardneh and Orcus vanished in a gargantuan blast of mutual annihilation, other folk had used certain surviving materials to construct buildings of their own design, for their own reasons, in this part of the valley.

The ground hereabouts also sometimes yielded fragments of stranger and more complicated devices. Much more rarely, by diligence or accident, someone turned up an Old World light, that still, amazingly, functioned. One of the Servants mentioned once seeing a set of what had been called binoculars, with powers that seemed miraculous. "Nothing but metal and glass, not a bit of magic—or so it seemed. But it made distant things look many times nearer."

LADY KUAN YIN CONFIRMED A STORY THAT CHANCE HAD HEARD RE-peated among the Servants: how, a few years ago, a band of extraordinarily wicked bandits in the nearby desert had erected an altar to some particularly nasty demon—("I think we can now be certain which one it was.")—but when they tried to incorporate materials once used by Ardneh into their design, the project had turned into a fiasco.

THE COMBINED PARTY WAS SETTLING INTO SOME OF THE MORE CON-venient of the cave's many rooms. Horkos had posted one sentry outside the cave, two hundred meters down the narrow approach to the entrance. He was also maintaining a regular watch right at the top of the twisting trail. Someone in the past had rolled and wrestled medium-sized stones into position to form a formidable, though somewhat narrow, breastwork at that point. It appeared to Chance that half a dozen well-armed and active fighters in that position might easily hold off a thousand attackers, who would be forced to approach along a steep and exposed path, virtually in single file.

For people in the cave, the bulk of the hollow mesa provided high walls on every side, many meters thick, making the inner chambers a fortress of stone that seemed immune to assault by any imaginable siege machinery.

MEANWHILE THE CAPTAIN, UNCONVINCED BY THE SERVANTS' PROMises that there was only a single entrance, took it for granted that there were bound to be, somewhere, other ways to get in and out. Before he had taken a dozen breaths inside the cave, he had dispatched small search parties to locate those secret entrances, wherever they might be, and if possible block them.

From just inside the entrance, the cave's floor went continually down, in some places by large, irregular steps, in others by a gentle slope. Rooms narrowed into mere passages, and passages swelled out again into rooms. The total volume of interior space would be hard to calculate, but there was certainly no shortage. One very large room on a slightly lower level, basically flat-floored and royal in its dimensions if not its furnishings, had been turned into a park for wagons. A vaulted nearby space became a stable. Stalactites and stalagmites gave these and most of the other chambers an unearthly and enchanted appearance.

AS SOON AS CHANCE BEGAN TO LOOK AROUND INSIDE, HE WAS READY to believe that Kuan Yin told the truth, and no one knew the cavern's full extent. Large natural tunnels and passageways branched away from the large entrance opening, burrowing into rock in several directions. Major passages split into smaller branches, some of which shrank in turn to dark, pinched cracks in the earth. The Servants reported that no one had ever made a serious effort to explore them all.

The cave's new occupants began to establish their personal quarters in a dozen or so of its interconnected spaces. Most of these appeared to be natural formations; Jervase gave it as his opinion that they had been eroded from limestone by the age-long trickle of water. Here and there human hands and tools had enlarged openings and leveled floors for human convenience. Abby pointed out where, in one or two places, entire smaller chambers had been reshaped and enlarged by previous occupants. Chance could readily imagine this cave had been visited over the centuries by wave after wave of refugees, explorers, or people simply seeking storage space.

SEVERAL HOURS AFTER THE CAPTAIN HAD DISPATCHED HIS SEARCH parties into the depths, equipped with torches, and balls of string to keep from getting lost, the last of them came back to near the entrance. This pair of men, even armed with string, had come near losing themselves in a bat-infested lower portion of the labyrinth. It was an area that was thick with guano and showed, as they said, no signs of ever having been previously entered by human beings. Nowhere had they found any additional openings to the outside world—but it was still impossible to swear that none existed.

DURING THEIR TWO MONTHS' OCCUPATION OF THE WALLED COM-pound, Kuan Yin and her people had not been bothered by any visitors more dangerous than a few beggars. But they reported hearing tales of robbery and murder in the wasteland at no great distance. And the altars and other ominous signs of demon worship were scattered through the region, impossible to ignore. The Director had already concluded, with regret, that whether their organization worked here or in the cities they would be forced to develop their own arm of guardian force.

One of the female novices said: "We are none of us eager to take up arms. Draffut would never hurt a human being."

Novice Benambra reacted scornfully to this idea. He thought it was practically a sin to submit to robbery without a struggle.

ABBY PASSED ON A WHISPER SHE HAD HEARD—THE SUSPICION, HELD by some of the Servants, that their visitors were really under Lord

Chance's command, and that the true object of their expedition (the Scholar being brought along only as a cover) was the priceless treasure of material wealth, gold and jewels and rare Old World materials, that many people stubbornly believed Ardneh had hidden somewhere in the area.

On hearing the rumor, Chance almost laughed. "If you had traveled half a day with our expedition—or, better, spent even an hour talking with Jervase—you'd know it's not at all like that."

He thought Abby was giving him the benefit of the doubt. She said: "But there are people among the Servants, friends of mine, who are convinced it is."

Chance sighed. "Tell them they're wrong."

He later passed word of the whispers on to the Scholar. Jervase, who had been tired of hearing similar stories even before he left home, tried to squelch the persistent rumor of material wealth just waiting to be dug up. While still at home, before he had the king's support safely in hand, he had thoughtfully allowed the stories to flourish.

"It is true that I have spent my life in seeking Ardneh's treasure— or something very like it."

Chance, with the jeweled scimitar flashing in his imagination, asked: "What could there be, that is very like Ardneh's treasure?"

"The treasure I always have in mind, the one I think we have a real chance of finding, is knowledge."

"Knowledge."

"Yes!" Jervase, as Chance would have expected, seemed to come alive. "A chance to learn the truth about the past. That includes the facts regarding Ardneh—even if the truth about him should turn out to be something different than what is commonly accepted."

Kuan Yin, busy at some record-keeping task nearby, had overheard. She smiled slightly. "I could not agree more. I mean, that we should search for truth, wherever that may lead us."

Thoughtfully the Scholar went on. "What we truly need to know is the truth about ourselves as human beings. Where do we come from? Where and how do we fit into the universe?"

Kuan Yin nodded. "Again, I heartily agree. But I think if we can understand Ardneh it will help us to deal with the greater mystery of ourselves.

"You are right, Scholar Jervase, many people create in their own minds their own versions of his legacy. Most, of course, see gold and jewels. Others imagine miraculous weapons, the possession of which will enable one to conquer the world. Such things spring up readily in the human imagination."

Horkos surprised them by interjecting a rare conversational comment: "Ardneh was interested in weapons, after all."

The Scholar granted the captain a thoughtful nod. But his main attention stayed with Kuan Yin. "Just what do you imagine the treasure to be, Director?"

"That is a question to which I have given considerable thought. If, as legend says, it is a Sword, it is not the kind that will cut human flesh. Do you know? Sometimes I strongly suspect it is not a hidden treasure at all; perhaps it is too big to be seen, too valuable to be appreciated." She looked at Jervase. "Perhaps it is not even so much knowledge, as an idea: that we, humanity, should help one another."

Abigail put in: "Perhaps, then, it is knowledge about ourselves."

Jervase was nodding slowly. "That is not the strangest theory I have heard. Certain scholars have claimed that it was not really Ardneh, but in fact the archdemon Orcus, who had amassed a hoard of treasure somewhere near the place where the two of them met their end."

He shook his head. "You see, there we are again; it must always be gold and jewels. Bah! What use has a demon for such stuff?" He shrugged. "But the mass of people will have it so."

BY NOW CHANCE HAD TOLD KUAN YIN ABOUT THE STRANGE CHIL-dren who had warned him about attacking bandits, and how they had told him accurately where to find the Servants' compound. The Director seemed as skeptical as the other leaders had been.

"Were they the same ones who asked you about the Key?"

"Yes."

"You've not been talking to a demon, have you?" The Director's forehead creased in a frown even as her lips seemed to be trying to smile. It did not sound to Chance like an entirely serious question.

Automatically his fingers groped inside his collar—but, as he had expected, Ardneh's Key was not available. Chance murmured some vague response. If he had in fact been talking to a demon, or demons, he seemed to have survived the experience unharmed. In any case, there was nothing he could do about it now.

NONE OF THE SERVANTS WERE READY TO ADMIT TO ANY DOUBTS THAT Draffut was completely real. Jervase continued arguing with Kuan Yin, and others, about at least some of the Servants' fundamental beliefs. It wasn't scoring debating points that the Scholar really cared about, it was determining the truth.

"I will gladly lose an argument," he was telling Kuan Yin now, "if I can gain knowledge."

"I believe you, Scholar. I would like to think that is my position too."

"Good! Then—have you ever entertained the possibility that Draffut is not, never was, a being of flesh and blood? But rather an allegory, a representation of all the good things that Ardneh did in the world?"

"I have heard the possibility mentioned—but I have not really entertained it. I would prefer to think, Scholar, that it is the bloody battles Ardneh's armies fight in Scripture that are mere allegorical descriptions. Descriptions of a war that was not waged with violence on Ardneh's side."

BENAMBRA CAME TO CHANCE, DIPLOMATICALLY HINTING THAT THE impoverished Servants of Ardneh could really use a contribution.

Chance ignored the hint; he truly had little money with him, and he thought that his mother had already given all that the Rolfson family could be expected to provide. So far none of the Servants had sounded him out on the chances of recruiting him to join their Order. But he supposed one of the more diplomatic and persuasive members would be getting around to that in time. The answer, of course, was going to be no. Healing people was an admirable thing to do, but it wasn't how he wanted to spend his life.

TWELVE

THE LEADERS OF THE COMBINED PARTY, MEETING IN CONFERence, were now generally satisfied that their people were ready as they could be to repel an attack and withstand a siege. Food would not be a problem for many days. The Servants' wagons and those of the Scholar's expedition had come amply supplied with dried rations. For more than a month the Servants had been prudently stockpiling the cool, dark lower rooms of their refuge with similar supplies—grain and roots, smoked fish and meat—against just some such emergency as this. Abigail said the chilly cave temperature varied but little from summer to winter.

Of course the food supply could eventually be exhausted, but not the water. At least three small, clear streams trickled steadily down the cave's interior walls, a couple of them forming tranquil pools of ample size to supply the needs of the defenders. A black abyss of a narrow crevice in the cave's floor even appeared to offer efficient waste disposal with little or no magical exertion.

On the other hand, stocks of fodder were comparatively modest. Feeding the garrison's loadbeasts and ridingbeasts would begin to present a challenge if the enemy's investment of the refuge should last more than a few days. But Horkos was not greatly worried on that score.

One of the veteran soldiers said: "That's not the most terrible problem a besieged fort can have. At worst we'll wind up eating the beasts before they starve."

EVERYONE WAS ANXIOUS THAT THE OWL SHOULD BE ABLE TO DO ANother scouting flight tonight. Abigail had examined Mitra's injured wing and pronounced it largely healed. But she had added a bit of magic, from which the owl seemed to derive benefit.

The Scholar and Chance tried to talk Mitra into repeating her last night's reconnaissance flight, and it seemed that the bird was willing.

Chance told Abby that they wouldn't know until the owl came back whether she had actually followed instructions or not.

Even down in the rocky vault where she had been carried, among the assembled wagons barely lit by torchlight, Mitra seemed able to discern the moment when darkness fell outside the cave. As soon as that happened, she took to the air, apparently without difficulty, and circled the room once before soaring away toward the unseen entrance.

Jervase watched with concern as at the same time a flight of bats came pouring out of some deeper chamber of the cave, also on their way to the open air. But the bats and Mitra ignored each other, even as their wing tips seemed to brush.

"Quite harmless," the Director assured her guests, speaking of the bats. "They eat only insects." Chance overheard Vardtrad murmuring something to himself about a possible source of food in the event of a long siege.

Dinner was served cold on the first evening in the cave, it being thought wise to conserve the limited supply of cooking fuel as much as possible. In a peaceful moment round the lamp where the leaders had gathered, Kuan Yin asked: "By the way, Scholar Jervase—what was it that really brought you riding up to our compound in the desert? Did you come only to give us warning, or to have your wounded cared for?"

Jervase smiled faintly. "At one time we had a story ready, to be told to strangers who might ask us about our business." He went on to tell Kuan Yin of the cover story—that young Lord Chance needed help for his sleepwalking—only to show how silly it was.

The Director looked closely at Chance. "Do you indeed have a sleepwalking problem?"

"Not really. It happened once or twice, when I was a child. You may have noticed that sometimes I stutter." He paused. "Not a problem that's worth launching an expedition into the desert."

Another layer of the expedition's cover story—it was to be revealed only under pressure, as if reluctantly—was that the Scholar and the Lady Ayaba had been sent under orders to seek out the infirmary to inquire about healing, on behalf of some very eminent person they had left at home, too ill to make such a journey.

As matters had worked out, there was actually no need to make up excuses for the caravan's presence; the fact that they brought in a couple of seriously wounded soldiers was reason enough, as was the need to unite against a force of bandits that had grown astonishingly strong.

When the move into the cave had been completed, and Chance and Abigail had seen that the Lady Ayaba's things were stowed away as well as they were able, Chance seized the opportunity to get some sleep, during which he endured his usual quota of evasive dreams. They bothered him but then danced away, evaporated, before he could bring his conscious thought to grips with them.

Awakening toward morning, he spent a moment or two in trying to remember where he was. Then he climbed out of the wagon bed and sat down on the driver's bench. Not being an owl, he had a hard time, when he was this deep underground, telling whether it was day or night. His guess, based on only a vague feeling, was that the hour was near dawn, which meant that Mitra could be returning at any moment. If she could see him on the wagon, that might induce her to land in the proper, familiar place; otherwise it would not be unprecedented for her to choose some other perch, and time would pass before anyone realized she was back. Then whatever news she might have brought would remain unreported for hours.

Around him the array of silent and empty wagons, the expedition's and the Servants' too, was quiet and peaceful. The encampment that they made was strange for being underground, and also larger than any to which he was accustomed.

Chance found himself halfway hoping that Abigail would stop by for another talk, but she was busy. Earlier he had caught a glimpse of her in candlelight, as she bent, chanting magic, over one of the wounded Sarasvati troopers. And like everyone else she had to rest sometime.

So did Chance. He still felt sleepy, and for all he could tell, dawn might still be hours away. The driver's bench was too short and narrow to allow any human of adult size to lie down on it with any hope of sleeping. That might have been arranged by calculation; there certainly appeared to be no danger of the wagon driver drifting off when he was supposed to be keeping a sharp eye on plodding loadbeasts just ahead.

THE NET, IN WHICH ONLY A FEW NIGHTS AGO SOMEONE OR SOME-thing had tried to catch the owl, was still lying just under the bench. In the press of other events, Chance had forgotten about it, but there it was.

He was running the lines of soft, pliable mesh through his fingers when he heard a soft sound inside the wagon. His body jerked to attention. It was surprising—though, when he thought about it, not totally impossible—that the bird had managed to find her way this deep into the cave, and had actually got into the wagon on which he sat, without his knowledge.

But perhaps Mitra had not yet returned. What stirred now inside the wagon's canvas shelter was much heavier than the owl. The weight of it made the twisted leather springs below the box frame creak.

Chance's hand went up reflexively to probe inside his collar. He felt an odd mixture of alarm and reassurance on discovering that the little chain holding its small mysterious burden was solidly present once again.

Turning his body on the seat, he reached out without hesitation to open the flap of the wagon's canvas door; the tension of not knowing who or what might be inside was greater than the fear that some danger might leap out.

What did leap out was startling light—dim, cool, steady illumination, such as Chance had once or twice seen when the Scholar showed him an Old World lamp. A moment later the sight of bright red hair came as something of a relief, and no real surprise at all.

Opening the flap fully, Chance found himself looking at an elderly woman he had never seen before, her hair a variegated mixture of bright red and gray, her slender form almost completely covered by a mottled cloak. She was clearly visible in the light of an Old World lamp that she held in her left hand.

The woman did not appear to be a Servant. Her back was to the astonished young lord, and she was tut-tutting as she looked upward, taking note of the mended tear in the canvas top. Turning to smile at Chance over her shoulder, she jabbed at the flaw with one bony finger, and shook her head.

Her speech shared some qualities with the voices of Moxis and Zalmo. "Yes, I did make a mistake, trying to catch Mitra in a net. That was foolish. There were other, better ways to manage your poor bird. But no great harm done, not yet. Come in, my young Lord, come in. You needn't be afraid of me. And your precious owl is not going to return for perhaps a quarter of an hour."

Chance pushed one foot forward through the canvas doorway. If this being had wanted to harm him, and if the charming power of Ardneh's Key could not prevent it, the damage would be done already. One thing the Key had evidently not done was turn him invisible again—at least not to this visitor's eyes.

For the moment Chance's anger and curiosity outweighed his fear, and he demanded: "How did you get in here past the sentries?"

The elderly woman ignored the question. She smiled as she took note of the torn net that Chance was still carrying in his hand. Leaning forward slightly, as if what she was about to say was confidential, she murmured: "Zalmo and Moxis have told me about you, young sir."

"I suppose you're really their grandmother?" It could have been a logical relationship—if anything about this red-haired crew turned out to deserve that kind of a description.

"That would be a pleasant way to think of me." Her voice continued sweet and strong. "In a manner of speaking, it is even true. Everything that Moxis and Zalmo know, I know. That includes all that they were able to discover about you, Lord Chance. What a fine, upstanding young man you really are! So ready and willing to listen to a different point of view."

She took him by the hand, pressing his palm gently, like a fortune-teller.

"Does it bother you, my dear one, not to be able to tell where Ardneh's Key is at any moment, or even if you still have it?—or perhaps we should say that it has you!"

Chance muttered something. Pulling his hand free, he felt reflexively for the Key again. It was still there.

His visitor was still smiling. "Do not let its odd behavior bother you, for that only testifies to the strength of your protection. Be glad that I was able to deflect the foolish bird, who would have given the great prize into the Scholar's hand and not yours. That would never do! Such a treasure would be entirely wasted on Jervase."

Chance was standing with his mouth open, unable to say anything.

The elderly lady sighed. "I would I might have seen you, met you, taught you, months ago, or even years ago. Together we might already have accomplished . . . much.

"Well, young Chance, one cannot have everything, can one? Tut tut, you look so lost, so puzzled. I am an agent, you see, of the Lord Draffut himself. And he and I are only doing our best to save your life."

THIRTEEN

As CHANCE'S VISITOR EMERGED FROM THE WAGON, SHE TURNED off her Old World lamp and caused it to vanish somewhere under her mottled robe. Evidently her eyes needed nothing better than the dim illumination filtering from other chambers into this vast one where a number of wagons had been parked.

Stepping down briskly onto the cave floor, the old woman's movements were firm and confident. Her arms were folded in the same way Moxis had once held his, as he stood waist deep in the icy pool. As she stood looking around among the wagons and hastily deposited piles of baggage, her green eyes seemed to glow and twinkle.

Her voice was cheerful. "Bless you, child, sentries do not pose me any problems. That is, if you are speaking only of the human kind, who stalk their measured paths with blades and clubs in hand." Chance had followed her, and she gave his arm a reassuring pat. "Oh, of course such have their uses in your situation here! Against your human enemies they may be very useful."

The young lord realized, to his relief, that he was not much afraid of this visitor. At least, no more than he had been of the children. "What other kinds of sentries are there?"

"Those who are much more difficult to avoid. Now, you need raise no alarm among your friends on my account; if you do, I will simply disappear . . . tell me, young Chance, how are you getting along with Ardneh's Key? Has it given you the power to do anything truly marvelous? Or presented you with unexpected problems? I am really curious."

"It once made me invisible." Here, it seemed, was at least one listener who was probably going to believe him.

"Ah, did it now?" Grandmother seemed pleased but not particularly surprised. "No doubt at a moment when you were in danger."

"That's right, I don't doubt it saved my life. Beyond that, about all I can tell you is that the thing keeps vanishing completely and coming back again. Right now it's hanging around my neck." The small irregular shape on its chain was currently quite visible, perfectly solid in Chance's hand as he pulled it out from inside his collar.

The lady shook her head. "I am sure that my gift remains with you, dear child, even if there are times when you cannot find it."

Before Chance could say anything else, the woman surprised him by shooting out an arm toward him in a gesture of amazing speed, as if she meant to seize the Key. Or perhaps her only intention was to touch it. Whatever her purpose, in the instant before Grandmother's hand could make contact with the object, she recoiled sharply. At the same moment an odd little yelp burst from her lips, as if great Ardneh's gift had bitten her, or stung her with a spark of the kind that came from shuffling across wool carpet on a dry, cold day. For just a moment Chance imagined he could see Grandmother's extended fingers tangling bonelessly, writhing like a nest of snakes.

A moment later, the figure before him had recovered its pleasant appearance and mild manner.

Grandmother's hands were meekly folded. "I see," she said in her sweet voice, its tones suggesting that some difficult point had just been made clear to her. "That is very interesting. Not that I want to take my great gift back, you understand. I was only testing. But even if I wanted to . . . it would not be possible. Even for me. At least not while you are still . . ." Grandmother's words trailed off, as if some inner train of thought had claimed her full attention.

Chance's right hand rose slowly up to hold the Key. He could touch it. It was his. "*Your* great gift? It wasn't you who gave it to me."

"Oh, yes it was. But never mind." She smiled brightly, displaying perfect teeth. Chance noted that they seemed completely human teeth, and of only modest size.

Grandmother went on: "The Key has . . . fully . . . *adopted* you, shall we say, and that is a very good sign. No one will be able to steal it from you. I hoped that something of the kind would happen. Everything seems to be working as blessed Ardneh intended, to eventually put his Sword into your hands."

"Oh yes, Ardneh's Sword! I might feel happier about that if I knew just what in all the hells it is."

"If *I* knew that secret, dear lad, I would assuredly tell you. But it is certain to be marvelous. There are wonders ahead of you, young Chance, even greater, much greater, than the Key. . . ." Grandmother kept shaking her head as her voice trailed off.

"You keep talking about great marvels, but you tell me nothing useful." Chance's anger was pushing his fear further into the background. "Who are you? What do you want? Why should I believe anything you say? And there's another thing: Are you working some kind of magic on me, to keep me from talking to anyone else about you—?"

Grandmother looked pained. "Well, *that* kind of magic . . . there is only just a little of it in place, my dear." She held up a finger and thumb that were almost touching. "To keep the situation from growing too complicated. . . ." The lady made a deprecating gesture. "Nothing harmful. The Key is still allowing it. Not very strong magic, for you *have* talked to others about me."

Chance was primed by anger to go on. "Don't tell me you're just those crazy children's grandmother. And don't tell me they're real kids. You are . . . the whole bunch of you are . . ."

His visitor's annoyance had vanished, or was once more well concealed. She clapped her hands. "What a clever young man! Oh, it will be a pleasure to work with you! I am, as I have told you, the Lord Draffut's chosen agent, and in his name I have delivered to you Ardneh's Key."

"Let's get things straight. It was the Scholar's owl, Mitra, who gave me the Key."

"But I was there, my dear!" The lady reached out to pat Chance on the arm again, and easily succeeded; to that simple contact the Key evidently had no objection. "I was perched with your beautiful owl atop this very wagon. My fingers forced the great prize from your dear bird's claw, so that it fell into your hand. Draffut and I wanted you to have it."

That name silenced Chance for a moment. Then he said: "Oh? Jervase has told me something about Draffut, too."

"Bah, Jervase!" Grandmother frowned and gestured scorn. "A young man filled to his eyebrows with misinformation. A pity you have learned so much from him, so much that is not so."

Chance would not be distracted. "What is your name?" he demanded. The true form of a name had ramifications, consequences, in the realm of magic even more than in society.

The lady nodded; she almost bowed, her posture and manner becoming those of an elderly servant, eager to please. "My own true name is Zalmoxis; yes, it really is. I reveal it to you freely. One of my true names, as useful to you as any other would be. And, as you may have guessed already, I have also used the name of Zalmo . . ."

". . . and also the name of Moxis."

"Yes, yes, of course. Do you know, dear Chance, how much trouble I have gone to, that you and I should be able to have this little, reasonable chat?"

"Tell me—Zalmoxis. How much trouble?" Was he being told the truth about anything? Chance had no means of deciding.

"Well. For our first meeting I wanted to make sure you would not be frightened, and so I clothed myself in the image of a little girl, the most harmless-looking human imaginable who would still be capable of speech." Grandmother frowned thoughtfully. "I admit I failed to foresee the accompanying difficulty—how could you take seriously anything said to you by so immature a child?"

"Then after Zalmo came Moxis . . ."

"Exactly!" Grandma Zalmoxis beamed. "I made the boy a little older than the girl, while keeping him almost as harmless in appearance. And so I intended to go on by stages, without making you too uneasy, seeking a balance between innocent appearance and sensible argument, until I could appear as a substantial adult, and we could have our reasonable discussion—and yet you still found the boy somewhat alarming."

"I did."

"So I thought I had better proceed cautiously. On the children's bodies I wore, as a demonstration, simple versions of Old World armor. Had Moxis been able to persuade you to wear that, you would now be enjoying some additional protection. Which I still fear you may need." The woman paused, thoughtfully fingering her chin. "You do not find my present appearance at all threatening, I trust?"

"No." Chance swallowed. "It's not your appearance that bothers me. And it's not your name either. What I want to know is what you truly—"

"Good!" The figure offered him a slight bow. "For a time I considered presenting myself tonight as Zalmo's older sister. But on reflection it seemed to me that any female of approximately your own age would probably prove too distracting. You would have looked at her and thought of her, and not paid much attention to what she was trying to tell you."

I would have looked at you and shuddered at the thought of touching you. Knowing you are not human, but . . . It was possible, Chance thought, that in the next moment Grandmother was going to reveal herself as a demon and grab him. But whatever happened, he would be better off for knowing the truth—one lesson he had learned well from the Scholar. "But you really built that waterwheel. Or you somehow . . ."

The lady was suddenly excited. "Oh yes, I built it. Definitely! And fabricated little Zalmo's fishing net as well."

"And the suits they wore?"

"No. No, no, no! I have been telling you the precise truth about those garments all along. They were a very valuable find, entirely serendipitous, during one of my explorations of Ardneh's anterooms—they are places not very far from here, but difficult to locate. It will be necessary for you to find your way inside before you use the Key. However . . .

"The suits are indeed from the Old World, notwithstanding whatever denials you may have heard from your mentor, a man who is lost in abysmal ignorance."

Chance cast a look around in the cavernous dimness. It appeared that he and his visitor were still alone among the dim shapes of the wagons. He said: "Jervase has told me that he has never heard of such a thing as Ardneh's Key." He omitted to mention that others had mentioned it.

"I have told you that man's ignorance is great." Momentarily the old woman displayed signs of pity and amusement. Then her appearance underwent some changes that put her very nature in doubt. For a moment it seemed that Chance was looking at a man of forty, and then a slender woman not much older than himself.

He shut his eyes for a count of three, and when he opened them again, Grandmother was back, as solid-looking as ever. "All right. And what's the real reason you were set on getting me to wear a suit?"

"Ah, what a clever young man! A pleasure to do business with you." Grandmother seemed to be wringing her hands, or washing them. "I have been trying to explain, but you will keep interrupting! The Key itself provides you with a certain measure of protection—as we have seen, praised be the powers of Ardneh! But its fundamental purpose is not to guard, merely to open certain doors, and I fear you are likely to need all the protection that you can get."

"Why?"

"Because you are carrying the Key, dear lad! Bandits, as you have seen—and there are going to be worse creatures than bandits, too—they are going to want to take it from you—or force you to use it for their benefit. I am exerting every effort to keep you alive, by convincing you to accept from my hands the same suit that Moxis offered you. Whatever inadequacies may exist in your present protection, I trust it will cover them."

"And it was you who tried to catch the owl? You ripped that slit in the canvas?" When he got no answer he pressed on. "If you won't tell me the truth about yourself, how can I believe anything you say?"

The lady drew herself up. "The owl's talon made the hole. I have admitted that my attempt to net your dear bird was a mistake. In my great endeavor to become human, or as close to human as I can possibly be, I have experimented with almost every form of human activity. Capturing birds is one such occupation. But while atop your wagon I was trying to do too many things at once, which had the unhappy result of injuring the bird and terrifying you.

"I was still in the process of learning how to present a convincing human face. Now I see I must apologize—expressing regret is a human action too.

"Happily I did succeed in my main goal, of providing you with the Key."

Chance took half a step forward. "But a moment ago I heard you say something else—that you are making some kind of effort—to become human? Did I hear that right?"

"You did, dear boy." The figure sighed. "Have I made a great mistake in telling you?"

"I don't know. And you still maintain you are the one who gave me the Key."

"I do—you see, that was more difficult than it sounds. Because great Ardneh has designed the little treasure to rest peacefully only in human hands, I was forced to enlist the bird to carry it for me. However carefully and craftily I picked the Key up, it flew away from me again." The lady looked sad, as if recalling great hardships.

Chance's fear had been suppressed, but it was not gone. Every few heartbeats he experienced a moment that had him hovering on the edge of flight, near turning and running away through the great cave, crying out for help—help from some grandmaster magician who was able to order about demons and other eldritch powers. But such help would certainly not be available.

So far Chance had sounded no alarm. He had often heard of demons taking the shape of seductive women or handsome men, but never of one that presented itself as a saucy red-haired child or babbling grandmother. If this was indeed a demon that confronted him, it seemed to be behaving in contradiction to all the rules of monstrous evil.

He drew a deep breath. "You still haven't told me. What are you, really?"

His visitor was looking tragic. "It seems I have deceived only myself in my efforts to become a human being. But trust me, I would be your friend."

"*What are you?*"

Grandmother drew back a step, and raised ten trembling fingers to hide her face. Her voice came out muffled. "I have told you my name. I beg of you, do not force me to admit in so many words that I am something other than what I crave to be."

Chance's old suspicions came rushing back. "I will have nothing to do with demons!"

The figure before him emitted the strangest sound he had yet heard from it, a startling and inhuman yelp, a cry of terror and surprise. It wrung its hands. "Is that what you suspect me of? Oh, pupil of a stupid teacher! *Would that I could have nothing to do with demons either!*" It seemed a heartfelt cry. "I will ask you for no sacrifice of blood! I have no altar, and want none. I am of the race of djinn, older than demons and far less understood!"

FOURTEEN

C HANCE, TO THE BEST OF HIS KNOWLEDGE, HAD NEVER SEEN A djinn before, but he had no doubt that such a class of beings existed. He remembered encountering them occasionally in the Scripture passages assigned him by the Scholar. Jervase had never disputed their reality. There, and in other ancient books, the djinn were only mentioned in passing, as far as Chance could remember, and their nature remained obscure. They were not demons, nor were they elementals; but what they *were*, exactly, Chance had never been interested enough to make an effort to find out.

How could he judge if the being before him was telling the truth?

Not wanting to reveal the dangerous depths of his own ignorance, Chance proceeded cautiously: "Zalmoxis. You say you are a djinn, and you are determined to work with me."

Grandmother folded her hands primly. "Both statements are very true."

"Why have you chosen me?"

"The choice was not mine. You are Chance Rolfson." The figure bowed, deeply enough to suggest that the gesture was really meant in mockery.

"This is maddening! That doesn't make any—"

"Because the great Lord Draffut *knows* you are Chance Rolfson, and for that reason he has chosen you to be entrusted with the power of the Key.

"As you have pointed out, to be a lineal descendant of Ardneh's foremost human friend and closest helper may mean little in terms of actual inheritance of flesh and blood. But it means rather a lot in terms of human society—and, I assure you, it is important in the mind of Lord Draffut himself.

"With the help of the Key, you and your associates should be able to enter the Workshop. But unless I am there to provide guidance and protection, you will probably find it impossible to locate Ardneh's Sword, even to recognize it when you stand in its presence. You must understand, it is highly unlikely that Ardneh's legacy will be a sword in the common, mundane sense!"

"But I suppose you *will* recognize it. Even though you say you don't know what it is."

The djinn nodded gravely. "That is true. I will have ways of identifying that which I seek to find. Also, no human will be able to control the powers that will surround you in Ardneh's Workshop." Zalmoxis had put on a distant look. "Jervase is right about one thing. What you discover there will not be gold and jewels."

"But you can't say what it will be. Or you won't. Meanwhile you keep talking about saving my life. How are you going to do that?"

The djinn burst out with a word Chance did not understand, some kind of incantation he supposed. With the flamboyant gesture of some stage conjurer, the woman-image produced, seemingly from nowhere, a small, shapeless bundle.

Her hands thrust the bundle forward. "Another gift for you. At first I toyed with the idea of simply leaving it beside you as you slept, for you to find. But then I decided that a few words of explanation were in order."

In another moment Grandmother had unrolled the bundle, with a dramatic snap of her slender wrists that seemed to promise great revelation—but produced only what Chance saw and felt as a crashing anticlimax. The suit in Grandmother's hands was notably larger than the ones worn by her earlier child-images, but otherwise looked very much the same. Still basically a set of long winter underwear, or it might have been a costume for some adult acrobat. The color scheme, a brighter mottling than Zalmo or Moxis had enjoyed, favored the latter interpretation.

Evidently misinterpreting Chance's silence as an effect of awe, the djinn thought it necessary to warn him against overenthusiasm. "Do not suppose that this, even in combination with the Key, will render you totally immune to harm. Take no unnecessary chances. Our most dangerous enemy here is very powerful."

Grandmother was holding out the suit, but the young lord had made no move to touch it. Instead, Chance retreated slightly.

"I'm not going to take any more chances than I can help . . . and I see no reason why I should put that on."

"That you do so is a matter of some urgency!" Zalmoxis shook the shapeless bundle at him, as if to scatter some of its benefits in his direction.

"Bah. Why should I trust you?"

Zalmoxis emitted another inhuman sound, suggestive of growing outrage and suffering, and shook the bundle again. "Have I not already given you the Key, and saved your life?"

Chance had to admit to himself that that might be true. On impulse he reached out to touch the suit. The fabric felt surprisingly soft, like fine cotton, even though some embedded component glittered in the dim cave light like bright metal, or perhaps like diamonds.

Grandmother was still supporting the garment with one hand. With the other she stroked the fabric gently, as if she too enjoyed the feel of it. "This should serve you well indeed against material attack."

Chance could detect no aura of magic from the garment; but he knew himself to be insensitive in such matters. "The idea is that I just pull it on over my other clothes?"

"No. The warriors of the Old World did not wear them in that fashion. For safety, there should be nothing under it but your skin. Then you will probably want to cover it with other clothing."

Fumbling at the garment's collar, Chance exposed some fine lettering that was just inside, only faintly visible in the dim cave light. It was in the same script, for the most part readable to Chance, that he had seen over the compound's gate, and on one or two of the Scholar's old maps. As far as he was able to determine, it said:

BODY ARMOR, LINER, LIGHT
MARK I

The word "armor"—if he was reading it correctly—was reassuring. "You say it offers protection. What exactly will it do—besides keep my feet warm if I go wading?"

"Much more! It is body armor worn by human warriors of the Old World—do not be deceived by its comparatively unexceptional appearance."

"I'll try not to be deceived—by anything."

Grandmother abruptly let go of the suit, so that it hung suspended by the end still gripped by Chance. "Then will you put it on?" the elder pleaded.

"I'll think about it."

The djinn—the little old lady—demonstrated agitation and impatience. "I had considered taking you away with me, for a time, to keep you safe. But alas, that would only draw the attention of a certain entity, the Bad Demon—hush, if you know his name, do not pronounce it. We must keep from him as long as possible the knowledge of what Key it is you carry."

"You mean he—the one whose name I'm not supposed to speak—he doesn't know about the Key already?"

"There is a chance that he does not."

Chance felt an impulse to tear out his hair. "You may be telling me the truth about all this. But how do I know?" He shook the suit. "How do I know this thing is any good at all?"

The woman-image seemed delighted to be able to offer a demonstration. She seized one leg of the suit and pressed the fabric tight against the nearest wall of solid rock. In the next moment the little old lady's right arm moved with a verve and ferocity more than adequate for any human warrior, and she stabbed at the garment fiercely with a blade she had apparently materialized out of thin air. The fabric of the shirt glowed subtly and briefly.

Amazingly, Chance could hear no sound of impact with the wall, but when the djinn tossed the dagger aside, Chance could see that the point was seriously bent. The shirt showed no evidence of damage.

Grandmother was about to make some comment when her gaze suddenly darted past Chance into the darkness of the cave behind him, and he fell silent. The face of Chance's visitor assumed a piercing look. The two hands holding the suit and weapon dropped abruptly to the creature's sides.

Chance turned to see Abigail approaching, still wearing her Servant's robe. The garment was stained and blotched by a hard day of physical work, but still its whiteness stood out almost glowing in the cave's near-darkness. The blue of the girl's eyes looked more striking than ever in the glint of distant torchlight, as her gaze darted from Chance to Grandmother and back again, her face a study in puzzlement. Obviously she was shocked to find a stranger in the cave.

The self-proclaimed djinn stood calmly, having nothing to say. Chance finally broke the silence. "Abby? It's all right. I think it's going to be all right."

The girl began to murmur something about having come to see Chance about some question having to do with the Lady Ayaba's things. But she lost the thread of her sentence halfway through, and let it drop. "I—I—who—?" She gestured helplessly at the figure of Zalmoxis.

"I don't know who," said Chance, looking at the image that still stood silent. "I'm not sure. That is exactly the problem—but I think it's going to be all right."

The old woman had regained her more or less ordinary appearance. She smiled at Abigail, curtseyed in her direction, and promptly turned to Chance.

Grandmother said to him: "You stand in greater danger than you realize. I will continue to guard you as well as I am able, and you must wear both of the gifts that I have brought to you. Still, the powers that menace you are very dangerous."

"The one who must not be named," he murmured.

"Oh, I can name that one, Avenarius. But I fear him even so." An expression of alarm suddenly came over the old woman's face. "I must depart, for the time be—"

. . . She had vanished like a popped bubble, right in the middle of a word.

Abigail stared at Chance helplessly. "Who was—she?"

"She said she was a djinn."

"Ah!" Somewhat to Chance's surprise, the girl seemed ready to consider that as a serious possibility.

"I don't know why she just—" Chance broke off there. The djinn's senses had evidently been keener than the human. Another moment passed before Chance and Abby were startled by the alarm of a trooper's bugle, sounded above them in one of the rooms closer to the entrance.

He was half-consciously fingering his throat, when Ardneh's Key, or some power residing in it, seemed to stir, giving a little jump that Chance took as a warning.

Abby was alarmed. "Ardneh defend us! What is it?"

ABBY WAS STILL A STEP AHEAD AS THEY BOTH WENT SCRAMBLING UP the stairs. There came the sharp sound of a slung rock shattering against a massive wall, the pieces ricocheting. Chance saw the blurring, speeding shadow of great wings, totally unexplainable, far larger than those of any owl. They had almost reached the head of the first stair when the bizarre shape of a flying reptile, its body bigger than a human's, went hurtling by, like nothing he had ever seen before. It was flying so low in the confined space that he thought he felt the brush of a wing tip.

A large irregularity in the rough cave wall presented a natural niche the size of a small closet. Instinct sent both young humans cramming into it together, while more hurtling, airborne shapes shot past them in near-darkness.

Abigail murmured in her terror: "Ardneh defend us! What are they looking for?"

"All I can think of—is that there's a good chance it's me."

There were glaring, probing fingers of Old World light, cold and pitilessly bright, playing through the blackness then vanishing again. Their niche grew momentarily as bright as noonday sunlight, then went dark again, leaving them dazzled and almost blind.

As soon as Chance's vision had cleared a bit he saw a human figure run by, whether male or female it was hard to tell. It was clothed like neither soldier nor Servant, but a bandit. The first amazing intruder was followed closely by a second, then a third, bearing what appeared to be an Old World light much like Grandmother's. Again a beam fell straight on Chance, cowering with his right arm wrapped tightly around Abby, his left hand at his own throat clutching the Key. The djinn's latest gift lay on the cave floor at his feet. All that happened was that after a moment the light moved on, the running, scrambling footsteps vanished in the darkness.

Abby sounded lost in sheer bewilderment. "I thought sure they— had us."

"I expect they didn't see us after all." Peering out of the niche, Chance saw a man vaulting to remount a grotesque, winged creature—he knew a griffin when he saw one, though he had never glimpsed one outside of old illustrations. In the griffin's rider Chance thought he recognized one of the pair of men who had been blinded by Ardneh's Key on the first day of fighting. As soon as the bandit was on its back, the beast spread wings of magic and was airborne, flying close under the cave's low ceiling.

"How could they not have seen us?"

Chance didn't try to answer that. Silence and darkness seemed to come rushing back. After a few moments there was distant shouting. Abby murmured: "What about my mother? And the Scholar, and . . . we must find out what's happening. And see that they know about the djinn."

"And tell them about the griffin, if they haven't seen it yet. It'll be hard to defend this place against things that can come flying into it at night."

Abby's fingers found his arm and clutched it, hard. Chance's eyes, recovering from that last flash of light, were beginning to make out her shape again. She said: "Wait a bit. What did the djinn—the old woman—what did she give you?"

Groping in front of him on the cave floor, Chance came up with the supposed Old World garment, and turned it over in his hands. In the gloom it appeared to be nothing but a simple, ordinary item of clothing, ready to be put on as if it were indeed long underwear.

Abigail was still holding his arm. She whispered: "Are you going to wear it? That's what she wanted you to do."

Still he could not quite make up his mind. Surprisingly, his strongest inner feeling was that he ought not to trust Zalmoxis. He said: "There's magic in it."

"Oh yes. I can see that."

"Had I better put it on or not?"

"How should I know?" Abby grasped the fabric of the suit with one hand and murmured something. "I can't sense anything *wrong* with it. But . . ."

"Yes. But."

"We must get back to the others. . . ."

"But I had better decide this first."

THEY HAD HARDLY STARTED TO LEAVE THEIR NICHE BEFORE THE SIGHT of more intruders sent them once more crowding back into it, trying to keep out of the sight and sound of human fighters who rode on the backs of flying griffins. Two human riders, armed to the teeth, were mounted on the next airborne monster that Chance saw. Something even stranger than a griffin came darting through the air, sporting two pairs of wings, looking half dragon and half dragonfly. Where in all the hells could this array of creatures be coming from? It was discouraging that the enemy kept coming up with new resources.

The only menace that had not yet shown itself seemed to be the great demon himself, Avenarius—Chance wondered suddenly whether the djinn's warning about that threat had been only misdirection.

FIFTEEN

I N ONLY MOMENTS, THE GANG OF INTRUDERS HAD RUSHED ON, leaving him alone again with Abigail. In a fierce whisper she began insisting that before they tried to rejoin their friends he must tell her everything he possibly could about Zalmoxis.

A distant clamor of alarm came echoing through the cave. "But hadn't we better first find out what—?"

"Chance, settling this may be the most important thing that we can do. Trust me on this. What sort of djinn did it say it was?" she asked.

Chance blinked. "W-what sort? I don't know. What do you mean?"

"Well, there are different types."

His eyes were once more growing accustomed to the semidarkness, and he could see Abigail frown as she went on: "My specialty is healing, not the study of the djinn. But I know they come in a number of different varieties. Sort of like elementals. I have experimented with raising those."

"Elementals?" That was truly a surprise. "I would have thought they had little to do with healing."

"Well . . . my mother has insisted that I focus mainly on medical magic. But when I have any leisure time—which isn't very often—I find other varieties exciting, too."

That was interesting. "Anyway, about the djinn, when he—she—talked to me we didn't get into any fine distinctions. How many species of them can there be?"

Abby had to admit she didn't know. "But tell me all you can about this one. We have to consider the possibility that it was not a djinn at all."

ONCE CHANCE HAD BEGUN WHISPERING THE TALE OF HIS WEIRD EX-periences to someone, someone who listened intently and believed the strange parts of the story even if she did not approve of the choices he had made or credit all the details, he found it very difficult to hold back anything.

Still the telling did not take long. In a few moments he was concluding: "The strange folk I've been running into—the little girl wading, the boy in the pool, the old woman you just saw—none of them were real people. They were all, well, just disguises, worn by the same creature. It was ready to admit as much."

Abby was looking more and more horrified. "And it claims to be a djinn, but I must warn you that quite possibly it is a demon!"

Chance could feel his own face mirroring the girl's changed expression. That was a horrible thought that had to be rejected. "No, I don't think so."

"Have you ever encountered a demon before?"

"I . . . no."

Her voice had fallen to a whisper. "You're forgetting what you just told me a few moments ago—about the terrible face that you saw, staring at you through the hole in the covered wagon's top. What about that? To me that sounds like what a demon really ought to look like."

"Zalmoxis explained that too. It—she, he, whatever—was still trying to perfect his imitation of the human form. Plus he had recently been experimenting with imitating a bird."

"A bird." That gave her pause. "Why in the world should a djinn try to imitate a bird?"

"*I* don't know. I can't imagine why it does half the things it seems to do. Anyway, what I saw through the hole had some characteristics of each species—no wonder it was monstrous looking."

Abigail sat back, and for a few moments the two regarded each other in silence. Then she spoke again. "But why you? Chance, with all due respect to your famous family, what do demons and bandits find so special about you that they must fight to get their hands on you? Don't tell me it's only because Rolf might have been your ancestor."

Chance's right hand had strayed inside his collar again.

"Abby, I told you before that the strange children mentioned Ardneh's Key. But they didn't claim to have it. The fact is that I do." And he demonstrated. "You see this, don't you?"

"Chance." Kuan Yin's assistant stared at the object. Something about it must have been convincing, for her eyes widened. "What are you going to do?"

TWICE NOW, THE DJINN'S FIRST GIFT HAD SAVED HIS LIFE. HE JUGgled the soft bundle of the second in his hand. "Maybe I'd better get into this before we show ourselves again. But maybe I should offer it to you—I mean, I can't give you the Key—but this, if it really provides protection—"

She moved back slightly, into deeper shadow. "I'm not going to put that on. Whether you should wear it or not, is, well—I don't know what to advise."

Somehow her hesitation made him perversely ready to move forward. "All right. Here goes. Excuse me for undressing." He began to pull his shirt off over his head. "You can look the other way."

"In this darkness?" Abigail's whisper sounded somewhere between outrage and amusement. When his head emerged from his shirt, her white-robed form was only faintly visible in the gloom. "I couldn't see you if I tried. Anyway, I doubt there is anything so special about the body of a Rolfson that a lowly practitioner of medical magic has never seen its counterpart in the flesh of ordinary men."

Chance could think of no good reply to that. In a moment he had kicked off his shoes and had turned slightly aside, stripping off his trousers, getting rid of every stitch. Whether some young female practitioner of medical magic might be eyeing him appraisingly through the shadows he did not want to know. He drew a deep breath, then stepped into the suit's soft legs, one after another, and pulled the garment up over his body, feeling it reassuringly warm, and comfortable as silk against his skin.

A moment later, just as he was starting to pull his pants up over his new protection, a different feeling started, and for a long moment he hesitated. The sensation was neither pain nor itch nor pleasure but contained something of all three, making it utterly strange. Chance's eyes were affected too, objects blurring into rainbows at the edges of his field of vision.

Looking down at his body, he saw that he did not appear to be clothed so much as blurred.

He fought to keep his voice from breaking in sheer panic. "I hope I can g-get this off again, when the time comes. But th-there's got to be a way to do that."

"Of course there will be." His companion indeed seemed to have turned into a nurse and medical technician, and was trying to be calm and reassuring. "We can figure this thing out."

Now, hers was the voice of an interested practitioner of magic.

"Come over here where the light is better." Abigail hitched up her white robe, sat down on a ledge of stone, and stared at him, as if, in his tight, mottled suit, he presented a truly fascinating problem. "Though if it truly has protective qualities, you had probably better leave it on for the time being. Is it at all painful?"

"No. Don't worry, I'll leave it on." His vision had cleared, the strange sensations were going away. He was still alive, still functioning. He started to put on his shirt. Ardneh's Key was still very much with him, hanging outside his new set of long underwear.

Shirt on, he noted with relief while reaching for his shoes that his vision had settled down to normal again, or perhaps even a little better than normal. The gift of Zalmoxis and Chance's skin were also reaching an accommodation. A sensation of intense itching up and down his torso lasted only a moment before being succeeded by a feeling like light sunburn, which in turn quickly faded into a pleasant faint warmth.

"How does it feel, Chance?"

"Not bad. Better than it did." The feeling suggested to him that the powers of the mysterious Old World had come to life and were working their way deep into his body.

WHILE THEY WERE TALKING, DISTANT NOISES OF ALARM AND STRIFE had faded into a babble of voices, sounding familiar and urgent but not desperate. With Chance's companion leading the way again, they groped their way through gloom to a short flight of stone stairs, then a ladder, and hurried to check in with the joint expedition's leaders.

Even as they hurried on, Abby questioned him further on his relationship with the creature calling itself Zalmoxis. Could he remember every word his mysterious visitor had ever said to him? How many meetings had there been?

As more details came to mind, he added them to his account of his encounters with the red-haired folk.

"You should have been telling people about all this before now," the young enchantress said. It was an accusation.

"Believe me, k-keeping it all s-secret is the last thing I-I have been trying to do! But no one wanted to listen to me, and . . . a-and there were other problems. Now I have you as a witness to back me up."

ON THE NEXT LEVEL UP, CHANCE CLEARLY HEARD THE VOICE OF CAP-tain Horkos, and soon Chance and Abby were able to rejoin their leadership.

Quickly, they learned from their companions as much about the enemy incursion as anyone had yet been able to understand. A strong squad of bandit infantry had come swarming up the narrow path to the cave's only functioning entrance, their arrival timed to coincide with that of half-a-dozen flying creatures, some of them large enough to carry humans on their backs.

Despite being taken somewhat by surprise, the captain's strong-point at the entrance had not fallen, and only the small airborne raiding party, six or eight humans and their grotesque mounts, had managed to actually get inside the cave. Casualties among the de-fenders had been light—the attackers had lost heavily only among the squad coming up the path.

The Scholar said: "It seems they weren't trying to overrun us, as much as they were simply looking for something. Or someone."

"It was me, I expect. But as before, they couldn't see me. Or Abby, wh-when she was—standing very near."

THE CAPTAIN, SOUNDING BOTH RELIEVED AND ANGRY, WAS DEFI-nitely determined that his young charge was going to go on breathing—and Chance had been given reason to believe that the

Lord Draffut himself might have the same idea. "Then I'll try not to get killed, Captain. After all, that would be my neck too."

The Scholar turned to him to say: "It appears that your mysterious informant was right. Or very nearly."

Drawing a deep breath, Chance determined that his failure to communicate had gone on long enough. No matter what, despite any magical influence that might be making it difficult, he was going to fully inform the Scholar and the other leaders about all his meetings with the djinn.

The leaders were evidently thinking along the same lines. The captain confronted him sternly. "It appears that you have not been telling us everything you should."

Jervase was standing by with folded arms. "It may be also that we have not been listening to you, when we ought to have been." He shook his head. "I wish you had questioned this strange visitant more closely when it told you it might be able to help you find old things."

Chance could wish that too; but the bandits hadn't given anyone a lot of time. And Zalmoxis had a great aptitude for not answering questions.

The young lord began to tell the story once more, from the beginning, and taking care to leave nothing out.

SIXTEEN

HIGH IN THE UPPER REACHES OF THE GREAT CAVE'S ENORMOUS entrance chamber, close under the curving ceiling of natural rock, some earlier generation of occupants had cleverly created an observation post. A long pole—the stripped and seasoned trunk of a tall, thin tree—had been propped up at an angle, its sides studded with driven pegs to serve as ladder rungs, the top fitted with a small platform and railing, creating an aerie to hold a single lookout. From this key position a watcher, looking out through the cave's broad mouth, had by far the best view of the outside world that it was possible to have from anywhere inside the cave.

The attempt at kidnapping Chance and his Key having failed, there were indications that the next attack was going to be more massive. A sentry in this elevated post had recently announced the appearance of a large cloud of dust, such as might have been raised by the arrival of a formidable force of bandits. What the captain's human scouts and the great bird had reported was finally confirmed.

When the enemy's advance party had moved two-thirds of the way up the twisting path, to within a hundred meters of the entrance to the cave, a single rider, leading another animal behind him, detached himself from the small group and came trotting easily on up. As the bandit drew nearer, he was seen to be a little man, very erect in his saddle, mounted on a large and imposing riding-beast, itself wearing fancy armor.

Watching, the captain mused aloud: "And the fellow comes leading a spare mount, by all the demons. I wonder what that's all about? As if he fully expects to have a companion when he rides away."

The enemy's representative pulled his ridingbeast to a halt some fifty paces down the trail, boldly putting himself within the range where any defender's missile, launched with skill, would be unlikely to miss him.

With a sweeping gesture of one arm, he managed a kind of mounted bow, and simultaneously introduced himself in a loud voice. "Nathan Gokard, at your service, gentlemen and ladies!"

Several moments went by in which no one answered him.

The flamboyant one was smiling slightly now, as if he interpreted the silence in the cave as a result of fear. He shook his head, "Might as well speak up, people. We know you're in there." He shifted in his saddle. "Captain Horkos, isn't it? Hiding behind the little rock on the end? How many of your stout troopers are with you today? There can't be very many."

If Horkos was surprised at being recognized and named, he showed no sign of it. After a look around to see if anyone else was eager to speak, he raised his head a little above the breastwork of rock. "There are enough," he finally called back.

The fellow who had introduced himself as Nathan Gokard nodded briskly, as if he found that answer satisfactory. Then he announced—in the manner of one assuming that the whole matter had already been arranged—that Chance Rolfson was going to be turned over to him at once.

"We know that young Lord Chance is in the cave. We know also that trying to separate him, alive or dead, from what he carries isn't going to work. So we are just going to borrow him and what he has attached to him for a short time—you people have nothing to be afraid of. We will even return him in good shape."

When Horkos and those with him remained silent, Gokard finally produced another statement of fact: "You will bring him forward now." Pause. "There can be no reason to delay." There followed another interval of silence, and at last a question: "Is there something you have failed to understand?"

Horkos grunted, glanced round at his colleagues again to give them a chance for input, then called back: "No, I would say our understanding is in perfect order."

"That means you will turn him over."

"No, it just means you have made an idiotic prediction, and we feel no comment is necessary, as the world is already awash in such damned foolishness."

"Ah? Then, good captain, you will let me hear what you consider an accurate forecast of events."

"Why, had I any faith that you were not really an idiot—"

"Your faith would be quite justified."

"—I might predict that you would promptly remove your horde of wretched and deluded followers to some far distant portion of the world, where we would not have to look at you, listen to you, or smell you. After which everything would be fine."

The bandit leader looked judgmental, as if disinclined to give high marks to that last bit of verbal fencing. Then, like a persistent salesman, he repeated his assurance that he and his associates would do the lad no harm, and that they would be generous to all concerned.

He concluded: "I would like to see the lad himself, and talk the situation over with him. You are still laboring under the delusion that you can change the essentials of what is about to happen."

Jervase was gesturing fiercely that Chance should remain in the background and keep quiet. Chance only nodded.

The captain, head and shoulders above the breastwork now, leaning on it with folded arms, nodded sympathetically. He too seemed to be enjoying himself, in his own way. He called down the twisty path to Gokard: "All of us crave prizes that we'll never have, imagine pleasures that will never happen. You may find consolation in the thought that serious disappointment is a common fate."

The bandit nodded in turn. "It seems we go to arbitration, then. My representatives will call on you." Turning his mount carefully on the narrow trail, he began to ride unhurriedly away, seemingly with no concern that he presented his small back as a target. But in the space of another breath he had turned back again, as if in afterthought. His voice was calm, and it sounded with a certainty more frightening than anger.

"We will have young Rolfson, and what he carries. You may have seen, somewhere, that my name is written close to another, a word you are afraid to say. And so you know that if I call upon that one he will come. When that has happened there can be no talk of letting people go, of doing folk no harm." And he turned and rode again, not waiting for an answer.

The captain shouted after him: "Then call your nameless monster, and be damned! Feed your whole bloody army to him, one at a time!"

THE ELEGANT LITTLE MAN DID NOT TURN BACK AGAIN, OR REVEAL BY any sign that he had heard. The small gathering of people in the cave's mouth watched in silence, until the lowest bend in the narrow path hid Nathan Gokard from their sight behind some rocks.

Jervase turned to his apprentice. " 'And what he carries'—that is what the scoundrel said. I don't suppose he meant your new suit of armor, did he, Chance?"

Chance sighed. "I'm sure he didn't, Scholar. He meant the other thing I've just been showing you and telling you about."

Benambra, with the air of one entitled to do so, had come forward to join the leaders at the cave entrance. "Lord Chance, may I ask if you have tried giving the Key away?"

"No, and I'm not going to. Anyway, I doubt that I could. The thing has attached itself to me."

Abby said: "It does seem to be Ardneh's will, not just the djinn's, that Chance should have the Key."

"In the first place," the Scholar mused, "I'd like to get a look at this djinn myself. In the second place, should we be convinced that that overdressed bandit is really capable of calling up a demon?"

"It might be so." Abigail looked and sounded somewhat lost.

Chance reminded his companions that he had seen the two names, Gokard and the demon's, together on one altar. "For whatever that might be worth."

Captain Horkos doubted that Gokard had been telling the truth. "I say the bandit bastard must be bluffing—if he really had some great demon at his beck and call, he'd be bringing it on the scene already."

Jervase observed grimly: "It has been my experience that those who claim the power to call demons are generally fairly reluctant to do so. It is a business not without risk for the one who does the calling."

The captain said: "We are in a strong position here, and I have no intention of being bluffed into giving it up."

"We are not going to give up anything," the Scholar said. "Ardneh's Key must be defended, until it can be used."

In the next moment Jervase reached out a cautious hand, in the direction of the object that now hung, perfectly visible to everyone, just outside the shirt of his apprentice.

But the hand stopped halfway through its movement. "First, let me assure your guardian powers that I do not mean to seize the prize—only to touch it, the beginning of an examination. Fascinating!" Jervase breathed, making gentle contact with one finger. Not wanting to push his luck, he quickly withdrew his hand.

JERVASE, AS USUAL INTENT ON INVESTIGATION, PROPOSED SUBJECT-ing Chance's armor to some kind of further test. Horkos agreed that would be a good idea. Tugging Chance's sleeve away from his wrist, they poked at the thin fabric with a knife point. The Key tolerantly remained present, but inert, while they did this.

Jervase expressed a keen wish that he might someday be able to try the armor on himself—never mind that he would be too tall—but he agreed that Chance probably ought to keep wearing it for the time being.

Kuan Yin said that she and her people would die before yielding to Ardneh's mortal enemies in such a shameful way, as to surrender anyone to them. The lady's opposition was made more firm by the fact that these bandits, their chief especially, were notorious demon-worshipers.

Chance felt a need to speak for himself, and added his own re-fusal to theirs.

"First of all, this—what I carry—must not be allowed to fall into the hands of demon-worshipers. I don't know what would happen if they tried to take it from me.

"Of course I want to save my own life. If I went to the enemy with this, I'd lose it—and much more."

The captain advised that Chance should not even show himself at the cave mouth. "If they don't see you, they can't know for certain that you're really here. Give 'em something else to feel unsure about."

Chance said: "The way I look at it is this: As long as I have the Key with me—or it has me—the powers of Ardneh cannot fall into the demon's hands. Or to any of his human slaves."

Abigail murmured: "It turns me cold inside to think of what the great demon might do. If he did somehow get Ardneh's Key into his possession—could he use it?"

And Jervase put in: "I think not directly. Ardneh—whatever Ardneh actually is—has seen to it that only human hands will have that power. But there would be no shortage of human volunteers to partner with a devil. There never is."

SOON CHANCE AND ABBY WERE ONCE MORE ABLE TO TALK ALONE. They had found a spot in the corner of one of the bigger chambers, comparatively remote from the broad entrance, from which faint daylight filtered in ghostly fashion.

Abby told Chance that some of the Servants were quietly outraged that such a mark of favor, as they saw it, had been granted to a youth who perhaps did not even believe in Ardneh.

Her eyes glowed in what seemed yet another shade of blue, as she wanted to know what Chance was really thinking about all this.

"I won't pretend to guess what Ardneh really may have wanted when he somehow created this Key, a thousand years ago." He paused, then demanded: "Do you believe Zalmoxis when he talks of being Draffut's partner?"

"I don't know what to believe. I will ask my mother for advice. But though she is wise, she is no magician. I doubt she will be able to help us much in this."

Abby had borrowed one of the Scholar's old books, and was digging into it by candlelight in search of useful information. Also spread out before her on the floor of the cave were several scrolls of text that she and Chance had discovered among the Lady Ayaba's things.

Chance sat beside her, nodding in agreement as she read aloud: "Listen to this . . . 'the djinn are no more like demons than men are like talking reptiles . . . rather like elementals, neither good nor evil in themselves. . . .'"

Abigail shifted her position and raised her eyes. "The magical sources all say pretty much the same thing, Chance. Sometimes the djinn can be subject to human control. But all authors warn against depending on them for anything of importance. They say that dealing with them can be more perilous than it seems at first."

Chance said: "All I know for certain is that this one is using me. Keeping me alive for his own purposes. Doing his damnedest to use me. We must try to find out how much of what he says is truth, and how much is damned lies. But trying t-to force him into anything is bound to be dangerous."

"Then what should we do?"

"We are facing perils on every side. If we can gain any power over him, and you are willing to take the risk, I say we should give it a try."

KUAN YIN'S DAUGHTER WAS NOT SHY, NOR LACKING IN DARING. THE uncertainty in her blue eyes had been replaced by determination. Suddenly she proposed: "I want to evoke him, call him up. Force him by magic to come to me and serve me."

Chance stared at her. "Can you do that? I—I thought your training in magic was only—well, in the field of medicine."

"Well . . . yes. But magic is magic, and I don't see why I can't make it work. I have tried elementals, and they are stronger beings than this babbling djinn."

Chance nodded. He didn't know enough to argue.

Abigail went on: "Besides, it seems to me that we have little choice. Zalmoxis is trying to get you under his control! I think we had better act first, and get him under ours! That might solve a lot of problems."

If we fail it might also create new ones. Chance could easily enough imagine such an effort having that effect; still, strong action of some kind certainly seemed called for.

He offered: "Can I be of help?"

"Perhaps you can. Let's go through Lady Ayaba's materials and tools once more. I may have overlooked something."

AFTER A LITTLE MORE SEARCHING IN THE LADY'S WAGON, ABIGAIL announced herself satisfied that the formula she had found was indeed the proper one. With the air of one reaching a final decision, she announced: "A mere summoning doesn't look too difficult. I think we must attempt it. What do you think?"

Danger loomed ahead, whatever course they followed. Chance said: "Go ahead."

Having put aside her books, Abigail gathered the small objects that seemed relevant, and arranged them carefully on the cave floor, creating a regular pattern. She said: "I don't see what the magical purpose of these particular items could be, unless they are to aid in evoking a djinn of technology."

Again Chance was reminded of a collection of toys for some artisan's children, whose doting father hoped sons or daughters would follow in his footsteps. Here were miniature hammers, wooden wheels, a tiny saw, small brace and bit, and other little models that the young lord was unable to identify.

AFTER DRAWING LINES ON THE GROUND AMONG THE ARRAY OF TOY tools, and making a few controlled gestures over them, Abby uttered in a low voice words that Chance could not quite hear. With an explosive puff of sound, fire was born in the air before the young enchantress. There came a belching of soot and acrid smoke, accompanied by a sound of rapid pounding, as of unseen crude and heavy implements beating on something hollow. The voice of the djinn rolled forth from a flaming, almost formless image, sounding one moment like splintering wood, the next like clashing metal. "I come as bidden, mistress! What is your command?"

Suddenly a shape that Chance found relatively familiar, that of Grandmother Zalmoxis, flared into existence, her red hair appearing and disappearing again, flickering like true flame, her lips gibbering in protest.

"Abandon your imitation of human shape!" the girl commanded sharply.

The form of the being before them flashed in and out of visibility, then soon dissolved in formless magic flame, taking the form of an unnatural torch topped with twisting and distorting fire. The clattering and clashing of its voice formed barely distinguishable words: "I hear and obey!"

Abigail's look of relief when the djinn yielded to her control belied the air of confidence with which she had begun the invocation. "You will speak more clearly," was her next command.

"Alas, great mistress, that will be very difficult—unless I can resume my poor effort at assuming human shape?"

The girl exchanged looks with Chance, then shrugged. "Very well. Until I tell you differently."

In a moment, Grandmother was back, and communication once more seemed crystal clear. The djinn offered Chance advice in full agreement with what his human companions had been telling him. "Should you be dull-witted enough to trust a bandit's promises, you would remain alive only until the Key could be extracted from your person—I can imagine several ways to do that, and doubtless one of them would succeed, with demonic help. All of which would be most unpleasant for the subject. Nor would your colleagues here be spared, once Gokard had gained his prize of tremendous power."

The enchantress demanded: "What can you tell us of the great demon?"

"Oh—there are some things I could tell you." Zalmoxis seemed to be trying to look wise.

"Such as where his life is hidden?"

"Certainly not!" The djinn looked fearfully about. "Are you mad, to ask me such a question?"

"I am not mad . . . then tell us this, are the bandits truly going to summon him?"

"Let us hope not! Let us try to offer no provocation that might cause them to do so, while at the same time giving way to the enemy on no important point."

Chance broke a momentary silence. "Since you present yourself to us as an ally, I assume that you are going to help us defend the cave."

The djinn seemed to pout. "I am already doing all I can. To attempt more could easily have unintended and unpleasant consequences."

Chance tried another tack. "You can be a great help by merely giving us some information. Where is the underground chamber where you found the suits of armor?"

But the djinn chose to be coy with that answer. "It is not in this cave."

"I didn't think it was. Then where?"

"Suits like the one you are now wearing are to be found in what I call the anterooms of Ardneh's Workshop. Not in the portion that remains sealed against entry."

"And you know where these several places are."

The djinn seemed almost offended. "Of course I do! I have lost count of the number of times when I have stood—with the Key in my possession, more or less—at the very door of Ardneh's Workshop. Again and again I found myself bewildered by strange illusions, and denied entrance."

"But you say you still know where it is. So tell us."

Grandmother smiled indulgently. "All in good time, impatient humans! It will be best to do that when the Great Demon and the bandits no longer present an immediate threat. In any case it is impossible just now for you to leave this cave and go there. If I can still be patient, after all I have already endured, then you can wait a few more days."

Abigail kept on trying to be strict. "What do you mean by saying, 'all you have endured'? Tell us about it!"

"Have I not been doing so?"

The djinn chattered on. He said he found it maddening, just as any human being would have, to know where the Key to unimaginable treasure lay, to be allowed to feast his eyes on it—and still to remain totally unable to put his discovery to any use.

Oh, he had been able to take possession of the Key, all right, in the sense of picking it up and moving it from one location to another. "But carrying it to and fro in such a way did me no good at all!"

For one of the race of djinn to try to put the Key to use was hopeless. "Did I say I have lost count of my attempts? There might have been a hundred!" Zalmoxis said he had tried every trick of magic that he knew, every ingenious deception that he could think of. But something painful or inconvenient had happened to him every time he picked up the gift of Ardneh. He would suddenly find himself transported a thousand kilometers or more away from the Workshop, in some situation that no decent djinn could enjoy.

"And the Key would vanish from my possession, only to be magically restored to its original hiding place—where Ardneh had decided it should remain until it should find its proper human caretaker."

After Zalmoxis had done this many times, the device began to avoid his touch altogether, vanishing every time he reached for it, not reappearing until he had traveled to a certain distance and returned. The djinn had found it necessary to commandeer the owl, simply to fetch and carry Ardneh's Key to the human being in whose hands Zalmoxis wanted to place it.

———

EVERY TRICK ZALMOXIS TRIED—AND THERE HAD BEEN SEVERAL—HAD only affirmed the inexorable conclusion that the Key could only be made to work in human hands. Its awesome creator had taken great pains to make sure of that.

Therefore Zalmoxis had selected Chance to be his partner—and so far it seemed that the partnership might work, to the great benefit of both.

His earlier attempt to take the Key back from Chance ("I merely wanted to see if that was possible.") had given the djinn a nasty shock—it made him think twice about the prospects of a being of his nature trying to match wits and strength with Ardneh—even after Ardneh had been dead for a thousand years. Any mere djinn entering such a contest was taking a frighteningly long step up in the category of competition.

Thus the tech-djinn had convinced himself that becoming human, or, failing that, learning to imitate humanity convincingly, was the only way he could achieve his goals.

"Patience, I say again, patience! As soon as you come within a day's travel of your goal, I will tell you precisely where it is. Provided that in the meantime we can keep from antagonizing the Great Demon, or even attracting his attention."

SEVENTEEN

CHANCE FELT CONSIDERABLE ADMIRATION FOR CAPTAIN HORKOS. Despising the attackers' greatly superior numbers, and their recently demonstrated ability to force their way into the cave, Horkos remained intent only on doing his duty as he saw it. He seemed to be managing to ignore the threat of Avenarius—since he could do nothing about it.

Jervase agreed in Chance's assessment, and also admired the captain. Horkos might easily be called upon to give up his life in pursuance of his duty, but it would be a happy death.

"I might even say that I envy him," the Scholar concluded, "except that I am aware of a similar capacity in myself. With the difference, of course, that his duty and mine are not the same."

"Yours is less likely to get you killed."

Jervase raised a thoughtful eyebrow. "In ordinary circumstances, yes—however, in our present situation . . ."

OUTSIDE THE CAVE, THE ENEMY APPEARED TO BE SETTLING DOWN TO their job in a discouragingly professional manner.

"No need for any of our scouts to go crawling out tonight," said Horkos. "The bird can have a look around. Anyway, I know what the bastards out there will be doing—extending their lines until they have this whole mesa effectively surrounded, making sure no one gets in or out. It's what I'd be doing in their place.

"If they have the guts to stage another raid, we'll try to make sure that one or two of 'em stay in the cave alive. With prisoners we could confirm that they're Yasodharan troops on loan. But never mind, it's got to be that. This demon-worshiping Gokard has worked out some deal with His Madness, who hopes it will bring him some of Ardneh's treasure. He must be crazier than we thought!"

Chance and Jervase exchanged looks. The ruler of Yasodhara did at times seem more than a little mad. Chance made a mental note that he must get around, sometime, to having at least one serious talk with the Scholar on the subject of politics, a subject in which his parents were always urging him to take an interest. But that was going to have to wait until some more immediate problems had been solved.

NOW AND THEN A SLUNG STONE CAME SAILING IN THROUGH THE cave's broad, high entrance, to pulverize itself against a solid wall, or, depending on its hardness and the angle of impact, rebound resoundingly down through one or another branching passage. But presently this sporadic bombardment stopped—Jervase supposed that the enemy had decided not to accept the risk of accidentally killing Chance, the Key-holder, while he was surrounded by other humans who might grab up the prize.

AS SOON AS DARKNESS FELL, THE DEFENDERS PREPARED TO SEND OUT the owl on another scouting mission. Chance and Jervase both tried to brief the bird on what was wanted, and to reassure her that flying reptiles were highly unlikely to be out at night, since they did not see well in darkness. Whether Mitra was totally convinced was hard to tell, but she did take off. Chance saw her dark shape silhouetted for just a moment against the dimming brightness of the sunset sky—then she was gone.

HAVING SEEN THE OWL LAUNCHED, CHANCE WENT TO TALK WITH Abby. The young lord proposed being more aggressive in their dealings with Zalmoxis.

"He brags about all the things that he had done, and will do some day, and he swears he's on our side. What if we demand that he get busy now, break the heads of a few bandits, and drive the rest into flight? Alternately he could provide us with some Old World weapon so we can do the job."

Abigail was doubtful. "I don't know . . ."

"I don't either. But it just seems to me that a creature who claims to be so clever and powerful, the right hand and confidant of Draffut himself, ought to be able to find some way to discourage a few hundred scruffy bandits—well, maybe soldiers—who have no more skill in magic than I do."

"Gokard threatened to summon . . ." She let her words die away.

"So he did. But maybe we should call that scoundrel's bluff. If they really have a monster demon on call, why don't they just use him?"

RETURNING TO THE OTHER MEMBERS OF THE PARTY, THE YOUNG ENchantress warned them that she and Chance were about to embark on a serious magical undertaking and ought not to be disturbed. Then Abby picked up the bundle of the Lady's magical artifacts, and followed Chance, who carried a single candle to light their way to the small, remote room she had selected for this business.

The chosen chamber was short and narrow, with no real ceiling, its upper limit quite out of range of a single candle's light, just an indeterminate closure between tall inward-leaning walls. When Chance had set down their taper in the center of the floor and spread the Lady Ayaba's goods around it, Abby seemed to relax a bit. She was beginning to look very tired.

"But I'm not sure, Chance," she began, running fingers through her hair, and looking at her companion worriedly. "I'm not sure how much control I really have. There are moments when I suspect the djinn is just pretending."

"Pretending—?"

"Allowing me to believe that I am his master."

Chance devoutly wished that he had spent the wasted hours of his childhood intently studying magic. But he had not. "You're sure you're using the right name—?"

"Yes. Oh, I have determined that his name is really Zalmoxis. That much I think we can rely on."

This time the summoning of Zalmoxis was quicker and less dramatic. The djinn took the form of a middle-aged man, robed in white like Grandmother. His body was on the small side, traces of red still showing in hair that was on the whole ever grayer than Grandmother's.

The young enchantress posed sharp questions. Redheaded Grandfather groaned, expressing his resentment that they had called him up at all—if Avenarius should find out that he, the powerful Zalmoxis, was subject to the control of a mere girl, that would be very bad!

Abby was still clearly uncertain as to how much authority she actually possessed.

"Is there a way by which I can force you to obey? I command you to tell me that!"

Zalmoxis appeared to be giving the matter dutiful consideration. At last he asked: "Have you yet discovered a way to force me to answer that question?"

"I am the one asking the questions! Does a way exist for me to compel you to obedience?"

"Oh, such a method does exist, I must admit it does." The djinn looked very sad, not at all triumphant. "But it seems I am not compelled to reveal it to you." There was a slight gleam in his eye, a hint of mischief in his voice. "On the other hand, if you suggest a formula, or method, I may be constrained to tell you whether it will work or not."

Watching and listening in silence, while the flame of the single candle flickered, Chance shook his head. There seemed no likelihood of making progress in an endless guessing game.

Further discussion between enchantress and djinn kept leading back to the same roadblock: Zalmoxis was much too frightened of Avenarius to oppose him openly. There might be ways by which Abby could force him, but he wasn't going to tell her what they were. But the djinn several times repeated that his intentions were entirely friendly: He insisted he would give Chance and Jervase precise directions to the Workshop as soon as they were within a day's travel of their goal; meanwhile he was concentrating on not drawing any attention from the demon.

"So," the djinn concluded, "he will not realize that I am having any dealings with the holder of the Key."

Chance put in boldly: "Talking about the great demon brings up another point. I'm not convinced that Gokard can just call up this mighty ally whenever he feels like. If he has that power, why doesn't he just do it, and have the demon destroy us all, and seize the Key?"

Zalmoxis, suddenly looking very human, made a graceful gesture. "Would that all your questions were as easily answered! Gokard is aware of his own severe limitations as a wizard, and hesitates to summon the Mighty One for the very good reason that the demon might turn on him—which would be quite possible.

"Once Avenarius is brought into this business he might easily decide to carry away the prize himself—depending, of course, on what it turns out to be. If the Mighty One should do that, who could stop him?"

"Ardneh defend us!" Abby murmured.

"May he, indeed," the djinn agreed. "Oh, by the way, young master Chance, if Avenarius should come to claim the prize, even he will have to rely upon the Key to enter Ardneh's Workshop. That means some human hand will be required to hold the Key for him, and turn it in the lock. The honor would necessarily fall to you, my youthful Lord."

Abigail asked in a hushed voice: "What good is treasure to a demon?"

Zalmoxis had to think that over a bit before he answered. "That depends, my noble young Lady, on what the treasure is. Some demons have been known to hoard gold. It does them no good that I can see—any more than a miserly human draws any benefit from his hoard."

Abby closed her eyes, muttered some new incantation under her breath, and opened them again, alight with a new idea. She spoke up boldly: "Zalmoxis, I command you to tell me—how is it possible to control this demon?"

An instant later she and Chance both recoiled, as the djinn let out a strangled cry, and rent his apparent garments. From nowhere, it seemed, he produced ashes and even coals of fire that he heaped on his own head, even as he groaned in terror and misery. "Oh meritorious mistress, I beg you to drop this line of inquiry. If I had such skill in magic, knew such profound secrets, would I not be using them on my own behalf? Making myself the ruler of half the world, instead of groveling before you?"

Chance thought that what Zalmoxis was doing did not fit any reasonable definition of groveling; but the young lord refrained from interrupting.

The enchantress was firm. "A simple answer is what I require. We do not need these extravagant demonstrations." She drew a breath. "Tell me everything you know about him—the one we are talking about."

"If you are still daring to ask me, noble mistress, where his demonic life is hidden, that I cannot say." The djinn paused, as if to draw breath for dramatic emphasis. "If you are inquiring about his history, know that a thousand years ago the one we speak of served as personal bodyguard to the last great human ruler of the East, Ardneh's enemy John Ominor."

Chance had the impression that a lump of ice had suddenly formed, deep in his gut. Abby's expression suggested that she felt it too. Believing what the djinn had just said would put them both well along on the road to being truly frightened. The name of Ominor was familiar to everyone who read in Scripture—it was also well-known to much of the world through legends and terror-tales used to frighten children.

For a time the little cave room was ruled by silence, broken only by a distant drip of water.

WHEN ABBY HAD RELEASED THE DJINN, AND SHE AND CHANCE HAD rejoined their human friends, they learned that Captain Horkos had once more been in communication with Nathan Gokard. The bandit had proposed that the defenders of the cave send over an emissary, who would then carry back to them a somewhat complicated proposal Gokard wished to make.

"That's interesting," said Jervase. "I suppose I should be the one to go."

"Not you, sir," Horkos growled. "You're worth too much ransom. And certainly not Lord Chance."

"Not you either, captain," Jervase said sharply.

"I was not about to volunteer."

The young novice, Benambra, was hovering within earshot, as he often seemed to be. The leaders were somewhat surprised by his offer to put himself into the bandits' power as messenger, but after a brief discussion they accepted.

Chance would not have given favorable odds on the young man's safe return, but Benambra was back, safe and sound, in less than an hour. Grimly he reported on his meeting with Gokard, who he said had shown him two children in a cage, ready to be sacrificed. The listening Servants murmured in horror.

"He said to me that 'Children, as you must know, are the best material for sacrifice.' But he insisted that he was still inclined to be merciful. Then he said: 'If the idea of human sacrifice offends you, and the Lady Kuan Yin and the Scholar Jervase, tell them it may still be possible to avoid such measures. Tell Jervase we are well aware of what brings him to this forsaken wasteland. Similarly, you all know what I want.'"

Kuan Yin asked: "And what did you understand him to mean by that?"

Benambra's voice dropped. "Well, it was plain enough, Director. He is after Ardneh's treasure."

Jervase looked up at those last words. "Here we are again," he muttered, almost to himself. Then he raised his voice. "Novice Benambra, I would like to know, as a matter of intellectual curiosity, exactly what you have in mind when you call something by that name. What do you understand the old stories to mean?"

The novice smiled, showing his teeth surprisingly white and even. He answered obliquely. "I think we will all of us recognize the value of true treasure when we find it."

"Perhaps. But my point is that we still don't agree on what it is. And none of us really knows—except perhaps the djinn, and he won't tell."

"But he seems very intent on reaching it. Despite the fact that a djinn is not going to be interested in jewels and gold."

"In Zalmoxis's case, I'm not so sure. He might be, if he thinks that's an essential part of becoming human."

The Scholar himself still sharply rejected the notion that Ardneh's treasure had anything to do with gold and jewels.

Someone else observed: "I've run into other people here and there who talked that way. Every one who says that money doesn't matter seems to have a good supply of it."

But the Scholar was actually saying: "If we do find any such stuff, the bandits can have it."

Horkos and his men would have a different idea about that.

WHEN THE CONFERENCE RESUMED, IT WAS IN THE FORM OF LONG-range shouting. Gokard demonstrated a clear voice and a good pair of lungs: "It seems there is a serious misunderstanding here. All I want to do is borrow Chance Rolfson for a little while, and all the rest of you can go free. Yes, and I pledge that we will even return the young man to you, unharmed, as soon as he has helped us with a simple task. It won't even take him very long. A day at the most. No, I'll make that half a day."

Horkos was unmoved. He shouted back: "I'm about as likely to loan you my own head."

The bandit's lips curved faintly. "Your head seems quite a good one, Captain. It might be of some use to me another time—not merely as a decoration. But not just now."

Jervase stoutly agreed with the refusal. "It would be shameful to yield anyone, even the lowliest stablehand, to such a demand."

Another bandit down below was making noises of disdain. "Ahhh! We're not going to do the lad much harm!"

"Damned right you're not."

"From what I hear, he's not cut out for a warrior anyway. And it's no matter of ransom. Nothing like that. There's just a little twist of magic, a certain seeking, that he's required to help us with."

But no one in the cave was listening any longer.

WHILE THE DEFENDERS MAINTAINED THEIR VIGILANCE AND HOPES, they continued to speculate and debate and argue about what kind of treasure Ardneh might have hidden—also about exactly what kind of door, or portal, the Key was supposed to unlock. And how could the bearer of the Key be sure of recognizing the portal when the moment came—?

MOST INTRIGUING OF ALL REMAINED THE IDEA, THE LEGEND, OF ARD-neh's Sword.

Most of those who focused on that name for the treasure believed that the Sword must take the form of some fantastic Old World weaponry, whose power would enable its wielder to defeat any opponent, win any war, perhaps claim mastery of the world.

The novice Benambra said to Chance: "We have all heard the legend of what was called the Elephant, discovered by your famous ancestor. That device was named for an animal though it had never been alive. Ardneh's Sword is named for a simple weapon, but . . ."

It was Jervase who answered. ". . . but it may not be a weapon at all. Is that what you mean? Well, there are many imaginable forms of treasure, and weapons are only one."

"I must admit, sir, that my own imagination runs to a different sort."

"May I ask you, young man—do you come from a wealthy family?"

"Once they were, sir—but no longer."

There came a new roar from outside the cave, a blending of many voices, not all of them human. Other forms of life were adding noise to the tumult that went up from the demon's human servants preparing for a sacrifice. The Scholar was distracted. Turning aside, he muttered: "Folk whose lives offer them nothing . . . will try to find hope somewhere. Even in a demon's promises."

Chance thought that must be true. Gokard had evidently promised his people some mighty payoff for success, and had doubtless threatened them with some terrible doom in case of failure. Or perhaps the threats and promises had come directly from Avenarius, the great demon! He to whom the sacrifice of children was the most acceptable—the great infernal demon, whose terrible name those roaring voices were speaking now, chanting it over and over, as if they would never stop.

EIGHTEEN

RYING TO GET A BETTER LOOK AT WHAT WAS HAPPENING OUT-
side, Chance followed Abigail, relying on her greater familiar-
ity with the cave. Other Servants were traveling more or less the
same route, squeezing through a narrow passage, then up a series of
crude ladders alternating with carved-in stairs.

Presently Abby was leading him out on a kind of balcony or mez-
zanine, high on the shadowed rear wall of the cave's vast entrance
room. Here a broad recess, its natural shape augmented by centuries
of intermittent stonecutting, offered room for several people to
stand on a floor of aged built-in timbers. Looking over a railing, out
through the cave's broad mouth, they had a wide-angled, elevated
view of the landscape before the entrance—not quite as good as that
from the single observation post which stood at an angle in front of
them, and even a little higher, but better than anyone else had from
inside.

Chance gazed out into several kilometers of clouded sunlight.
The weather had reverted to something very much like winter, with
a thin wet snowfall hazing the horizon and blurring the outlines of
nearer objects. The stuff was melting about as quickly as it came
down, and only dampened things it fell on instead of covering
them.

———

MUCH CLOSER THAN THE HAZED HORIZON, LESS THAN HALF A KILO-meter from the cave, a number he estimated as several hundred of the human enemy, mere dots at such a distance, were moving about in some kind of organized activity. Here and there some larger, in-human creature moved among them. From the balcony it was possible to hear the sound of the Bad Demon's name quite clearly, as the seemingly endless chant went on and on out there. "Av-en-ar-i-us, Av . . ."

Another Servant beside Chance on the balcony was squinting into the cloudy distance. "Looks like they're building a new altar, right outside our door. Gokard must be getting ready to call on his big friend."

It was sickening to realize that the evocation of the demon was going to be energized by human sacrifice, as the bandit chief had threatened. That seemed almost certain, though at the distance, Chance could discern no victim, nor could he tell exactly what any of the distant dots were doing. Then suddenly a thread of smoke be-gan to rise from the center of their activity. They were kindling fire . . . he felt a sudden certainty that these flames would not be for simple warmth or cooking.

"But I didn't think they used fire in their sacrifices," Abby said. "Surely they can't hope to smoke us out—burn us out?"

Then she paused, struck by a new idea. "I wonder . . . I wonder if someone over there is trying to raise a fire elemental?"

Another Servant, standing nearby, said: "If so, let it come. We have the power of Ardneh on our side."

But Ardneh is dead, thought Chance. "There's no point in our watching this," he said aloud.

"No, there isn't," the girl beside him agreed.

Together they made their way down from the balcony, to join a gloomy conference of leadership in one of the nearby rooms. Here too, the possibility that they would have to face a fire elemental was being raised.

All agreed that the demon-worshipers must be preparing some new and fearful assault—and trying to burn them out of the cave seemed all too likely.

One voice disputed the seriousness of that threat. "What can even a fire elemental do to us? Our walls are solid rock."

"But our clothes, and food, and weapons are not," said Abigail. "Neither are our bodies." Faces turned toward her, as the best available authority on any kind of magic.

Several people began to question her at the same time. "What can we do against it?"

"The first thing must be to quench all our own fires right away," Abby answered quickly. "Put out every spark of our own flame. The thing might be able to seize on a campfire and build it into an inferno. Then pass word to all our people to separate their flint and steel."

"What else?"

"Try to deny it fuel, as much as possible. Wrap our bodies in wet cloth—better to feel a chill, waiting for the thing to come after us, than to burn when it does. Fortunately we have plenty of water."

"Anything else?"

The girl pondered what was obviously a more difficult question. "Well. There are spells, direct countermeasures that a first-rate magician could take—I'm afraid those things are far beyond my power. If it were a matter of raising an elemental instead of quenching one, I might try . . ." Abigail's voice faded, as her attention seemed to turn inward, upon some new idea.

"You said we must deny it fuel?" someone was objecting. "We can't destroy our own food supply!"

"No, we can't," the girl answered abstractedly. "Save the food, even if it's flammable."

Someone was eyeing a stalactite overhead, hanging like a spear, point down. "Good thing it's not a rock elemental they're calling up."

"Is there such a thing?" asked one Servant, sounding appalled.

People looked at one another in fresh uneasiness.

"Yes, there is." Abigail still had her faraway look. She seemed almost entranced. "But they're not going to try that, because . . . I suppose because they don't want to bury us under this hill, and the Key with us."

"What are you thinking?" Chance questioned tensely.

Abigail's chin came up. "*I'm* going to raise an earth elemental, if I can. Please hear me out! If I raise it, I can direct it away from the cave. I'll aim it out there . . . Chance, if I can energize mine before they get theirs going, maybe I can spoil their plan."

The Director looked worried. "You're sure an earth elemental won't bring the cave roof down on top of us?"

"I'm not absolutely sure of anything, but I think I can control it. And we must do something drastic. The point is, my elemental will drain away the energy that theirs needs. No one will be able to evoke another elemental of any kind in this region for months, maybe years!"

It was Horkos, commander of the cave's defense, who overrode a discussion among the leaders that threatened to become a debate: "Then do it. Do what you can, and quickly!"

Abby nodded. Suddenly she looked a trifle pale and haggard, but her voice remained firm. "I'll try to aim it so it comes plowing up from underground, right under the lines of those . . . those people and their things out there."

When she turned away from the group, Chance started after her. "Can I help?"

"Not this time. This I must do alone." And she withdrew.

Someone was muttering: "Yes, but I mean . . . an elemental. Can a little girl create something that's so . . . so . . ."

"It is not a question of creation." The Director sounded proud of her daughter, and at the same time very worried. "No human could do that. Abigail will only awaken sleeping forces, tap them, and channel into the thing she wants to see, then set it free. If she is skillful, and lucky, she will be able to keep herself and all of us out of its way."

NOT MORE THAN A QUARTER OF AN HOUR HAD PASSED BEFORE THE fire elemental bloomed in the sky over the enemy camp. Moments later it came sweeping through the air toward the cave, swirling in a thin veil of blue and orange, broader than the cave's broad mouth, making the air around it dance in waves of pure heat. But suddenly it shrank and smoked and sputtered, as if its fuel had been cut off.

At the same moment people in the cave screamed loudly, as the solid rock beneath their feet gave a preliminary lurch.

"Saying 'rock elemental' is near enough to the fact, though most folk won't call it that." Someone said: "I've seen a mountain elemental—once—and we're lucky there are no true mountains within a hundred kilometers."

CLOSING HIS EYES, CHANCE THOUGHT HE COULD SENSE THINGS HAPpening that were beyond his power to see or hear, as in a dream. The earth elemental was being born from the coming together of the strains and fiery heat of rocks that rested many, many meters below the surface of the earth. . . .

Suddenly there broke a vast rebellion against the power of gravity. Sentience came seemingly from nowhere, and in a flash. A great knot of mindless, urgent need, the creature battled its way toward the surface, sending before it from the body of the planet a deafening eruption of shattered rock, geysering water, splattering fountains of mud.

The cave echoed with screams of terror as the cornice of overhanging rock above the entrance started to give way. Chance saw giant chunks break free, and with a terrible slowness begin their fall toward the sharp slope just before the entrance. There the hard stone surface of the earth seemed to be simmering, bubbling, like liquid in a pot just brought to boil. But it was not heat that stirred the soil and shook the rocks.

From the attackers' point of view, much of the heat in the sudden waves was being wasted, scorching only air and rock in the top portions of the high cave chambers. Bats aroused in broad daylight swirled up in spirals of sheer panic.

All other forces of magic blurred within the narrow locus of the elemental's influence. It stirred and moved with purpose, as full of life and ferocity as some giant predatory cat. Subterranean waters burst forth as steaming geysers, there jetted more fountains of hot mud.

At last the thunder of the erupting earth was quiet.

Many tons of rock had fallen from above the opening to the cave, most of it spreading out before the entrance, and much more rock had erupted from below in the same area, filling in and blurring the sharp dropoff that had so well protected the people under siege. Where before the only approach had been by means of a narrow path, there was now an altered landscape, a much more gradual slope, offering comparatively easy access.

ROBBED OF ENERGY BY ABBY'S COUNTERATTACK, THE FIRE ELEMENTAL had weakened and died before the bulk of it could reach the place where it had been directed. A few of the people in the cave were lightly blistered, and some wooden objects, including bows and arrows, had been consumed. Some damage had been inflicted on wagons, clothing, and the wooden parts of weapons, but the actual movement of the earth had been quite small.

———

THE SCHOLAR, AS USUAL GIVING THE IMPRESSION OF ABUNDANT PHYS-
ical courage, continued to carry his sword with him at all times. But
to Chance he grumbled quietly that he was impatient for this military foolishness to be over, so he could get on with his life's work.
Chance was astonished to see what an active role Horkos assigned
to Jervase in the defense, and how matter-of-factly the Scholar accepted.

Chance himself was an exception to the assignment of active
duty. Horkos sternly ordered him to stay as far out of the way as he
could and protect himself—the enemy would have to locate him
again before making another attempt to snatch him away.

The earthquake had frightened the enemy and disrupted any
provisions for attack that might have been under way. But the great
majority of them had avoided falling rocks, jetting steam, and opening crevices in the earth. There was no sign in their camp of any
mass panic or flight.

Inside the cave, Kuan Yin had her hands full trying to treat minor
burns and tamp down panic, among Servants and troopers alike. As
soon as the shaking and spouting of the earth had stopped, Chance
hurried to Abby, in her small isolated chamber, to make sure she was
all right.

HE CARRIED HIS OWN LIGHT AS HE MOVED FROM ROOM TO ROOM,
and noted with relief that the enemy's fire had not penetrated here.

The first sign that something might be wrong was the silence and
darkness in the small room where Abigail had labored. The candle
by whose light she generally worked was out. Calling her name,
Chance entered, raising his torch before him—its light fell upon the
girl, who seemed to be peacefully asleep, lying on her side, padded
from the stone floor by her pack and several blankets. Scattered
around the extinguished candle on the floor in the center of the

room were the pebbles and artifacts she had been using to raise the elemental.

Chance had just started into the room toward her when, from the corner of his eye, he spotted an unfamiliar figure. It was that of a man, recognizable as neither trooper nor Servant, who had been standing there in silence, waiting in the dark with folded arms, only two or three paces from the sleeping girl.

Momentarily certain that he faced another intruding bandit, Chance turned toward the stranger, raising his torch, his free hand going to the hilt of his knife. But this man appeared to be unarmed, and his clothing was very un-banditlike—actually conservative, upper-class garb that suggested a teacher, a minor wizard, or perhaps a lesser academic. His hair was short, carefully arranged— Chance noted particularly that it was dark rather than bright red. Walking on a city street in Sarasvati, he would have been totally inconspicuous, a trifle shabby but basically respectable.

But at a second look, Chance found him also very improbably familiar.

Incredulous, Chance blurted: "Master Miyamoto?" Thrusting his torch nearer still, he recognized the countenance, the hair, the clothing, of a teacher Chance had had as a child and seriously disliked.

But, even in the moment of recognition, he knew quite firmly that this could not be. With a second mental jolt, even sharper than his first surprise, Chance recalled hearing from someone, perhaps a year ago, that his old teacher was dead.

NINETEEN

THE VISITOR WHO SEEMED TO HAVE BEEN WAITING SO CONTENT-
edly in darkness and silence greeted Chance with a faint smile.
At the same moment he began a small, continuous nodding motion
of his head and body—whether it was meant as a greeting or was
unconscious was hard to say.

He said quietly: "I must introduce myself, Chance Rolfson. You
have seen my real name, carved in stone, but have been afraid to say
it." The voice was smooth and deep, not at all that of Chance's remembered teacher. "As you must realize, I have only borrowed the
esteemed Miyamoto's form for the occasion—I thought his shape
one of the least likely to alarm you. Now come a little closer to me, if
you please. Stand just over here." The man's small, neat hand made
an elegant, economical gesture.

Chance felt numb. Somehow his brain refused to supply him
with a reason to refuse. He moved forward until he was little more
than an arm's length from the intruder. Looking into the man's dark
eyes at close range, he discovered depths in them, terrible depths
that seemed to go on forever. . . .

But the voice continued soft and pleasant. "Yes, lad, I am Avenarius. You can pronounce my name, if you like, and nothing horrible
will happen. The word won't bite you—words rarely bite anyone.

You really mustn't believe all the gems of wisdom these fools around you keep trying to impart." The figure of Miyamoto kept nodding, smiling, just standing there with folded arms.

Chance dreaded what might happen when the feeling of numbness in his mind wore off. Seeking reassurance, he shot another glance toward Abigail, lying wrapped in a blanket, head pillowed on her pack. Yes, by all appearances she was just sleeping peacefully, unharmed.

Turning back to the standing figure he said: "Outside . . . Gokard and his people . . . they're doing some kind of a summoning. I thought . . ."

His visitor dismissed such matters with another small wave of his hand, suggesting that this was a favorite gesture. "Oh, you may safely ignore those fools most of the time. I generally do. Mmm-hmm. I suppose you thought I was going to appear out there, five meters tall, roaring and bellowing and spouting flame? Tut-tut. I let them imagine that they can command me. That if they order me to come and go, then I will . . . come and go."

Again the man-image, nodding, nodding, gave Chance what seemed a friendly little smile. The expression was both pleasant and impenetrable, like those worn by many human faces. "The reality is quite different," Avenarius assured the young lord.

"But you are a demon."

Miyamoto raised an elegant eyebrow. "Oh yes, indeed I am. What you see before you is by no means my only shape. Be assured, I can provide you with the most spectacular example of a ravening monster that you have ever seen. Mmm-hmm. But to what end?" A slight shrug of the shoulders, narrow and neatly clothed. "I have not come to terrify you. Why should I?—desperately frightened people do unreasonable things. The state of mind I hope to induce in you is calm, and rationality." The smile deepened.

Chance was not aware that he had started backing away, not until his shoulders and elbows were brought to a stop against a wall of cold solid stone, and he could feel that his body wanted to melt into it. His voice had fallen almost to a whisper. "What do you want?"

Neat demonic eyebrows lifted. "Why, what I want, young man, what I will have, is Ardneh's Sword! The same thing that all of us in and around this cave desire so very urgently . . . though none of us can be absolutely certain of what it is. Only one of us is going to carry it away—but perhaps one or two others can gain some profit."

Avenarius stopped nodding. "I propose that you and I here and now conclude a deal. Just between the two of us, Chance Rolfson. Or perhaps it would be more accurate to say among the three of us." He nodded toward the sleeping Abigail.

Chance made a small sound.

The demon was gazing at Abby with seeming fondness. "Oh, but didn't she handle the elemental smoothly, craftily? Mmm-hmm. That shows rare skill, in one so young and inexperienced. Still guarding her virginity, as no doubt you can testify. If she manages to grow to full womanhood, she may become a practitioner of the art who is not easy to ignore. So powerful an enchantress that . . . well . . . that possibly I shall have to watch my step! Hey? Ha ha!" He seemed to find amusement in the prospect.

Chance's feeling of mental numbness was wearing off, a bit, and he was having trouble getting his throat to work. "How is she . . . why her?"

The demon frowned; it was time to concentrate on business. "You mean, why and how is Abigail Yin involved in our agreement? Just this extent, young man: I will not do her any harm—nor you either, of course—provided you help me, to the best of your ability, obtain what I desire to have."

Two light and casual steps brought the Miyamoto-figure right beside the girl, to crouch down gracefully and smooth her brow with what seemed a gentle hand. Abby's eyelids twitched, and the faint line of a frown momentarily creased her forehead—but she slept on.

Avenarius, straightening up again, gave a little whispery chuckle.

Chance could feel his own body trembling. He had been on the verge of darting forward, trying to knock the demon's arm away from the girl's head—but in fact he had not moved.

The voice of Avenarius flowed smoothly on. "On the other hand, should you fail to cooperate with me wholeheartedly—try to scheme against me—or should you even tell anyone about this little talk we are now having—then you will probably not recognize the young lady at your next meeting. And I fear that encounter would be in an unhappy place. Yes. You would find that—quite unsatisfactory."

The demon's eyes turned fully on Chance again. He could not look away from them, although he desperately wanted to, because there seemed to be nothing inside their blackness. Nothing at all. How could nothing be so terrible?

As if he were reading Chance's mind, Avenarius said: "Yes, I know you have the Key, my boy—that is why we are having this conversation. I need its power. But it will not help you against me. Not a bit. Cleanse your mind of that illusion. Neither will the armor that the fool djinn has provided."

Key and chain were hanging inertly at Chance's throat. A toy, a trinket, meaningless. It had not rendered him invisible to Avenarius. His suit of armor was doing nothing but absorbing sweat. He heard himself asking: "What do you want me to do?"

The demon's eyes were bearable again, his friendly little smile back in place. "What I ask of you is very simple. Mmm-hmm. First, it is important that you retain your Key. In my own hand I would find it useless, perhaps even harmful—no more help to me than it was to the djinn. Next, for the time being you should just go on as you have been going, with your respected Scholar and your dear girl at your side. I bear them no ill will."

Abruptly Avenarius moved a step closer to Chance. Suddenly he seemed taller than before. "But when the moment comes—and it will be soon—when the Key turns in your hand and the door to the Workshop opens, I intend to be standing very close to you indeed. Closer than any other. From that moment on, as we enter and approach the treasure, you will obey my every command, and instantly!"

The demon edged a little nearer still—as if something about Chance, or something on him, was suddenly so attractive that it was hard to remain at a distance. Now hardly an arm's length away, Avenarius tentatively reached out his very ordinary-looking hand—Chance noted dazedly that his schoolteacher's fingers wore no rings at all—as if he intended to touch the Key—but at the last moment the demon pulled sharply back.

What had happened? Nothing, really. Except that, momentarily, Chance had felt as if some enormous weight was hung around his neck.

A moment later, Avenarius was gone. Chance's legs seemed suddenly unable to support him, and he sat down on the cold stone floor. His hand that still held the torch was trembling. It seemed he had hardly had time to gasp for breath when Abby, across the chamber, began to stir. In a moment she was sitting up and stretching.

"I needed that rest." Her voice was small and sounded tired. In the torchlight her face looked pouchy around the eyes. "But you don't look good, Chance. What's wrong with you? Why are you sitting on the floor?"

"I'm all right." Unable to face her for a moment, he turned away and started to get to his feet.

Her soft voice called: "Don't go! Stay and talk to me for a moment, Chance. I had an . . . ugly dream."

He dropped the torch to the cave floor, where it continued burning, the flames guttering and dancing now, sending their shadows in an even wilder dance across the walls.

How it had happened, he did not fully understand, but both of them were standing now, and she was in his arms. How different, this, from any fumbling with a servant girl. How infinitely more. But there was only one kiss, and then she was feebly trying to push him away, mumbling something about how all her energy must be conserved for magic. Her virginity preserved.

She whispered: "I can't . . . even if I wanted to."

A great lump seemed to be stuck in his throat, and he kept trying to swallow. "I don't think that I could either. Not right now." *Somewhere, invisible, nearby, Avenarius might be watching.*

Abigail was beginning an effort to tell him of a frightening dream she had just had. Some man had been bending over her, she didn't want to say what the man was doing. Chance wanted to close his ears against the story, but it was necessary to let her talk.

She was saying: "But I mustn't let it bother me. It will get in the way of my doing magic."

"Maybe you've been doing too much magic."

"I'm not doing it for fun, you foolish man. I'm doing it because we have no one else who can."

Faintly, in the distant background, he could once more hear Benambra reading.

DURING THE NEXT HOUR OR SO, A COUPLE OF OTHER PEOPLE REMARKED to Chance that he was looking haggard.

From one room of the cave to another he bore the monstrous secret that he now shared with Avenarius. He feared the burden of the demon's threats might kill him if he carried it much longer—but he thought it would certainly kill him if he let it go.

———

AT NIGHTFALL THE GREAT BIRD FLEW OUT AGAIN.

The novice Benambra, no longer required to carry messages to and from the bandits, was reading from another scroll of Scripture, while outside the bandit voices kept on chanting, trying to summon their great demon.

Someone in the room with Chance was murmuring gloomily: "Another fire elemental will cook us in this cave, like ducklings in an oven."

"Abby says that they can't possibly evoke another one. So let 'em try."

"We hope she's right."

And another contributed to the grim mood. "Another try at raising an earth elemental will bury us!"

"It looks to me like the first one has already sealed our fate. Did you see how the surface of the ground has changed out there? As soon as Gokard has his people ready, they can march up to the entrance and come right in."

Yet another faint tremor ran through the bones of the mesa, and some small bits of rock fell from overhead.

For the time being there was nothing for most of the defenders to do but huddle in what seemed to them the safest shelter, and try to keep themselves alive. Outside, the wind was beginning to rise, creating in Chance the irresistible feeling that powerful, storm-like forces were contending against each other.

Jervase was wondering aloud: "Do you suppose the damned demon-worshipers could have a really powerful wizard with them after all?"

Chance couldn't think of an answer. The background chanting was going on, as it seemed to have gone on for a hundred years already. There were moments when he thought it would drown out the reading novice's clear words.

TWENTY

"HOLD YOUR PLACES!" HORKOS HAD A GOOD COMMANDER'S tone, loud but calm. "That last spark was only a touch, they're just trying to frighten us into running out into the open. Or turning over Lord Chance."

One of the troopers snorted. "Hah! Trying to scare us, are they? I'd say they're coming pretty close."

Benambra went on reading in his smooth voice, not stumbling even when the sound of high-pitched screams came drifting in from somewhere far outside the cave.

The voice of the reader still did not falter. "*And the god Ardneh said to the men and women of the Old World, once only will I stretch forth the power of my hand to save you from the end of your own folly, once only and no more. Once only will I change the world, that the world may not be destroyed by the hellbomb creatures . . . called up out of the depths of matter. And once only will I hold my Change upon the world, and the number of the years of Change will be forty-nine thousand, nine hundred, and forty-nine.*

"*And the men and women of the Old World said to the god Ardneh, we hear thee and agree. And with thy Change let the world no longer be called Old, but New. And we do swear and covenant with thee, that never more shall we kill and rape and rob one another, in hope of profit, of revenge, or sport. And never again shall we bomb and level one another's cities, never again . . ."*

What was a hellbomb creature? Chance found himself wondering, with the part of his mind that was almost always ready to be distracted. He would have to ask the Scholar.

There came a new crash of noise that sounded like more rock dribbling from the cracked upper rim of the cave's entrance onto the newly created slope just outside. If only the whole top of the mesa could fall in, he thought, blocking the entrance . . . but if that happened, probably all it would really do would be to kill everybody inside. That might be the best thing that could happen to us, he thought. He ceased to listen to either words or noises, his thoughts drawn back, almost helplessly, to focus on the menacing problem of the demon.

As far as he could tell, the Key had done nothing to protect him when Avenarius came threatening. There was no reason to think that Abigail would have derived any benefit, this time, from Chance putting his arms around her. No reason to think that actually giving her the Key, assuming that it would allow itself to be given away, would do her any good. The attempt might only have put her in greater danger.

But . . . maybe the Key had taken no action to protect him because the demon had not been trying to do him any harm.

The only hope Chance could find to cling to was that somehow Avenarius might still be afraid of the Key's creator. Ardneh, slayer of the archdemon Orcus and the evil emperor John Ominor; Ardneh, who had driven a hundred demons, some of them stronger than Avenarius, from the field of battle, and shattered the evil domination of the East. Ardneh, whose power was still channeled across a thousand years of time to focus itself in the Key and the yet-to-be-revealed Sword.

When Chance thought back, it seemed possible that the demon

had simply not dared to attack him as long as he held the Key. There had been a moment when Chance had expected Avenarius to simply reach out a hand and kill him, snatch away the power that hung around Chance's neck. But in the end the demon had not tried to do anything of the kind.

Avenarius might have been bluffing when he said the Key would be ineffective against him. Avenarius might have been afraid.

If only he, Chance, could learn to use it . . . the power of Ardneh . . .

The young novice was still reading. "*. . . and when the full years of the Change had been accomplished, Orcus, the Prince of Demons, had grown to his full strength. And Orcus saw that the god Draffut, the Lord of Beasts and of all human mercy, who sat at the right hand of Ardneh in the councils of the gods, was healing men and women in Ardneh's name, of all manner of evil wounds and sickness . . .*"

Benambra paused to clear his throat and drink from his canteen. Then he read on.

"*. . . in all the Changed World, only Ardneh himself was strong enough to oppose Orcus. Under the banner of Prince Duncan of the Offshore Islands, men and women of good will . . . rallied to the cause of good, aiding and supporting Ardneh. And under the banner of the evil Emperor, John Ominor, all men and women who loved evil rallied . . .*"

The floor of the cave was quivering.

A last stirring of the earth-elemental's power—well, they could hope it would be the last—was shaking the ground below and the walls around them. For a long moment even the unshakable Benambra paused, but this time the basic remaining structure of the mesa and the cave's roof of rock held fast. Only pebbles and dust came dribbling down.

Someone called out: "Where is our enchantress? She had better make sure that her monster isn't coming back."

Chance hurried to look for Abigail, found her in the small room that had become the laboratory and headquarters of defensive magic. As he approached, he dreaded to find Avenarius once more with her—but this time she was wide awake, and her only visitor was Zalmoxis, who was again wearing the image of Grandmother.

Chance said to Abby in an unsteady voice: "Your rock elemental hasn't entirely gone back to being lifeless rock."

She still sounded vaguely resentful—as well she might, having probably saved all their lives. "But nothing is ever simply anything—any more than rock is ever utterly without life. Else there would be no magic in the world."

Turning to the djinn, she asked: "How would the people of the Old World have dealt with such a problem? Might they have created some technology of strength, powerful enough to hold up a cave's roof when it threatened to come crumbling down?"

"They might have, great enchantress." The djinn sounded sweetly reasonable.

"Do not mock me! I am no great enchantress, and you know it. And do not evade the question. Can you not do as much as the people of the Old World did?" Turning aside momentarily to Chance, Abby reassured him: "The elemental will be quiet now."

"I am better at collecting ancient technology than I am at reconstructing it." Zalmoxis sounded almost proud of the fact, as if he considered himself above doing manual labor. "And there are many skills I have forgotten. Forgetfulness is a very human characteristic, do you not agree?"

"Do what I tell you!"

The djinn was all regret and self-effacement. "As you know, mistress, I am compelled to obey. Of course it will take some time to repair this roof."

"How much time?"

"Probably years."

Chance sighed. "It seems to me, Zalmoxis, that you have ways of following the letter of a command while violating its purpose."

"I have heard similar complaints in the past," the djinn admitted. "Thus is it ever with slaves, dear master. Still, the wizards of Ardneh's day could have told you something of how important and dependable an ally they found me to be—so could your illustrious ancestor, young sir."

It took a moment to sink in. "You *saw* Rolf? Spoke to him?"

"Oh yes, my dear. On several occasions. You couldn't have been paying attention a little while ago, when I discussed how he and I both took part in the attack on Som's citadel." The djinn brightened. "Perhaps it is that you already think of me as human, so I could not possibly be that old!"

Chance looked at Grandmother closely. He thought that the details of the image were everywhere improved, compared with her first appearance. "Well . . . you do look human—or very, very close to it."

"Thank you! That is an encouraging thought. But, alas, somewhat premature. To me in my present mode of existence, a thousand years is no great gulf of time."

GOING TO REJOIN THEIR FELLOW HUMANS, CHANCE AND ABBY FOUND Benambra was still reading aloud, in the background, while Jervase was in the middle of a low-voiced argument with Kuan Yin. She was telling him: "You had never seen a fire elemental before today, yet you had no doubt that one might appear."

"That's different."

"Really? I don't think so. If so, why do you stick at believing in Draffut?"

"Show me the evidence, and possibly I will be convinced."

"I hesitate to tell you this, but because of the situation we are in, it is best that you should know." Lady Kuan Yin went on to explain that she and her companions had reason to believe, or at least to hope, that the Beastlord's return was imminent.

Jervase blinked. But his voice betrayed no surprise. "What reason?"

"The fact is that we have lately been trying our best—there are certain secret, traditional ways—to summon him."

"Really."

"Yes." The Director sighed faintly. "I gather you do not believe we can succeed."

"I do not believe your Beastlord can be a real, flesh-and-blood being, surviving from the days of Ardneh. No. Tell me: Why do you keep this appeal that you are making a secret?"

"Because, if such a summoning should fail—people might lose faith in our whole enterprise."

"I see." The Scholar made his thoughtful little noise. "So you are not certain it will succeed?"

Kuan Yin was hesitant, uncomfortable. "Of course I do not know," she finally admitted. "The Lord Draffut is not our servant, that any human can order him to come and go."

"But Ardneh could."

"Presumably."

Once more Jervase made little meditative sounds. "And what will your Lord Draffut be able to do for us—for you—if he does choose to appear?"

"I do not know that either. We can only hope that he will help us."

The Scholar did not sound triumphant. He simply went on, in his dry voice. "There are a number of reasons why it is difficult for an intelligent human to believe in Draffut. In the first place, I know of no living person who claims to have seen him."

"I know of several."

"Reliable?"

Kuan Yin did not answer.

Jervase grunted faintly. "In the second place, he is one of a kind, and fits no known category."

Kuan Yin would not concede the argument. "A wise human might think that a good reason to credit his existence."

INTERRUPTION CAME IN THE FORM OF A NEW BURST OF SHOUTING from outside, hundreds of enemy voices raised in great excitement. People inside were springing to their feet, a small crowd of them moving toward the entrance.

Something was about to happen out there—no, the sound of shock in the voices strongly suggested that whatever it was had happened already. Chance, shivering, could envision only too clearly what it must be: Avenarius had lied to him, or had changed his mind. Or maybe the great demon had now materialized in solid form, finding himself compelled, after all, by the power of some unspeakable sacrifice, to do Gokard's bidding. The demon's worshipers and his enemies alike were going to get a look at the monster, and somebody was probably going to be eaten.

TWENTY-ONE

ALL TREMORS AND SPARKS HAD DIED AWAY. THE ELEMENTALS OF fiery wind and shaking earth had both exhausted themselves. Or, at least, the run-of-the-mill human magicians who had brought those monsters into being, Abby, and whoever her counterpart might be among the bandits, had been unable to tap into any new sources of energy to keep the elementals going.

Shortly before dawn the owl reported that Gokard's irregular troops, clad in their bandit's motley and carrying their assortment of weapons, were massing, more than a hundred strong, below the chaotic incline of jumbled rocks that Abigail's earth elemental had pushed up from below and shaken down from above. The new slope that had thus been created was much too rugged for human legs to mount it in a running charge. But attackers could make steady progress, crawling and climbing forward on a relatively broad front, finding plenty of places along the way that offered shelter from defenders' missiles.

In the air above and behind the bandit infantry, large winged reptiles and even larger fantastic griffins were gliding in circles, while some roosted in nearby trees, ready to join in Gokard's next attack as soon as his infantry started forward.

At the strongpoint just inside the entrance, Horkos was once more rallying his determined handful. Those defenders who had been forced to throw away their arrows and bows when the fire elemental set them alight made ready to hurl rocks and fight with knives.

Chance could hear Abby, close beside him, muttering some desperate emergency appeal to Zalmoxis—and getting no reply. It seemed certain that her power over the tech-djinn had seriously declined. Chance supposed that Zalmoxis might have taken himself away to some great distance—or might even have joined the enemy. There seemed a worse possibility—that what the djinn had dreaded all along had come to pass, and the great demon had devoured him. In that case Zalmoxis had seen the last that he would ever see of daylight and humanity.

ON THE GROUND THE BANDIT TROOPS, WITH MUNDANE WEAPONS IN hand, were just beginning their renewed advance. But this latest attack faltered, was broken off before it had been fairly launched, its human component abandoning the effort, in defiance of shouted orders, when a wave of disturbance spread through the enemy ranks.

At first the defenders did not know what to make of this. Some assumed it had to be a trick. "Stand your ground! Stand your ground!" The captain's voice sounded as solid as the rock beneath their feet.,

"I don't think that they are playing games," said Jervase. "At this stage they have no need for that."

THE WOUNDED TROOPER WHO MANNED THE HIGHEST LOOKOUT POST was the first of the defenders to react with more than puzzlement. He was letting out one strange tongue-tied cry after another, as if he could not find words for what he wanted to convey.

Chance holstered the hunting knife he had been sharpening,

more to give his hands something to do than in any hope of improving his effectiveness in combat, and left the spot where Horkos had commanded him to stay. Disobeying orders did not particularly worry him; he was no soldier, and no one was going to have him flogged. He climbed as high as he could, mounting a kind of jagged natural parapet that had been broken by the latest rockfall. For the moment he was ignoring the possibility of flying missiles or more falling rock.

Abigail had begun to follow him, and Chance seized her hand and pulled her along, feeling that as long as she stayed close to him she might benefit from the Key's protection.

Another wordless cry came from above. Turning his head toward the lookout, Chance saw that the man clung to his precarious perch with one hand, while pointing as best he could with his bandaged arm, indicating something in the distance. Despite the fact that at least ten people below were shouting up at him, demanding information, he continued to have trouble finding words to tell them what he saw.

Chance stared out of the cave in the direction of the sentinel's pointing arm. Almost a kilometer distant, well beyond the Servants' abandoned compound, a strange shape had appeared, more than half obscured by snow and mist. It was steadily moving straight toward the cave, gradually taking on solidity and form. It appeared to be roughly human, the outline of a walking man, but there were things about it that made Chance rub his eyes.

In the moments when the figure's head and limbs and body could be seen most clearly, they had the look of being covered in shining fur. Also there appeared to be something wrong with the scale of distance. As the shape drew near the abandoned compound, it towered over the single-story buildings.

In the next moment, it had braced one shaggy arm atop a waist-high wall and vaulted over gracefully, easily clearing a barrier that Chance remembered as far higher than his own head. As the advancing marvel left the compound behind, a pair of what appeared to be midget humans, bandit stragglers or foragers, broke from cover in its path and appeared to be running for their lives, the movement of their tiny legs just visible at such a distance.

The cause of their mad flight ignored them. He—or it—came striding on, heading purposefully for the stronghold. No sex could be discerned directly, but an angular body and thick limbs suggested maleness.

Two legs of proportional, but still incredible, length carried the towering figure forward at a steady walk, faster than most young men would be able to sprint. Now and then it dropped from sight behind an intervening hill, but always reappeared. It was still coming straight toward the watchers in their half-shattered citadel.

Something else in the scene had changed. Chance was startled to realize that there were no longer any griffins or magically-augmented reptiles to be seen. The sky had suddenly been emptied of everything but small and innocent birds.

Another change was also taking place. Chance watched as the mundane forces of the besieging enemy began to part in front of the intruder, bandits scattering like drops of water encountering a ship's prow.

IN THE NEXT MOMENT, A RISING MURMUR WENT UP FROM THE GATH-ered onlookers. The air was no longer clear of trouble. One griffin, larger than his fellows, had rematerialized, and the sound of its angry scream carried to the cave as the monster fell on the intruder in an angry dive.

The flying monster's eagle-head bobbed and swayed at the end of the long neck, along which feather and scale commingled. The hooked beak opened when it screamed. Its wings spread and sailed, seemingly no more than banners or balances as it ran on wind and nothingness with driving, pounding legs, energized by magic. It snorted fire. . . .

The target of this attack, instead of cowering away, stopped on two braced legs and raised a pair of giant arms, ignoring the demonic howl and jetting flame. The griffin's dive turned into a tumbling fall—whatever magical power had sustained the massive body in flight had been snuffed out like a candle. Two great hands clamped on the winged shape and snatched it out of the air. In the next instant it was unceremoniously torn apart, wing from leg from body, like some hapless chicken in a barnyard.

The high rocks just slightly below Chance and Abigail had been overrun with onlookers from within the cave, and a chorus of gasps went up when smoke instead of blood burst from inside the griffin's shattered torso. The destroyer wiped his hands of smoking offal as he resumed his march straight toward the cave.

Chance yearned for some yet higher observation post—or for some marvel of Old World technology to bring the action nearer. But none was available.

Both of Abby's hands were gripping one of Chance's arms, and he could feel her nails bite; had he not been wearing the djinn's armor they would have drawn blood.

Abby was pointing. "Look!" In the middle distance at least a score or two of their human enemies, mounted, were in the process of fleeing for their lives, putting the speed of ridingbeasts to good use, whipping their animals to get away.

Around Chance and below him, the voices were no longer clamoring for information, but simply marveling, awestruck at this apparition come marching out of a storybook into their own lives. People were grabbing and shoving each other, trying to get themselves into a position to see. Fighters on both sides were becoming aware of what was happening in the attackers' rear.

ABBY'S FACE HAD BEEN TRANSFORMED WITH JOY AND HOPE. BUT IT seemed that she, like Chance himself, could find no words to say.

"Lord Draffut!"

The name had already been shouted inside the cave a hundred times, but only now did it fully begin to register with Chance.

Close beside him, one of the Servants, dressed and armed for battle beneath a tattered white headcloth, shouted in a breaking voice: "It is our great lord come to our rescue!"

The advancing figure was now so close that it had fallen out of sight beneath the cave's projecting lip, and people scrambled to find new positions from which to see what happened next. Screams of joy went up from many of the Servants, and one or two actually had run down the ascending narrow path to meet their savior. Farther down the slope, one bandit running to get away collided with another fleeing madly in the opposite direction.

Abigail had already let go of Chance's arm and was beginning to work her way down to the level of the entrance path. He followed as quickly as he could, hopping and sliding from rock to rock, trying to contain the fierce new hope that had suddenly exploded in him.

In Chance's fears, Avenarius stood as a monument of awesome and evil power, surpassing all human strength. But Avenarius had not appeared. Chance still carried Ardneh's Key, and now everything had changed. Lord Draffut himself was on the scene.

Chance quickly caught up with Abigail, who gave him a strange speculative look, and they advanced together. In moments they reached the strongpoint at the entrance, the place where only minutes ago Captain Horkos and his small dedicated band had been digging in for a final stand. Those men were all scattered now, like their fellows mainly concerned with finding better places from which to watch. In another moment Chance and Abby had passed

Kuan Yin, who stood staring straight ahead, as if she had been turned to stone. Her hands were gripping each other fiercely.

The novice, Benambra, mouth hanging open, for once fit in with everyone around him, the whole group virtually paralyzed.

The Beastlord's advancing form had once more dropped out of sight, behind tall trees on a small hill. Now he came into view again, no more than some two hundred meters down the trail, entering the area where it had recently been possible to watch the enemy fighters massing for attack. The place where the sacrificial fire had burned was abandoned by them now.

The closer Draffut came the more amazing he appeared, reminding Chance of some gigantic bear reared on two legs. Seen at close range, the shaggy figure was obviously different from a man. His fur was radiant, of many colors or of none. His countenance displayed enormous ugliness and power, more beast than human certainly, but gentle in repose.

The giant showed no hesitation as he moved in among the bandit ranks. His approach was one of methodical devastation. Wading into a phalanx of about a dozen warriors, men who had been too foolhardy or too slow to get out of his way, Draffut spread his arms wide, gathering a pointed contribution of long spears into a bundle. Whether their owners might be trying to retain the weapons, thrust with them, or simply let them go seemed to make no difference. Draffut wrenched the bundle away from a multitude of clinging hands, raised it in his own two, then casually broke it over his shaggy knee, like a man snapping twigs to build a fire.

In the next moment, each of Draffut's hands had plucked a sword from somewhere close before him. Chance held his breath as he watched those fingers of silver fur tie the two steel blades together in a knot, the metal flowing momentarily as if the power of his living grip had melted it. And yet there was no glow of heat.

Swiftly the space close around the Beastlord emptied of all humans and their creatures of war. But in the next moment the situation changed, as a few of the most fanatical demon-worshipers dared to charge the intruder. Howling like demons themselves, the madmen tried to stab the towering figure with their spears, puncture him with arrows. Chance could see no blood gushing from the shaggy body, no sign that the wounds—if blades in human hands could wound this lordly creature—were having the least effect. Arrows simply lodged in his fur, to be brushed away like leaves or twigs a moment later.

Draffut's inhuman mouth had opened wide, and he was shouting something in some language that Chance could not remember ever having heard before. The volume was deafening, even at the distance of the cave. At the same time the Beastlord gestured with both mighty arms. The effect was to galvanize fifty or a hundred of the attackers' ridingbeasts and loadbeasts into action as one animal. The ones carrying riders shed their human burdens as they went galloping off, scattering in every direction where there was space to run. Others were jumping, plunging in circles, uncontrollably amok. All organized effort and activity among the bandit army ground to a halt.

"How can he do—such things?" Abigail was murmuring. "In such a way?"

Somehow her face, her tone, conveyed to Chance just what she meant: that since coming into sight, Draffut had not only broken the besiegers' circle, but had accomplished the feat without killing or injuring a single human being.

DAZED, CHANCE COULD HEAR SOMEONE IN A STUNNED VOICE RECIT-ing from memory:

"... and Orcus saw that the god Draffut, the Lord of Beasts and of all human mercy, was healing men and women in Ardneh's name ..."

Another shout broke in: "Look at that!"

The enemy had abandoned all thought of pressing an attack. They were having all they could do just pursuing their frenzied mounts on foot and trying to recapture them. Hours, perhaps days, must pass before any substantial number could be rounded up, and Nathan Gokard might have to resign himself to the loss of almost all his livestock. Perhaps getting back more than a few of his men would prove just as difficult.

JUST WHEN IT SEEMED THE FIELD HAD BEEN WON, AND A RAGGED cheer was going up from the defenders, Chance could feel a sudden alteration in the atmosphere, a darkening of light and air.

"The demons," Abigail breathed. "There was a swarm of them. I hoped they might have gone away . . ."

There was something hovering in the air. A disturbance, a thickening, that was more like the roiling of heat above fire than like rain clouds. Something the sickly color of bruised flesh, lit from inside with dull orange flame, had detached itself from the vague disturbance in the air, like a swirling of half-visible bats in twilight, and was swiftly taking on more tangible shape.

"Gronzero!" went up a triumphant shout in a distant, single human voice. Chance thought he could identify it as that of Nathan Gokard.

"Not Avenarius," someone nearby breathed.

The monster hovering in the air, and he who stood two-legged on the ground, were exchanging communications, roaring cries. Some part of Chance's mind was able to decipher the roaring out of a great challenge, and to the sounds he thought he could fit an approximation in human words—something like: *you big dog—you son of a bitch—don't look so tough—*

Lifting his gaze to the defenders in the half-shattered entrance of their cave, and raising his voice so that his words would carry to them, Draffut switched languages to announce calmly and clearly: "You will excuse me for a moment."

The blot of orange and purple plunged toward him, at the same time assuming solid form: not a human giant in armor, as Scripture said the great demon Zapranoth had once become, but some kind of ravening cat—or was it in fact a dragon?

The High Lord Draffut's drawn-back lips suddenly revealed enormous fangs studding an abruptly carnivorous mouth, that snarled and tore at the enemy, and spat, and then made human words again: "Where have you concealed your life, you squalling wretch? Never mind—if I cannot kill you I may make you wish that you were dead."

The demon's struggle with the High Lord of Beasts lasted perhaps for the time a man would use in drawing four full breaths. At the end of it Gronzero abandoned solid form, melted in abject surrender to go yelping, screaming, in desperate retreat. There was a blurring and a streaking in the air, that before Chance had counted five more heartbeats had vanished over the horizon.

Once again the victor spat out something, a gob that steamed and fizzed and vanished soon in smoke. For a long moment Draffut, his shaggy chest heaving like some human athlete's, stood looking after the routed demon.

Then the giant turned again toward the cave. His words were firm and carried clearly: "I think that one will not bother humans again for several decades. Perhaps even a century."

Moments later, the Beastlord was beginning to climb the switchback path. One after another, spots on the stone and hard packed gravel of the path seemed to stir briefly with life as his shaggy feet came down on them. A few stray snowflakes swirling near him no longer trembled on the verge of melting. It was as if instead they gained new vitality, spinning away and rising through the air again in a kind of joyful dance.

TWENTY-TWO

ALL FEAR FOR THE TIME BEING SWEPT ASIDE, SOLDIERS AND SER-
vants together were climbing into exposed positions along
the newly jagged lower rim of the great cave's broad opening. Shouting back to their comrades who were still deep within, they reported
jubilantly that the siege was broken. The only attackers who could
still be seen were in full disorganized retreat.

Meanwhile, he who had shattered the enemy's lines was finishing
his climb, with long, sure strides, to the strong point guarding the
cave's entrance. When he got there Draffut paused, and began to
talk to the people gathering to welcome him. Seen at close range, he
was easily six meters tall, three times the height of a big man. The
Beastlord's face was not human—certainly it was not—but neither
was it merely bestial. His towering, massive body was clothed from
head to toe in long fur, a covering subtly radiant with its own ener-
gies. The suggestion was of light on the edge of vision, its colors in-
definable.

Suddenly timid in this overwhelming presence, Chance hung
back like the people around him. His forward progress slowed to a
halt. Only an easy pebble-toss in front of him, the Lord Draffut was
nodding to the nearest troopers, who bowed and saluted and murmured awkwardly in return, fumbling with their belts and caps and

weapons. When the High Lord of Beasts moved on again, passing so close that they might have touched him, they shrank back in timid silence.

Moments later, the giant had found himself a comfortable place to sit down, a ledge of solid rock formed on the proper scale. Once settled there, he appeared to draw a deep breath, and closed his eyes.

But the great visitor was not to be allowed much time to rest. He had hardly time for a second deep breath when confusion in the form of a hesitant onrush of humanity swirled around him, maintaining a wary distance of at least four or five meters. First one, then two, then half a dozen of the Servants, emerging from deeper in the cave, had rushed past Chance to throw themselves prostrate on the ground before the giant visitor.

The Lord of Beasts opened his eyes again. Chance found it hard to read any reaction on Draffut's inhuman face, but the only tone in his clear voice seemed to be that of restrained annoyance. "Stand up. If you would please me, stand. Or sit, if you are tired."

Kuan Yin, having at last regained the power of movement and of speech, had not thrown herself upon the ground. She came forward bowing lightly, offering a more formal, low-voiced greeting, which the great guest acknowledged with a seated bow.

Meanwhile, the Scholar, with a look on his face that Chance had never seen there before, was advancing more slowly toward the mountainous, living presence that he had been convinced no one would ever see. Slowly the Scholar passed Chance and Abby to take a stand between two novices. The ledge of rock where Draffut sat was itself as high as an adult human, but his head still loomed far over those of the tall men who stood before him. It crossed Chance's mind that this was an odd way to entertain an important visitor. But of course it would have been hopeless to invite this particular guest to enter any of the small rooms within the stronghold.

TURNING HIS HEAD TO FACE THE SCHOLAR, THE NOVICE BENAMBRA asked him, in a whisper: "Is that the real thing, Scholar, sitting before us?"

Jervase's voice was not much louder than a whisper, and for once it sounded a little shaky. "He must be genuine. He must. What we have just seen him do could not have been done by some impostor."

Meanwhile, Abigail, who for a few steps had lagged a little behind Chance, had come up close beside him. Her face was alight with joy, showing no trace of fear. But she could find no words to speak. Gazing at her, Chance wondered that he had never realized before how close she was to becoming a beautiful young woman.

Jervase slowly moved forward again, passing Kuan Yin, until he was standing closer to Draffut than any other human being. The man stood gazing up at the giant figure that in turn gazed down at him. For what seemed a long time neither spoke. Then at last the Scholar introduced himself.

The Lord of Beasts acknowledged the name with a nod, and continued looking back at him with quiet patience.

"For once," the Scholar murmured after another pause, "I must be glad to have been proven wrong." And he bowed deeply.

Draffut in turn slightly inclined his enormous head. He seemed to require no explanation of just what the Scholar thought he had been wrong about. His great voice rumbled: "In my time I have been guilty of a mistake or two as well."

Jervase had pulled himself together, and was going to be equal to the occasion. The world was a different place than he had thought, but he was no less anxious to find out the truth about it. Turning, he beckoned Chance forward, and said: "Lord Draffut, this is my student, and also my associate in my search for truth—Chance Rolfson."

Chance had to respond, to make himself do something more than stand and stare. Moving forward on suddenly unsteady legs, he was thinking that if any being could be trusted to offer wisdom and provide good advice, it would be the one who rested before him now, monstrous and regal at the same time. At the moment he could believe that Draffut would be a match for any evil demon in the world.

Coming to a halt beside Jervase, Chance could hardly wait to get the words out. *First make sure he knows about the Key,* he cautioned himself. *Then warn him about the demon, if possible so no one else can hear. Let the High Lord Draffut decide how best to deal with that terror.*

The dark gaze of those great eyes rested on him.

Chance raised one hand in an awkward gesture. "Lord Draffut. Sir. I am c-carrying . . . I have b-been g-g-given . . ."

Having got that far, Chance suddenly froze; his fingers, groping inside his collar, discovered that the Key was gone once more.

The Beastlord regarded his confusion with rocklike patience. The huge voice rumbled: "I see that you are wearing Old World armor." Chance's outer clothing completely covered the djinn's contribution, but apparently to Draffut's vision that did not matter.

"Th-that w-was a g-gift, f-from—"

"Wait." The great furred hand came to rest softly on the boy's head, then gripped his throat briefly and gently, between huge thumb and forefinger. Draffut rumbled: "From now on, speak clearly. In a little while I will talk to you alone. But first, there are others who need me more."

Turning his head slightly, the Beastlord said to Kuan Yin in a louder voice: "Where are your wounded? Let me go to them."

"Lord, I fear the passageway would be too small. We will bring them here at once." She turned away and gave crisp orders.

Meanwhile, Chance had been taken by a small fit of coughing. He cleared his throat, turned his head aside and spat out—something. He wasn't sure just what, but he needed to be rid of it.

Beside him, Jervase was saying: "We thank you, High Lord. You have undoubtedly saved our lives." The Scholar seemed to be the only human capable of looking steadily upward, meeting that dark gaze.

"You are quite welcome," the huge voice rumbled.

"You accomplished it so"—the man made an uncertain gesture—"efficiently. Beautifully."

"I have long experience in dealing with disagreeable humans," Draffut observed mildly. With one enormous hand he gestured vaguely toward the world outside the cave. Somehow Chance could hardly take his eyes from their visitor's huge hands, which despite their subtly glowing fur were certainly five-fingered, and of human shape . . . but far more powerful and beautiful.

With the Servants in general still awed into silence, it seemed to fall to the Scholar to carry the main burden of conversation. Jervase was certainly willing. "As far as I could tell, Lord Draffut, you did not kill or even injure anyone."

"Direct violence against humans has never been an option for me," the answer rumbled. "And long ago I learned that other methods are usually superior."

One of the Servants had, somewhat belatedly, brought bandages and medicines. Looking up at the tremendous visitor, she asked: "Were you wounded, sir? Not that I mean to doubt your—your—powers."

Draffut's great head turned slowly from left to right. "If you are asking whether I can be hurt, the answer is yes. But nothing that happened here today has caused me any harm."

BY NOW THE HANDFUL OF WOUNDED SOLDIERS WERE BEING BROUGHT up from their shelter in a lower room. Some were leaning on comrades as they arrived on the scene, a few hobbled without assistance, others were carried on stretchers. These last were the first to be brought forward.

Chance heard Draffut muttering something to the effect that his powers of healing were not what they had been in Ardneh's day, when the whole Lake of Life had been at his disposal. But meanwhile the injured men and women were being brought directly to him, in obedience to his gesture. His huge hands reached out to touch them briefly, one after another. Behind the seriously wounded, an impromptu line was already forming of folk with minor wounds and injuries. A new murmur went up among the onlookers when they realized that the men who had been carried up on stretchers were all standing and walking now.

A SERVANT WHO HAD COME OFFERING THE GREAT VISITOR DRIED fruit apologized for not having any fresh. "Which we know that you enjoy, High Lord." Others were bringing bread and biscuits, roots and grain.

Draffut ate, almost daintily for a being of his size, of this and that, as things were spread before him. Then he mildly suggested: "Water would be welcome. I assume you have a good supply available—?"

Consternation; somehow no one had thought of that. "Of course, sir! Our apologies for not thinking of it sooner."

Servants with their eyes still glazed by awe went scurrying in a search for fancy goblets, in the existence of which Chance could see no reason to believe. Abby grabbed up a nearby large bucket and lifted it in Draffut's direction, giving him an inquiring look. When a nod of the massive head had given approval, the human quickly filled the pail from a nearby stone cistern fed by one of the cave's several springs.

Hauling the filled bucket within reach of his giant hand, sparing him the trouble of getting up, she commented: "Our selection of fine goblets is somewhat limited, Lord Draffut."

"Thank you. So is my experience of them." His hand engulfed the bucket and his great mouth drained it in a gulp. "Another, if you please. And I think one more after that."

"I will be honored."

THE LORD OF BEASTS DRAINED HIS THIRD BUCKET OF COLD CAVE WA- ter, spilling hardly a drop, and graciously handed the empty con- tainer back. Chance thought he could see the outer surface of the bucket, dull battered metal in its ordinary state, swirling momentar- ily with impulsive life in response to the giant's touch.

Captain Horkos was standing by in silence, the alert pose of a sol- dier ready to be commanded. Other people were hesitantly edging closer, hoping to engage the Beastlord in conversation or perhaps to ask some favor.

Suddenly Abby, moving close to Chance and whispering, called the young lord's attention to the fact that there was one notable ab- sence from the group gathered around Draffut.

Chance looked around and nodded. In his concern for other matters he had forgotten about the djinn entirely. "Zalmoxis . . . yes. Has something happened to him?"

Her voice was very quiet. "Should we hope that it has, or that it hasn't?"

Chance let out breath in a sigh. He wondered whether Draffut might already have dispatched the djinn on some mission? Or, had the tech-djinn already offered the great visitor some kind of private welcome? Or . . .

Someone else in the slowly growing assembly of humans was clearing his throat. "Sire—great Lord—"

A vast hand waved in annoyance. "Call me Draffut. Or Lord

Draffut, if you are more comfortable with that. I am no king or potentate, I hold no human rank. If I am lord of anything, it is only of the lower forms of life. Never of humanity."

Kuan Yin was finding her voice again: "What can we do, High Lord, to demonstrate our gratitude?"

"You have thanked me, given me food and drink, and soon you will find me a place to rest. That is enough." The great dark eyes swung back to Chance. "There is one among you with whom I would briefly speak alone. If the rest of you will graciously allow us a short time?" The towering figure rose to its full height.

Chance could only nod, while others, Jervase prominent among them, stared at him and murmured.

Rather than trying to get the small crowd to disperse, Draffut beckoned to Chance to follow, then led him partway down the rugged slope recently created by the fall and slide of stone from roof and wall.

When it became evident that the boy's progress on this terrain was going to be slow, the Beastlord scooped him up in one arm and carried him as easily as a baby, while stepping swiftly over obstacles as tall as men. In a few moments the two of them were alone on the far side of one of the larger fallen blocks, effectively out of sight and sound of other humans.

From this new location, Chance had a wider view than when looking out through the broad cave entrance. The vista was broad enough, stretching far beyond the nearby hills, to give the impression that some considerable portion of the world, the vast desert that had been Ardneh's final battleground, was spread out before them.

Here the Beastlord set his passenger down gently, and attempted, with only limited success, to find himself a comfortable seat.

Then he faced Chance. "You were trying to tell me you had been given something of importance. What was it?"

As concisely as he could, Chance related the essentials of his situation, and the main events of the last few days. As he spoke he was aware—but only as a matter of secondary importance—that he did not stutter once.

After listening to the story with close attention, the Beastlord took thought for several moments. Then he said: "The existence of Ardneh's Workshop is no news to me, but I have never been there. It must lie at no great number of kilometers from where we are. And for centuries there have been stories, some of them possibly true, about a Key to open it."

Chance pounded himself on the chest with both hands. "Sir, I swear to you that the thing itself was here—right here—hanging on a chain around my neck—only minutes before you arrived! Now it is gone."

"I am inclined to believe you."

Chance waited, but Draffut only continued to gaze at him in silence. Finally the boy burst out: "But—sir, Lord—there is a greater problem. A demon has appeared to me, in secret, here in the cave—I don't know whether I ought to speak his name or not. He threatened horrible things if I told anyone about him—please, tell me what to do."

The Beastlord remained unruffled, as if he dealt every day with such reports. "Tell me all you can about this demon—for the moment omit his name."

Chance did so, as succinctly as he could. The telling did not take long.

It was impossible to read any strong reaction in Draffut's face or voice.

Chance waited a moment for an answer, then could wait no longer. "Can you protect us—me, Abby, all of us—from the demon? Or may the Key be able to do that? Do I press on to try to find the Workshop?"

The Beastlord opened one huge hand, and let it close again. "If this demon appears before me, I can very likely deal with him. Experience in such matters has given me valuable insights. If he does not appear I can do nothing. But remember not to trust his word on anything he told you."

For a few moments Draffut lapsed into what seemed a meditative silence. Then he said: "Your story is a strange one, Chance Rolfson. All I can tell you with certainty is this: Whatever this Key may be, it is a matter between Ardneh and humanity." The great head was shaking slowly back and forth. "I am not able to tell you what to do."

Chance knew a shock of surprise, and then a sinking feeling. "But . . . Lord Draffut . . . what about the demon? Can he do the things he threatened? Can he? . . ."

Draffut seemed to shrug. He seemed maddeningly calm, as if great demons were a part of everyday existence. Perhaps in his life they were, but appearing only as occasional details, nothing to be really worried about.

He sat back a little, shifting his weight on a stone seat that must be proving less than comfortable. "Descendant of Rolf, I truly wish that I could fight your demon for you, and tell you where to find the treasure. But I can do neither.

"You must realize that, while I served Ardneh at the Lake of Life and elsewhere, I very seldom saw him. Believe it or not, Ardneh was not much concerned with me. We seldom spoke, he told me very little. I was a useful helper, a happy accident, having become as I am from long dwelling in the Lake of Life." Again Draffut shook his massive head.

Chance drew a deep breath. "The djinn tells us—the girl Abigail and me—that he, the djinn, visited the Workshop several times before Ardneh sealed it off from the world. That he knows its wonders. But can such a being be trusted? He also says that you and he are making a great effort to keep me alive. I wish I understood."

For a long moment Draffut sat silent and motionless. Then he asked: "Here I too lack understanding. You speak of me—and the djinn. What djinn is that?"

Chance could only stare, for the space of several breaths, at the inhuman face that loomed above him. Then he managed an answer. "I mean the djinn called Zalmoxis, Lord. One whose power lies in technology. The one you . . ."

"Ah." The tone of the word suggested only that Draffut had now grasped what Chance was talking about; still, Chance could read no expression on the inhuman face.

Chance pressed on. "Abigail—she is Kuan Yin's daughter—has some skill in magic, and she has established some control of Zalmoxis—exactly how much we are uncertain. He has told us several times that you and he are constantly working together. He gave me this armor that I wear."

Draffut heaved a mighty sigh, an almost human sound, and again sat silent for a little time. At last he said: "So Zalmoxis is here. Oh yes, I know the one who bears that name, he is not easily forgotten. But over the past . . . well, say five hundred years . . . he and I have had only the most trivial contact. Whatever he may have told you about being my partner or helper was a lie."

Chance felt no great shock of surprise, only a rising bewilderment. Fear of the demon loomed so large that whatever happened regarding Zalmoxis seemed only incidental. "Then how could he—?"

One great hand made a gesture, as of throwing something away. "You ask, how could he dare to make such a claim? I tell you the tech-djinn has his own goals, his own plans, and I doubt they have changed much in a few centuries. For a long time his great desire has been to become a human being."

Chance nodded. "Then at least he has been telling us—Abigail and me—the truth about that. I wasn't sure."

It seemed that the more time Lord Draffut was allowed to think about Zalmoxis, the more Zalmoxis bothered him. The Beastlord rose majestically from the rock where he had been sitting to pace and gesture as much as was practical on the steep irregular slope.

He paused momentarily to touch—not pick—a flower that was sprouting most improbably, yearning toward the distant sunlight, from a crevice in what had been the outer surface of one of the fallen slabs . . . again Chance found his attention drawn to the enormous shaggy hand, very like a human hand in shape but far more powerful and beautiful. It might caress a flower, or tear a ravening griffin into pieces.

Draffut said quietly, in his reasonable and almost human voice: "Zalmoxis can be of help to you, as long as he thinks you can be of use to him. But I fear he would as readily kill you if he believed that would be useful! So, I warn you, trust him not!"

"Ah."

Draffut frowned deeply, taking thought. At last he spoke again. "One thing more occurs to me: The apparition you took to be a demon may very well have been the djinn himself, working his trickery in yet another disguise!"

The suggestion hit Chance hard—he could find no words to say. Soon Draffut went on: "Since he gave you the armor you are wearing, I would advise you to take it off. More than likely there is some trick connected with it. But of course that is for you to decide."

Chance stared in silence for a moment, then hastily began pulling his outer shirt off over his head. If the Old World's version of long underwear held some potential danger, he would rid himself of it at once, taking his chances against ordinary weapons.

"I swear to you, Lord Draffut, he did tell us that the two of you were somehow—intimately associated." Chance's belt and trousers quickly fell.

"A proof of how he lies." Draffut was gazing into the distance, as if he searched for something in his memory. He demonstrated a unique laugh, a kind of spasmodic rumbling. "For an hour or so, Zalmoxis and I were . . . thrown together, I may say. Very intimately indeed. It happened on one of the days of battle when Ardneh fought against the East, when the djinn of technology and I were . . . yes, very closely."

"At the last battle!" Chance breathed. His fingers worked at undoing the fastenings of the djinn's gift, stripping and peeling it from his body. At first, the chill spring air felt good on his skin.

The Beastlord blinked at Chance. Emotion deepened in his voice. "No, I was not present there. At that hour other humans had great need of me, kilometers to the south of the place where Ardneh and Orcus fought, that later came to be called Ground Zero. It was on a different battlefield, somewhat earlier, when the djinn and I shared a common fate."

Chance had thrown the gift of the djinn aside, and was pulling on his trousers again. He dared to ask: "And what was that?"

"We were devoured by the same demon. His name was Zapranoth."

At least those were the words that Chance, listening intently as he tucked in his shirt, *thought* he heard. *We were devoured.* Then he realized it had to be some kind of figure of speech . . . didn't it?

"But let us spend no more time just now on historical matters," Draffut was going on. "I have traveled a long way in a great hurry to reach this place, responding to the Servants' summons. But I cannot linger. Another duty calls me far away again, and quickly."

"Yes sir," said Chance automatically. At the same time he felt a chill. "But . . ."

"I can stay here no longer than about two days. But, leaving, I can take with me as many of you, whether Servants, soldiers, or mere bystanders, who wish to go. I will escort as far as Cascadia Oasis all who wish to flee this area. Whoever comes with me will be able to escape its demons, its bandits, and its cursed past."

Chance was having trouble finding words. "Thank you, sir," he got out at last. "I'm sure that some of the Servants . . . there will be a number of people who will be very happy to be able to get away."

"And you?"

"I still carry the Key," said Chance simply. "And the bandits have been driven off—for a while, at least. And I have no doubt that Jervase will still want to go on."

"You still carry the Key." The Beastlord's wide-set eyes fixed him with their stare. "Chance Rolfson, what would you do if you should be granted great power? Take your time, consider your answer carefully."

Fully dressed again in his own clothes, the djinn's armor cast away, Chance did so. He thought about the question for what seemed to him a long time. At last he said: "That is something I never wanted."

"Good. That is the kind of answer I hoped to hear. What *do* you want?"

"Nothing but . . ." Chance flailed his hands in awkward gestures. "Nothing but to be let alone by all the demons and bandits in the world. Just to get on with my life. But somehow or other things have worked out so I seem to be stuck with the Key. Now Jervase and the soldiers and I . . . well, we should be able to get on with the job, what we came here for. I don't see how any of our party can go with you to Cascadia."

The Beastlord nodded slowly. "As good an answer as I had any right to expect. The question may not have been fair, but I had to ask it. Remember that power is a very dangerous drug for human beings to take—perhaps the most dangerous one there is. But there are rare occasions when the alternative is even worse."

What seemed a long time passed before Chance asked, almost in a whisper: "Lord Draffut, even if the apparition I saw was not the real demon, I must settle this business of the Key. Can you tell me nothing about what is inside Ardneh's Workshop? About the thing that is called his Sword? What kind of power will it give me?"

Draffut was shaking his head slowly. "If you are still convinced that I knew Ardneh . . . well, that is incorrect."

"He trusted you."

"Oh yes. Probably *he* knew *me*. Whereas I—I only lived in the same world with him."

"The Scholar, Jervase, thinks that the treasure revealed by the Key will be—great, useful knowledge."

Draffut shrugged. "If the Key leads to anything, it will be power of some kind, so your Scholar may be correct. But it seems pointless for me to speculate." Then he drew an enormous breath. "It is time that we rejoin the others. Perhaps some of their problems are of a kind that I can solve."

Ready to move on, Chance asked Draffut what he should do with the Old World armor.

Draffut gazed for a long moment at the crumpled, innocent-looking garment. "You might hide it here, somewhere among the rocks," he suggested.

Chance wondered if Zalmoxis would know at once that he had taken it off; but however that might be, he would a thousand times rather put his trust in Draffut.

Once more scooping Chance up in one arm, the Beastlord briskly strode uphill over the tumbled rocks, making short work of what would have been an awkward climb for merely human arms and legs. At the top of the rugged slope, the handful of people who had assembled and seemed to be waiting, Abby among them, cast jealous looks at Chance.

TWENTY-THREE

Envious and curious stares followed Chance as soon as the High Lord Draffut had set him on his feet and turned away to converse with other people. For a moment Abigail appeared as jealous as anyone else. Drawing Chance aside, she demanded: "What did he say to you?"

He walked with her a little farther from the others before whispering his reply. "Told me I'd better get rid of my armor."

She stared at him. "Did you?"

"Yes. Tell you about it later." His head was whirling in an agony of indecision. How much ought he to tell this girl? Would knowing all that he knew help her, or only seal her doom? By confiding in Draffut, he had already defied the demon's orders—if the small, threatening man-image that had announced itself as Avenarius had truly been the demon, and not the treacherous djinn, playing some new game of disguise.

"What else did he say?" Abby sounded breathless.

"Uh—Draffut?"

"Yes, of course! Who else?"

"The bad news is that he's leaving us very soon, can't stay more than a day or two. The good news is that he'll provide an escort, as far as Cascadia Oasis, for any of us who want to get away."

"Ah." She stared at Chance thoughtfully. "That's good to hear. I know my mother will want to take as many of our people as she can to safety. What are you . . . ?"

"I don't have much choice, Abby, with this Key around my neck. And Jervase certainly isn't going to walk away from Ardneh's Workshop, not when he has a chance of making the greatest discovery in a thousand years. Not when the bandits have been driven off, and Horkos is still here with fifteen troopers in case Gokard still wants to make trouble. By Ardneh's ears, I think it would take fifteen troopers to drag Jervase away."

Chance paused, afraid of what the answer to his own question was going to be. But he had to ask it. "What will you be doing?"

Abby was shaking her head slowly. "The first thing I must do is talk to my mother. I have taken a Servant's vow that I must keep."

FOR THE NEXT FEW HOURS, EVERYONE, EXCEPTING THE SENTRIES WHO kept rotating short tours of duty at the cave's mouth, enjoyed a welcome opportunity to rest. Many people went right to sleep, healing their exhaustion in one or another of the sanctuary's rooms. But there were some Servants, and one or two soldiers, who despite weariness found sleep all but impossible with the High Lord Draffut actually in their midst.

Jervase was foremost in this latter group.

Draffut had withdrawn somewhat deeper into the cave, to a room accessible through a broad, high doorway, where he was trying to rest, though still surrounded by a gathering of people he evidently lacked the heart to chase away. With all fear of elementals past, several fires had been kindled for warmth at places in the room where natural chimneys drew away the rising smoke.

CHANCE HAD LAIN DOWN AGAINST ONE SIDE OF THE BIG ROOM, HIS body wrapped in a blanket, his head pillowed on a folded coat. He managed to remain awake long enough to hear the Beastlord telling those who had gathered round him something of his various adventures over the years.

Draffut said he chiefly regretted having wasted a lot of time, a total of many years, even centuries, pursuing rumors that another Ardneh-like entity existed somewhere else in the world.

In other parts of the world, Draffut had been able to discover a few constructions vaguely similar to those in this valley; but on going there he had found only fragments of inanimate slave stations, large but insentient complexes of machinery that had once been in close communication with the living Ardneh. All of these auxiliaries had ceased to function a thousand years ago, at the time of Ardneh's destruction or shortly thereafter. If in one or two places there were indications they had not died totally, still they had become ineffective, useless to the Beastlord in his quest.

Pursuing those stories, one by one, Draffut had satisfied himself that all were false.

SOME OF THE SERVANTS GATHERED IN THE DEEP FIRELIT CHAMBER OF the cave were at least as eager as Jervase to question the Beastlord further. But their feelings of awe and reverence held them back, and they were content to hang on every word of the Scholar's conversation with their lord.

Chance had turned to exchange a few words with Abigail, who lay similarly blanket-wrapped nearby. When he looked back, Draffut was saying: ". . . what I remember of a thousand years of wandering would fill many books—and I fear that what I remember of all that time is small, compared to what I have forgotten."

During the past ten centuries, Draffut had spent a lot of time looking for Ardneh Two—that the human creators of the great original had duplicated their efforts was too much to hope for, but still he could not rid his mind of the nagging hope.

"For a long time I was convinced that there had to be a second Ardneh in existence—somewhere. Where this idea came from I do not know, nor what caused me to believe in it. But it grew to dominate my thoughts."

He described how gradually that hope, too, had died away. "Now I do not believe there ever was a second Ardneh, or ever will be."

His fondest hope of all was that a second Lake of Life might still exist, somewhere in the world.

Either Jervase had not yet heard Draffut say his stay would be cut short, or the Scholar thought he might change his mind: "High Lord, are you going to come with us? Stand beside us when Chance Rolfson uses Ardneh's Key to open the Workshop?"

"That will not be possible." Draffut's refusal was calm and immediate.

Plainly that was not the answer the Scholar had been expecting, and for once Jervase looked confused. He glanced toward Chance, then returned his gaze to the High Lord. "Forgive me, sir, if I seem impertinent. But my need for knowledge compels me to ask you why."

"There is no offense to forgive. The answer is that I have a duty that I must fulfill."

At that moment, with the fall of darkness outside, there came the almost silent passage through the large room of a horde of bats, up and out from some of the cave's inner recesses.

The owl, too, emerged in flight from the lower cave. But instead of flying straight up and on to the open air, she paused, turning abruptly in flight to land and sit contentedly on the Beastlord's great furry wrist, as if they were old acquaintances.

The bird was too big for any ordinary human to carry her long on wrist or shoulder—and few humans would be willing to trust those talons to rest on their own skin.

Draffut turned his head, and his throat produced a surprising sound, a low, cooing hoot that might have come from Mitra herself, and to which she responded in similar tones. After another exchange with the bird, Draffut reverted to human speech, noting that the owl's species had degenerated sadly over the past thousand years, and was now probably on the verge of extinction.

Translating the owl's speech for the listening humans, the Lord of Beasts informed them that Mitra thought she had been hatched somewhere in this region of hills and desert. "She also says, as nearly as I can make out, she has been told she hatched from an egg laid in a nest constructed out of some Old World materials."

Jervase put in: "It seems plain that the great owls of Ardneh's day had more intelligence, were closer to full partnership with humanity."

IT SEEMED THAT ABBY WAS NOT ASLEEP AFTER ALL. SHE RAISED HERself on an elbow and asked: "How did Mitra come to live with you, Scholar? I have heard there is a story to that, but I have not heard the story. Did you raise her from an egg?"

"Hardly." Jervase was still sitting upright, though now he had pulled a blanket round his shoulders. "There is a story, but I doubt it will clear up anything that you find mysterious."

Chance had heard bits of the story before, but had never been curious enough to press for the whole. To him the owl might have simply seemed part of the Scholar's equipment, like his collection and his books.

Jervase was telling a fuller version now. The bird had been a featured performer in some kind of traveling show, playing tricks among the audience, sometimes answering questions in her hooting voice. The show had been playing in the old quarter of the capital city of Sarasvati, and something had drawn the Scholar to take a break from his studies and research, and pay a small coin to watch a performance.

"When it came my turn to ask a question, I looked at Mitra perched on the back of a chair before me—the trainer had dressed her in some cheap foolish costume, and decorated her with a couple of foolish feathers taken from some gaudier bird—and it suddenly struck me that this talking bird was worthy of some better fate.

"I told her, half in jest: 'Find me something like this.' And I held up one of my choice specimens, that I just happened to be carrying with me. It was a small piece of finely machined metal that seemed virtually indestructible—what its function was supposed to be, I never learned."

Mitra had stared at the artifact for only a moment. Then she had slipped whatever leash she had, and flown away.

"More than a full day passed before she returned. When she did come back, she had rid herself of the costume and the foolish extra feathers. And she came back, not to the abusive charlatan who had claimed to own her, but to me, in the rented rooms where I was staying at the time.

"When I went to answer her sharp rapping at the window, she was carrying a small object that she dropped immediately into my hand—a blob of jelly the size of my fingernail, encased in an impenetrable skin. What this strange object was supposed to be, or do, I had no means of guessing, nor have I discovered to this day. It resembled what I had shown her only in that both were incredibly durable, genuine artifacts of the Old World—the small skill in magic that I possess enabled me to verify that.

"Long before the bird came back, of course, the showman had despaired of her ever returning. He had found out where I was staying, and had begun complaining bitterly to me, saying it was my fault she had escaped." Jervase shrugged. "I paid the man off—about half of what he was demanding, as I recall. But it was enough to shut him up.

"Ever since then, Mitra has chosen to remain with me. She has also demonstrated a continued knack for identifying and picking up mysterious fragments of Old World technology. Not, of course, that she can find one every time she searches. If only that were possible!"

Kuan Yin asked: "But what is the owl's purpose in gathering them? What is going through her rudimentary mind? Simply a wish to please the one who rescued her from a kind of compulsive slavery?"

No human knew for certain.

"Interesting questions," Draffut was saying. Those words seemed to reach Chance's ears from a great distance. For he was tumbling slowly into a deep abyss of sleep . . .

. . . FROM WHICH HE WAS BEING DRAGGED BY THE NOISE OF SOMEone screaming—realized that it was he, himself—he was being shaken awake—

—and, looking around, saw that he could not have been asleep for long.

Several people were looking at him anxiously. Abby was the closest. "What was it?" she demanded.

"What did I say?" Chance's heart and lungs were slowly regaining something like their normal rhythm. For once, a complicated sleepvision had not entirely fled.

"Nothing. You were just—screaming."

Turning to the giant figure in the background, Chance said: "I dreamt of you, Lord Draffut. You were holding a sword in one hand—a weapon no bigger than a man might wear at his side, and so it looked very small in your grip. You were standing among a group of—I want to say that they were people, but that is not entirely right, for they were something more . . . their heads looked strange. . . ."

The Beastlord had pulled himself into a sitting position and was paying close attention. "If they were something greater than humanity, what could that be?"

Chance said, in a small, lost voice: "I don't know."

Draffut leaned back against the wall. "Indeed, it is hard to know what humans are, let alone what they might be if something more were added. For thousands of years I have been trying to answer these questions. It is certain that Ardneh did not create men and women; equally certain that Ardneh himself was the work of human minds and human hands.

"In a sense human beings, working through Ardneh, also created me. For I was born as something very different from what I am."

No one had any immediate reply to that. Through Chance's mind there flashed a memory of the ridiculous tale he had heard somewhere, of the Beastlord having been born a dog; but it would be unseemly and insulting even to allude to that.

CONVERSATION HAD DIED AWAY, THE FIRES HAD DIED DOWN, AND Chance was on the verge of drifting off again, when he heard Abby's nearby whisper, saying that as soon as they had rested, she intended to summon up the djinn once more.

Chance roused himself sufficiently to whisper back. "We should ask Draffut first."

"It was his suggestion, made to me when we two were alone for a moment. Draffut wants to see him, too."

TWENTY-FOUR

THE SUN WAS HIGH IN THE SPRINGTIME SKY, ITS LIGHT REFLECT-ing and filtered down from the cave's broad entrance into the inner rooms, making them about as bright as they were ever going to be. After getting some much-needed hours of sleep, Chance and Abigail had breakfasted with their companions, hearing the results of the owl's reconnaissance during the night just past. The bird's report was confirmed and amplified by a pair of the captain's scouts, returning to the cave at dawn.

Gokard and a hard core of his loyal followers were far from giving up. They had succeeded in reclaiming perhaps half the animals that had been driven off. Many humans had deserted the bandit's cause after Draffut's destructive passage through their ranks. But the scouts agreed that Gokard probably still had fifty fighters on hand. Even aware that Draffut was still on the scene, they gave no sign of being ready to abandon their ambitions entirely and go home.

Jervase summed up the situation. "So we must make the best possible use of the limited time in which the Lord Draffut will still be with us."

CARRYING A CANDLE TO A DIFFERENT ROOM OF THE CAVE THIS TIME, Chance stood ready to help while Abby began the process of once

more summoning the djinn. By now Chance was sufficiently familiar with the process that he could be of real assistance, handing her
certain objects at the proper time, even pronouncing a word or two
when it was helpful to add another voice to hers.

Before beginning, Abigail had made sure that Draffut was indeed
lying in wait (there being not quite enough headroom for him to sit
up straight) in the next room. The Beastlord had expressed a strong
wish to talk to Zalmoxis as soon as the chance arose.

This time there was no difficulty in summoning the tech-djinn,
whose arrival was preceded by the usual smoky fanfare. Scarcely
had Zalmoxis assumed the visible form of Grandmother when Abigail said to him impatiently: "Draffut tells me that you have been
trying for a long time to become a human being."

Chance, standing a few meters off, was also staring hard at the
djinn. Privately the young lord was wondering what would happen if
he flatly accused Zalmoxis of counterfeiting the appearance of the
great demon. But before doing that he would certainly have to tell
Abby the whole story, and be guided by her advice.

The djinn had put on a what's-this-all-about expression, and
looked at Chance, as if calling him to witness the kind of outrageous
accusations he was forced to put up with. Then Grandmother, looking and sounding injured, faced back to Abby. "That only confirms,
my powerful young mistress, that I speak the truth! Have I not been
telling you the same thing?"

Chance, standing with arms folded, confident that Draffut's help
was nearby if he should need it, put in an accusation of his own:
"You do not always speak the truth. The High Lord gave me very
convincing evidence of that."

"That only goes to show you, young master"—the red-haired apparition grimaced—"judging from the tone you have adopted, I
suppose I must get used to having you as my master now?—that I
am making substantial progress in my emulation of humanity."

"Why should that be so important to you?" Chance demanded.

Zalmoxis seemed to marvel at the question. "Well, being human is important to you, too, is it not?"

Then he drew a deep breath and seemed to reconsider. "But your question deserves an answer. Many years ago—a very long time before you were born—when my investigations began to reveal to me the awesome complexity of the human brain, I began to be obsessed with this incredible machine. Since then my fascination has only grown, almost to the point of my being compelled to worship it. My attitude toward humanity . . ."

Slowly the djinn's voice trailed off.

Draffut, lying in a prone position, his chin held up off the floor by his arms folded beneath it, had just maneuvered his head and shoulders into the doorway connecting to the next room. From this position he contemplated the djinn, the Beastlord's face wearing its usual unreadable expression.

If Zalmoxis was totally surprised, he concealed it well. After staring back for a moment, he said smoothly: "Many years have passed since we have had a chance to talk to each other, noble Draffut."

"Perhaps too many," the giant rumbled. "No, don't bother to change your form on my account."

"Certainly not," said the djinn, whose image had wavered momentarily. "By the way, I have been telling our human friends here about the interval of great pain and peril that you and I shared as comrades, on a day of memorable battle, long ago."

"I hope you told them the truth about it."

"But of course." Zalmoxis cleared his throat, a very human sound. "It was on that occasion when the two of us agreed to form a permanent alliance against all demons—"

One of Draffut's eyes screwed almost shut, his face becoming more expressive than Chance had seen it yet. "We did *what*?"

"—and it was fortunate for us that during that interval the demon Zapranoth found himself too busy trying to preserve his own life to devote any time at all to devising imaginative entertainments for his captives."

Abby was watching and listening in silence, her mouth hanging open; looking at her, Chance realized that his was in the same condition.

Draffut had abandoned his attitude of doubt, and nodded solemnly, agreeing with what Zalmoxis had just said. "Still, it was a period of memorable suffering."

"Memorable! Is that all you can say?" The djinn tried two or three dramatic gestures; somehow none of them looked quite right. "I would hope that between us we could enable our young human friends to grasp the searing impact of that experience. Help them to understand why I, having survived that, am now most reluctant to do anything to provoke a powerful demon's wrath!"

Draffut gave another nod or two. "Of course the demon who chiefly menaces us today is hardly in the class of Zapranoth. Avenarius is not going to swallow me . . . I only wish that he would try! But unfortunately he is probably too intelligent to make that blunder . . . remember that I cannot come to grips with one of his kind directly unless he takes on solid form."

Zalmoxis shuddered. "*He* can still come to grips with *me*, however. . . ."

"So far you have been nimble enough to avoid that fate," Draffut observed dryly. He turned his gaze back to Chance and Abby. "It seems to me that our task is to protect those humans who stand in the greatest danger."

The djinn sounded almost indignant. "I have been doing my best along that line. Doing rather well, I think."

"You gave me that armor—" Chance put in.

"Yes I did! And it has saved your life at least twice."

"—for which I am grateful. But I think perhaps that there was something wrong with it."

Zalmoxis paused. He seemed to be taking careful thought. "There may have been some minor defect. There *may* have been, I say."

Abby was bristling. "Just what was the nature of this flaw?"

"Oh, highly technical! You must understand that all devices of the Old World are very old—"

Draffut's rumble overrode the bickering: "Time is flying, and the armor, whatever its imperfections, has been cast aside." His gaze bored at the djinn. "The fundamental question is whether you can be trusted. In truth it is your envy that dominates your attitude toward humanity. Am I not right?"

"Ah, but is not envy akin to love?" Zalmoxis admitted that there were moments when he felt his own further existence would be impossible, life perhaps unendurable, unless he could have for himself a set of the marvelous machinery constituting the human brain. "The veriest peasants are endowed with this miraculous tool!"

Chance and Abigail had been edging closer to each other, as if instinctively, and now he reached out for the girl's hand. Somehow he had started to fall into the habit of thinking of Zalmoxis as a clown. There was truth in that—but it was far from the whole truth. The djinn could also be frightening, and dangerous, and was a very powerful being in ways wherein humanity tended to be weak. When Zalmoxis spoke of his desires and problems, Chance could get a glimpse of savage anger showing through.

But at the moment the djinn was displaying only his pleasant demeanor. He rhapsodized: "Of all beings in the universe, humans are most to be envied!"

For the moment, he was ignoring the two young humans in his presence. And except for the fact that Draffut continued to use the humans' language, it seemed to Chance almost as if the Beastlord had forgotten their presence as well. "Is that the reason you wish to join them? Foolishness! Abysmal foolishness!"

"Wish to join them? *Wish?*" Again Zalmoxis was almost screaming; Chance could well imagine other people in the cave being alarmed, wondering what was going on. But perhaps the troopers and Servants had grown accustomed to strange noises emanating from these magical sessions. "I have labored at it for centuries! It is my heart's desire!"

"As you admit that you lack a brain, what makes you think you have a heart?" Draffut sounded sour. "Being the most envied, you must realize, is hardly distinguishable from being the most hated by the other orders of creation."

"Ah, but who would not be willing to endure a modicum of hatred!" The djinn was no longer screaming, but he gestured extravagantly with Grandmother's hands. For a moment he allowed her to wave with three arms, then four. "That would be a small price to pay indeed. Given the complexity of a human brain to think and work with, given such intricate entanglement of things that are material and things that are not—what could I, what could any djinn or demon or elemental, not accomplish!"

Draffut muttered something.

Zalmoxis was going on. "When I began to comprehend the true nature of this most intricate mechanism, this meaty marvel that lies between even the most foolish pair of human ears, suddenly all my work up to that point appeared to have been in vain. I realized that I was no nearer to my goal than when I started."

In a moment the djinn had raised its hands to its head. "Look! Look at this . . . let me show you." In the next instant he was pulling apart the simulated skull of its own avatar-image, bloodlessly scooping out most of the contents, which appeared mainly as infinite complexities of glistening whitish fiber.

Holding the brain-image in his left hand, Zalmoxis pointed to it with his right forefinger, dramatically calling attention to certain details of the convoluted marvel. Meanwhile, he was ignoring the fact that his mouth, his whole face, had virtually collapsed into a small wrinkled mass of illusory flesh. The sound of his voice emerged as clear as ever. "There are Old World devices that make things that are too small to see grow large enough . . ."

Chance, confronted with what appeared to be a human cranium torn apart, felt the start of a rebellion in his stomach, and had to turn away lest he lose his breakfast. Abby, the experienced medical worker, displayed an opposite reaction. She kept staring at the djinn's performance, obviously more fascinated than revolted. She said to Zalmoxis: "It would be very helpful in my work if you could, sometime—show me the inner workings of a complete body?"

"Of course!" the djinn exclaimed mechanically. Then he pressed on, seeming totally unaware of the effect he was having on a portion of his human audience. Lightly tossing what appeared to be its own brain in one hand, his image said: "It is a wonder that must remain forever beyond my power to duplicate."

Draffut seemed strongly interested, and in no danger of getting sick. He said: "There is a great craving, and not only in humanity, to destroy the treasures one can never have!"

The djinn made a swift lifting and stuffing motion with his left hand. Instantaneously his head was back in perfect shape. "Tell me, Lord of Beasts, do you never wish to be a human being?"

The answer was short and simple. "I am what I am."

A FEW HOURS LATER, DRAFFUT WAS RESTING AGAIN, AFTER REPEATING to the expedition's leaders his warning that he must soon be leaving, and his offer to escort in safety all who would come with him.

No one could doubt that the bandits still represented a serious danger—or they would, as soon as Draffut was no longer present.

All evidence suggested that there were among Gokard's people enough fanatical demon-worshipers, not to mention people strongly motivated by sheer greed, to keep them in service to Avenarius, in close pursuit of what they thought would turn out to be awesome treasure.

AFTER SOME HOURS OF REST AND RECUPERATION, KUAN YIN AND CAPtain Horkos, with the approval of Jervase, convened a general meeting of Servants and troopers near the cave's broad entrance. The pair of sentries standing guard were able to attend without leaving their posts.

The Sarasvati soldiers whose wounds Draffut had healed were among the first to join the group, weapons gripped firmly in strong hands. Chance saw some of them displaying the faint, fresh scars that were no longer wounds, and heard them voicing vows of eternal loyalty to Draffut. The Beastlord himself was elsewhere at the moment—Chance had heard him say something about talking to the bird again.

CHANCE WAS SURPRISED TO SEE ABBY APPEAR WITHOUT THE WHITE Servants' garments she had been wearing since they met. Instead she had on a common blouse and trousers, such as any working man or woman might wear; somehow the change made the elegant slimness of her body more apparent. Her Servants' footgear had also been replaced by shabby boots of a Yasodharan army type. These looked somewhat worn, as if they might have been stripped from a dead enemy. She also had a hunting knife, much like Chance's, at her belt, and she said that the small backpack she had put on contained all that she and Chance had salvaged of the Lady Ayaba's magical equipment.

Looking around, Chance realized that the appearance of other Servants had also changed markedly. Over the period of siege and combat, their white clothes had all become more or less tattered and begrimed, and many of them had put on other garments, borrowed, pulled from their own stores, or scavenged from the enemy. Here and there some portion of a Servant's original robe was still in evidence, no longer white. Their bodies were adorned with packs and canteens, sword-belts, slings, bows, and arrow-quivers.

ABBY'S EYES SEARCHED CHANCE'S AS SHE TOLD HIM AND JERVASE: "I am coming with you to the Workshop. You are doing Ardneh's work by carrying his Key, and my mother agrees that I can best serve Ardneh by helping you. It seems you must depend upon the djinn to guide you to your goal, and only I will have any hope of controlling him. He is hardly trustworthy."

Chance felt a sense of relief so deep and strong that it surprised him. "Good! I actually think you will be safer with me than walking away with Draffut—as long as the Key is with me too." In a few days at the most, the protection of the Lord of Beasts would be withdrawn from all of them.

Abby was motioning another Servant forward. She told Chance: "Novice Benambra has convinced my mother that he can best do Ardneh's work by joining your party too—if you will have him."

Chance was not surprised to see that the tall young novice had changed his white robes for a blue coat and trousers—these fit him so well that they were probably his own. Benambra had armed himself with a short sword and a dagger, and was still wearing the money-pouch at his belt, though it looked flat and empty now. Chance supposed its contents had been turned back to Kuan Yin.

The Scholar was on hand. He studied the tall youth for a few moments, then said: "If the decision is up to me, yes, let him come. He seems dependable, and we've seen that he can use a weapon when he has to."

"Thank you, sir." Benambra seemed to feel it necessary to offer some explanation. "Sir, the Servants, as you may have noticed, are perpetually in need of money. Now more than ever, sir. They—we— are going to have to rebuild, reestablish ourselves, somewhere. I want to earn a share of Ardneh's treasure, so we can carry out Ardneh's work."

"It seems a worthy objective." Jervase studied his latest volunteer. "But you must realize that I have been quite serious, all along, in saying that I am not after gold, or any treasure of that kind. I don't expect that we will find any."

"Yes sir, you have made your ideas on the subject very plain. But in a place like Ardneh's Workshop—we don't really know what's in there, do we?" The tall youth spread open hands in a questioning gesture. "It's possible we will discover your kind of treasure and other kinds as well."

"Certainly, very many things are possible." Jervase sighed. "All right, then. If you understand that I promise nothing."

"Thank you," Benambra repeated. "I will make every effort to achieve the common good."

"All of us in this enterprise must expect that of each other."

KUAN YIN BEGAN THE SEMIFORMAL MEETING WITH AN EXPRESSION OF thanks to the Lord Draffut. In the next breath she announced in a tired voice that the Servants were going to have to abandon the cave.

"We're not going back to the compound?" One of the slower acolytes had to ask the question.

"We are not. The enemy is still in the field and is beginning to reorganize. Lord Draffut cannot stay with us. Our compound is still indefensible—and so now is this cave." The speaker gestured toward the entrance, drastically altered by masses of displaced rock.

"Where are we going?"

"The High Lord Draffut has promised he will escort us as far as Cascadia Oasis. From there we should have a relatively safe route overland to Sarasvati, where Lord Chance assures me we will be welcome. There we can catch our breath and make new plans. Of course we who have dedicated ourselves to the ideal of healing must soon get on with our chosen work, in Sarasvati and wherever else we can establish ourselves.

"As most of you know by now, two of our number have expressed a wish to join Scholar Jervase's party. One of their number carries Ardneh's Key, and I believe they are doing Ardneh's work in their own way—though perhaps the Scholar would not describe his efforts in those terms.

"His expedition will need the special skills of magic that only novice Abigail, among us all, is able to provide. Novice Benambra has told me he feels called to join their expedition also. He has promised to donate whatever things of value he may gain to the Servants' treasury to support our work of healing."

The young man spoke up. "There is no denying the fact that we are going to need large sums of money. For new buildings, wherever we decide to settle. For supplies of all kinds . . . yes, even to hire mercenaries for defense if it comes to that."

There was a murmur of objection from some of the Servants listening.

Benambra was ready to debate the point. "If it is morally correct to defend ourselves, then why should it be wrong to hire mercenaries to do the job? Their mere presence may deter attack."

"I don't know," someone in the small group murmured back.

Benambra argued: "Nothing that we can build or achieve is going to last unless it is protected."

SERVANTS AND TROOPERS ALIKE BEGAN, WITH MIXED FEELINGS OF hope and reluctance, to prepare for another move. This time the packing would be somewhat easier, for many of the bundles and boxes they had so recently carried into the great cave had not been opened. Draft animals and ridingbeasts were made ready to hit the road again. It was agreed that on leaving the cave the two parties would continue to travel together, until the djinn gave the treasure hunters notice that their route must diverge from the path leading to Cascadia Oasis.

BEFORE THE LATEST EVACUATION GOT UNDER WAY, KUAN YIN SENT A trusted aide back to the compound they had previously abandoned to take a quick look at the situation there.

In less than half an hour, the mounted scout came cantering briskly back up the narrow path to the cave entrance. His report confirmed the decision to abandon the facility the Servants had so recently established. The enemy had burned some of the buildings, and much that would not burn had been broken, probably in a foolish search for hidden valuables. Sheer demonic vandalism had probably also played a role.

The scout reported grimly that yet another altar to Avenarius had been hastily erected, right in the center of the compound. Certain ugly evidence indicated that the unspeakable sacrifice spoken of by Gokard had indeed been offered.

"I fear it was a child," the scout concluded. He gave no further details. Chance saw tears in Kuan Yin's eyes, and Abby's.

But the Director quickly pulled herself together, and in her crisp voice cheered up her people by assuring them that eventually—someday—some of them might be able to return to the compound that had been so profaned, and cleanse it of all traces of evil occupancy.

LEAVING BEHIND THE HALF-RUINED STRONGHOLD OF THE CAVE, THE combined caravan set out in the early morning of a warm spring day. There was no longer any trace of snow, even in shadowed spaces on the ground. An occasional glimpse of a single flying reptile, or more exotic flyer in the sky behind them, strongly suggested that the combined caravan was being shadowed at a respectful distance by the bandits.

ONE OR TWO OF THE SERVANTS WERE SUCH WORSHIPFUL FOLLOWERS of Draffut that they had decided their highest priority must be simply to remain with him. These people the Beastlord made some effort to discourage, without actually ordering them to stay away.

No, he insisted, no matter how devoted they might be, they would not be able to accompany him everywhere he went. He had warned them a day would come ("And it will be sooner, rather than later.") when they would not be able to keep up.

Draffut told the undecided people that if pleasing him was really their primary goal, they should devote their lives to helping other humans. In the end they accepted his advice.

When Draffut happened to come near the demon-altar that had so recently been put up just outside the cave, he turned aside and spent a few moments smashing it into fragments, hurling stone against stone and scattering the pieces, carrying out this work in savage silence.

WHEN THE MARCH HAD BEEN UNDER WAY AGAIN FOR A FEW MIN-utes, Chance could not resist the impulse to ask just once more: "You cannot come with us all the way to the Workshop, Lord Draffut?"

The massive head shook slowly, patiently, back and forth. Draffut did not seem annoyed, but neither was he flexible. "I have made a pledge that must be honored. I cannot stay with you all your life, watching for a demon who may never come.

"Besides that, what happens in the Workshop will be up to you. Ardneh decided that the Key, his pledge to humanity, will be useful only when it is in human hands."

"Will demons be able to enter there?"

"Wherever you humans go, you are likely to bring demons. But the Workshop itself may provide better help than any I could give you."

TWENTY-FIVE

THE SPRING CROP OF GRASS HAD MADE GOOD HEADWAY IN ITS growth during the days of siege, and people were counting on it to feed the livestock during the next period of travel. Ten loaded wagons rolled out of the cave, half of them loaded with Servants' cargo and the other half with the goods of the Sarasvati expedition. Meanwhile the majestic figure of Draffut stood with folded arms, silently encouraging the humans to waste no time. Descending across the band of altered landscape just below the entrance, the loadbeasts and their drivers began to establish a new, winding path of their own design.

Two hours later the combined column had left behind not only the cave and mesa, but the whole cluster of hills, and was setting out across a wasteland, under an enormous sky, moving into territory where few of its members had ever been before.

Draffut continued to lead the way. Behind him, some people were mounted, some walking, while others rode in wagons. From time to time the Lord of Beasts looked back, as if to make sure he was not going too fast. He was now walking at a much slower pace than he had used when charging toward the cave, restraining his long strides to match the speed of human feet and slowly rolling vehicles.

Chance was driving Mitra's familiar wagon, with the bird inside, snugly hooded and covered as on earlier peaceful days of travel. Abby was in a different wagon, still communing with the Lady Ayaba's magical equipment.

At the start of the move Jervase had been riding at the head of the column, trying to get in as much conversation with the Lord of Beasts as he possibly could. But now the Scholar, astride his usual mount, had dropped back to talk to Chance.

Still sleepless with the excitement of having met Draffut face to face, Jervase wanted to share with someone the joy of having been able to talk with him at length—and the tragedy, as the Scholar saw it, of being forced to separate from him again so soon.

Jervase said he had made repeated efforts to learn the nature of the commitment that was compelling Draffut to hurry away. But the Lord of Beasts refused to be drawn into giving explanations. Nor would Draffut reveal where he was going, when he might visit this part of the world again, or where he might be found a month or a year from today. He had finally insisted on being allowed to take a break from the interrogation.

Benambra was walking nearby, his long strides easily matching the slow pace of the loadbeasts that drew the wagon. He said: "I suppose, sir, that pressing the High Lord to answer questions could be counterproductive."

The Scholar nodded. "I was beginning to realize that fact. Oh, there are a thousand more questions that I want to ask him. I suppose if I made them less personal, he might be more likely to answer them."

Chance could sympathize with both of them. "And you couldn't very well refuse to grant him a break."

"No I couldn't. Without actually saying much, he managed to get across the idea that I might regret it if I kept nagging him on the subject. Oh, I don't believe he was threatening me with violence—I think that could never happen. But somehow he made it plain that there could be consequences I wouldn't like."

Benambra was still thoughtfully keeping pace. "Perhaps, sir, Draffut does not see the accumulation of knowledge by humans as the greatest good."

Jervase blinked, and looked surprised. "Perhaps he doesn't. I tend to forget the fact that he's not human." The man brightened slightly. "He did assure me that if I cared to delay our hunt for Ardneh's treasure, I would be welcome as any other human being to accompany him on his journey—beyond Cascadia Oasis, if I liked, as far as I could get on my own power. He said again that once he left there, no human, even mounted, would be able to keep up with him for long."

Chance yawned. His gnawing worry about the demon was making it difficult to get any restful sleep. "Having seen how Lord Draffut moves when he's in a hurry, I can believe that. And what did you say?"

"I said that, tempting as his invitation was, I could not possibly accept. Of course I would very much like to travel with him for a few more days; but not at the cost of missing the exploration that you and I, Chance, are about to make." The Scholar's voice fell to an intense whisper. "Opening Ardneh's Workshop must come first." His eyes probed at Chance, as if seeking to make sure his student was still committed to the job. "I trust that you still have the Key?"

"Of course I do. That is, I assume I do." Chance was learning to rely upon its unseen presence as a matter of faith. It would be there, hanging around his neck, as soon as it was needed.

If they could somehow keep bandits and demons from interfering, Jervase would be the second or third human being ever to enter Ardneh's secret domain—Chance was sure he would have given anything to be the first, but that did not seem to be in the cards. Once the Scholar got inside, not only secrets of the past would lie open to his inspection, but also wonders existing in the here-and-now, that were known to no one else. There could also be strong clues about the future. Jervase's personal search for knowledge could be enormously advanced. Essential discoveries would be made.

Chance bitterly envied Jervase his freedom to enjoy his great dream. He himself dared hope for nothing but some way to get free of the cursed demon's threats. And the only reason he could find to hope at all was his possession of the Key.

Appealing to the High Lord Draffut had brought him no assistance—unless he counted Draffut's suggestion, advanced only as a possibility, that the great demon might not have been a demon after all.

Nor was there any relief to be found in trying to think the matter calmly through. Mental steps in any direction foundered at once in a great bog of uncertainty. For the time being, all Chance could be certain of was that he must drive the wagon.

Struggling to suppress another yawn, he asked the Scholar: "What did he say to you about the demon? Anything?"

"Demon?" Obviously Jervase was living in a state of blessed freedom from worry about such creatures. To him Avenarius was still hardly more than a name. "No, nothing. I'm coming round to the belief that Gokard is bluffing with his threats. His murderous sacrifices seem to have produced only one smallish specimen of the tribe—Gronzero—and the Lord Draffut disposed of him."

Chance wished devoutly that Draffut's suggestion could be true, that the secret apparition calling itself by the name of Avenarius had been only another trick played by the djinn. But even if that should prove to be the truth, the real Avenarius could be lurking nearby— the Lord of Beasts had given him no reason to doubt that.

Jervase was still speaking, as much to himself as to Chance, on the subject of Draffut. He implied he was not yet entirely confident about the Beastlord's true character and motives. It was hardly possible that the reality could be as noble as the glorious legend.

That was not exactly what Chance was hoping to hear. "You're not suggesting that he's—he's—"

The Scholar for once appeared uncertain. "I'm not sure what I'm suggesting. It is only . . . well, I keep coming back to the fact that Draffut . . . simply is not human. Everything he decides and everything he does may not always be in the best interests of humanity. It is even possible that everything he tells us may not be the truth."

ON THE FIRST NIGHT OUT FROM THE CAVE, HORKOS ORDERED WAG-ons drawn into a circle and established sentries. The feeling of security in Draffut's presence was so complete that the captain allowed bright campfires, as if they were some mighty army. The Beastlord himself offered no opinion on the subject.

Evoked by Abby inside the wagon that had been Lady Ayaba's, the djinn said Jervase and his party should simply continue for one more day to accompany Draffut and the Servants on the road to Cascadia.

KUAN YIN AND JERVASE STILL ARGUED, AS IF THERE MIGHT BE SOME-thing to be settled between them before they separated.

Jervase was saying to her now: "If Ardneh lives on in any form, it is only in the sense of dreams and visions."

"A little while ago, you were certain that Draffut could not be living either."

Jervase was frowning. "Obviously I was wrong about that. But I still don't expect Ardneh himself to come out to meet us when we reach his Workshop."

"Nor do I."

"And on that point the Lord Draffut himself agrees with me—I have questioned him about it. What I do not understand, then, is in what sense does Ardneh live on?"

Kuan Yin remained unruffled. "He lives, in a very real sense, in us, his followers. I do not expect you to understand."

"I've never understood what kind of being Ardneh was, or was supposed to be. It seems possible to eliminate all categories, one by one. Certainly he was not a demon."

"Absolutely not. Rather the very opposite. An archenemy of demons, and great friend and benefactor of humanity."

"But not a human being either."

"No. Definitely not."

"An elemental, then? Or djinn?"

"Hardly. During his lifetime, some were determined to worship him as a god. And some still are. But he steadfastly refused to claim that classification."

The Scholar had another question: "Lord Draffut, there is another phrase, sometimes appearing in the ancient writings, that has often puzzled me. 'Twenty megatons.' Those words in literal translation only specify a certain amount of weight, or mass—I take it to indicate the size of a large hill or small mountain. What this has to do with an explosion, a violent flying apart, seems utterly mysterious. Can you offer enlightenment?"

To Chance it sounded as if Ardneh and Orcus might have been killed by a mountain falling on them. That made about as much sense as any other explanation he had heard.

Draffut seemed to hesitate. "What I can give you—is not precisely an explanation—I doubt whether I even ought to offer it."

"I wish you would, sir. Anything that you can tell me—anything at all—"

"Then stand with me, in your imagination, where I was standing, in the open air, at the moment when Ardneh and Orcus died."

Jervase said softly: "I will try." Kuan Yin bowed her head and murmured something.

Draffut raised his own gaze, looking toward the horizon. "I was at a great distance from the event, something like a hundred kilometers away.

"But I remember, as if it were only yesterday, how at that instant the sky seemed to become pure light, even in broad day. The light died swiftly. But then, minutes later, the ground shook, even at the distance where I stood marveling and afraid. I remember how the winds roared, first sweeping out away from the terrible center, then rushing back again. How the thick column of dust and smoke went mounting up—up—up for kilometers into the sky."

At that point Draffut paused, and his silence went on and on.

It was the Scholar who broke it finally. "Lord Draffut?" Jervase looked around at his fellow humans, who stared back at him with eyes as innocent of comprehension as his own. "Lord Draffut, I—we—do not understand."

The ancient being before him was shaking his head slowly. He had no more to say.

AT THE CONCLUSION OF ARDNEH'S WAR AGAINST THE EAST, ZALMOXIS, the tech-djinn, had been too far from the great blast that ended it to serve as a reliable witness. But, as he told Chance and Abby, he had heard and pondered the stories of a number of humans, and of others who were not human, who had been somewhat closer to that event, while still remaining far enough from Ground Zero to survive.

Ground Zero was another incantatory phrase harvested from the old writings. The Scholar was telling what he knew. "The literal meaning in the old language seems to be 'a place where there is no ground.' That might refer to empty air, or space. Some argue that, in a philosophical sense, it is where fundamental reality fails in some mysterious way. Other dispute those interpretations. One of the few things the sources generally agree on is that somewhere in this river valley is the place where the power called Ardneh died."

"And the archdemon Orcus died with him."

Jervase nodded. "No one seriously disputes that Ardneh and Orcus perished together."

It was still hard to understand. "But how did they die? I mean—" The speaker made an awkward gesture; he seemed to be using the fingers of both hands to point in ten directions at one. "Strangling each other? Stabbing each other with iron blades?"

"I don't think so. Both entities were capable of taking physical form, but their struggle was more likely in the realm of pure magic. Different legends tell, as you know, different versions of the event. Beyond the fact that they fought, and neither one survived, we know nothing with any certainty."

He glanced briefly in the direction of Abby and Benambra. "A few of our friends who want to devote their lives to serving Ardneh will tell you that he still lives. In opposition to that, I have met people who assured me that the great demon was the only survivor."

"That sounds like an idea that our friend Gokard might put forward."

The Scholar smiled faintly. "People, especially demon-worshipers, are likely to say anything. We may be sure that Orcus did not survive. Approximately a thousand years have passed since the great struggle, and if he still existed, by now he would have eaten up the whole world, along with all the people in it."

The other grunted, as if unconvinced. "And Ardneh?"

Benambra cut in, as if it were important: "Excuse me. You said that Ardneh was a . . . what did you say?"

"A god."

The novice frowned. "Sorry, sir, I am not familiar with that word."

Jervase smiled faintly. "I would have expected a Servant to be trained in Scripture."

"No doubt the fault is mine, Scholar Jervase. Since joining the Servants of Ardneh I have been kept very busy with practical matters."

"I see. Well, very few people, other than Scriptural scholars, are familiar with the word. It appears several times in the so-called sacred writings, where it refers to a supposed class of supernatural entities, beings-deserving-of-worship, superior to all others in power and majesty and wisdom."

A few people were absorbed in the discussion, while others wandered off.

The Scholar went on. "In the Old World, existence was claimed for literally thousands of gods, arrayed in various pantheons. No one believed in them all, of course. Some people believed in a great number of them, as I say, while others prayed only to one, an omnipotent creator."

Benambra seemed interested. "But you say that even Ardneh refused to place himself within the god-category."

"Indeed, more interesting than you can have yet realized. After all, it seems only logical that there must be some being, or class of beings, superior in power to all others."

AS TIME PASSED, ABBY SEEMED TO GROW MORE SUSPICIOUS ABOUT BEnambra's motives. She said to him: "But everything you find will go into our treasury."

Benambra: "Yes, of course. That is what I said. Do you doubt me?"

She seemed to pause for just a heartbeat before she answered: "No."

AT SUNRISE ON THE NEXT DAY, THE DJINN APPEARED TO TELL ABBY that this was the point where the two parties would have to separate. From here on the route for those who sought the Workshop's secret entrance must diverge from the desert trail leading to Cascadia.

Kuan Yin's words and actions, when she came to say farewell to her daughter, made it clear that she, like the great majority of Servants, had no intention of giving up their dream of an organization dedicated to medical service.

"My little girl . . . it is hard, but I must force myself to see that the time has come for you to be grown up. Now we each have our own work to do. Send a message whenever you can . . . I would like to be able to hope that you will hurry back to me."

DRAFFUT SAID FAREWELL TO THE MEMBERS OF JERVASE'S EXPEDITION simply and briefly. When he came to Chance he said: "You are troubled, and I wish that I could be of more help. One bit of advice I perhaps can add: Trust yourself."

"Trust—myself?"

"I have said that Ardneh seldom spoke to me. But he did tell me that humans, by all appearances so small and weak, have innate powers that no demon can ever match."

Moments later, the Beastlord had taken his place at the head of Kuan Yin's party. Mitra, heavily hooded against the growing light, was perched on the giant's shoulder. Draffut had said that he would send the bird back to Jervase at nightfall, either tonight or on the following night, bringing any new information about bandits that might become available.

When the humans signaled their readiness, Draffut turned his back on them and began to walk. The Director's people and their animals and their five wagons began to move, heading out on the faintly marked trail that led in the direction of some distant hills and would eventually bring them to Cascadia Oasis.

THE SCHOLAR'S EXPEDITION WAS ALREADY INDEPENDENTLY IN MO-tion. The two small trains of wagons drew farther and farther apart under the enormous sky that spanned the open country.

———

EVEN IF THEIR DRIVERS WERE SPURRED ON BY A COMBINATION OF FEAR and anticipation, the loadbeasts pulling the Scholar's wagons over the rough ground could still make only a few kilometers between sunrise and sunset. Always one or more of the expedition's members rode on ahead to scout, and very often Jervase himself assumed this duty.

Now that the Sarasvati expedition was back very nearly to its original strength, it seemed to Chance ridiculously small.

FOR SOME HOURS ZALMOXIS HAD BEEN NOTABLE BY HIS ABSENCE. AS the time approached for Abby to summon the djinn again, she told Chance: "I have no doubt we will soon be seeing him, whether we try to call him up or not. We might well find him waiting at the door of Ardneh's Workshop."

"That's one place we are certainly not going to find him if he never gets around to telling us exactly where it is."

"Oh, he will, he will. What he has been telling us seems to make sense. He has to guide the Key-bearer to the door if he is ever going to see it opened. So I think it will be better if I order him to stop this coming and going. Why should he not remain with us, allow our companions to see him in some form?"

"If he doesn't want to, he will tell us some reason that may or may not be the real one."

"If he will obey me in this, that ought to help me establish some firmer control over him. On the other hand, if he is able to refuse a direct order—well, that will tell us something that we ought to know."

"You are managing very well." Chance paused, his conscience clamoring that Abby ought to be told everything about the appearance of Avenarius and his threats—if anyone had a right to know, she did. But suppose the threatening visitor had been the real demon? There was no escaping the fact that the very act of telling her could put her in terrible danger.

Feeling overwhelmed by stress, Chance suddenly burst out with: "I wish that the Key had come to someone else."

"But it didn't," was Abby's response. Her hand came to rest on Chance's shoulder. After a pause she added: "When I think about it, I'm glad you are the one who got it."

At last the young lord tried to approach the subject from another way: "Abby, I fear Zalmoxis may be trying to fool us with some new imitations."

"He may. But I think I can manage your great playmate. Yes, I am sure we will hear from Zalmoxis again, as soon as Lord Draffut is well out of the way."

"Playmate!" Chance heaved a sigh. "That's an interesting title for him."

Abby gave him a crooked little smile. "I must call him something light and humorous, you see. Otherwise I will be too much afraid of him."

"Whatever we call him—whatever happens—I want you at my side. Close at my side." The words had burst out before he could think about them. He had no wish to call them back.

Now she did indeed look flustered. "I am sure your mentor Jervase will be determined to occupy that spot at the Workshop door— as long as he's unable to snatch the Key away from you."

"Well, I have two sides, don't I? At least."

CAPTAIN HORKOS HAD SOMETHING TO SAY TO THE OTHER LEADERS AND Chance. "I foresee a possible problem."

"Yes, Captain?"

"It's all one to me, gentlemen—and lady—but I hear the men talking, and it's best to get such things out in the open. What my troopers would like to know is, can they all hope to have some share in this treasure, when it's found?"

Benambra shifted uneasily, as if he might be about to explain once more why he was interested in treasure. But he thought better of it and remained silent.

Chance was ready to answer the captain. "I don't know what we'll find in Ardneh's Workshop. If there is treasure, I don't know how much control I will have over its distribution. So the only promise I can make regarding it is this: If we discover gold, or coin, or jewels, or"—here he looked at Jervase—"or if it should be knowledge, then each man or woman who comes with me can have as much of it as I keep for myself."

Jervase was nodding, smiling gently. "Tell the men they can each take as much as they want—of the things that I want—and my share will not be diminished."

TWENTY-SIX

BY NOON ON THE DAY WHEN THE TWO PARTIES SEPARATED, THE five wagons of the Sarasvati expedition were entering another range of small hills. The reasonably ordinary landscape through which they had been traveling soon turned into a mazelike complex of broken slabs of rock. Jagged pieces the size of ordinary houses were strewn about, standing on their sides or edges, suggesting that some violent conflict on a gigantic scale had taken place here at some time in the past.

This landscape was swiftly becoming the strangest that Chance had ever seen. It was new to Jervase also; none of his earlier explorations had brought him very near here. Presently there appeared certain funnel-shaped dark openings in the earth, the like of which no one could remember seeing anywhere. Wind and water erosion had been at work for centuries, adding their changes to those made so long ago by Ardneh as he prepared for battle, and to the damage caused in the final struggle.

Progress was difficult through the afternoon. At dusk, the wagons had not gone as far as Zalmoxis had anticipated when he laid out the day's route. Abigail's latest effort to contact the djinn was not successful.

As the young enchantress finally, reluctantly, stuffed the little set of toy carpenter tools back into her pack, she and Chance discussed this ominous development, before going to rejoin the others.

He took her hand.

Once he had kissed her—but he was not going to kiss her now, and he wondered if he ever would again. They both knew that the djinn might appear at any moment, and might be near, invisibly, at any time, and watching them. That was bad enough. Infinitely worse for Chance was the fact that he could all too easily imagine the great demon looking on as well.

Next morning, inside the moving wagon, with a trooper driving and Chance looking on, Abby tried again with the toy carpenter's tools, and this time had success. When Zalmoxis appeared, and appeared startled to discover that Jervase and Horkos were present, she warned him immediately that he could no longer refuse to meet the other members of the expedition.

The djinn muttered something to the effect that it had only been the Servants and their leader that he had been trying to avoid.

"You cannot avoid all of Ardneh's Servants, for I am one of them," Abby proudly proclaimed. "Whether you like us or not, there are some answers that we need. The directions for travel you have given us are taking us through the middle of these cursed hills, where there seem to be no roads. Getting the wagons through some of the tight spots is very difficult. We're lucky we haven't broken an axle yet."

"Ah yes, the wagons." Grandmother's voice turned condescending, as befitted one who lived above the plane of such mundane, material things. "I have been meaning to discuss that point. It will soon become necessary to abandon them, and your animals as well."

"Abandon them?" Jervase was immediately upset; he had been looking forward to being able to cart home whole wagonloads of books, maps, and Old World instruments. "Why, in the name of all nameless demons?"

Zalmoxis was nodding to himself, in a way that reminded Chance forcibly of another apparition who had nodded too. The djinn said: "I may as well reveal to you now the fact that you will soon be required to spend some time beneath the surface of the earth."

The humans exchanged stunned looks. Chance demanded: "What do you mean, 'some time'?"

Zalmoxis considered. "You will almost certainly be underground for many hours. Perhaps for days."

"I thought—"

"I am trying to explain that our search will not end at the moment you use the Key. The Workshop is as large as a small city. When we enter, the object we are seeking may not be immediately apparent. There will be plenty of water available underground, but you must carry with you several days' supply of food, as well as weapons."

Captain Horkos, for once forgetting himself in the young lady's presence, remarked on the various body parts of Ardneh. "Underground . . . I don't like this. What about lighting?"

"Certain areas within the Workshop will be illuminated, though it would be unwise to depend on that entirely. Whatever is not essential from the contents of your wagons will have to be abandoned, along with your animals—with the exception of the owl, whose natural talents you may find invaluable."

Chance burst in: "You've been telling us you know exactly where the treasure is! Now you say that we must search!"

Zalmoxis made soothing gestures, as an adult dealing with fretful children. "What I have told you is that I will guide you precisely to the Workshop's door. Of that location there is no doubt. The Sword of Ardneh is somewhere inside, and once we are in, we will inevitably find it. But, as I have said, the interior is large. Exactly how long the search will take is impossible to predict."

"But . . . abandoning the wagons! To have to leave my collection behind, my library unguarded . . ." Jervase displayed disgust. "You might have let us know about this days ago. We could have made some other provision for the wagons."

AS FAR AS CHANCE COULD REMEMBER, ARDNEH'S KEY HAD REMAINED out of sight as long as Draffut was near. When the distance between Chance and the Beastlord grew great enough, Ardneh's gift was back again where Chance could see it, hanging on its chain around his neck. He took the Key's reappearance to mean that Draffut was no longer near enough to be of any help in case of emergency.

CAPTAIN HORKOS URGED ON HIS TROOPERS, SOME OF WHOM WERE RE- luctant to penetrate this unearthly landscape any farther, especially with demons in the air like vultures—this looked like it might be the monsters' very homeland. The men were beginning to wonder if, deprived of Draffut's mighty protection, they were all going to wind up as food for Avenarius and his associates.

Were they being led into some bandit's trap? To Chance, the air-borne reptiles seemed slightly closer each time he looked up at them. Sometimes he could see three of them instead of only one or two.

From the way that the captain talked about their goal, it was obvious that his martial imagination was beginning to be stirred by the idea of Ardneh's Sword. To him that name suggested the world's most powerful weapon; and, whatever the details proved to be, his mind filled with thoughts of what a good military man would be able to do with such a marvel in his hands.

Of course, he would still be loyal to the monarch of Sarasvati, and the government he served. Of course.

Chance had little doubt of what was going through the captain's mind. He could only hope that all of the troopers still with them would be so loyal.

THE NEXT TIME CHANCE SAW THE DJINN, HE TOOK NOTE OF THE neatness of Grandmother's fiery hair, the fineness of the networked wrinkles on her face, and could not resist an attempt to probe. "You are getting better and better at imitations, Zalmoxis."

"Thank you, oh percipient young master." The djinn spread his hands gracefully. "I assume that your remark was intended as a compliment."

"Oh, it was, indeed. How difficult would it be to imitate a demon?"

The djinn's busy hands halted in mid-gesture, and he looked perplexed. At last he answered: "Whyever should I want to do that?"

"Possibly if you wanted to scare people?"

From the corner of his eye, Chance could see that Abby had turned her head and was giving him a slightly puzzled look. He kept his own gaze closely on the djinn.

Zalmoxis struck a pose, as if posing for a statue of Thought, eyes gazing skyward, one forefinger propped against his brow. Holding the pose did not stop him from slowly beginning to nod again. "Mmm-hmm . . . yes, a good demon-imitation should certainly have that effect. Perhaps, young master, you are suggesting that, should we suffer a recrudescence of bandits, I could frighten them away. The trouble is that any such effort might set me back in my progress toward becoming human—and I do not choose to accept that risk."

TWENTY-SEVEN

A N HOUR AFTER SUNSET ON THE FOLLOWING DAY, A RAGGED cheer went up from the Sarasvati camp, as Mitra came plunging out of a fading sunset sky to land atop her wagon, as she had so many times before. Draffut had kept his promise to send back the bird.

The cheering quickly stopped; the bird arrived noisily, squawking her outrage, complaining at having been attacked when she was almost home. As the Scholar came hurrying up, Mitra stretched out her right wing to display a slight injury. Chance, arriving with a torch, saw to his relief that the damage amounted to very little more than a couple of feathers knocked loose, along with a few drops of blood.

A small group of humans was swiftly gathering round the owl. "Where are the bandits?" several of them wanted to know. Were the Servants being attacked?

A trooper had shaded the bird's eyes against firelight. With hootings, and gestures of her good wing, she conveyed that the Servants were all safe with Draffut. When she left them they had been making camp some twenty kilometers away, after a day's good progress toward the oasis. As for Gokard and his people, they were also far away, too far away to worry about tonight. But the immediate problem was near at hand.

"Then who shot you?" Jervase demanded.

Mitra's answer to that question was a little more difficult to understand. "Two-o-o—two-o-o hu-umans. O-only eggs and a little mo-ore!"

"Two—*eggs*?" Jervase was scowling as if he smelled a bad one. "What—?"

Chance, who during the last month had spent more time than anyone else trying to converse with Mitra, did his best to interpret. "I think she means that whoever took a shot at her was very young. A child, perhaps."

Moments later, Jervase, steaming with indignation, was climbing into the saddle of his ridingbeast. A minute after that, he was leading out a small scouting party, consisting of Chance and a couple of troopers. The owl, more shocked and outraged than disabled by her wound, went fluttering with them as guide. Abby called after them, saying she would soon follow.

When Chance's hand went routinely up to his throat, checking for the presence of the Key, he discovered to his surprise that it was gone again. Riding into darkness to look for an armed unknown, he found it comforting to have some indication that he was in no particular danger.

SOON THE OWL WAS FLYING IN A TIGHT CIRCLE OVER ONE SPOT, marking for the hunters a small thicket from which, she claimed, the offending arrow had come darting up. The party surrounded the clump of bushes, and a moment later Chance saw a ridingbeast, saddled but riderless, burst out of cover at a frightened gallop. There was hardly room remaining for any menacing force of bandits, and Jervase advanced with drawn sword, shouting and threatening. The bushes quickly emptied, producing two frightened children, barefoot and clad in nothing but shabby adult-size shirts, tails almost long enough to drag on the ground.

Chance, urging his mount forward, caught his breath at the torchlit sight of two heads thick with reddish hair . . . but even in that moment of minor shock he noted that this was not the shocking red worn by the djinn's imitations of humanity. These children were not Zalmo and Moxis.

But it took him a moment to be sure of that; the resemblance in both cases was too striking for sheer coincidence. The smaller child was a girl of six or seven, a close match for Zalmo in age and general appearance. He who was evidently her brother, a boy of about twelve, closely approximated Moxis. Chance, sliding quickly from his saddle, seized him by the sleeve of his oversized shirt, and beckoned a trooper to come closer with a torch. The visual resemblance held up at close range, but this lad had the look and feel and smell of genuine unwashed humanity. As he came out of concealment, the Moxis-model had thrown down a businesslike bow of the same type the bandits used, and a half-filled quiver of arrows.

Moments later, with a trooper grabbing the boy's other arm, and Jervase barking questions, the captive admitted, in a piping voice that Chance thought he had heard before, having used the bow to try to bring down a bird for food.

". . . an' it scared me, scared me like demons, when the bird started talking back some words at us!"

The girl had darted to her brother's side, where she clung weeping and saying nothing helpful. Both children were obviously terrified.

Jervase, with a disgusted gesture, ordered the troopers to let go of them and step back. Then he squatted down and began to ask questions in a calm, quiet voice. "Who are you? What are you doing here?"

"Please!" The little girl squeaked. "The bandits had us."

"Yes," her brother agreed. "The man called Gokard."

Jervase straightened up and offered food, which was greedily accepted. While the children chewed on dried meat he continued his calm questioning. Soon talking freely, the youngsters said that their names were Jemmy and Cress, and their parents were long dead.

Cress and Jemmy had been taken by the bandits a long time ago—how long they could no longer even guess—from a caravan in which they had been traveling with an aunt and uncle. The man named Gokard had immediately marked them for use as virgin sacrifices, and had made sure they understood they were going to be ritually slain as soon as he decided the proper moment arrived for him to summon up his great lord demon. Jemmy and Cress had seen signs that two other children, whose names they did not know, had been killed in the same way a few days ago.

"How did you get away?"

Before that question could be answered, Abigail had arrived on the scene and was briskly taking over. In a moment she had put aside her magician's demeanor to become motherly and comforting. Stroking Cress's grimy hair, she assured the little girl: "We're not bandits, Gokard and his scum are our enemies too. No one's going to hurt you now!"

AS THEY WERE PROCEEDING BACK TO CAMP, CHANCE MADE SURE THAT Abby understood the strong resemblance between these red-haired youngsters and the first two images shown him by the djinn.

Of course Zalmoxis had not bothered to mention the existence of any living models for his imitations. When Chance told Abigail, she was furious with the djinn, and wished aloud that she knew how to inflict painful punishments at a distance.

"So, he must have been using these two for models." Abby's maternal instincts, and her training as a healing Servant, were in full sway. "All the while letting them . . . letting them remain as the prisoners of demon-worshipers, waiting to be killed."

She heaved a giant sigh, and made a gesture of helplessness. "Now what are we to do? Feed them, obviously. Even your Scholar knew that much. Then find them some clothes. But that may be difficult, all our spare things have gone off with mother."

ONCE THE CHILDREN WERE ESTABLISHED IN THE RELATIVE SAFETY OF the nightly camp, and had been fed more systematically, Abby began to ask them if they knew anything of a djinn. They only stared at her blankly, with apparently no idea of what she was talking about.

Questioning brought out that Cress and Jemmy had not been physically mistreated by the bandits—apart from being locked into a cage during almost the whole period of their captivity. They had been given adequate food and water—the bad people had seemed to think it important that their bodies be kept fresh and undamaged. But some of the bandits had enjoyed describing to them how horribly they were going to die.

For a moment or two, when the enormous furry monster who walked on two legs came rampaging through the bandit camp, they had been sure that the demon was coming for them as promised. But instead, the bandits had all run away. Loadbeasts running in blind panic had tipped over the metal cage, knocking one side of it loose, creating a gap large enough for the children to manage to squeeze out.

None of the evil men and women were paying them any attention, only running crazily about in an effort to save themselves. Jemmy and Cress had hidden under a wrecked tent until most of the noise had died away. Then they had crept out of concealment and fled the deserted camp, delaying only long enough to grab up such items of food and clothing as came immediately to hand. Jemmy had also picked up a bow and arrows that some terrified bandit had dropped in his flight—long ago, someone, somewhere, had taught the boy something of archery.

Once out of sight of the camp, the pair had started following the river, with a vague idea that it might lead them into familiar territory. About a day later they had come upon a saddled ridingbeast, obviously one of the animals that had stampeded out of the bandit camp. The beast had calmed down by then and was ready to be caught. Since then brother and sister had been riding it, consuming the food and water they found in its saddlebags, and doing their best to stay out of the way of bandits and demons.

When they came upon the trail left by Jervase's party they had begun to follow it, in hopes that it would lead them somewhere. They no longer had a home to try to reach. The water their mount had been carrying was quickly used up. They had come to the stream shortly after sunset, to get a drink, when the great bird flew overhead. The boy had thought it might be good to eat. The recital faltered to a halt.

Abby, as she listened to the story, was already whittling at a spare pair of sandals, trying to make them small enough for Cress to wear. From time to time Jervase and Horkos shot unhappy glances toward the children; it seemed that they possessed no useful information. Still, there was nothing to do but bring them along.

CHANCE, IN HIS DREAM-WANDERINGS THAT NIGHT, FOUND HIMSELF standing at the foot of a cliff, gazing in wonder, through a glowing mist of bright dream-moonlight, at a huge door that was just starting to open in the base of the sheer rock wall before him. The panels of the door were marked in concentric circles, like some giant archers' target.

He had just started to move forward—what else to do with a door, but open it?—when he realized that a half-familiar figure was waiting for him just beside the portal. It was the demon, in his Miyamoto-form again, leaning there with folded arms.

"But," objected Chance, in the ghostly whisper that was the best he could manage at the moment. "But I am dreaming."

"Is it so strange to dream of real things?" Avenarius asked him smoothly. "It has become extremely urgent that I speak to you alone, and this method was easiest to arrange."

"What—what is it, then?" Chance could feel the stirring in his belly of the sickness of great fear.

If only it could be something like simple poisoning . . . but he was afraid that it could not. *Ardneh defend me*, he thought to himself. Something he had picked up from Abigail.

He turned around slowly to behold the figure of Avenarius, in the almost-familiar form of Miyamoto, nodding, nodding.

The demon allowed a long moment to pass before he smiled and said: "I have not come to punish you . . . not yet."

"Then . . . what? . . ."

The face before him was not quite Miyamoto's, not any longer. It might have belonged to one of the teacher's relatives—if any of his relatives were mass murderers. It said: "You have already disobeyed me once. This one time, this one time only, I will not punish your disloyalty. The great beast gave you no help at all, did he, when you told him about me?"

"No." Chance could barely hear his own whisper.

"Learn from that fact. Would it help to stiffen your resolve if I were to describe in detail what will happen to dear Abigail's young body— and to yours—if you should be foolish enough to betray me?"

"No."

"Well said! Why should you even have to listen to such things? No doubt you are wise to decline the experience . . . it might keep you from getting any sleep at all."

The demon glided a little closer. "But at least you should do this much. Mmm-hmm. Let your imagination do its worst—its very worst—in conceiving what your torments and hers would be. Then consider how much stronger, how vastly more experienced, my imagination is than yours. . . ."

Chance had never had a dream go this bad without being granted the relief of waking up. But then the horror eased. It was as if Avenarius realized that his tool was in danger of going mad and might be of no use in that broken condition.

"You see, my little lordling, if I could devise some plan that would allow me to avoid entering the Workshop altogether, I would adopt that method—but I doubt that will be possible.

"It will be necessary to rely upon you—and I am sure you will be my faithful servant."

And nightmare faded into a welcome oblivion. . . .

IN THE MORNING, WHEN ABBY HAD RECEIVED FRESH DIRECTIONS FROM the djinn, the party moved on. It was another day of slow and difficult progress. At sunset Jervase tried to dispatch the bird with messages for Draffut, but Mitra only circled, and almost immediately came back to land on the wagon, complaining that her wing was too sore for such a lengthy flight.

Benambra seemed interested in the owl. After trying to talk to her, with limited success, he wondered thoughtfully just how much people would be willing to pay for that kind of oracle. Regretfully, he concluded that it would probably not be much.

Abby stared at the novice Servant with wide eyes. "But she is not for sale."

"Oh. No, of course not."

ZALMOXIS TOLD ABBY AND CHANCE THAT THEY WERE NOW VERY NEAR the place where they must go underground. One more day should do it.

TWENTY-EIGHT

J ERVASE WAS NOT PLEASED TO HAVE HIS EXPEDITION BURDENED
by two useless refugees, whose presence seriously distracted his
only skilled magician from her essential work. "Still, as a civilized
man, I feel an obligation to help them if I can."

"Of course you do," said Abby decisively. She was still wearing
boots that had been liberated from a fallen bandit, and had passed
along to Jemmy her only spare footwear, a pair of sandals that fit the
boy well enough. The tentmaker soldier had offered to contrive
shoes for both children as soon as he had time, but as long as they
were in a wagon or astride an animal most of the time, this was not
a vital necessity. The weather had warmed enough so that the outsize
shirts they were wearing served well enough for the time being.

Ongoing instructions from the djinn kept the treasure hunters
essentially following the narrow, winding canyon of the Rivanna
somewhat deeper here than where Chance had first encountered the
djinn's images. At irregular intervals lesser ravines and gullies, many
of them completely dry, came twisting in to join it. Their course was
leading them deeper into a seemingly interminable wilderness of
small hills and broken rocks.

———

FACED WITH THE PROMISED NECESSITY OF GOING UNDERGROUND, Horkos and Jervase pondered the option of leaving the wagons and draft animals on the surface of the earth, maybe under the guard of one or two men, taking a chance on being able to reclaim them after finding the treasure. There was some suggestion of leaving the children, too.

Abigail was outraged. "Really? Where the bandits will be sure to find them?"

But the idea of leaving anyone behind was soon abandoned. The captain was decisive. "It would mean dividing our party, which is awkwardly small to begin with. Besides, when the bandits track the wagons down, as they can hardly fail to do, a couple men guarding them would do no good."

Jervase was nodding. "Not only that, Gokard will be sure that we have gone underground, somewhere nearby. But what else can we do?"

And Chance put in: "The djinn had no helpful advice to offer. We certainly can't count on him to do more than he has promised."

Abby said sadly: "I have serious doubts that we can even count on him for that."

Taking an inventory of the remaining supplies of food, the leaders calculated the number of days for which the amount available would support the party. Marshaling names and numbers in his head, Chance arrived at a total of twenty-three people.

When sunset came round again, Mitra still complained of pain in her injured wing, and continued to refuse any lengthy missions. There was no way to compel obedience.

"We can hope she'll feel better tomorrow," Jervase mused. And even were Mitra healthy, she might well be unable to catch up with the Beastlord, once he had passed Cascadia Oasis and began traveling at something like full speed.

ONE OF THE CAPTAIN'S SCOUTS, WHO HAD BEEN RANGING TO THE rear, caught up to report that the bandit leader and the sturdy remnant of his followers, perhaps fifty humans, were still on their trail. Gokard, depending on his own scouts in the form of flying reptiles, seemed content to follow the expedition at a distance of four or five kilometers, making no effort to catch up. The bandits' modest baggage train, consisting of three or four wagons, was following at a somewhat greater distance.

"I'd say there must be at least forty people in his main force, sir, men and women, about half of them mounted. From what we've seen of their women so far, they're no shrinking flowers that will fold up their petals at a touch."

"All still well-armed, I take it."

"Yes sir. And many of 'em are good friends with demons—or think they are. Almost every time they stop they put up another of their little altars."

Abigail asked: "Are they planning more sacrifice? Have they any prisoners?"

The bearded scout looked at her. "Not that I could tell, ma'am. Might be some in the baggage wagons."

"What about demons?"

"Couldn't see any, ma'am. Doesn't mean they're not around."

Jemmy and Cress looked frightened.

ZALMOXIS, AT HIS NEXT APPEARANCE, SAID THAT THE BANDITS' LEADER had threatened his followers with punishment by the Great Demon should they ever desert his ranks.

"But still they turned and ran," said Abigail, "when the Lord Draffut walked among them."

The djinn displayed a tiny smile. "Yes, they did. But at that point, they had not yet seen Avenarius—and possibly they now have. I think they are unlikely to turn and run again."

Jervase put in: "Whatever the reason for their persistence, we must accept it as a fact. By this time Gokard will certainly have noted that the Beastlord's trail and ours diverge. He knows we no longer have Draffut's protection—so, what's the son of a demon waiting for? Why doesn't he come after us?"

Abigail said: "The answer to that is plain enough. He will be waiting for us to find his goal for him, and for the Key in Lord Chance's hand to work its magic. The moment, the very moment, that the door of the Workshop opens—that is when Gokard will try to pounce on us, with all the force that he can gather."

"I suppose you're right. I suppose that all we can do is—be ready."

Chance was thinking to himself: *If only I could believe that human bandits will be the only ones who pounce. . . .*

Jervase and Chance were generally in the lead, often walking or riding side by side, as their party continued to advance following the next morning's clues. The landscape around them was getting even stranger—Chance took that as a hopeful sign.

Even Jervase, whose attention was almost always focused elsewhere, noticed that Chance did not look well.

Abby and Chance went apart from the others to hold their nightly communication with the djinn. Abby scolded Chance for becoming absent-minded. "You must pull yourself together!"

"Yes, I know I must." He was having a hard time directing his thoughts to anything except his most powerful and dangerous enemy, the chief object of the tech-djinn's terror, the great Bad Demon, Avenarius.

Chance, in his private thought, kept reminding himself of another fact, this one solidly in the waking world, that gave him reason for optimism: He had never seen Avenarius and Zalmoxis at the same time. He also reminded himself repeatedly that the High Lord Draffut carried the wisdom of ages inside his huge, shaggy head—therefore Draffut's suggestion that Chance might have seen only the djinn pretending to be the demon—perhaps the djinn driven mad by trying to be something he was not—that was almost certainly the case.

ZALMOXIS APPEARING AGAIN, CHANCE SAID TO HIM: "I HAVE SEEN your models for Zalmo and Moxis. Their names are Jemmy and Cress."

Zalmoxis seemed totally unconcerned. "Oh yes, the two who were to have served as fragrant, juicy sacrifice." He paused, reflecting. "Does it surprise you that I used human models for my experimental forms? Is that the point you are trying to make? I had thought that you probably understood as much. Is there some objection?"

Chance accused: "It's not that you used them as models. It's that you didn't even try to set them free."

Abby nodded fiercely.

The djinn blinked at them blankly, looking from one to the other without comprehension. Grandmother's expression indicated: *What did you expect of me, young crazy humans? What are you fussing about now?*

Finally Zalmoxis said: "How would my freeing them have helped you? Can you not see that their presence in your camp may irritate, unnecessarily, a certain powerful enemy who so far has not attacked you?"

"If you don't understand . . . never mind." The young lord pressed on. "I suppose Grandmother is also a near-duplicate of someone?"

Zalmoxis shook his finely modeled head. "No. No single fleshly counterpart exists for the image you see before you now. This is rather a—what should one say?—a composite. An extrapolation. Drawn from many. Many—shall I say glorious?—specimens of humanity."

" 'Glorious'?"

The tech-djinn was suddenly wistful. "But you all are glorious, don't you see? No, I don't suppose you do. The more humans I encounter, the greater does my passion grow.

"But enough of that. I have given you directions. Why do you not push on?" Then, teasing: "Is it possible you do not realize how close you are to Ardneh's Workshop? I have just given you the last directions you will ever need. Tomorrow should find us at the Door!"

Jervase sprang into action.

TWENTY-NINE

THIS TIME THE DJINN'S DIRECTIONS HAD BEEN PRECISE AND FINAL. He said that the door to the Workshop was embedded in the side of a small hill—the land had shifted in recent years, and exactly where in the hillside it could now be found would be up to them to discover.

The place, when they reached it, looked very much like a thousand others the party had passed during the past few days. Most of the visible surface of the land consisted of massive slabs of rock, many tilted crazily, leaning against one another in such a way as to create the appearance of myriad doorways in between. It was the boy, Jemmy, scampering about with more energy than anyone else could muster, who located the exact spot: Inside one triangular gap between slabs, a designed passageway began to go twisting narrowly down a smooth decline.

A few heartbeats later, the rushing vanguard of their party, Chance and his close companions, discovered the entrance itself, several meters beneath the hill, where the passage widened at its end into a smooth-walled anteroom. The door ahead of them was massively designed and formed in two side-by-side panels, half again as tall as a man, and proportionately broad. Its wide surface was marked with concentric rings like some target designed for giant archers—not an exact duplicate but a close analogue of something he had seen in his most recent dream.

Abigail close on Chance's right side, and the Scholar on his left, the three of them advanced into the space formed by a broadening of the passage to stand within reach of the door. The air around them immediately began to glow with gentle light, coming from no detectable source.

Close behind Chance were several soldiers, one of them carrying the hooded form of Mitra on his padded shoulder. Jemmy, the discoverer of the passage, was very near as well, his sister tagging at his heels, with Benambra towering over both of them.

A few strides farther to the rear, Horkos was barking out quick orders, telling some of his troopers to unload necessities from the wagons, then drive the vehicles away, scatter them at half a kilometer's distance or more. He also posted a guard just inside the surface entrance.

CHANCE TURNED HIS ATTENTION FORWARD.

At the center of the massive door's concentric rings, bisected by the vertical division between two panels, was the bull's-eye of the painted target, its shape symbolic of an ordinary keyhole.

Jervase's voice on his left was so low that Chance could hardly hear it, but extremely tense. "Let us not waste any time. We may not have any to spare."

Oddly, it had not occurred to Chance until this moment that to actually use the Key he might have to lift its short chain off his neck. But when he took the artifact of Ardneh in his hand, the chain that had been solid metal felt ready to stretch out easily, like springy thread. The young lord had no difficulty holding the Key out at arm's length, applying it directly to the painted keyhole at the center of the door.

Abby and Jervase were still pressing close on either side, as if they half expected him to disappear in a puff of magic smoke—not the worst thing Chance could imagine happening at that moment. In the instant before the Key could touch its goal, Chance almost let it fall. He had suddenly become aware of a new presence materializing in the confined space, a figure leaning over Abby's shoulder . . . a moment later he groaned inwardly with relief when he saw that this was only the djinn.

"I see that you are all ready." Grandmother's voice was low and tense and hurried. Her wizened, well-modeled face shot looks to right and left. "This glorious moment should belong to you alone, Lord Chance—to you and of course to these, your faithful human followers. Therefore I leave it to you. I advise you to enter the Workshop quickly, before anything happens to . . . quickly, I say!"

Abby had turned to the djinn, opening her mouth to give him some command. But before she could utter a word the djinn had disappeared.

He's run away, thought Chance. Enormously grateful that the figure he truly dreaded had not appeared, he continued the interrupted motion of his arm, pressing the Key forward against the door with something close to violence.

For a moment it seemed to him that nothing had changed. Then many things happened in rapid succession.

The target design had disappeared from the great door's towering panels, that now seemed to be of smooth and solid bronze. To right and left they went swinging majestically back, opening into a broad gray haze that at first glance seemed to be neither night nor day. The space in front of Chance was spotted with a chaotic distribution of multiple smaller doorways—or might they be large windows?—in a dark hazy wall.

In another moment the bronze panels, the entire door, had disappeared entirely. What had seemed a simple, if rather large, doorway was somehow unraveling at its edges, becoming a broad opening that went on lengthening into the distance on both right and left, exposing little on either side but more haze, more shadows, quirky lights, and additional openings. The opening of the door had been more like the destruction of a wall. The entire space beneath the hill seemed to be changing into—something else.

Abby was clutching Chance's right arm and calling on the name of Ardneh. On his left, Jervase was muttering something about the Gate of Horn, through which true dreams enter the world. Chance, facing steadily forward, saw ahead of him an immediate choice of doorways, labyrinthine branches all susceptible of exploration. Opening upon opening, to right and left and straight ahead.

Abby was wondering in a lost voice: "How are we supposed to know which way—?"

It seemed that the Key was going to be of no help in making that decision. Chance allowed it to fall back on its chain, to once more rest inertly on his chest.

THE BARRIER AT THE WORKSHOP'S ENTRANCE HAD NOT ONLY BEEN opened but totally abolished. No longer was there any barrier at all, no longer any obstacle to human beings, animals, or demons entering. The artificial glow had faded, and daylight came filtering more brightly down into the anteroom, as if the small space had suddenly gained a hundred more entrances from the sunlit surface of the earth above.

While Chance hesitated about which way to move forward, Jervase, quickly conferring with Captain Horkos, decided that there would be little use trying to post a guard to keep the bandits, or anyone else, from following them in. "Have the men all follow us. There appear to be multiple passageways, but for the time being we should all stay together."

The djinn had rematerialized, and seemed upset as he peered over Chance's shoulder at what the opening of the door had revealed. As before, he muttered that things had been drastically rearranged since his last visit.

Jervase challenged him: "Which way do we go, Zalmoxis? Which way to Ardneh's Sword?"

Gazing at the chaotic assortment of misty, irregular doorways, the djinn admitted he did not know which would lead them most quickly to their goal. "But I will recognize the Sword of Ardneh when I see it."

"That's great," Chance muttered. "But where is it?"

"Chance." Abigail was prodding him. "It seems that you must choose."

He was already moving. Seeing no reason to turn to right or left, he followed the path of greatest convenience and moved straight ahead. The others crowded after him, into a passage where they must go single file. The haze seemed to clear in their immediate vicinity as they moved into it, but there were increasing shadows, odd lights radiating from nowhere in particular, and everywhere strange objects, unfamiliar shapes.

Glancing back before he had advanced more than a few steps, Chance took note of the soldiers and the owl, of two small red-headed figures in ill-fitting shirts, determinedly following. Benambra was also staying close, and Zalmoxis closest of all—he could fit his immaterial image-presence into any sliver of space available.

THEY WERE INDEED ENTERING A DIFFERENT WORLD, ONE WITH NOTHing natural about it. Chance moved warily forward, the others staying close behind him, as the passage they were following widened into a buried room with gray smooth walls and flat ceiling panels from which cold light still flowed tirelessly, as if in some eternal glow that might not have ceased since Ardneh's day. The light fell uselessly on masses of ancient machinery, giving the impression the hardware was decayed beyond all usefulness. Here and there some little, mouse-sized life form went skittering away.

After traversing several more rooms full of cold light and ruined machinery, Chance, in the lead, found himself confronted by deep darkness, through which he would have to grope his way. It was time to get some torches lighted, and in a few moments a soldier had passed one forward.

Grandmother, as if grudgingly, produced her Old World light, but retained it for her own use as she, for the first time, moved ahead to scout.

THEY HAD GONE LESS THAN A HUNDRED METERS, WHEN THEY ARRIVED at a grand intersection that seemed to Chance a good place to pause. Here no fewer than six passages debouched into a common room, where good light glowed from panels in the smooth floor and ceiling. Zalmoxis murmured something and went flitting on ahead, testing one branch after another.

Abigail promptly took advantage of the stop to remove several small objects from her pack and spread them on the floor. She was muttering over them—she said she was trying to use some magic to help them find where they should go, but not having much success.

Chance said: "We can hope that the djinn will be back in a minute. He should make a better scout than anyone else—except perhaps Mitra, if the passageways were big enough to let her fly."

Jervase was pacing back and forth, staring down each darkened passageway in turn. "Better? Better? He would be excellent, superb, incomparable—were he not absolutely useless. What good is a scout who conceals his own secrets, whose reports cannot be trusted?"

Benambra added: "Also he tends to be—or pretends to be—paralyzed by terror just when he is most needed."

Zalmoxis was suddenly back, pointing to the opening beside him.

"This way, if you will, my friends. In another fifty meters we will come to a large room—do not allow yourselves to be dismayed by what you see therein. Interpreted correctly, it is actually encouraging." And the djinn bowed himself aside, gesturing for Chance to once more lead the way.

A score or so of paces later, rounding a corner into the largest room they had yet discovered, Chance was confronted, in the sudden glare of the djinn's Old World light, by the horrific face of some kind of frozen monster, caught in the immense thickness of a crystalline wall.

Jervase muttered that he had seen insects trapped, in just such a way, in amber.

The thing embedded in the half-transparent segment of wall was all fangs and claws and jagged crests, armed with a poisonous-looking tail. Certainly no insect, though it shared some of the features of that unbreathing race. It was bigger than a loadbeast, but its size was the least important thing about it.

"It is a demon," Abigail pronounced with certainty.

"What else could it be . . . looking like that?" some trooper muttered.

"It is caught in one of Ardneh's traps," the djinn explained.

Zalmoxis explained to them that there were other demon-traps about. "I must be wary of falling into them myself. No two are quite alike, I think."

Chance wondered privately how much Avenarius knew about demon traps. It was doubtless too much to hope for that he could find some way to maneuver the Bad Demon into one of them. . . .

There still burned steadily in Chance's memory the pledge of Avenarius to be at his side at the moment of his entering the Workshop—but since they passed the doorway he had seen no demon. There had been only his usual group of human companions.

And of course Zalmoxis, coming and going with his usual blend of urgency and anxiety.

The other members of the party came crowding in behind him—this room was big enough to hold them all—to stand shocked into silence at the sight of what a demon-trap had caught.

After a moment or two of horror, Jervase was able to regard the frozen monster with the same cool analytic gaze with which he studied everything.

"All I want to know is, is there any chance of the thing getting out?"

Scowling at the thing that seemed to be frozen in clear ice, the gray-haired private Vardtrad muttered: "Look at that face—if you can call it that. A demon appealing for sympathy, by Ardneh's eyebrows! What can possibly happen next?"

Abigail, though she was getting used to hearing soldiers' talk, winced slightly at the blasphemy.

Zalmoxis, looking about him nervously, felt called upon to give an explanation. "Its life is probably hidden elsewhere, so Ardneh's snare could not destroy it. Perhaps it would not move even if it were able, for it is caught up in a dream."

"How long will the dream last?" Abigail breathed in wonder. Jemmy and Cress were behind her, their backs pressed against a wall, putting as much distance as they could between themselves and the frozen thing.

Zalmoxis signed his ignorance. "How long will the sun shine, and the moon? This is one reason why a certain being, our chief enemy, is reluctant to enter the domain of Ardneh."

ZALMOXIS HAD MOVED ON, SCOUTING AHEAD. THE PEOPLE HE WAS guiding had all slumped down, resting, with their backs against one wall or another, when a loud inhuman voice suddenly spoke in a strange accent. It took a moment to be sure that the words were issuing from the slab of crystal that held the demon in stasis.

It was a voice like none other that Chance had ever heard before, and it said simply: "You are humans."

Everyone was on their feet again, startled out of weariness. A swift murmur of alarm rippled around the group. Zalmoxis was back on the scene, so swiftly that Chance wondered how far away he could have been. The djinn gave them all a look of reassurance, saying: "It is the trap and not the demon that speaks to you; it will be safe to answer."

Jervase was whispering in awe. "It is *alive*?"

"Servants of Ardneh who derived their vitality from the Lake of Life do not die easily. Answer, some of you who claim the name of human."

It was true that the demon showed no signs of having moved; its great green eyes still stared at nothing. Chance had just opened his mouth to say something when Jervase beat him to it. "We are human, yes."

Now Chance could see in the depths of the crystal slab a faint ripple of movement; a subtle thing suggesting vibration in a clear jelly. Nothing that looked strong enough to hold the monster it had engulfed—but there the monster was.

Words came again, matching the faint movements of the deep ripple. "What has happened to Ardneh?" the demon-trap wanted to know.

Jervase answered: "Ardneh is dead—but there are still demons in the world."

And Chance put in: "A bad one may be pursuing us."

The crystal rippled again. "It is my task only to hold the one I hold. I can be of no help to you against another. But in the Workshop you may find other machines that can."

"Where will we find them?" Captain Horkos demanded.

"I do not know."

"Which way to Ardneh's Sword?"

"I do not have that information."

The humans were on the point of moving on, when the voice from the wall spoke once more, asking them where Draffut was.

This time it was Abby who replied. "The High Lord is many kilometers away."

"But still living? That is good. I wish the Beastlord might come back."

"We certainly wish that too."

There seemed to be no more to say. The people and the djinn moved on.

THE CHAMBER OF THE FROZEN DEMON WAS NOW BEHIND THEM, AND the djinn still leading them forward by fits and starts. Benambra moved forward as eagerly as anyone, his body taut with controlled excitement. The two children continued to tag along, beginning to be more excited than frightened by the wonders around them. At first they stayed near their rescuers, but seemed to enjoy being in this new environment.

Horkos, looking uneasy, caught up with Jervase to report that he had brought all of his troopers down into the underground, with orders to a couple of them to lag a bit behind. They were to bring reports on how quickly the bandits managed to pick up their trail underground—the captain did not doubt that Gokard's people would do so somehow—and how closely they would be following.

PEOPLE WERE BEGINNING TO WONDER, ALOUD, HOW FAR THEY HAD been walking underground. Certainly by now the distance would be measured in kilometers. In certain tunnels and chambers of the sprawling complex, the Old World lighting was comfortably bright, while in other places obscurity was the rule.

Here too, as so often on the surface portion of their journey, the sound of rushing water was frequently nearby, sometimes rising to a roar and filling the nearby air with mist, though the stream itself was rarely visible. Chance could only assume that the familiar Rivanna, in which Zalmo had caught fish, and Moxis built his waterwheel, had somehow followed them beneath the surface of the earth.

"But I can't be sure," Chance complained to Jervase. "Take it out of its natural banks, and one small river looks a lot like another."

"Which way do we go now?" Abby asked him.

"I don't know."

WHEN THEY PAUSED FOR A REST IN ALMOST PERFECT DARKNESS, JER-vase said it was one of the things he ceaselessly wondered about: how does an Old World lamp, certified by magicians to be devoid of what was usually called magic, keep shining, year after year, century after century, without ever exhausting its source of power? Trying to open such a lamp for examination only destroyed it—perhaps violently.

Zalmoxis, the tech-djinn, gradually growing more nervous as they proceeded, still looking over his shoulder as if he expected something unpleasant to descend upon him, remembered his own efforts to investigate that question. "One answer I came upon was that the lamp simply keeps on emitting the same light, over and over."

Chance thought about it—or at least tried to think about it. "But that doesn't make any sense."

"Perhaps the world is not required to make sense." The djinn did not seem keenly interested in the question.

The Scholar rejected that idea. The answer seemed finally to convince him that the djinn was never going to be a great source of knowledge about technology.

"Nuggets of truth are there, no doubt, in what he tells us, and what he could tell us; but rare, and difficult if not impossible to find in the rubble of confusion and lies."

Abigail offered: "The stories in Scripture say that the tech-djinn was sometimes very helpful to the wizards who worked with Ardneh."

"The old stories may be right, they often are. But that was a thousand years ago." Jervase looked grimmer than ever. "Perhaps Zalmoxis has gone insane since then."

SOMEHOW BENAMBRA GAVE THE IMPRESSION OF BEING RATHER ODDLY at home down here in the deep dark, in places where an owl might be the only member of the party able to see without carrying a light. Every now and then Chance could hear the novice humming a small tune.

Benambra was jingling the few coins, presumably of his own money, that he had brought with him in pocket or pouch. He seemed a rather different man now that he had gone underground. Some of the change was no doubt due to his change of clothing; but it was more than that.

He was flipping a coin and catching it in his large, pale hand, trying heads or tails to decide which way to go. Chance noted the head of an ancient hero on the obverse of the flipped coin—he knew, from seeing others of the familiar type, that it bore a supposed image of his own illustrious ancestor.

Light flickered, somewhere, and perhaps it startled Benambra, for his small coin went astray, falling and bouncing, carrying with it the image of Rolf's face down a narrow crevice.

The loss seemed a matter of concern to the tall young novice. He stood there looking after his lost money until Abigail tugged at his sleeve.

"Come along, Benambra. There's no way to get it back."

"I suppose there isn't."

"Then come. The treasure ahead of us ought to be somewhat greater."

THIRTY

As they moved forward, Abby again took Chance by the arm. "What happened to Cress and Jemmy? It's been a while since I've seen them."

Who? What? She had to repeat the question before he could get his distracted mind to focus on it. "I don't know."

Turning his gaze back through the chamber holding the frozen demon, to the shadowed rooms and passages in the direction from which they had come, Chance could now see no sign of the children. But other intruders were coming on the scene—the age-long exclusion of humanity from Ardneh's Workshop had come to a conclusive end. At the distance and in near darkness, it was impossible to tell if these newcomers were bandits or more of the captain's troopers, or even whether all of them were human. The sound of shouting, then a scuffle with the clash of metal, left no doubt about the nature of some of them at least.

A soldier muttered: "The bandits are somehow on our trail."

Grandmother was back again, reporting, in tones of fresh anxiety, that the horde of demons who had been following them for days were now swarming more thickly than ever in the air above the Workshop's sprawling underground expanse.

The djinn added: "For the time being, I am going to remain inside the Workshop. If there is any place where demons are reluctant to intrude, it would seem that we are in it now."

Chance looked closely at his inhuman companion, trying to make out some hint that the one who wore the mask of Grandmother could put on the Miyamoto mask as well. "If demons cannot reach you here, just what are you afraid of? Not bandits, surely?"

"I fear that Avenarius may be ready to take the risk. The others will all be fearful of his gaining the treasure, dreading the increase in strength that Ardneh's Sword may afford him if he can find it and put it to use. Each of them will crave that power for himself."

"Then they know what it is."

"I doubt very much that they do."

"*You* know what it is, Zalmoxis."

"Not so, young master. It is only hope and fear that drive me forward toward our goal, not knowledge."

"Your hopes or fears must be very strong if they can hold you here in our company, Grandmother. You could flee at any time, vanish into the air like steam before a demon could get his hands on you. Right? I've never understood what treasure you hope to gain that keeps you with us in spite of all your fears."

Zalmoxis said wistfully: "It is truly not the same one that you seek."

"It is not the Sword? . . . what, then?"

"Do you still not understand?" Grandmother made one of her extravagant gestures. "What have I been telling you for days and days? Unless I live with humans, strive with them, identify myself with their cause, how can I hope to become one? The only treasure I crave is the one you poor fools already have, and do not realize you have: humanity."

The djinn soon vanished from their sight again.

Abby, who was staying close at Chance's side while he continued to move forward, murmured her awe at their surroundings.

No two chambers seemed to contain exactly the same sort of thing. There were plenty of strange objects in sight, more in every room. Some vanished as people drew near them, to reappear in the distance behind them when they had moved on again. Chance was nagged by the feeling that he could be looking directly at Ardneh's Sword and never realize the fact.

From time to time the owl let out a mournful hoot. The humans were still taking turns at carrying her, shifting the burden from one padded shoulder to another, hooding Mitra's eyes for her when lights grew bright. Now and then Mitra scouted on ahead of the glow of Old World lamp and torches, fluttering and stalking through darkness, coming back with reports that tended to be hard to understand.

"The treasures of Ardneh . . . Squawk! Whee-whooh! The treasures of Orcus!" And the great owl tilted her head, as if pondering the implications of what she had just uttered.

The humans moved on—Chance lived in quiet desperation, expecting that the real demon would appear before them at any moment.

Jervase walked most of the time with one hand on his sword's hilt, and the other holding a light—or ready to grab up his notebook, or scroll, in which he liked to record observations and events as soon as possible after observing them.

Despite all problems and dangers, Jervase looked happier than he had for days. Chance heard him musing to himself: "We are probably the first human beings ever to stand in this spot."

Benambra, close behind, had turned his head to listen to sounds of fighting. He said: "Well, we will certainly not be the last."

Unless, thought Chance, *Avenarius or some other power should wipe out that whole stampeding herd of humanity before they get this far.* That certainly seemed a possibility.

Jervase gestured toward the soldiers or bandits, figures unidentifiable in shadow, who were visible with weapons drawn in the middle distance. "Look at them. They look like the demons gathering outside. Ready to kill to gain a prize, even before they have any idea of what sort of prize the crime will gain them."

He still had a hand on his own sword.

THE WORKSHOP'S DARKNESS AND ITS PECULIAR SHAPES CONTINUED TO give its explorers an impression of immense size. There seemed to be so much space to roam about, that perhaps fighting between the human factions who had entered might not be inevitable. Chance could imagine whole groups of people searching, wandering through these rooms for hours, for days perhaps, without ever coming into contact with each other.

CHANCE NOW REALIZED THAT, FOR SEVERAL DAYS BEFORE ENTERING the workshop, he had thoughtlessly been assuming that many of his major questions would be answered, even if the demon did appear, once he had used the Key. But opening up the domain of Ardneh had only plunged him and his companions into new uncertainty. He suddenly began to doubt if there was any way for important questions ever to be answered.

Even now he could still hear, somewhere off in the distance, the damned demon-chanting of Nathan Gokard and however many bandits he had managed to bring with him. They never gave up, but went on worshiping a horror that paid them only slight attention, and that only to derive amusement from their suffering. They could be getting ready for some new sacrifice.

———

THE EXPLORING PARTY, CHANCE STILL IN THE LEAD, WERE ON A NAR-
row path, skirting a feature of their surroundings that Ardneh could
not have planned, a deep crack in the earth that was a long stride
wide and of unguessable depth. From far down in the blackness of
the crevice there echoed a distant, muted roar of falling water, the
sound accompanied by a hint of rising mist.

Abigail suddenly turned to Chance. "I've lost sight of Benambra
for a while."

"We're not sending out any search party."

"No, of course not. But the children are missing again and I
worry about them. How long since you've seen them?"

"I don't know, I don't remember. By Ardneh's blood, don't keep
nagging me!"

And Abby moved away, keeping silent.

Zalmoxis had suddenly popped out of one of the branching passages ahead, gesturing excitedly. He wanted Chance to lead his party
on a new course, away from the river. Presently the rumbling roar of
its endless fall was fading steadily toward silence as the cavern-
tunnel the explorers were following bent, and bent again, and led
them ever farther in a new direction. There was only the slow drip of
water coming from somewhere much closer at hand.

They had advanced less than a hundred meters on their new
course before their surroundings had changed again. The djinn
looked hopeful, saying he had found the way into a different section
of the Workshop, more familiar to him from the time of Ardneh.

Here none of the visible surfaces were of natural rock. Rather they
had been lined with some wondrous artificial substance—here Ardneh had moved to take control of a portion of the world completely
away from nature. The smooth-floored tunnel through which Chance
now led his followers seemed to have been cut or bored through
something that was less like rock than like diamond, or incredibly

tough ice, transparent and warm. Some inner component of the stuff went drifting through its form like smoke seen through clear glass.

Still, the overall maze-like pattern of the place continued. They passed through room after room, crossing other passages, down which they could see, in several directions, other chambers, plus un-countable irregular spaces. Most of these rooms, large and small, seemed to be arsenals of grotesque machinery, which Chance took to be Ardneh's failed attempts at achieving his great purpose.

"THESE ARE ARDNEH'S FAILURES, IT MAY BE," ZALMOXIS WHISPERED, the image of elderly Grandmother seemed to be gliding rather than walking beside Chance.

Someone commented on how worried Zalmoxis seemed.

He heard the remark, that merely human ears would never have managed to pick up, and rounded on the speaker. "If I am more worried than you, perhaps it is because I see more—and remember more. To me Ardneh was not always friendly." He shuddered faintly. "But I would truly hate to be a demon in this place."

GRADUALLY THEIR SURROUNDINGS WERE CHANGING YET AGAIN, AS the party of explorers moved on. All things around them were silent and dark and frozen, as if nothing might have changed or moved in this place for a thousand years. Trying to deal with this wreckage, thought Chance, these failed experiments, the wisest of humans would be no better off than children, liable to provoke some acci-dental disaster with every move they made.

Zalmoxis, in what sounded like awed appreciation, observed that when Ardneh chose to be cunning, he had been as devious as the archdemon Orcus himself!

Chance heard an anonymous voice behind him whisper a fearful suspicion: "Did great Ardneh go mad in his last days?"

No one was going to try to answer that.

SOON ABBY REPORTED WITH RELIEF THAT SHE HAD SEEN JEMMY AND Cress again, and Benambra had also managed to rejoin the party. After marveling at the cocoon-objects, he again began to lag behind the others. The young lord heard the novice muttering: "These lamps alone would be worth . . ."

"They might be worth your life if you don't keep watch."

LONG HOURS—CHANCE COULD NOT TELL WHETHER THEY HAD added up to days—had passed since the djinn warned them that the Workshop was as big as a small city. But the full meaning of that had not really sunk in until now.

How many kilometers they had traveled underground Chance could not have said. They had reached a domain partly lighted by Old World lamps—Chance counted first six, then eight, then ten, and twelve, and gradually more and more, until he gave up numbering—casting circles of illumination. The lamps were turning themselves on, one at a time, as the explorers drew near, then extinguishing themselves as the intruding humans left them behind.

The presence of the djinn alone in a room or passage turned on no lights, no matter how solid his image looked and sounded. He murmured to Chance: "It is fortunate that I see better in the dark than you do."

The fact that some substantial portion of the vast cavern, perhaps even more than half of it, remained in shadow even in the rich glow of some half a dozen Old World lights, aroused in Chance the eerie feeling that the full extent of it might be infinite.

ASPECTS OF THE ROOMS THROUGH WHICH THEY TRAVELED NOW WERE as much a revelation to Zalmoxis as to any of the humans, and Chance saw the djinn darting about like some giant hummingbird, vanishing in one place and instantly reappearing somewhere else, looking for the richest source on which to feed his curiosity.

CHANCE ADVANCED A LITTLE FARTHER, THEN CAME TO A HALT, LOOK-ing to left and right. Listening intently, he could hear only the eternal trickle of water, and far off the dismal chanting. In his mind there was growing, like some noxious weed, the hideous conviction that he and his whole party were doomed to wander this strange sunken world until they died.

"The Key was not enough," he burst out to his companions. "Ardneh ought to have left some kind of guideposts also!"

Jervase: "We must remember that he—the creator of all this—was killed before his work was finished."

Abby suggested that perhaps the Key would give guidance, if Chance watched it carefully, tried hard to sense which way it wanted to go.

He snapped at her: "Don't you think I've been doing that? It's showing me nothing at all!"

Benambra was finding a number of things to interest him. "These strange materials might be valuable, useful for something—but what? Ah, it might take years of work to thoroughly investigate all these racks!"

Some trooper grumbled faintly: "Years, hey? I keep thinking that we'll be lucky if we have a few more minutes."

CHANCE PICKED UP SOMETHING, SOME FRAGMENT OF ONE OF ARD-neh's failed or unfinished projects, a twisted staff or rod that looked as if it might have been meant for the leg of a giant mechanical grasshopper, then in frustration threw it down again. "But this is wasting time! I feel no closer to Ardneh's treasure than I was before I used the Key."

GRADUALLY THE SCHOLAR'S EUPHORIA AT ENTERING THE DOMAIN OF Ardneh was turning into renewed dissatisfaction. Here he was, surrounded on every side by Ardneh's work and Ardneh's secrets, and so far he had been able to understand almost none of it.

While the party was resting, Zalmoxis came to talk with the humans.

"Where are we, djinn?" Jervase was sounding angry. "You said we were entering a part of the domain that you recalled from Ardneh's day."

"So we have done. It is only a matter of time until we find what we seek."

"Are you experimenting on us, or what? Just to see how long you can keep us going?"

Zalmoxis drew himself up, gaining a hand or two of height in the process. "I assure you, sir, my investigations into human behavior are always conducted in the most ethical way!"

"Conducted on living bodies, I have no doubt!"

The djinn seemed outraged. "I have done nothing to cause harm to any living human!"

Zalmoxis admitted to being in a general way familiar with where and how Gokard and his people were accustomed to keep their hostages and the various other materials for ritual sacrifice. But he had done nothing to aid the bandits in that nefarious practice. "You have two former victims in your party now—I just saw them somewhere about. You should ask them if I was in any way responsible for their plight."

Chance made an imitation of Draffut's skeptical grunting sound.

Benambra suddenly stepped into the argument: "It seems to me that you can think as shrewdly as any human being, djinn, and can do as much . . . what am I saying? You can do much more. You could fly away from here in a moment, if you wanted to, and soon be halfway around the world. In fact it is we who should envy you, for you are not burdened with all this meaty, aching, tired, and hungry substance."

With an airy wave of Grandmother's small hand, Zalmoxis dismissed such arguments, as if he had long ago considered and rejected them.

"I do think more effectively than humans in some ways, but less so in others. I am what I am, Lord Chance—borrowing a quotation from the great Lord Draffut—I still am what I have been up till now—and I know my limits. You are what you are, a human; but you do not begin to understand what that means."

"And I suppose you do!"

"Indeed!" Zalmoxis lamented. "But what good does it do me to have the understanding, even the attributes of humanity, if I am denied the thing itself?"

For a long moment he fell grimly silent. Then he mused, in Grandmother's gentle voice: "The origin of humanity is lost in the remote past. Billions upon billions of men and women have been formed out of the dust of the earth . . . why should there not be one specimen of the race who is constructed of finer material?"

Jervase gave a short laugh. "So, you mean to improve on the original design."

Zalmoxis: "Would you believe it? There are moments when I toy with the idea of abandoning my ambitions to be human, times when I long to revert to what I was in the days of Rolf and Ardneh. Then I want to say: 'If humanity will not have me . . . then neither will I have it.' "

"But I take it that these moments do not last." As usual, the Scholar sounded genuinely interested.

"Oh, they do not. As soon as I give the subject any thought I realize that I have probably idealized my memories of what happened ten centuries ago."

BENAMBRA, WHEN QUESTIONED, STILL SPOKE OF WORKING FOR THE Servants, gathering wealth to help them carry on their important work.

After all, Ardneh's constant thought had been for the welfare of human beings, had it not? And what could be more conducive to human welfare than the discovery of fabulous wealth? It seemed to the young novice necessary to keep looking . . . and then looking again, just a little farther on. It ought to be here somewhere. . . .

To Chance, Benambra was murmuring: "But I think that somehow Lord Draffut understood me. Knew that if I came here I would find wealth. . . . I am going to take a look down this way."

Chance tried to see what lay in the distance, far down the passage indicated. But he could make out little beyond a shimmering haze—perhaps the haze did appear somewhat yellower and brighter here than it had elsewhere. He said to Benambra: "Doesn't look very promising to me. Be careful."

"Of course."

In a moment, shadows and darkness had intervened, and Novice Benambra had passed out of human sight.

THIRTY-ONE

THE SKYLESS, TIMELESS DARKNESS AFFORDED THE PARTY NO CLUE
as to how long they had been underground. But there arrived a
moment when Jervase firmly declared a halt. Weariness and hunger
demanded rest and food. "We're staggering and stumbling, and this
place is too dangerous to tolerate that."

The djinn was of course an exception to the needs of the flesh,
able to dart tirelessly ahead, examining one room, one container,
one shelf, or machine, or bin of stored material after another—but
he was nervously reluctant to do so, unwilling to be away from
Chance and the Key for longer than the time of a few deep breaths.

"Zalmoxis!" This was Abby. "Tell us, how long have we been underground?"

Zalmoxis answered distractedly that he had not been keeping
time. Then he added: "What does it matter? You will be here until we
find the Sword—or until you die."

The djinn seemed far from at ease here, despite his claim of being
familiar with this domain of Ardneh. He was anxious to get on with
the search, begrudging the humans any time they found it necessary
to take for rest.

Chance groaned at Grandmother's image: "Someday, Zalmoxis,
when you have achieved your great goal and become a human

being—then you will find yourself compelled to stop for rest and sleep like all the rest of us. Your bones will ache with weariness, and your mind will ache with fear."

Grandmother's face looked haggard. "Talk to me not of weariness, young human—someday perhaps I will discourse to you upon that subject. Very well, sleep if you must. I will look ahead, a little way, and in an hour at the most I will return to wake you."

EXHAUSTED AS HE WAS, CHANCE STILL EXPECTED TO HAVE TROUBLE sleeping. The fine edge of excitement he had felt when opening the Workshop's door had been quickly dulled by uncertainty. His sense that they might have only a few more minutes before the bandits caught up with them had been replaced by a dragging anxiety. There were moments when it seemed to him that it would be possible to wander in this netherworld forever.

For a few moments he was still aware of the sound of running or dripping water. Then he seemed to tumble into nothingness.

CHANCE COULD NOT TELL HOW MUCH TIME HAD PASSED BEFORE ZAL-moxis was back, shaking him awake as promised. But he had slept, after all, he had finally rested. There was a new note of hope in the djinn's voice as he announced that he had discovered a passage leading to territory with which he was more familiar.

Abby seemed determined to be optimistic. "We have seen no demon yet."

"That is true—except for the frozen one."

"Then perhaps he will be unable or unwilling to enter the Workshop after all."

Clearly the djinn would not allow himself to believe that. Avenarius was far more dangerous than any of the others of his kind who swarmed above. The great demon was not going to allow himself to be kept out of Ardneh's territory. The door had been utterly destroyed, so there was nothing to keep him from entering—if he dared.

The djinn concluded: "And he will dare . . . were I he, I would have done so; I would now be lurking invisible in the background, watching, waiting . . . uneasily. He will not strike until we have found and identified Ardneh's Sword for him."

"But you, Zalmoxis, you would know if he was watching."

The djinn made his familiar motion of looking right and left. "Oh yes. Of course. I would know. He is not watching yet."

As an attempt at reassurance, it was sickeningly unconvincing. Chance and Abby exchanged a glance.

IN CHANCE'S PRIVATE THOUGHTS, THE IDEA THAT THE DJINN WOULD be motivated to imitate the demon seemed frighteningly plausible. Chance could not really believe Zalmoxis's protestations that he wanted only to become human. It seemed that he, like all the other players in this game, must be determined to gain Ardneh's treasure for himself—which strongly suggested that he knew more about its nature than he had admitted.

DURING A PAUSE FOR REST, CHANCE AND ABBY HAD TAKEN MITRA and gone apart a little from the others, into an alcove as big as a small room, part of a larger chamber. They were hoping to persuade the bird to try to fly again. The owl was sulking and their efforts made little headway. Presently Abby murmured that she needed rest, and in a matter of moments she was sound asleep, curled in a corner, her head resting on her backpack. The great bird was in an opposite corner of the small space, and seemed to be sleeping too.

Chance aborted his second yawn just as it was starting. The sickeningly familiar shape of Miyamoto had appeared, leaning against the wall with folded arms.

The demon wasted no time in greetings. "I would like," he informed Chance, smiling, "to hear from you some convincing pledge of your firm loyalty. Of your undying eagerness to deliver into my hands whatever of value may come into yours. Hmmm?"

There followed a long moment in which Chance was almost able to convince himself that he faced a fraud, that the being he confronted was nothing worse than Zalmoxis in disguise. The idea, the hope, gave him nerve and strength. "Understand, I still have no idea what this cursed treasure is. I can't be sure that it even exists—if it does, whether I can even move it. Suppose there's one nugget of gold that weighs a ton."

"Ah, prepared to argue, are we?" The Miyamoto-thing raised an eyebrow. "The points you raise do have some force," it admitted. Then its dark shape flickered suddenly across the room, to bend over the sleeping owl, extending one hand, on which the digits were suddenly no longer fingers but filthy-looking claws. Digging a talon into the slight wound on the bird's wing, the demon provoked a writhing spasm of pain—but something prevented Mitra from waking up. Something also prevented Chance from trying to interfere.

"Mmm-hmmm!" This time it had the sound of a high-pitched giggle as the demon straightened up again. "It will be a while before you fly on *that* wing, hey? He, he!"

Chance made a helpless sound.

The demon, utterly in control, all the time in the world, let his gaze dwell for a moment or two on sleeping Abigail before he turned slowly to face Chance. "You are probably right, my young Lord. Handing over treasure, which may perhaps appear in the form of some extremely powerful weapon, is not the sort of task that one can trust to a subordinate. So I do not mean to retire outside the Workshop and wait for you to carry it out to me"—and he leaned closer, menacing—"I do insist that you devote your whole being, heart, mind, and soul, to—to the goal of getting it—getting it—into—m-my possession."

For just a moment, the demon had seemed to be losing the thread of his thought—just as if, Chance realized suddenly, the being before him, like Chance himself, was under some tremendous mental strain—

Abruptly Avenarius was giving the impression of being on his guard. He had paused, looking keenly to right and left, as if he were focusing on some sound, some subtle warning, that Chance had not detected yet—

Then Chance saw it, approaching in the background. Over Avenarius's right shoulder, only faintly visible to human eyes, a rippling movement came darting swiftly through the fabric of one of this large room's solid walls. At least the wall had appeared, until this moment, to be completely solid—but maybe it never had been. The thickness of it contained a slab or panel, translucent though not completely transparent, very similar to another strange sight Chance had seen in the recent past. The blob of translucency kept sliding slowly along and at the same time through the wall—as if it might be possible for a window opening in a solid surface to adjust its own position.

The cause of this phenomenon was not immediately apparent, but the presence of Avenarius did seem to be a key factor in its progress. The glassy panel kept gliding, slowly, silently, through each bend and curve in the boundary of the large room, until it had come as close as it could possibly get to the demon where he was standing, fiendishly alert but, it seemed, still totally unaware.

Don't watch it, Chance was telling himself. *Keep looking at him instead.* But it was hard to do.

"Young Chance." The dead demonic eyes had come back to focus on him, the voice of Avenarius was suddenly weary. "If I thought there was any possibility that you . . . that you . . ."

It had stopped directly behind the monster. A strong bulge in the center of the region of transparency began to show itself and it was reaching for him. (*Don't look at it, don't give him warning!*) It swelled out from the wall's smooth flatness in a way that at first suggested a huge watery bubble. But in a moment or two it had stretched itself too long and thin to have anything to do with water.

There surfaced again in Chance's thought the possibility that the creature before him was really only the djinn, the one being who might be able to identify Ardneh's Sword . . . but the boy was given no time to follow that thought to its conclusion.

Because the blob struck. Much too swiftly for the human eye to follow it.

As a great fist of crystal closed on Miyamoto from behind, his eyeballs bloomed, transforming momentarily into the heads of snakes, forked tongues darting from their small, fanged mouths. Sound burst from him in a great, wordless, elemental shout.

For a moment, the air around Chance seemed to swirl, as if an elemental, born of something more profound than rock or fire, had it in his grip. The demon was not trapped, not yet, not totally. He lurched forward with mad ferocity, exerting incredible strength.

The crystal blur had detached itself completely from the wall—no, the demon must have torn it free!—leaving a gaping hole. The Miyamoto-shape, half-covered in what looked like boiling ice, rebounded from one wall to go smashing through the barrier of yet another. Desperately the demon fought to escape the snare that had been been designed to freeze him for eternity. Chance saw with horror that Ardneh's stealthy artifact might not be able to complete the job; the centuries might have worn it down, sapped its strength. It had not been quite fast enough, or strong enough, to swallow up its prey in one clean grab—

Chance stumbled back, recoiling as he would have from a falling building. Because the demon, having somehow forced its way partially free, was coming after him.

Still half embedded in the glob of boiling ice, dragging it along, the monster was almost on him. The right hand of Avenarius shot forward in a frantic grab for Chance's throat—or perhaps the demon's intent was to reach the Key that hung there. The hand was no longer a hand, but the taloned paw of a raging beast. At the same moment a bloodcurdling roar of rage and hate burst from the demon's fanged and expanded mouth.

Chance went stumbling back, two steps, three, before he fell. The form looming over him had grown larger than human life, its eyes were slanted, jaws gaping with fangs that seemed to blur like the teeth of a spinning sawblade. . . .

"Ardneh defend us!" Abby, jarred awake by noise and light, was screaming. The bird too had awakened, and was fluttering and crying out in pain.

Avenarius, babbling, seemed to gasp as if in need of breath in the middle of his desperate struggle. Yet he seemed to be prying himself free of the demon-trap. The image arose in Chance's mind of some rat-killing dog, aged and weary from ten centuries of waiting, starving, now overmatched against a tiger. . . .

At the extremity of his lunge, Avenarius managed to clamp the grip of one hand on Chance's helpless body. But behind Avenarius the thousand-year-old ally of humanity, the child of Ardneh, exerted a new surge of effort and spun the demon himself backward, forcing him to release his human prey.

Thank Ardneh, Abby had not been caught. She was running, getting away, but had tripped and fallen. . . .

For a moment longer, Chance, his body briefly airborne, saw the shadowed mysteries of the Workshop spinning around him. He landed hard, went bouncing into soft things, unidentifiable objects that broke and scattered before the impact of his fleshly weight. No bones broken, Chance scrambled to all fours and began to crawl away. Six meters from him, Avenarius went on ranting, smashing

Ardneh's things, his failed experiments, going mad with anger as he pounded the would-be demon-killer into pieces—

"Ardneh defend us!"

The cry was even louder this time, bursting from a girl's throat. Something in it brought the raging demon to a stop. He turned slowly to face Abigail.

The voice of Avenarius sounded almost human once again, though his shape was no longer anything like a man's. "I have known your Ardneh, little fool! I have been closer to him—yes, much closer—than any of you can ever be, mortal enemies though we were. Who is the stronger now? I still live, and he is dead. *Dead!*"

The demon's imaged face had been restored to that of a middle-aged schoolteacher. He clenched his modest teacher's fists. "On the day great Orcus died, I warned John Ominor, the last of human blood to bear the title of Emperor . . . warned the overbearing human that though he thought he had defeated Ardneh there was still some trick, some trap to be avoided."

WHETHER THIS WAS TRULY A DEMON, OR THE DJINN'S TRUE FACE, this was not a being that Chance could deal with. But somehow he kept on moving . . . yet one more effort by the demon-killer, torn and beaten as it was, delayed Chance's enemy, giving the young lord time to turn, get on all fours, and begin to crawl away through one of the places where a wall had just collapsed. There loomed above him an ancient-looking arch with an engraved inscription.

Abby was screaming out the words: "In the Emperor's name, forsake this game, and do not pass!" Her head was thrown back, and she seemed to be reading from the arch.

Chance couldn't remember when he had first heard the word, the name, of Emperor . . . Jervase had taught him that in ancient times, the title had meant something very different from this magical incantation—a human of supreme power in the world, able to exact tribute from kings and hold them under his dominion.

It almost appeared that Avenarius had lost interest in his crawling human victims. The demon, absorbed in confirming the defeat of his ancient opponent, was shattering the glassy blob into smaller and smaller fragments. He had gained a partial victory over Ardneh. But Avenarius had been hurt too . . . he gave the impression of having been dazed, half blinded.

Turning again, he staggered across heaps of broken artifacts and masonry toward the arch. But there he stopped. It seemed he could not pass through under the smooth curve of the inscription . . . or did not want to.

In what might have been partly the exaltation of victory, partly sheer exhaustion, he was raving, babbling—mad. "Ominor ran away, he dodged . . . or tried to. But he could not flee far enough, dodge fast enough. For Orcus had been twenty megatons when he was born—much greater than I; much, much greater—and was no smaller when he died, and in those days we neither of us had any comprehension of how much twenty megatons could do. . . ."

The babbling had ceased to make any sense at all to Chance. Abby, on all fours beside him, was tugging at his torn sleeve, and now they were both crawling on, getting farther from the demon-image. Chance heard a few more words from it: "I will see you again, before you expect me!"—before it faded from their sight.

REACHING A PLACE OF DARKNESS AND SILENCE, THEY RESTED FOR A time. Soon Mitra, dragging herself painfully along, managed to find them in the dark.

Some time had passed before they were able to move on.

"Where did everyone else get to?"

"We must warn them . . . of the demon."

HEARING A MURMUR OF VOICES AHEAD, TONES TIRED AND HUSHED rather than excited, Chance and Abby, carrying with them the injured bird, dragged themselves on into the next room, then the next after that, moving toward increasing light and the faint sounds of humanity. At last they entered what was perhaps the second or third largest chamber they had yet encountered. Here the small crowd of their human companions were arrayed in a rough semicircle before the homely form of Grandmother. Chance noted in some corner of his distracted mind that Jemmy and Cress were absent from this gathering. Zalmoxis was sitting as if rapt in contemplation of a certain object, which lay on one of a long row of similar racks against a wall.

One of the humans bawled a challenge at the djinn, accusing him of leading them on a crazy path to nowhere.

Zalmoxis seemed to ignore the accusation totally. Instead he only pointed at the thing he had been looking at.

"This is possibly the second most complex object I have ever been privileged to examine—the most impressive is still the human brain, of course."

One of the troopers cried out: "What are you babbling about, you damned ghost?"

Zalmoxis sprang to his feet. His voice was very human and very loud. "Damned ghost, am I? Then what are you?—only stupid animals, too stupid to recognize your treasure when you find it. The Sword is *here!*" The djinn screamed out the last words, almost sizzling with excitement.

Everyone crowded forward.

THIRTY-TWO

DESPITE THE IMPACT OF THE DJINN'S ANNOUNCEMENT, SOME OF the people turned to stare in silence at Chance and Abby as the pair approached. Only now, in this room where the light was better, did Chance realize how they had been marked by their clash with the demon. Their clothes were smeared and torn, and Chance's elbow was caked with blood from a scrape sustained in his rolling fall.

His throat felt almost too tight and dry to speak, but he managed somehow to get out a few words: "We have met Avenarius."

"Where?" several voices demanded at once.

"Not far—somewhere back that way." Chance gestured vaguely. "It couldn't have been far. You must have heard the noise."

Jervase explained: "We heard something that we thought was possibly an earthquake, or a landslide. We . . . talked it over, and decided not to investigate." It sounded like there might have been an argument on that point.

Haltingly, Chance continued his account, Abigail chipping in with a few phrases. Between them they conveyed what seemed to be the essential information. Abby concluded: "We left him there, still intent on smashing up the demon-trap."

Jervase demanded: "Any chance that it will kill him? Or hold him frozen?"

"I don't think so."

Meanwhile, with plenty of water and reasonable light available, Abigail had started washing Chance's elbow, getting ready to put on a light bandage. He noted that warning everyone about Avenarius seemed to have been a futile exercise. There was nothing that any of them could do.

Grandmother was regarding Abby and Chance with impatience. Chance suddenly demanded of the djinn: "How long have you been here?"

"In this room? I arrived shortly before you did." Zalmoxis was definitely irritated to have attention diverted from his great find. "What does it matter?" He pointed again at the row of objects in front of him. "*Here* is the only answer that you need! Here, the Sword of Ardneh! Here!"

Chance stared at the long row of waist-high racks, all apparently connected to more elaborate machinery that was built into the wall. Each rack held a small and unimportant-looking bundle of what looked like some ordinary brown cloth. The sight provoked only a familiar sinking feeling of disappointment.

Jervase, as usual, was first to move forward. Gingerly he touched one of the objects, observing that it felt warm. In another moment he had pulled the small bundle of fabric out of its rack, and remarked in a vaguely disappointed voice that it was almost weightless.

As the thing unfolded in his hands, it plainly took the shape of a garment designed to fit the human body. There were four limbs, corresponding to those on any normal human frame, and an opening for a head.

The djinn was still talking, going on about the noble plan in which Ardneh had invested his last and greatest hopes for humanity. The weapon that would give men and women the best chance of fighting demons effectively would have to be built on the foundation of humanity's own natural powers.

"What you see before you," Zalmoxis was claiming, "is the necessary weapon, the true Sword of Ardneh. It offers you your only real chance against the demons."

Disappointment was building in the surrounding ring of human faces. Lord Chance moved forward. His own rage, long suppressed, against demons, against bandits and djinn and the unfair world in general, came boiling out. "Are you telling us that *this* is what we've almost killed ourselves trying to find? The great treasure, the great secret? Another of your lousy tricks! Another damned suit for someone to put on." His rage was growing, and he did not care. "I *wore* something very much like this, the first time I trusted your advice! It should have been the last."

The djinn was swiftly sobered, conciliatory, almost humble—and at the same time, it seemed, offended. "Quite the contrary, young sir. *That* suit I could carry about and hand to you—this one I dare not even touch until a human hand has claimed it from its rack."

Jervase let go of the suit he had picked up. The garment drifted to the ground, looking as light and ineffectual as thistledown.

Zalmoxis uttered something like a groan. He turned about, looking into each face in the silent ring of humanity that had formed around him. "Is there some curse on all of you, that none believe me? I was with Ardneh in those days, and I know! Daily he contended in deadly war against the East, fighting powers for whom dread Avenarius might have served as pet or plaything. Ardneh had no time for leisurely contemplation. He decided that the protection of humanity could be most efficiently achieved by building on the existing foundation of Old World body armor."

Around them the other human members of the group were moving about uncertainly. At the moment Zalmoxis was paying no attention to anyone but the holder of the Key. "Look closely, Lord Chance—the resemblance between this and the armor you once wore is quite superficial. That was completely primitive, a prototype, a very tentative first step. Even so it had value, protected you at times. This—"

"This looks much flimsier," Chance interrupted.

"But what it *is* . . . is what a sage of the Old World might have described as a quantum leap in progress."

Chance was still bitterly suspicious. "Then maybe you should put one on yourself."

"Are you not listening? I will not dare even to touch this—until I have achieved humanity."

Abby put in: "This looks more—more ordinary than the last suit you gave Chance to wear."

Zalmoxis made a scornful sound. "Perhaps Ardneh lacked your fine regard for fashion."

"Zalmoxis." Abby's calling of his name seemed to compel the djinn to look directly at her, though he did so only reluctantly. "Do you still consider it a bad idea for humans to be granted the power that Ardneh wanted to give them?"

"Were I able to experience full humanity myself, I might better answer that worthy question.

"The question that great Ardneh had to face was this: Would it truly benefit humanity to bestow such godlike powers upon only a few members of the race? Or would it doom them to destruction? The great majority would be left practically helpless before the chosen few. Would the few who were granted immense powers use them for the benefit of the whole race? What Ardneh knew of the long story of human history did not inspire optimism."

The djinn went on to claim it had been his arguments that had finally dissuaded Ardneh from taking such a step. He, Zalmoxis, according to his own account of events of a thousand years ago, had strongly protested that human beings were already powerful enough!

Raising a hand, the Scholar interrupted the flow of grandiloquence. Pointing to the suit that he had dropped, he said: "You say that this is truly Ardneh's Sword—but that you argued against its creation. So in the end Ardneh did not take your advice?"

"Ah, but he did! A number of Mark VII suits were manufactured, as you see. But they were never distributed.

"The more Ardneh considered the program, the more rigorously he tested his chosen materials, systems, and devices . . . and the more he considered the nature of humanity, its strengths and limitations, its bloody history . . . the greater grew his doubts about his own wisdom in offering such power to only a small segment of humanity.

"I must in fairness warn you of another possibility regarding the Mark VII suits—that a human who dons one may undergo a devastating loss of memory, in effect a near-destruction of personal identity. Had Ardneh lived for one more day, perhaps only for one more hour, he might have destroyed these utterly, and tried to find some other plan by which humans could defend themselves."

Abby, her voice a screaming parody of its usual tone, burst out with: "Chance, what are you going to do?"

"I don't know!" He had carried the Key for them all, he had opened the damned door for them, he had wrestled with the damned demon and had been nearly killed. Wasn't that enough?

Feeling all eyes upon him, he reached out to take the specimen from the nearest rack, and looked inside the collar. The legend in neat permanent Old World symbols said:

Mark VII.

At least Zalmoxis seemed to have been telling the truth about the nomenclature—but however the numbers might have gone up, this was still only another suit. Chance opened his hand and let the garment fall to the ground. He wasn't going to put it on to please the djinn who lied, who probably played the role of demon—

Abigail, terrified by a sudden realization, was looking wildly to right and left. She burst out with a distracted and distracting question: "Great Ardneh! Where are the children?"

For a long moment it seemed that no one wanted to answer, or even think about the question. It was Zalmoxis who finally responded, tersely, trying to dispose of a distraction without lifting his gaze from the suit that lay at Chance's feet. "Some time ago, the pair called Jemmy and Cress strayed back into a part of the Workshop occupied by Gokard's people, where they were recaptured. I think you will not see them again."

Abby, shocked beyond speech, let out a half-choked scream of outrage.

The djinn gestured impatiently. "I regret that you find their loss so upsetting—but it was not my fault. Or yours. And it is of trivial import compared with the issue before us. We must concentrate upon—"

The girl had regained a partial command of speech. "You fiend! You will never become a human being!"

At last, someone had said something that seemed to hit the tech-djinn hard. Grandmother's image flickered. For the moment the djinn ignored Chance and the other people, several of whom were now edging closer to the long array of racks. They had all been disappointed, but this might be the only game in town. A few were gingerly touching the merchandise the djinn was trying to sell. So far, no one had snatched up a bundle. But caution was not the dominant trait of any in these folk.

Several heartbeats passed before Zalmoxis answered. "You mean if I had saved them—?"

"If you had even *tried*!" Again Abigail almost screamed.

"Ah. Although to try might well have enraged the one the sacrifice was meant to please." Suddenly the djinn seemed in an agony of doubt. "But do you really think—? There are many humans who would not risk their lives to save members of their own race."

"Even children? *Some* might not. If you can call such people human!"

Zalmoxis was still staring intently at Abigail. For the moment he might even have forgotten Ardneh's Sword. "To accept the gravest risk to my own life . . . the benefit going entirely to others . . ."

Suddenly his eyes lighted. "But going to *humans*! Aye! That would establish, would it not, a most vital connection between us? And thus between myself and all humanity. I never thought of that! And it is true, I have seen it happen, there are folk who do such things!"

The girl cried at him: "Of course there are, many, many! Any mother would sacrifice herself—would—would—"

Zalmoxis, musing, uttered a single word: "Mothers."

"Yes! Though certainly they are not the only ones—they sacrifice themselves all the . . ."

She let her words trail off. The djinn had vanished.

CHANCE AND ABIGAIL LOOKED AT EACH OTHER. ONE OF THE NEARBY troopers, puzzling over the peculiar, fuzzy, lightweight object he now held in both hands, was saying to his comrade beside him: "Didn't the tech-djinn just say that these were meant to help us deal with demons?"

A little farther down the row of racks, Horkos was coming to his own decision. He had caught Chance's eye, and spoke to him: "Give me no argument, young man. Our situation is desperate, and I'm going to put one on. No reason why you should have to bear the weight of every trial."

Even as Horkos was declaring his intentions, Jervase had already accepted the challenge. Having laid aside his pack and weapons and canteen, the Scholar was sitting on the ground, still fully clothed, and trying to shove his feet into the garment's legs. But evidently that process was more complicated than it looked, and he was meeting some kind of resistance.

Perhaps the ineffectual appearance of the suit at rest had been deceptive. Bursts of dazzling light were beginning to flash from the garment Jervase was struggling with. A splashy radiance outlined his legs, which were half-immersed in it. A sound like the faint howling of a wind was being generated somewhere.

The flashes soon became a daunting glare, and the wind-howl swelled into bursts of crackling noise. The Scholar was making slow progress in getting the garment on, grunting as he struggled with its unexpected tightness. His eyes met Chance's, and he grunted: "There are strange sensations . . . not altogether pleasant . . . should have had someone taking notes while I did this . . . Chance? . . ."

"Scholar?" Chance could hardly recognize his own voice. But the important transformation was happening to the shape before him. He had to shield his eyes from its radiance. "Scholar, you are changing." He wondered helplessly if he should have cautioned Jervase to take off his ordinary clothing first.

When he looked away from Jervase, swept his gaze around the room, it seemed to him that even its shape and size were changing.

Abby too was squinting into the glare, her wonder so great that she had even forgotten the children for a moment. She demanded of the figure at its center: "Are you—Ardneh?"

"Ardneh?" The owner of the strange voice might never have heard the name before. "*Who?*" Then: "No . . . not that . . . but . . ."

The glare abruptly died away, the noise fell silent. Jervase's body—
the body of the being who had once been Jervase—stood in the exact spot where moments ago the Scholar had been sitting. But the
head that turned to regard Chance in the dim light was that of a
long-beaked bird.

Every shred of the Scholar's clothing, including the suit he had
just put on, had disappeared. It seemed incredible that the man
himself had not been consumed by the fierce glare of the melding,
the metamorphosis. But his body had not been charred, or even
blistered. Far from it.

From the neck down the Scholar's new form was still that of a
man, though it had taken on aspects of a heroic statue. Muscles and
bones had swelled, bulking his frame into an unfamiliar shape of ele-
gance and power.

And he was taller, by a full head—though his was no longer a human head. Instead it was smoothly feathered in solid black, topped
with a thin crown of silvery metal.

With the feeling that he must be dreaming, Chance recognized
the Scholar's new head as that of an ibis, a wading bird of the
seashore marshes. For a moment the image seemed to flicker, and
Chance seemed to be gazing at a seated baboon with its whole torso
covered in feathers. The form shifted rapidly back and forth a few
times, touching briefly on other shapes even more exotic, creatures
Chance could never have named, before returning with finality to
that of a man with a bird's head. The shape of the being's silvery
crown persisted, reminding Chance of a crescent moon surmounted
by a moon disc. The great bird's long, thin, downward-curving bill
looked as strong and sharp as the sword that the man Jervase had
laid aside only a short time ago.

LIGHTS WERE FLARING IN OTHER PARTS OF THE LARGE ROOM, AND
the noise was mounting up again. Reassured by the fact that Jervase

still moved and showed no signs of drastic suffering, spurred on by the urge to imitate, other people were hurrying to put on suits. If this was Ardneh's treasure, they were not going to be left out of the division of the spoils. If it made you look like a great bird, well, that was doubtless only some kind of a disguise.

Chance caught a glimpse of Captain Horkos, now well along in his own personal transformation. Private Vardtrad seemed to be launching himself into the process. Chance still recoiled when someone tried to offer him a suit—he felt sure that the alterations in Jervase had gone far deeper than a mere matter of disguise.

Where had Abby got to? He had no more than missed her when he heard her voice, crying from the next room, which was unexpectedly far away. He ran toward it.

What sounded like one of the djinn's voices issued from there as well, babbling something about the Scholar turning, or having turned, into the god called Thoth. Chance could not tell if Zalmoxis was elated or outraged. "Oh, we are to have the gods again! I half suspected and half feared something of the kind. . . ."

THE IMAGE OF GRANDMOTHER WAS STANDING BEFORE ABIGAIL. AND flanking the djinn, one of his arms round each of them, were Cress and Jemmy. The children's faces were blank with shock and horror. Gone were their bandit shirts; Zalmoxis had somehow managed to clothe his living salvage in tight-fitting Mark I suits that looked to Chance like the same ones their imitations had been wearing when he first met them.

"If you hope to keep them this time, you must guard them well," Zalmoxis was telling Abigail at the moment when Chance came in. "I dare not stay."

"Thank you! Thank you very much!" Abby sprang forward, grabbed each child by an arm and drew them to her. But then the look on her face, alive with joy, suddenly faded to match the grim expression of the djinn's. In a hushed voice she demanded: "Avenarius is still alive?"

"So you assured me, not long ago." The djinn was not triumphant, but utterly subdued. "I have not seen him lately."

"Does saving the children mean you'll be in trouble?" She threw a glance toward Chance. "We'll do everything we can to help you."

"There is nothing you can do." The voice of Zalmoxis had turned remote, his attitude fatalistic. "Having offended Avenarius, my chance of survival is very small—smaller than I expected. It is not the torturers' knives or flames I fear. It is something much, much worse. I must hurry back to the cage and occupy it myself before any of Gokard's people find it empty—or, Ardneh forbid, the demon should learn what I have done! Playing the part of two humans at once will mean dividing my powers, so I fear the illusion will fail as soon as there is an attempted sacrifice, and flame or blade touches my . . ."

The djinn's words died away. Grandmother's features blurred, became in a moment those of a generic human being, no more personal than a crude computer graphic. But its expression was plain, a mask of tragedy, eyes staring fixedly over Abigail's shoulder.

Just behind her there had flickered into existence the form of Avenarius in his schoolteacher guise. The image was speckled with small fragments as of sparkling glass, or diamond—Chance could recognize the broken fragments of Ardneh's smashed and trampled demon trap.

For a long moment no one moved. Chance, his last hope shattered by the sight of djinn and demon both visible at once, could only keep looking back and forth between them. His brain had not been given time for utter terror as yet. He stuttered words: "But—I thought—"

Whatever he might have been thinking a minute ago meant nothing now. The djinn had vanished again, in desperate flight, abandoning Cress and Jemmy, Chance and Abigail, all four standing as if paralyzed.

But Avenarius, for the moment at least, did not appear interested in them. Instead he went immediately to the doorway, peering back into the larger room where more people were struggling to put on Mark VII suits. He ignored them, and ignored as well the ones who brandished useless swords or spears, and those who turned to run away. In the blink of an eye the demon had moved to stand beside the row of racks.

Chance followed, and Abby followed him. Avenarius had grabbed up one of the small, lightweight bundles from its rack, and was considering it. Then he muttered something scornful and threw it down. He seemed relieved. He spoke as to himself. "Then this is it, the famous Sword? Is this all? The very best my ancient enemy could do? It looks to me like another species of feeble protection." He turned directly to Chance: "This treasure you need not bother to bring me. Hah!"

Chance was witnessing an echo of his own first reaction, but then a thought came whispering from somewhere: *The Sword of Ardneh was designed to look like this! So that no demon would take it seriously at first. . . .*

Avenarius had already moved on, frowning with the impact of a new thought. "What was Zalmoxis babbling about, a few moments past? Playing some game of pretending to be a sacrifice?"

Abigail had come up beside Chance and held his arm. "Oh no," she said. "I don't think it could have been that."

The demon giggled. Extending a suddenly elongated arm, he chucked Abby playfully under the chin with dirty fingers, and a moment later did the same to Chance.

He said: "I look forward to an intimate relationship with both of you—quite soon. We are going to spend a *long* time in each other's company. And if there is another demon trap about, I wish you would point it out to me—that little workout was quite enjoyable. . . .

"But first, another matter remains to be settled . . . the stupid djinn has overstepped the boundaries. It is time, and past time, that he be disposed of, once and for all."

The demon smiled, and disappeared.

CHANCE REMAINED STARING AT THE SPOT WHERE AVENARIUS HAD vanished. Now was their opportunity to try to run—but suddenly it all seemed totally futile—hope vanished, leaving them no chance at all. . . .

Abby was trying to shake Chance out of his state of shock or rouse him from a faint. "Wake up!"

Finally he was able to focus on her. Cress and Jemmy, looking thin in their Mark I model suits, hovered at her sides—until she roused herself and ordered them fiercely to run into the next room and find some place to hide there. This time they were terrified enough to obey at once.

The children were barely out of sight, when movement at the far end of the big room caught Chance's eye, and he turned to see Gokard and a handful of armed bandits entering, their weapons raised.

They had hardly burst in when they paused, effectively stunned by the spectacle before them. People trying to put on suits were bathed in dazzling flashes of light, booming with noise— earsplitting cracks, loud rumbles, enough to drown out human speech.

Presently Gokard was advancing slowly in the general direction of Chance, crying something as he waved his sword. He seemed to be calling on his enemies to surrender.

Whatever response the bandit might have expected could not have been the one he actually got. Most of the people already in the room ignored him. Chance's hand had gone to the hilt of his hunting knife, but he did not draw it.

A moment later, Gokard, his sword drooping in his hand, had approached them closely. For once the little man seemed to be utterly at a loss, having trouble in finding words. "What's going on?" he finally demanded, shouting to be heard above the din.

Chance gestured vaguely. "Just what you see."

Behind the bandit leader, there was an ongoing scramble as more of his people, and still more armed men and women after them, came entering the space, their eyes alight for treasure, their fingers practically grasping for it in the air. But immediately confusion and astonishment began to claim them.

Gokard was focusing on Abby. "We have been performing sacrifice," he told her loudly and distinctly—ready to feast on her reaction, wanting to make certain that she heard every word.

"Have you indeed?" she asked.

"Ah yes. You will be pleased to know, my lady and lordling, that the little victims' sufferings were not prolonged. Their bodies were untouched by sacrificial fire, they could not be dismembered. At the first touch of my knife blade on their skin, they disappeared."

"There was no blood upon my hands this time," he marveled, more to himself than to his listeners.

"That means? . . ." Chance prompted.

The bandit chieftain was elated. "What could it mean, except that the Great One devoured them intact, so eagerly did he accept my gift! Surely he will share with me the Workshop's treasure, as soon as it is found!"

Chance was desperately trying to make some plan. "Then you don't know . . . that this around us . . ."

"Know what? What about this?"

Another presence was suddenly looming over them. Avenarius, in the form of a three-meter giant, one hand held behind his back, looked angry with Gokard. In a low and savage voice the demon demanded of his worshiper: "What kind of insulting tricks do you attempt to perpetrate on me? Do you expect me to play the fool, for you and the damned djinn?"

And he brought his arm swinging round from behind his back, clutching in one hand Moxis and Zalmo by the collars of their Mark I suits, to hurl the two child-images sprawling at Gokard's feet.

Gokard, on becoming aware of the demon's presence, fell on his knees at once. "Master!"

And began to tell of the glorious sacrifice he had just performed with his own hands. Of the many services he and his people had performed. . . .

His boasting was not well received. "You have done me no service at all—have had to do everything of importance for myself. Besides that, your whining wearies me. I do not even want you stewing in my gut!"

The demon's mouth stretched out, impossibly far open. The man's scream choked off as he perished in a blast of flame.

THIRTY-THREE

GOKARD'S CHARRED BODY LAY STILL TWITCHING ON THE ground, polluting the air of the Workshop with an odor like burnt pork. The demon roared at the two child-images sprawling beside it: "Enough of your idiotic games, Zalmoxis. I command you, retain your present form!"

Someone screamed.

The cowering children with bright red hair, both dressed in tight-fitting early models of Old World protective armor, were so convincing that Abby tried to put herself between them and the demon.

Zalmoxis, gibbering in terror, fell on his four small knees before Avenarius, and in a shrill-voiced duet strenuously denied that he had tried to interfere with the demon's plans in any way.

Moxis and Zalmo shrieked out their plea in chorus: "Oh Mighty One, forgive me if I have transgressed! Fool that I am, I saw the matter only as a challenge—trying to emulate two humans at one time."

"Your endless jabbering is an irritation, and it is not my habit to suffer irritations long. And what is this kneeling nonsense? Have you finally convinced yourself that you are human?"

In the next instant it was the shape of Avenarius that changed again, transforming into the most ghastly monster that Chance had ever imagined, its fanged and slavering mouth gaping wide enough to swallow a loadbeast.

Even as Chance lunged for Abby, trying to snatch her away from the horror, he saw Moxis and Zalmo snatched up and thrust into it, emitting gurgling yells of despair even as they disappeared.

HAVING DEVOURED THE DJINN, AVENARIUS BEGAN TO LOOK ABOUT, anger for the moment satisfied, seeking his next source of amusement.

His voice was calm once more. "There is not much psychic nourishment in a djinn, whatever form he happens to be in . . . say what you will, humans are the best of all. Where is my faithful Keybearer? There you are. Come, young man. Before I devour you we are going on a tour of the world. There are several other places where I wish to try what Ardneh's passport in a human hand can do to open things that have been locked and sealed away."

Chance thought of trying to run away. But that would be useless. Hoarsely he cried out: "Ardneh defend us! In the Emperor's name . . . the Emperor's name . . ."

"Ah, memorizing inscriptions, are we? Well . . . I might not be able to eat you, as long as you wear the Key—yet I am sure you will afford me intense pleasure, as you watch what I do with one other who has caught my eye." And the demon turned his gaze on helpless Abigail.

Then he was struck by another thought. "By the way, what has happened to Jervase?"

Chance said: "He is around—somewhere."

And Abby, at the same time: "We don't know."

The demon was paying little attention to their answers. "It seems your Scholar's intuition was correct—Ardneh had decided that the most valuable treasure he could leave to his human clients was knowledge—which I suppose these latest suits are meant somehow to impart. But knowledge in itself wins no battles."

IN THE NEXT MOMENT, THE MONSTER HAD REGAINED THE PROSAIC form of the elderly teacher, lightly dusting his hands together, smacking his lips and swallowing. Turning to Chance, his old teacher politely asked him: "You will not really miss Zalmoxis, will you, my Lord? Will you, Miss Abigail? But if you think you will, be not cast down too much. The prospects are really quite good that all of you will soon be reunited!" And with a burst of maniacal laughter, the image rippled and distorted into horror.

AVENARIUS LOOKED AROUND. NONE OF GOKARD'S FOLLOWERS WERE still in sight. Some had already fled in screaming terror—and some indeterminate number had already succeeded in putting on the mysterious-looking garments that had been claimed to be components of Ardneh's Sword. Others were still in the middle of that process, still thrashing about uncertainly in the remoter regions of the enormous chamber.

"Yes, it does appear that they are on their way to being transformed . . . but into what? This is interesting."

In general the demon seemed to feel reassured by what he had been able to observe thus far.

"I had feared worse. But now . . . perhaps I need not have worried. It is time for some entertainment."

The demon clutched Abby by her long dark hair and drew her close to him. "What portion of this virgin domain, this tasty morsel, ought I to nibble at first?"

Chance clutched the power of Ardneh in both hands, and, charging, thrust it forward toward his enemy. As it had when Chance opened the Workshop door, the chain holding the Key had grown longer and springier, strongly suggesting its readiness to be put to use.

Avenarius at first observed his mad rush with amusement. The demon put up a casual hand to catch him the moment he came in reach. But then, at the last second, a faint frown on the schoolteacher's face, the dawn of apprehension—

There was a jolt, of blinding, staggering force—

Chance had been knocked back a step. As his vision cleared, he saw that Avenarius—still dragging Abby with him—seemed to have been knocked back three times that far.

Chance charged again, thinking: *If I had only thought, only dared, to try this with the Key, while he was fighting to escape the demon-trap—between us we might have beaten him.* But it was too late now to think of that.

There was another savage impact, another staggering recoil. This time when Chance's senses cleared he could see that Avenarius had been driven yet farther off. Abby looked unconscious now, her body sagging as the demon supported her with one hand.

In the next room, or somewhere within earshot, someone—Chance supposed it might even be Jervase—was uttering strange cries, adding to the racket of the ongoing process of multiple transformations going on around them. The noise was enough to drown out what the demon shouted, screaming at Chance before retreating again, hauling with him the unconscious girl.

Chance hurried in pursuit, through the bedlam of other humans trying to pull on suits and being changed. The writhing of some of their forms, and the wild cries escaping some of their lungs, strongly suggested that the resulting transformations were in many cases going beyond anything the experimenters could have expected, or even imagined.

Not only were their bodies being altered, but their immediate environment. The floor of the chamber seemed to be buckling up, and

Chance stumbled on it in his haste. He kept after the demon, determined to rescue Abigail as she was continually dragged away by the stumbling, ranting monster, who was twitching with pain and rage.

Entering the next room, they were all confronted by the being who had once been Jervase—in the form of a powerful nude man with the head of a giant ibis.

The demon demanded: "What in the name of Orcus are you supposed to be?"

The voice from the bird's head sounded as a penetrating drone, a ringing whine. Still, the words were very clear. "The name of Orcus is nothing to me. I am Thoth, and I do not suppose anything; I only seek the truth."

THIRTY-FOUR

S UDDENLY CONFRONTED BY THAT FIGURE, AS TALL AS HIS OWN but enormously more human, the maddened demon stopped, mystified, brought to an utter standstill by the sight of the marvel that confronted him.

Chance thought he could read confusion in the demon's face and attitude, but nothing like fright. Not yet.

Chance cried in agony: "Jervase!"

There was no response.

The great demon's hesitation lasted only for a moment. Then the creature lashed out in rage at this phenomenon before him, eager to destroy whatever power Ardneh might be trying to pit against him. . . .

The blow seemed to have no effect at all. But the ibis-man's first attitude of leisurely curiosity immediately changed.

"It is time for judgment," the bird-voice said, a piercing drone. He who had called himself Thoth reached out with both hands. One caught Avenarius by a shoulder, and the other briskly tore off the demon's head. The swordlike bird-bill went probing into the help-less demon's torso, to be withdrawn a moment later, dripping with bits of what seemed rotted meat.

The harsh voice of the destroyer bellowed. "What, you have no heart? There is no real life in you to kill? Then be a worm, and crawl away!"

The demon's body did not crawl. It utterly collapsed, expanding as it did so into a pile of steaming wreckage. Chance saw what looked like greasy ashes, and the suggestion of a mound of corpses on a battlefield. It seemed the ruin of a vastly greater creature than the demon's projected images had ever shown him to be. There were also dancing, transient images, suggesting spinning hoops of steel.

But life quickly stirred amid the ghastly wreckage. There followed the emergence of a harvest of rescued beings, a majority of them human, enough of them to have filled the hold of a sailing vessel, who came crawling, walking, oozing forth. For the most part they just wandered away confusedly, and Chance saw several of them staring with the fierce gaze of madmen at the remaining rack of suits.

The destroyer with the bird's head stood watching the process with some interest.

"Jervase!" Chance cried out in terror and hope.

Abby cried something too.

He who had been the Scholar was gazing thoughtfully at the spectacle of continued demonic disintegration . . . amid the confused heap of beings now restored appeared two forms Chance found familiar, brother and sister in their two squirming bodies, still wearing their Mark I suits.

Chance seized the smaller of them as they drew near; the little body in his arms was solidly human, its human lungs, freed of demonic magic, gasping greedily for air.

"Zalmoxis?" he asked, in doubtful wonder.

In a moment tiny Zalmo had recovered sufficiently to choke out fearful words of explanation through her childish throat. . . . "Your friend and mentor has become a god. The deity named Thoth. One of the class of beings whose existence your Scholar for so many years denied."

The sight of children who might be in need stirred Abby out of her shock.

Thoth took brief notice also. He said to them: "Never again will you appear as anything but what you are."

Moxis was murmuring to Chance and Abby: "Do you know . . . I could never quite decide . . . whether I ought to be male or female when I turned human? And now that problem has been solved . . ."

". . . for we are both," chimed in the voice of tiny Zalmo. "Now it seems that the difficulty has been overcome; we are both male and female, having become not one human being but two."

And Moxis: "We . . ."

"I . . ."

"We . . ."

"We were the djinn—"

"—and now—"

"—we are—"

The conclusion came in a piping duet: "—two human beings!"

JEMMY AND CRESS HAD EMERGED FROM HIDING TO STARE IN DOUBT-ful wonder at their own near twins. Chance and Abby were waiting until the confusion, the gathering of what Zalmo and Moxis said were new gods, should be cleared away. Then they could leave. They remained huddled somewhere with the four children, all of them watching the strangest show that any of them had ever seen. Thoth had some of his new colleagues with him—most of them were at least as human-looking as he, though some were not. All were on a scale larger than human life.

These other new gods, Zalmo added in a whisper, were probably not going to care much for demons either.

CHANCE, STARING AT THE GIANT HALF-BIRD AS IT STALKED ABOUT ON human legs and torso, saw that the black eyes of the ibis were widely separated, set bird-fashion—one on each side of the black feathered head. The new god tilted his head sharply to turn one of his bird-eyes directly at the small group of humans. The droning voice that spoke from the beak, still dripping and steaming with the dead demon's quasi-material entrails, was clear and crisp.

"I am Thoth . . . but who are you, humans?" The eye fixed on Chance was black as the demon's had been, but far from empty. "What business have you to come here, pushing in so impertinently among the gods?"

"Jervase . . . Sir . . . I came here seeking knowledge."

"Ah." But before the god could say more, he was distracted by a sudden clamor that had broken out among his peers, who seemed a quarrelsome and excitable lot.

MOXIS AND ZALMO, TWO INDEPENDENT HUMANS NOW, STILL RETAINED memories of when they had been one djinn. Moxis, in his boyish voice, was murmuring: "So we humans are to share our world with gods again. They are not the first of their kind that I have seen—but that was long ago . . . but, do you know? I think it was so long ago that I had almost forgotten."

The small girl piped up: "It seems to me that the ones I saw so long ago did not look very much like these . . . but that might be wrong." She shook her head, making her untidy hair fly wildly, a blazing flame. "It seems I too am beginning to forget . . . so many things."

Sighing, Zalmo's brother turned to Chance a haggard face that seemed half child and half old man. "Esteemed descendant of the noble Rolf, your distinguished Scholar has metamorphosed into the deity known from ancient times by the name of Thoth, who is, among other things, the patron god of knowledge and of scribes.

"However scholarly, Thoth is not entirely bookish. Clinging jealously to his role as judge, he is subject to certain violent moments, in which he is wont to behead the enemies of truth, human or otherwise, and tear out their living hearts."

THOTH, MEANWHILE, HAD TURNED HIS BACK AND MOVED AWAY FROM the mere humans who gaped at him. He seemed much more interested in conversing with an elephant-headed colleague who had just come into view. One of the boys at Chance's side, the one whose hair was brightest red, whispered to him: "That is Ganesa, lord of hosts. And god of wisdom, among his other attributes."

Presently the titanic figure of a human warrior in armor, fully the size of Draffut, went striding by.

"If only that *was* Draffut," murmured Chance.

"But it wasn't," Abigail reminded him. "I think . . . I think that might—might once have been Captain Horkos."

"Maybe, before he changed—but I would have said Private Vardtrad."

Zalmo's shrill but still non-childish voice pronounced the verdict: "Whoever it might have been, it is now Mars, god of war."

Chance shook his head. For all that he could tell, Mars might previously have been a bandit, or one of the maddened humans who had just been freed from the dead demon's gut.

Moxis said, in a voice that quavered up and down the scale: "They have already forgotten who they were . . . I fear . . . I fear I am beginning to do the same thing."

And the little sister chimed in: "But they already understand—in a way—what they have become. And we don't!"

Chance was thinking that in making the Mark VII suits Ardneh had tapped into greater powers than even he could understand. . . . Probably not even Ardneh could have foreseen what the result was going to be, in this world that had once more been changed.

However wise and powerful great Ardneh might have been, he was never omnipotent. His dead hand reaching from the past could not control what he had been unable to foresee. It was plain to Chance that the sudden access of divinity was leaving them all somewhat confused, and not entirely happy.

Abby was tugging at his sleeve. "We must get these children to safety."

"Wherever safety may be found." But, tired as he was, Chance was more than ready to move on.

WHEN NONE OF THE GODS SEEMED TO BE LOOKING AT THEM, THE SIX humans came out of their niche and began to climb. They had not gone far in their progress toward the outer world before Abby hesitated. "Chance, are you sure?"

"Sure of what?"

"If we went back there and looked around on that long row of racks, we might find two more of Ardneh's Swords that haven't been snatched up."

He grunted. "Or we might get our heads torn off, if some god's feeling playful. But Abby, I don't want a suit. I don't want to be a god. I've been carrying this Key for what seems like years, and that's enough." He paused. "But if you want one . . ."

"I don't! Having seen what we have seen already . . ."

They climbed on. But Zalmo and Moxis were beginning an urgent conversation between the two of them. Chance caught snatches of their whispering. Having become human, are they now eligible to become gods? Should they join the rush to put on suits—what gods would they become?

They are certainly human now, Chance thought to himself. *As soon as they get what they have been craving, they are dissatisfied and must have something else.*

"On the other hand," the little girl was saying, "we have not yet been human for even an hour! We should allow ourselves some time to enjoy what we have craved for so long."

"I intend to take all the time I need," Moxis agreed. "Maybe a whole lifetime."

Abby was tugging at his arm. "Chance . . . look back there."

He looked. The wounded owl Mitra had come to sit on the shoulder of some tall, grave goddess who had stopped to chat with her colleague Thoth. The goddess stroked the bird's damaged wing, and Chance saw Mitra suddenly stretch it out to its full healthy length.

Chance for a moment considered calling to Mitra, but before he could try to nerve himself to do so, the tall goddess had departed, taking the owl with her.

THIRTY-FIVE

ABBY AND CHANCE PRESSED ON, TRYING TO MAKE SURE THE children did not stray. To their relief, they were not beginning their retreat as far below the surface of the earth as they had feared, and here seemed to be a steady infusion of natural light. There was a gradual brightening in the air, suggesting an early stage of morning twilight. Chance wondered if some god, perhaps simply curious as to how Ardneh's Workshop was put together, had decided to tear away the layers of earth that made its roof.

As they climbed, the half-familiar passages of the Workshop around them were for the most part very quiet, except for an occasional distant and triumphant howl. To Chance this suggested that some new divinity might be enjoying his or her sporting pursuit of demons. He wished the gods good hunting.

Presently the six young humans emerged cautiously on the surface of the earth by an opening in a rocky hillside much like the one through which they had entered the Workshop days ago. Chance gave a gasp of relief. There was not a demon in sight anywhere. He could see only a few gods, individuals he could not hope to identify, rushing away through the air, flying faster than griffins. Their raucous voices drifted back, as if they were disputing with each other, reveling in their new powers.

"I suppose," said Abby, emerging from the opening in the rock to stand beside him, "they have all forgotten who they were?"

"Jervase certainly did."

Moxis and Jemmy, looking like one set of almost-identical twins, followed by Cress and Zalmo, looking like another, came right behind Abigail. For the time being all six people were still staying close together. Abby added: "When we were down below, it looked to me like some of them were burrowing deeper into the earth."

Chance very much wanted to lie down somewhere and sleep. But first he wanted to get as far away from gods and Workshop as he possibly could. He said: "Jervase . . . I doubt he's going to want his books any longer. I wonder if that means I've inherited them?"

No one had an answer to that. Chance started to move again—if he once sat down he would fall right asleep. The others followed.

Moxis, walking near Chance, stretched out his own hand, and turned it back and forth, and looked at it. He made a fist. He said at last: "I wonder who I am?"

His little sister was looking up at him. She sounded frightened. "You're Moxy, aren't you?—I—I'm forgetting everything. Where were we—yesterday?"

Cress, who had about seven years' more experience at being human than Zalmo did, was looking at her new near-twin in sympathy and wonder. Then Cress fastened her gaze on Chance, as if she expected him to have an answer.

"We're going to have to decide who you all are," he told the children. Then added thoughtfully: "It's probably going to take a while. But it'll be all right."

CHANCE, WITH ADVICE FROM ABBY, WAS STEERING THE GROUP IN THE direction of where they thought the entrance to the Workshop might once have been. In that area it might be possible to find a ridingbeast or two, or perhaps a wagon and some animals to pull it.

"There could have been more than thirty people down there," Abby was saying. "In the room where the suits—where the Sword was. Horkos and about fifteen troopers, to begin with—and we don't know how many of Gokard's men and women got in."

"Or how many other folk are going to find their way. Tomorrow, or the next day—or next year. There's no longer any door, or wall. I don't see how the place will ever be closed up again."

"Unless some of the gods decide to close it."

"Right." Again Chance scanned the skies. There was no sign that Thoth or any of his new peers were about to do anything like that.

Abigail was saying: "And we don't know how many more copies of Ardneh's Sword might still be there."

"Therefore we don't know many new gods there are going to be."

"No idea . . . we never did discover, did we, where Avenarius had hidden his life."

"Doesn't matter now." Chance felt an involuntary shudder race through him. "It looks like if a god decides to kill you, then you die."

"Unless you happen to be a god yourself."

THEY HAD WALKED A LITTLE FARTHER BEFORE ABIGAIL ASKED: "WHAT about Lord Draffut? Can we get word to him of what has happened?"

"I don't see how," said Chance. "He and your mother and the other Servants must have passed through the Oasis days ago. They've probably moved on from there. If the owl comes back, we can send her to Draffut with a message . . . but somehow I doubt she's coming back."

Abby nodded. "Mitra might well stay with Jervase—with Thoth. Or with the tall lady who was standing—"

"I remember her—I think." Moxis whispered absently. "Her name's Athena."

The name meant nothing to Chance.

Looking back along the way they had come, he could see a few of the new gods drifting in the air, all of them quite unfamiliar to his eyes. No doubt they could easily see the handful of wearily trudging humans in the middle distance, but were paying them no more attention than to a party of climbing, struggling ants.

The voices of divinity, loud and careless, carried strongly. One of the new gods was saying he had what was certainly a great idea for a game. "But it will need a lot of thinking first. Maybe a century or so of preparation. And then it will be a job to convince the others . . . ah well, someday, perhaps. We now have all the time in the world."

Immediately there was argument, voices raised in quick dispute. Who needed a new game, anyway? Chance got the impression that no two of this unfamiliar class of beings were likely to agree on anything.

Abby was tugging at his arm. "Quick, this way! I can see one of our wagons, about a kilometer away."

Dispute among the gods had flared briefly into a violent struggle. Chance, feeling too tired to run, and running would be futile anyway, simply turned to watch. He saw a slumping figure supported between two others, and heard one god bark at another: "Now you've killed him!"

The answer was more puzzled than excited. "Killed? No, one thing we cannot do is kill each other." And indeed it seemed that the victim was recovering his senses.

A third put in: "*Of course* we can't. We are immortal—that's what gods are supposed to be."

Two of the gathered entities looked blank. One asked: "Gods? Is that what we are?"

And the other: "What are 'gods'? I don't know the word."

He who had been the Scholar answered. "Well, that I do remember. And I remember it quite clearly. Old Scripture has some use after all, for now it tells us what we are—what we have always been. For we are very old . . . older than I can remember, or imagine.

"We who are gods can never die."

"Never die?" One seemed to find that prospect puzzling.

"Never. And we have all power to rule the world. Humans, demons, elementals—all other forms of being must bow down before us. That is what gods are."

ANOTHER VOICE OF NEW DIVINITY WAS SAYING: ". . . EVERYTHING I could remember only a moment ago is gone. I don't know what that strange cave is, that we just came out of, or how I got here. But all those things are rather unimportant. I don't need them because . . . well, for one thing, I now have—*new* memories. Yes, that's it! Memories of what it is like to be a god."

"Where did such memories come from? Have you been a god before?"

"I . . . I am not going to worry about that."

"I have always been a god! It was only a delusion—only a temporary dream—that I was merely human."

"All humans must bow down to us. And all demons too."

"They too must bow down? To us?"

"Of course! Didn't you see what just happened to Avenarius, when he dared to be insolent?"

"Let's try!" The speaker looked round eagerly. "Where can we find one, to try things on?"

"They seem to have vanished. There are only people hereabouts. Want to see what we can do with a person?"

Enthusiasm quickly drained away. "Anything we want, I should imagine. What fun is there in that? They could offer us no challenge."

Some of the gods were actually fearful at first, not trusting in their own new powers. And some of the demons, in their ignorance, were rash and arrogant.

There was a fierce clash, in which several additional demons were totally annihilated. The survivors of their evil race were awestricken by the unexpected power of the gods.

HARDLY HAD THE BATTLE, IF YOU COULD CALL IT THAT, WITH DEMONS been concluded, when the intramural skirmishing among the gods began.

There were pyrotechnics, but no one was killed, none seriously hurt. The squabble soon broke off inconclusively, with the gods all scattering around the world, still suspicious and jealous of each other, some seeking solitude in which to try to understand themselves.

For the time being, humanity was going to be left in possession of the earth.

THE SIX HUMANS HAD MOVED ON ANOTHER KILOMETER WHEN ABBY paused to look around at their small company. She said to Chance: "It appears that what we will be bringing home with us will not be exactly Ardneh's treasure."

"I'll be bringing home more of it than my family expected." Chance tightened his arm around her waist.

"I never belonged to Ardneh, you know, even though I took a vow. It was a cautious, conditional kind of vow. He accepts only voluntary service."

"I think I will try to persuade you to replace that vow with another. Less cautious. I think we should find one that is large enough to accommodate two."

"I might be persuaded. But will the eminent Rolfson family be pleased?"

"The eminent Rolfson family will have to understand that they might as well get used to it."

"That sounds very firm."

"You doubt me. But it will happen—I'm still the heir to the family name, and to most of the property. In large matters I am not going to be pushed around."

"That's good—and will you be continuing your scholarly quest for knowledge?"

"Eventually. But first I want to digest a few large lumps of fact that are almost big enough to choke on."

They trudged a while in silence. Then Jemmy started whistling to himself. The sky in the east was brightening, and soon the sun would be giving them more light and heat than they really wanted.

After a while Chance said: "We will have to tell everyone something about Jervase."

"More people will be asking us about the soldiers than about Jervase—and more people will ask about the treasure than about the soldiers."

"Sad for the families—those who have any—but no real surprise. Soldiers are always going missing. As for Jervase, we can say he seemed happy when last we saw him. Confident, still on his quest for knowledge. All true enough?"

"Yes . . . 'confident' is something of an understatement."

"Fortunately the Scholar has no close family, no one to mourn for him if it turns out that he is . . . well, is gone for a long, long time."

"My mother will want to know what happened to Novice Benambra."

"Again, we can tell the simple truth. He disappeared, going off on his own to look for treasure. It might even be that nothing terrible has happened to him. In truth I would not be too surprised if he showed up again."

"Yes, perhaps with gold in hand," Abigail mused.

"I say we also tell the truth about the treasure, or lack of treasure—but not the whole truth. No use our trying to explain about suits and gods. Right?"

"Correct."

"The main thing is, we did find the place that was Ardneh's Workshop—but in it we discovered no trace of gold or jewels. Right again?"

Abby seemed ready to agree. "There were only a lot of strange machines. Nothing we could bring with us."

"Perfectly true. People who don't believe us are free to come and see for themselves. They may manage to locate what's left of the Workshop or not—I suspect it's going to look different."

After a period of silence the girl said: "You don't know my mother, when she wants to find things out. I am going to have to fill in a few more details. No, a lot more."

"I thought I was sort of starting to get to know her, Abby, when we were all together—so she doesn't scare me all that much."

"The treasure's not going to be the first thing she asks me about."

"I realize that. I intend to be standing right beside you when she wants to know about us." Even in his weariness Chance had to laugh. "Our two sets of twins will doubtless be there too—*that* she won't be expecting. For once your mother will be surprised."

Abby was giggling too. "Especially as one set seems not much younger than we are. How will you explain that to your people?"

They were almost at the wagon, which seemed intact. Chance gave an awkward shrug. "Whatever I tell them, they may not believe me. I am known to have strange dreams."